Here Comes the Bribe

Auntie Mayhem

Murder, My Suite

Major Vices

A Fit of Tempera

Bantam of the Opera

Dune to Death

Holy Terrors

Fowl Prey

Just Desserts

Here Comes the Bribe

A Bed-and-Breakfast Mystery

Mary Daheim

HARPER LUXE

An Imprint of HarperCollinsPublishers

HERE COMES THE BRIBE. Copyright © 2016 by Mary Daheim. All rights reserved. Printed in the United States of America. No part of this book may be used or reproduced in any manner whatsoever without written permission except in the case of brief quotations embodied in critical articles and reviews. For information address HarperCollins Publishers, 195 Broadway, New York, NY 10007.

HarperCollins books may be purchased for educational, business, or sales promotional use. For information please e-mail the Special Markets Department at SPsales@harpercollins.com.

FIRST HARPERLUXE EDITION

ISBN: 978-0-06-239304-3

HarperLuxe™ is a trademark of HarperCollins Publishers.

Library of Congress Cataloging-in-Publication Data is available upon request.

16 17 18 19 20   ID/RRD   10 9 8 7 6 5 4 3 2 1

In Memoriam
Dale Douglas Dankers
1929–2015

Author's Note

The story takes place in May 2006.

Chapter 1

Judith McMonigle Flynn got out of her aging Subaru, slammed the car door shut, and realized she'd locked her keys inside. "Damn," she said under her breath. But all was not lost. No doubt the back door was open. It was a pleasant May afternoon with the old cherry and pear trees blooming in the garden behind Hillside Manor.

As she reached the porch steps, her mother sailed her motorized wheelchair out of the house and down the ramp. "Good luck, Toots!" Gertrude Grover cried. "There's something really ugly in the kitchen."

"What?" Judith called over her shoulder, wincing as the old lady narrowly missed Sweetums, who had been lurking by the birdbath. The cat hissed before slinking off into the shrubbery.

2 · MARY DAHEIM

Gertrude kept going to the converted toolshed that served as her apartment. Apprehensive, but even more curious, Judith went up the steps, through the hall, and entered the high-ceilinged kitchen. To her surprise, Joe Flynn was taking the last of a banana cream pie out of the refrigerator.

"Why aren't you on your surveillance job?" she asked.

"It's done," her husband replied, setting the pie on the kitchen table. "The adulterers skipped town. You know I won't go outside the county since I'm semiretired."

Judith kissed Joe's cheek. "I didn't see your MG. Is it parked out front?"

Joe shook his head. "It wouldn't start when I left the apartment building across the ship canal. I had to have it towed." He put the piece of pie on a small plate and sat down. "Face it, the MG's old. It's entitled to have some problems. Where've you been?"

"At the bank," Judith replied, sitting across from him. "Some guests paid cash this week. I don't like keeping money on hand, not even in the safe." She paused, gazing around the kitchen. "Mother said something ugly was in here. What is it?"

Joe's round face was droll. "Me, probably."

"Oh. I should have guessed." Judith felt sheepish. "I locked myself out of the Subaru."

Joe's green eyes twinkled with amusement. "How come? That's not like you."

"I guess I'm still upset about Mike being transferred to the Bread Loaf Wilderness in Vermont. Could he and his family be farther away?"

"Technically, yes," Joe replied seriously. "Hawaii or Florida or—"

Judith waved an impatient hand. "Stop! Admit it, it's not like they can drop in whenever they have time. During the years he was at the national forest an hour away, it was perfect. He and Kristin could come by with the two boys whenever they had a day off. They could even spend holidays with us. Now . . ." She let her hand trail away.

"Hey," Joe said, leaning closer. "We'll go back there in the fall, okay? Maybe the Joneses would like to come along. Your cousin is the only one of us who's been to New England. It'd be a great trip."

Judith remained glum. "Renie got shot at when she was in Maine."

"Your goofy cousin took the wrong road during hunting season," Joe reminded his wife. "She should've known it wasn't the highway to Canada. It was gravel, not pavement."

"She was enjoying the autumn scenery," Judith asserted. She brightened. "Are you serious about going to New England in the fall?"

Joe shrugged and swallowed his last bite of pie. "Why not? Bill and I feel a little guilty over our Great Barrier Reef fishing trip this past winter. You and Renie got stuck house-sitting for Auntie Vance and Uncle Vince. Spending a weekend on the beach in January couldn't have been a lot of fun."

"It was kind of . . . dull," Judith murmured. She and her cousin had sworn each other to secrecy about the corpse they'd found on their first outing at Obsession Shores. There was a limit to how much mayhem Joe and Bill were willing to put up with when it came to their wives getting in serious trouble. "I need your key to get mine out of the car," she said, standing up and holding out her hand.

Joe delved into his pants pocket where he kept the extra Subaru key. "Here. Cheer up. You've got a full house this weekend. The B&B's been busy this spring. Lots of visitors in town. You ought to be happy."

Judith clutched the keys tightly. "I'd be happier if so many of them didn't decide to move here. Have you looked at how real estate prices have risen lately? Especially here on Heraldsgate Hill."

"Location, location," Joe murmured, getting out of the chair. "I'd better call to see if Ron up at Hillcrest Auto Repair has had a chance to look at the MG. By the way, he mentioned some guy had come nosing around to ask if he'd be interested in selling his business, property and all. Of course he said no."

"That's curious," Judith murmured. "Carrie at the bank said someone had offered big bucks to the hair salon down the street. They also said no."

Joe nodded. "The hill has gotten too popular the last few years. Close to downtown, yet sort of off the beaten bath. It's become a really hot commodity. Secluded, in its way, since people don't come up here unless they have a reason."

"True," Judith agreed. "When I was growing up here, it seemed like a separate world. Oh—did you put out the barbecue?"

"Yeah," he replied, his green eyes fixed on the refrigerator. "We can start using it. It's still got quite a few briquettes left over from last summer. Hey—what happened to the rest of the banana cream pie? There was only that one slice left."

"Ask Mother," Judith said. She tried not to stare at Joe's slight paunch. "I didn't eat it. Neither of us needs pie during the day."

"Speak for yourself," Joe murmured, and headed up the back stairs.

Judith went outside to retrieve her keys. On the way back into the house, she almost ran into Phyliss Rackley, who was carrying a load of laundry up from the basement.

"Careful!" her cleaning woman warned. "Is Satan after you again?"

Judith caught her breath. "I didn't find him in my car."

"He's everywhere," Phyliss said gloomily, her gray sausage curls bobbing as she kept going up to the second-floor guest rooms. "Beware!"

Shaking her head, Judith continued on to the kitchen and glanced at the old schoolhouse clock. It was ten to two. Not only would she have all six guest rooms filled, but she was hosting a marriage ceremony at noon on Saturday. She'd had some experience with weddings at Hillside Manor over the years. Counting back, this would be the seventh such celebration, though four of the events had been only for the receptions. All of this weekend's guests were connected to the bride and groom, a young couple from the Los Angeles area.

The phone rang as she was about to call the florist.

"What time should I show up tomorrow?" her cousin Renie inquired, not sounding very enthusiastic.

"Ten thirty?" Judith suggested warily.

Renie let out a sigh that traveled up and over and down the other side of Heraldsgate Hill. "You know I'll be barely conscious at that ungodly hour. Why didn't they schedule an afternoon wedding instead of high noon? That's a stupid time. And why do I have to come so early? It's all too primitive."

"You know damned well why," Judith retorted. "I need your help. Phyliss doesn't work weekends. She goes to her weird church both Saturday and Sunday. And don't ask why because I never have and I don't want to know."

"Ooooh," Renie said in mock chagrin. "Somebody's crabby. Do I detect rebellion?"

"Just . . . stress." Judith suddenly had an idea. "How about a compromise regarding your wake-up call? Why don't you and Bill come for dinner tonight and get acquainted with who's who for the wedding party? That'll save time tomorrow morning. They won't get here from the airport until going on six."

Renie didn't answer right away. "Well . . . just don't expect Bill to pretend he's polite and talk to these people, okay? You know he's not a social animal. He can fake it if he has to, but . . ." Her voice trailed off.

"Never mind," Judith said. "Tell him I'm making Auntie Vance's beef noodle bake. He likes that, right?"

"Yes," Renie replied. "It suits his Midwestern origins. How many years were we married before I could coax him into eating Dungeness crab? I finally told him that in this state, not eating it is legal grounds for a native's no-fault divorce."

"It should be," Judith agreed. "See you at five thirty?"

"Got it. I have to work on that mailing design for Gutbusters Warehouse. How do you convey buying in large quantities to get their deep-discount prices?" Renie didn't pause for an answer. "I've got it! A Jolly Green Giant juggling cases of string beans. Bye." She hung up.

The afternoon passed in its usual busyness of making hors d'oeuvres for the guests' social hour, starting dinner preparations, and dealing with Phyliss's concerns over the morals of the wedding party.

"I saw your guest list on the bulletin board," she said, her gaunt figure virtually shaking with indignation. "Two of those couples aren't married. How can you allow such depravity under your own roof?"

"The bridal couple is about to be married," Judith pointed out, "and Dr. Sophie Kilmore is married to Clayton Ormsby, but she goes by her maiden name."

Phyliss scowled. "Kilmore isn't a very good name for a doctor. It gives a bad impression. She should be Ormsby."

"None of my business," Judith murmured, watching Sweetums try to wedge his orange-and-white furry body into an open cupboard near the sink. "Are you done for the day?"

"I should hope so," Phyliss asserted. "I have to catch the bus in ten minutes. They've changed the schedule. Again. Changed my stop where I get off, too. I have to walk an extra block past an ungodly tavern. I reek of satanic fumes when they leave the door open. I have to change, too—change my clothes right away, even my undies." She glared at Sweetums, who was now sitting a couple of feet away and glaring back at the cleaning woman. "Speaking of Satan . . ." she murmured—and stalked off down the hall, grabbing her black raincoat along the way. "Enjoy your sinners!" she called as she left the house.

Joe appeared in the kitchen shortly before five thirty. "The news from Ron isn't all that great," he said, reaching for a bottle of Scotch. "It's the gearshift and the engine and—"

"Stop!" Judith put her hands over her ears. "Please! How much?"

Joe set the bottle on the counter and gently removed Judith's hands so he could be heard without shouting. "At least two grand. They'll let me know Monday. Maybe the MG's not worth the expense."

"You bet your fat butt it isn't," Gertrude declared, rolling into the kitchen. "You and your fancy foreign cars! Why not buy a Chevy?" She turned to Judith. "And where's my supper? You know I like to eat at five o'clock. I'm wasting away out in that stupid toolshed while you two get tanked before your gruesome out-of-town guests show up."

"Renie and Bill are coming to dinner," Judith said. "I thought you might like to join us."

Gertrude narrowed her faded blue eyes at her daughter. "At six? I'll have passed out by then. That's when my TV shows come on. I've seen my niece and her husband before. The programs are new."

"What comes on at that time except news and sports?" Judith asked, keeping one eye on Joe, who was making their cocktails.

Her mother briefly looked puzzled. "The news is always new. That's why they call it *news*, dummy." She glanced at her son-in-law. "Say, I wouldn't mind having a shot of that stuff. It's good for what ails me."

Why not? Judith thought. Her mother had come of age in the era of bathtub gin. She could probably drink paint thinner and not show any ill effects. Every time Judith saw the old framed photo of Gertrude wearing a cloche hat and short skirt while behind the steering wheel of a Model A convertible, Judith figured her mother would easily reach the century mark. And beyond . . .

"A GT?" Joe inquired.

Gertrude nodded. "How come I'm surprised you know some of the letters of the alphabet, Dumbo?"

"I finally concentrated," Joe replied drily. "During my years on the police force, I only learned APB, WINQ, and MOE."

"MOE?" Gertrude echoed. "That must've been you. Which one of the Three Stooges was your old partner, Woody?"

Before Joe could answer, Renie and Bill entered through the open back door. "We're early," Judith's cousin announced. "My husband likes being early."

Judith glanced at the clock. "It's five thirty-one," she noted.

Bill looked exasperated. "I knew we'd be late." He grimaced at his wife. "You just *had* to change your shoes."

"I wasn't wearing shoes," Renie asserted. "You know I never wear shoes inside the house. Hi, Aunt Gert." She leaned down to kiss the old lady's cheek.

"What are you, Serena?" Gertrude demanded. "A hillbilly? Why don't you wear shoes like normal people? What does your mother think about that?"

"She thinks I'm weird," Renie responded indifferently. "Oh, ugh, gin. Bill and I are allergic." She frowned at Judith. "You know that, coz."

"We weren't going to force it down your throats," Judith said wryly. "Scotch for Bill, bourbon for you."

But Bill shook his head. "Vodka. It's spring."

"Make that two screwdrivers," Renie said. "We always change liquors the first week of May. Unless we forget."

Gertrude took a big swig out of her glass. "I forgot I'm not staying here for dinner. My lazy daughter's trying to starve me into submission. I'm heading back to my cardboard shack to watch the news and find out which high-placed politician got busted for romancing a possum and letting it drive his limo. Or would that be a she instead of an it?" The wheelchair spun around as the old lady whizzed off down the hall and out of the house.

"Someday," Joe murmured, "I'm going to ticket my not-so-loving mother-in-law for speeding in that thing."

"I want one of those," Bill murmured. "It'd come in handy when I nod off during a session with one of my zany psychology clients. I could claim the visiting nurse was coming to see me. I wonder if she'd look like Eva Marie Saint?" He gazed at his wife. "You don't."

"Thanks," Renie muttered. "My self-esteem is shattered. Again."

"Everything's under control for dinner and the guests," Judith declared. "Let's sit in the living room."

The foursome adjourned through the swinging half doors into the dining room, across the hall, and on to the spacious living room.

"I made a copy of the guest list," Judith said after they'd sat down on the matching blue sofas in front of the dormant fireplace. "Here, have a look." She handed over the single sheet of paper to her cousin.

Scanning the list, Renie made a face. "Rodney Schmuck? Is that his real name?"

"Apparently," Judith replied. "I always check driver's licenses."

"Hey," Joe said, leaning toward Bill, "want to see the way I put together the album of our fishing trip?"

Bill practically vaulted off the sofa. "You bet. Let's do that somewhere else. Like Peru. Say, ever think about fishing off the coast of Chile during . . ."

The cousins exchanged irked expressions. "Why," Judith murmured, "can't men be as interested in people as they are in fish?"

"Because, as my mother would say, 'Men aren't like other people—dear.' You have to add the 'dear' so Mom gets credit for saying it. Often."

Judith smiled. "I always liked that comment. It's as pithy as Grandma Grover's 'There are worse things than *not* being married.' I often thought of that during the nineteen years I was stuck with Dan before all four hundred pounds of him blew up."

Renie's expression was sympathetic. "The rest of the family felt like you were in exile out in the crummy Thurlow District while you were married to El Blimpo. We hardly ever saw you. Between you working two jobs while Dan worked not at all, he kept you a virtual prisoner."

Judith nodded. "The nightly phone calls with you after Dan went to sleep or passed out were a lifeline. They helped keep me sane." She gestured at the list. "Rodney and Camilla Schmuck are the bride's parents. Note the daughter's name is Arabella. She likes to be called Belle. Oh—Camilla prefers Millie."

"Belle also prefers not being a Schmuck anymore," Renie remarked. "I assume her roommate, Clark Stove, is the groom."

"That's *Stone*," Judith said. "My handwriting's a bit cramped."

"That's an improvement over Stove." Renie studied the list again. "Clark's parents won't be on hand?"

"His parents are divorced," Judith explained. "I don't know anything about the father, but Mom is Cynthia Wicks, second husband is Stuart Wicks."

Renie shrugged. "The Reverend George Kindred and Elsie Kindred. I assume he's marrying the happy couple?"

"I guess so," Judith replied. "I wasn't informed otherwise."

"Charles and Agnes Chump. Dare I ask?"

"That's Crump." Judith spoke through gritted teeth. "My handwriting isn't *that* bad."

"Yes, it is," Renie argued. "You should've typed it out on the computer. That's what I would've done."

"Good for you," Judith said sarcastically. "You spend more time on the computer than I do. Get over it."

Renie wasn't perturbed by the comment. "Last, but I assume not necessarily least, are Dr. Kilmore and Mr. Ormsby. Married or live-ins?"

"I assume they're man and doctor. I mean, wife," Judith said. "The reservation noted that Clayton Ormsby is Sophie Kilmore's mate."

Renie turned to the grandfather clock across the room near the big bay window. "It's ten to six. If their flight's on time, they should show up soon. Will the wedding be in here or in the parlor?"

"I prefer the parlor," Judith replied. "That way I can set up the food during the ceremony. It just seems a better way to do it. For all I know, they may have some other guests coming for the reception. They could have more relatives and friends staying elsewhere in town."

"They didn't let you know?" Renie asked, frowning.

Judith sighed. "After going on twenty years as an innkeeper, I've learned to be flexible. To quote Grandma Grover again, 'It'll all be the same a hundred years from now.' "

"I was never sure what that meant," Renie mused. "Won't it be a lot different? Consider the early 1900s and all the changes since then. We had no computers or freeways or blenders or—"

"I think," Judith interrupted, lest her cousin go on, "she meant it'd all be the same to *us* because we'd be dead."

Renie looked affronted. "She couldn't be sure. People are living longer. I was probably two the first time I heard Grandma say that."

"You're being obtuse," Judith declared. "Stop. I think I heard a car pull up out front."

"It can't be your guests," Renie said. "They need a bus."

Judith ignored the remark. "I'm going to see if it's them. If it is, you'd better join me so you can figure out who's who."

As Judith stepped out into the hall, Joe poked his head around from the dining room. "Bill wants to know if we're eating at six. His ulcer, remember?"

Judith glared at her husband. "If Bill's ulcer is bothering him, he can have some of the hors d'oeuvres I made for the guests. But don't let him get near the wedding cake." She continued on to the front door and peeked out to the street. On the near side of the huge laurel hedge that separated Hillside Manor from Carl and Arlene Rankerses' property, Judith could see a pickup truck belonging to one of their sons.

"False alarm," she told Renie. "It's a Rankers. Your husband wants to eat now."

"He can wait," Renie said. "I'll dish up dinner while you go through the formalities with the guests. Is Aunt Gert staying in her self-imposed prison or deigning to join us?"

"She's staying in the toolshed." Judith heard voices. "That must be them." Hurrying to the door with Renie right behind her, she saw a silver stretch limo in front of the house. "Wow!" she exclaimed softly. "They travel in style. I should've charged more for the wedding festivities."

"Add surcharges," Renie suggested. "That seems to work for everybody else these days."

A tall man who looked to be midforties was the first to emerge. He turned toward the porch. "Here comes the bride!" he shouted.

"That must be Arabella's father," Judith whispered. "Rodney Schmuck. You got that?"

"Yes. One down, eleven to go," Renie grumbled. "Why don't you make them wear name tags? I'm not good with faces."

"It's not a convention," Judith murmured. "Welcome!" she cried as the tall man was followed up the steps by a strawberry-blond girl and a curly-haired young man. "I'm Judith Flynn. You must be . . . ?"

The middle-aged man moved in front of the younger couple and grinned at Judith. "You can't imagine how I've waited for this moment," he said, beaming even more widely. "Do you recognize me?"

"Uh . . ." Judith stared at the newcomer. "Not offhand. Have you—"

Before she could finish the query, her guest enveloped her in a bear hug. "Gosh, it's so wonderful to finally meet you!" he exclaimed, his voice shaking with emotion. "It's a miracle!" He finally released Judith, holding her at arm's length. "It's me, your long-lost son! Are you as happy as I am?"

Chapter 2

W hat?" Judith shrieked, reeling at the man's incredible statement. She would have fallen if he hadn't still held on to her hands.

"Watch it!" Renie yelled, stepping out onto the porch. "If you're her son, you damned near smothered your mother! Are you insane?"

"I am not insane," he stated calmly, no longer beaming and making sure Judith could stand on her own before letting go of her. "Judith Grover Flynn is my mother. I have proof."

"You c-c-can't b-b-be," Judith finally stammered. "I only have one ch-ch-child, Michael McMonigle. He's really Flynn, b-b-but . . ." She didn't feel like explaining that she'd been pregnant with her fiancé's baby when she married Dan after the woman known as Herself had hijacked a drunken Joe off to a Vegas JP.

The young blonde found her voice. "Could we come inside? We stood in enough lines at the L.A. airport. Then our flight was delayed and we didn't get in until after five."

Judith noticed that the rest of the party had exited the limo and the driver was pulling out of the cul-de-sac. "Yes, come inside," she said in a tight voice. "Please sit in the living room. I'll get your information."

Renie held the screen door open after Judith hurried inside. "Keep going," she urged the guests. "The living room's the second door on your left . . . you weirdos," she added under her breath. "Holy crap. What next?" She waited for Judith in the hall. "Are you okay? You're limping."

Judith nodded. "I moved a bit too fast on my artificial hip," she murmured. "Is this crazy or what?"

"They're crazy," Renie replied. "We're not. Should we call in the husbands? Can Joe arrest them? Or call Woody?"

Judith shook her head. "They haven't actually committed a crime," she said, leaning a hand on the staircase balustrade. "They can only be charged with confusion at this point."

"That's good enough for me," Renie muttered as they moved on to the living room, where her guests were foraging at the appetizer tray while a plump middle-aged redhead poured glasses of Vouvray from the wine bottles. "I'm rescuing our drinks from the coffee table," Renie said. "We need fortification. I'll top them off in the kitchen."

Judith took her time to join the newcomers. "Mr. Schmuck," she said, sounding more like herself. "Could you please sign the guest register? And may I see your driver's license?"

"Sure thing," Rodney replied, digging into the back pocket of his summer slacks. "I'm a southpaw. Are you? Always wondered where that came from. Figured it had to be on my mother's side. Of course I'm not sure who my father was. You got any ideas?"

"I certainly don't," Judith retorted. "Let's not discuss this mix-up right now. In case you've forgotten, you're here for a wedding. There are some details we should go over before you all go out to dinner."

"Oh, yeah, right," Rodney said. "You should meet the rev. He's in charge." He motioned at a thin, balding fiftyish man who sported a jet-black goatee. "Over here, Georgie. Mama wants to meet you."

Judith forced herself to hold her tongue. The rev loped toward her, extending a pale hand. "My pleasure, Mrs . . . ?" He looked at Rodney. "Finn? Flint? Flipp?"

"Flynn," Rodney informed him. "She was a Grover way back when. Right, Mama?"

Ignoring her bogus son, Judith shook the reverend's hand. "What abomination . . . I mean, *denomination* are you?" She wanted to bite her tongue.

"Not any of the usual ones," the rev replied solemnly. "Our sect belongs to the world. It's called the Church of the Holy Free Spirit. We welcome each and every lost soul. Have you been saved?"

"I'll find out later," Judith replied. *Like a hundred years from now when I'm dead.* "Have you tried the hors d'oeuvres?"

"Not yet," the rev said. "I fast between meals."

"Prudent," Judith responded, noting that the goatee looked as if it had been blackened with shoe polish. "I should show you the parlor. I've had weddings here before. That's the best place to conduct the service because it's so cozy, private, and intimate."

"Very nice," he murmured. "I trust your judgment. We'll talk more tomorrow. I must pray for a few moments." With a slight bow he moved away to the bay window.

The strawberry blonde was tugging at Rodney's short-sleeved shirt. "When are we leaving for dinner? This wine sucks donkeys." She sneered at her half-empty glass. "It's not from California. Or France. Yuck."

Judith felt obligated to stand up for the local vineyards. "I try to show visitors that we have our own wineries here in this state. Many of them are excellent."

"Not this one," the blonde shot back before her azure eyes widened. "Am I supposed to call you Granny? I'm Belle."

"Call me Judith. Please. I can find a different wine if you'd like."

Belle shook her head. "No thanks. We have a seven o'clock reservation somewhere on the bay." She turned around. "Where'd the nerd go?" She moved off to the far end of the table where a skinny man with a shaved head and a shapeless woman with long, straight gray hair were filling their faces with appetizers.

"The nerd?" Judith said to Rodney, who'd already drained his wineglass and was fingering a cigar in his shirt pocket.

"She means the groom," he explained. "She calls him that because he's a tech wizard. Makes big bucks with Zootsky. Huge honkin' deal up in Silicon Valley, one of the biggest high-tech companies around. Started there when he was only seventeen. Guess he'll be runnin' the place in a couple of years. Great to be young, huh?" He grinned again. "I bet you must've had a pretty hot youth yourself, Mama."

"Studying to become a librarian was very rewarding," Judith said, reverting to her previous tight tone while handing him the guest book. "If you'll sign this and show me your driver's license, please . . ." Out of the corner of her eye, she saw her cousin enter the room.

Renie paused briefly by Judith. "The husbands are eating dinner," she announced, and kept going toward the buffet table.

"Not this husband," Rodney said, scowling while handing over his wallet. "Truth is, I'm hungry. The airlines are cheap about snacks these days. I remember when you got a real meal."

To Judith's relief, the California driver's license looked authentic. She already knew the Visa card was good, since the Schmucks had paid in advance and the charge had already cleared. "You should meet the missus," Rodney was saying as he signed the register. He turned and shouted across the room. "Millie! Get your rear in gear and meet Mama."

Judith assumed Millie was the tall woman who wore her dark hair in a French roll and had a red patent-leather purse slung over her left shoulder. She batted what looked like false eyelashes and appeared to mouth the word *later*.

"Oh, well," Rodney muttered. "She's enjoying herself. Guess I'd better do the same."

"By all means," Judith said. "Oh—I noticed you signed the register as 'self-employed.' What do you do for a living?"

Rodney beamed again. "I'm a motivational speaker. And a damned good one. Aren't you proud of me, Mama? I'll show you my proof of maternity after we unpack." He patted Judith's shoulder before heading to the buffet table and barely avoided a collision with her cousin, who was eating Brie on a cracker.

"They're all a little weird," Renie declared. "Let's eat what's left of dinner. Joe took your mother's meal out to the toolshed. Did you convince Rodney he's not your long-lost son?"

"I couldn't convince Rodney it's Friday," Judith replied as they left the living room. "He's either nuts or . . ." She paused, setting the guest register down on the new marble-topped credenza by the staircase.

"Or what?" Renie inquired.

"I don't know. That's what bothers me." She gave Renie a bleak look. "I'm not sure I want to find out."

———

Joe Flynn was disgusted. "Let me handle this goof-ball," he said after Judith had recounted Rodney Schmuck's incredible declaration.

Renie waved her fork. "Hey, turn him over to Bill. He can probe his psyche and find out why he's goofy."

Bill looked exasperated. "I can't figure out what's really wrong with my squirrelly patients. I just sit there and think about what I want to watch on TV after dinner. It's the only way I can stay awake."

Renie gazed at her husband. "Tell them about the Hindi woman you had the other day."

"What's to tell?" Bill replied with a shrug. "It took me fifteen minutes to realize she was speaking in Hindi. Or something. The only odd thing was that I closed the window on her sari. Then she really became unraveled. Kind of interesting." He shot a sly glance at his wife.

Renie's brown eyes snapped. "Stop. Or you'll be the one who's sorry about the sari."

Bill shrugged again and attacked his boysenberry pie à la mode.

Judith looked at Joe. "Will you talk to Rodney tonight?"

"That depends," he replied, "if they get back before eleven. I'm not staying up to interrogate your latest loonies. I can do that at breakfast."

"Okay," Judith agreed. "But they should be back fairly early. Their dinner reservation was for seven. I won't stay up late either. I refuse to have to listen to Rodney insist I'm his mother just before I go to bed. I might have nightmares. Why would he do such a thing?"

"Maybe," Renie suggested, "as Uncle Al would say, he's 'got an angle.' Are you sure he's a motivational speaker? I don't think Schmuck could motivate me to leave a burning building."

"I only know what he told me," Judith admitted. "I didn't get a chance to ask if other guests were coming to the wedding."

"Forget it for now," Joe advised. "Maybe the guy's delusional. Or he's got you mixed up with somebody else. You can't be the only Judith Grover in this country. Both names are common. When your parents had you, Judith was a very popular name for girls."

Renie had forked in a mouthful of noodles and ground beef, but it didn't stop her from jumping out of her chair. "Ahmgundchwakrdznaw." She hurried into the kitchen.

Joe looked at Bill. "What did she say?"

"Who knows?" he responded. "She doesn't always make sense when her mouth *isn't* full."

Judith glared at both men. "She's going to check the name via the Internet. I *can* translate when Renie's eating. We're only assuming that my maiden name is the one Rodney researched, but it makes sense."

Renie's return was quick, mercifully after she'd swallowed her food. "There are pages of Judith Grovers. And Judy Grovers. I stopped after the first two. They're all over the place."

"That's a relief," Judith said. Then she added softly, "I think."

By five to eleven, the wedding party had not returned. The Flynns headed up to bed on the third floor's family quarters. Just as Judith was about to drop off to sleep she heard voices through the open bedroom window. The Schmucks and their companions let themselves in and apparently headed to the second floor. There had been no opportunity to give them their room assignments, but they could sort that out for themselves. Judith nestled her head into the pillow and fell asleep. Tomorrow was another day— and a busy one. She needed her rest.

But when she dreamed, it was of a baby version of Rodney in a bonnet and diaper, grinning as he shook a blue rattle and shrieked, "Mama, Mama, Mama!" Judith woke up just after two. Joe was snoring softly while the wind rustled the cherry tree in the backyard. She stayed awake for what seemed like a long time.

When she finally went back to sleep, she dreamed her mother was trying to run over Sweetums with the wheelchair. That was ordinary and somehow comforting. Judith awoke, feeling reasonably refreshed.

Joe was already in the kitchen when Judith arrived downstairs a little before seven. Unfortunately, so was Millie Schmuck, who was wearing a crimson Japanese robe.

"You *can* read, can't you?" she was saying to Joe, who was holding a typed sheet of paper.

"Only if I run my finger under the words," he replied, his round face innocent. "We *have* had guests with allergies and other dietary restrictions before. How do you feel about gruel?"

Millie sniffed. "As you can see, some members of our party have restrictions about what they eat. Is it gluten-free?"

Joe kept a straight face. "Yes. I was a dietitian before I retired."

"Very well." Millie ignored Judith with a swish of satin and left the kitchen. "No mistakes," she called over her shoulder. "Stuart is a lawyer."

"And I'm not," Joe muttered.

"You certainly weren't a dietitian," Judith murmured. "When did you start telling lies to people?"

Her husband shrugged. "I guess your knack for lying has rubbed off on me."

"I never lie," Judith declared. "I only tell small fibs to be tactful or to explain my reasons for asking questions that might seem inappropriate or what—"

Joe waved an impatient hand. "Skip the excuses, I get it. What if I make my own version of Joe's Special and call it Something for Everyone with Gastrogut Gripes?"

"You're going to lie to guests again?" Judith asked in a tone of reproach.

"Why not? You do. And I don't usually have them hovering over the stove while I'm making breakfast," he asserted, his usual morning cheer absent. "Are you sure the Schmucks' credit card went through?"

"Yes. They must have money. The stretch limo didn't come cheap."

Joe removed a ham from the refrigerator. "Let me handle the so-called proof Schmuck says he has about being your son. You don't need that kind of hassle. Then I'll see if I can get somebody at headquarters to run him through the system."

Judith frowned. "You think he's a crook?"

"I don't know what to think," Joe said. "But I'd like to find out if he has a rap sheet. If not, we could deal with him merely being nuts."

Judith, who was mixing waffle batter, was briefly silent. "Let me talk to Rodney first. I'd like to see his alleged proof for myself. Then you can take over and check out whatever he shows me."

Joe smiled. "You think your people skills are better than mine?"

"Well . . . in this setting, I *am* the innkeeper," Judith replied diffidently.

"You are at that," Joe conceded. "Okay, but I'm still going to chat him up. I haven't had a chance to meet the guy yet."

Judith nodded. "That so-called pleasure is all yours."

After they'd eaten their own breakfast and Judith had delivered Gertrude's scrambled eggs, ham, toast, grapefruit, and coffee, the first of the guests entered the dining room. Guessing that the skinny man with the shaved head and the long-haired shapeless woman were the doctor and her husband, Judith extended her hand and introduced herself.

"I'm Sophie," the woman said, keeping her hands at the side of her dun brown sacklike dress. "I don't shake hands. I'm a surgeon."

"Oh," Judith said as Clayton Ormsby's grip proved rather flaccid, "I understand. What kind of surgery do you perform?" she inquired of his wife.

"Cutting edge," Sophie replied with what might have been a smile. "Clayton blogs." She turned to her husband. "What's your topic today?"

"Gloom," he replied. "In all its forms."

Judith thought that was an apt subject for the long-faced Mr. Ormsby. "By midmorning the clouds will lift," she said for lack of a more cogent comment. "Most of breakfast is already on the buffet. French toast and muffins are on the way."

Back in the kitchen, Joe asked if Rodney had shown up yet. Judith informed him he hadn't, but heard more guests entering the dining room. She peeked over the half doors. "The bride and groom," she whispered. "And the Crumps. They're both short and stocky, like matching salt and pepper shakers. He's also got a bad comb-over. At least I *think* I'm getting these people sorted out. I heard someone greet Agnes."

"I figure she's the dumpy, frumpy woman," Joe said as Judith joined him at the stove where he was taking out the muffins. "What did Millie Schmuck do after she got up so early? Go back to bed?"

"I guess," Judith said. "Maybe it takes her that long to put herself together. She didn't look so hot when she was down here earlier."

Judith put the muffins in a basket and carried them into the dining room. "Just out of the oven," she announced.

Dr. Sophie set down her glass of tomato juice. "Are they whole wheat?" she inquired.

"No," Judith replied. "They're corn-bread muffins."

Dr. Sophie didn't comment. Nor did she look up when Reverend Kindred and his wife, Elsie, arrived. The couple offered everyone a blessed morning. The man Judith thought was Charles Crump voiced a hearty "Amen, brother!" He slapped the Reverend on the back, almost toppling the gaunt man of the cloth. Judith suppressed a sigh and went back to the kitchen.

"Still no sign of . . ." she began, but stopped when she saw Millie Schmuck coming down the hall from the back stairs. Mrs. Schmuck was dressed in a lime-green pantsuit, her makeup applied with a considerable amount of care.

"My husband is ailing this morning," she told the Flynns. "Too much excitement, perhaps. He's very sensitive to the feelings of others. I do hope he improves in time for the wedding ceremony. It means so much to him to give our daughter away."

"I can understand that," Joe said with only a faint touch of irony.

"Do you have a daughter?" Millie asked, somehow making it sound like an incredulous possibility.

"I do," Joe replied, "from my first marriage. Caitlin's still single. She's a dedicated career woman who works at a laboratory in Switzerland."

Millie looked askance. "How very ambitious of her. Excuse me. I'm going to fetch some juice to take up to Rodney. It may help settle his stomach."

Both Flynns watched her passage from the kitchen to the dining room. "Tied one on last night, I'll bet," Joe murmured.

Judith shrugged. "That's what wedding parties often do."

"We didn't," Joe pointed out, giving his wife a quick hug. "We had a nice rehearsal dinner and a church wedding like respectable people. I don't remember the Vegas ceremony with Herself. For all I know, the JP could've been Howard Hughes." He sniffed the air. "Damn! I left the French toast in the oven! I'll bet it's ruined."

As soon as he opened the oven, a cloud of smoke billowed into the middle of the kitchen. Joe swore under his breath as he rescued the charred French toast. Before he could dump it in the garbage can under the sink, the smoke alarm went off.

Judith hurried into the dining room. "It's okay," she asserted calmly. "Just a minor mishap. No need to panic."

But several of the guests did just that. Clayton Ormsby began to cough. Dr. Sophie hauled him out of his chair and insisted they go to the front porch. Stuart and Cynthia Wicks followed them to make sure Clayton wasn't choking to death. The Crumps glared at each other as if one of them were somehow responsible for whatever had gone wrong in the kitchen. The Reverend Kindred's call to prayer went unheeded, while Belle Schmuck and Clark Stone kept eating.

"We should smoke some weed before the wedding," Belle said to her groom. "You got that good stuff? This place smells like bad stuff."

Judith returned to the kitchen. "This," she whispered to Joe, "is a fiasco! I wish these people had never come here. They're a hex."

"Relax," Joe said, chuckling. "They're a peculiar bunch, but all that happened is some damage to half a loaf of bread. Stop fussing. You'll wear yourself out before the ceremony."

Judith put her hand on his arm. "You're right. It's not as if the oven hasn't smoked before. I should've reminded Phyliss to clean it yesterday. It was overdue for a scrubbing."

Five minutes later, the guests had reassembled in the dining room. After a few more remarks about how unsettling breakfast had been, their conversation turned to the wedding and the reception. Judith eavesdropped, hoping to learn if more people would be on hand. Finally she went back into the dining room, and after apologizing for any inconvenience, she asked Belle if they planned to hold a reception when they returned to L.A.

"Not the formal kind," Belle replied. "After we get back from Japan, maybe we'll throw a big pool party. How come you don't have a pool?"

"The backyard's not that big," Judith replied. "My mother has her own apartment out there."

"Your mother?" Belle said in surprise. "She must be a thousand years old."

"She's working on it," Judith murmured, noticing that someone had opened the dining room window that looked on to the Rankerses' imposing hedge. "Good," she said to no one in particular. "It's airing out."

By a little after nine, the guests had returned to their rooms. Or so Judith assumed. "I suppose," she said to Joe while they cleared the dining room table, "they're preparing for the wedding. I heard Cynthia Wicks say something to Dr. Sophie about getting manis and pedis. I wonder if they're going to that new spa where . . ." She paused, seeing Rodney Schmuck come down the hall clutching at his plaid bathrobe. "Good morning," she greeted him. "Are you feeling better?"

"Not as good as I should," he replied, leaning against the fridge. "I've got a problem." He grimaced. "I think Millie's dead."

Chapter 3

Judith thought she must have misunderstood. "You think your wife is . . . *what*?"

Rodney was obviously weak in the knees. He started sliding to the floor, but Joe caught him before he hit bottom. "Here, sit," he advised Rodney, pulling out a chair from the kitchen table. "I'm going up to check on your wife. Which room are you in?"

"Ahhh . . . the first one on your left," Rodney replied. "Room One, maybe? But Millie's not there. She's outside by the birdbath."

"Are you certain she's . . . dead?" Judith asked, leaning against the counter for support.

Rodney nodded. "No pulse. Not breathing. Odd color. Poor Millie!"

"I'll check," Joe said, moving briskly to the back door.

Maybe Rodney was mistaken. But even so, given Judith's vast experience with dead people, she was surprisingly flustered. It had been a long time since anyone had died or even fallen ill on the premises. It took her a moment to find the phone, though it was in its cradle on the counter. "I'll call 911," she said. To her relief, she didn't recognize the voice of the operator who answered. Help would be dispatched at once. That was much better than having some sarcastic grump at the other end who knew her history with corpses.

Judith disconnected. "Would you like a drink of water?" she asked Rodney, who was slumped in the chair, holding his head.

A grim-faced Joe came back inside before the question could be answered. "He's right. No response. She's dead." He looked at Rodney. "I'm sorry."

"I called 911," Judith said.

Joe nodded. "I'll go back outside and stay with . . . Mrs. Schmuck. I wouldn't want your mother to come outside and get upset. She might have a stroke." The idea seemed to cheer him.

"I need a real drink," Rodney declared. "A stiff one. Bourbon'll do."

Judith poured almost an inch of Jack Daniel's into a glass and added a couple of ice cubes. "What happened?" she asked.

Rodney downed half the bourbon in one huge gulp. "I'm not sure. I was in the can across the hall. When I came back to the room, she was gone." He made a face and shook his head. "I thought she'd headed back for breakfast. I had a pounding headache, so I came down to see if you had some aspirin. I got to the bottom of those stairs and felt light-headed. I opened the back door to get some air and—" He broke off.

"Take your time," Judith cautioned. "There's no rush."

Rodney licked dry lips. "I didn't know why Millie went outside. I thought she'd fallen down. So I went to help her . . . but she didn't move. I mean, she wasn't even breathing. I couldn't feel a pulse. Dang!" He drained the glass. "More, okay?"

Judith hesitated, but Rodney was obviously distressed. "Of course." She poured a refill. "Has your wife been sick lately?"

"Millie? Sick?" He shook his head. "She hardly ever gets a cold."

Sirens could be heard in the distance. "The emergency people are almost here," Judith said. "The fire station's only a few blocks away."

The phone rang. Judith snatched it off the counter.

"It's me," Joe said. "I'm staying with the body. The cops are pulling into the cul-de-sac. Oh, damn! Arlene and Carl are welcoming them. Maybe she'll bake them a cake. I'd better make sure they come out back instead of stampeding through the house." He clicked off.

But someone had already rung the doorbell. "I'd better let them in," Judith muttered, exiting the kitchen.

To her relief, she didn't recognize the two on-duty officers. "Are you the one who called?" the tall, rangy, young African American patrolman inquired.

Judith noticed his name tag identified him as Roland Pugh. "Yes. This is a B&B and I'm the innkeeper, Judith Flynn."

Roland exchanged a quick glance with his burly, fair-haired partner, who Judith noted was Ivar Soderstrom. Maybe her reputation had preceded her. "Where is the deceased?" Ivar asked as the fire trucks and the medic van pulled in.

"Out back," she replied. "My husband, Joe Flynn, is with the body."

"Joe Flynn?" Roland said in surprise. "He's not the one who was Captain Price's partner, is he?"

"The same," Judith responded. *Maybe,* she thought, *they'll show me a little respect instead of treating me like a meddling ghoul.*

The officers started to turn away, but Belle and Clark had just come down the stairs. They gaped at the policemen. "Hey, man!" Clark exclaimed. "What's up? We're clean."

The cops looked at each other and shrugged before trudging off the porch. The bridal couple lingered in the hall. Judith braced herself to deliver the bad news. "I'm afraid your mother's had . . . an accident."

"Not again!" Belle cried. "Did she borrow your car? Don't worry, she's got insurance. I think."

"Stop." Judith's voice carried calm authority, the tone she'd often used on Dan McMonigle's rowdy drunken customers at the Meat & Mingle Café. "Your mother collapsed and is unresponsive."

Belle's almost pretty face sagged. "Mom can act like she's not paying attention sometimes, but . . . what do you mean?"

"Your father saw her lying in the backyard. He couldn't rouse her," Judith explained. "The medics will try to revive her. We called as soon as your father told us. He's in the kitchen."

Belle's head swiveled, first to the stairs, then in the direction of the kitchen, and finally back to the stairs. "Come on, Nerd, let's go check out Mom. This must be some kind of nutty joke. Mom's always had a weird sense of humor." She grabbed Clark's hand and started racing for the back door.

Judith felt a headache coming on. She was turning toward the kitchen when someone called her name from the front porch.

"Mrs. Flynn," the smiling firefighter said. "Remember me? I'm Jess Sparks."

"Jess!" She was so relieved to see a friendly face that she hugged him, heavy gear and all. They had met the previous year when the young man was a recent hire and had been on a call in the cul-de-sac. "We're fine. I mean, Joe and I are fine, but one of the guests apparently dropped dead in the backyard. Her husband's in the kitchen."

"That's too bad," Jess said. "I guess there's nothing we can do about that. Mr. Rankers thought maybe you'd had a kitchen fire. One of my crew told me that happened a while back."

"Oh. Well, there was some smoke, but that was it," Judith said. "The dead guest is another matter."

"I guess." Jess's slightly crooked smile turned grim. "Is it true that you've . . . um . . . had . . . some other . . . accidents here?"

"No. I mean, yes, but they weren't really accidents. They were . . . premeditated."

"Wow! I guess the guys weren't kidding." Jess grimaced. "I'd better let you get back to . . . whatever you need to do next."

"Right," Judith said. "Nice to see you again. Take care."

Judith arrived in the kitchen to find Rodney drinking straight from the bourbon bottle. "On'y way t' cope," he mumbled. "Millie wash a goo' wi'. She'd ha' liked ya, Mama." With that, he slid out of the chair and passed out on the kitchen floor.

Ten minutes later, Rodney was on the sofa in the living room with an ice bag on his head. Judith had taken two Excedrin and Joe had finally returned to the kitchen.

"Heart attack, probably," Joe said. "No sign of trauma."

Judith put a hand to her head. "What a relief!"

"I had a feeling you'd say that." He sat down at the kitchen table. "I wonder if they'll still have the wedding. The last I saw of the bride, she was semihysterical."

"Someone will have to make that decision," Judith said. "It's after ten. Where's everybody else? I thought I heard some of them go out after the firefighters left."

Joe shrugged. "No clue. Maybe the other women decided to go ahead and have their nails done. The rev's meditating in the driveway. I hope he doesn't call on your mother and ask her to join him."

"Mother!" Judith exclaimed. "She has no idea what's happened. I should tell her."

"Why? She won't care. She's used to your disasters. That old girl has lived through two world wars, the Great Depression, the jazz age, the threat of nuclear holocaust, rock and roll, labor strikes, race riots, desegregation, the Beatles, several recessions, and almost twenty presidents. Nothing short of the Second Coming would jar her. In fact, she'd probably tell Jesus he was late."

Judith smiled. "That sounds about right."

"I guess I'll hold off moving the furniture in the parlor," Joe said, brushing at his graying red hair that had receded a bit over the years. He tensed. "I'll check to see if they're removing the body."

Judith decided to avoid that sad scene. Instead, she offered a silent prayer for Millie and her family before cleaning up the breakfast clutter.

"She's gone," Joe announced. "In more ways than one. The emergency people are all leaving."

Judith sighed. "Good. Maybe the rest of the wedding party will leave. Of their own volition, I mean."

"Right," Joe said, taking the garbage bag out from under the sink. "This thing's full. I'll put it outside."

He'd gone out the back door when a tearful Belle and a self-righteous-looking Dr. Sophie entered the kitchen. The older woman spoke first. "Ms. Schmuck is requesting an autopsy," she declared. "It's only appropriate under the circumstances. Her mother was in excellent health. It would be gross negligence not to have her death investigated."

Judith was dismayed, but tried not to show it. "I suppose that's true. Is . . . was Mrs. Schmuck your patient?"

"Yes," Dr. Sophie replied. "And a close personal friend."

"I understand," Judith said. "You should probably see to Mr. Schmuck. He's collapsed on the sofa in the living room."

"I shall." Dr. Sophie took Belle's hand. "Come, dear, we must tend to your poor father."

They left the kitchen. Joe was coming down the hall. "Did I hear the dreaded word 'autopsy'?"

"You were eavesdropping," Judith accused him. "Yes, the usual guff about a seemingly healthy person suddenly dropping dead. I guess I can't really blame the daughter for wondering why. If nothing else, parents' medical conditions can affect their children and grandchildren."

Joe frowned. "A complete autopsy can take several days. If they wait for the results, they'll have to find another place to stay after Sunday night."

"That's true," Judith said. "I've only got Room Two free Monday night, but another reservation might come in."

"Yoo-hoo," Arlene Rankers called, entering via the back door as family and friends usually did. "Is everything all right? Except for the dead person, of course. Goodness, you do have some bad luck. Are you sure whoever it was died of natural causes? That's not like your typical corpse. I didn't hear a shot, so could she have been strangled or stabbed?"

"The medics didn't seem to think so," Judith replied.

"Hmm." Arlene didn't seem convinced. "I left out a blunt instrument." When Judith didn't respond, her neighbor continued in an ambiguous voice. "They should know, I suppose. Unless they don't."

Judith was used to Arlene's contradictions. "People *do* die of natural causes."

"Not around here," Arlene pointed out. "Oh, well. I guess there's a first for everything. Is the wedding still on?"

"I doubt it," Judith replied. "I don't know what to do with the cake and all the food for the reception."

"Well . . ." Arlene looked thoughtful. "Could you freeze it?"

Joe had been reading the newspaper at the kitchen table. "There's not much room with all the fish I caught still there."

"You can put some in our freezer," Arlene offered. "We also have room in our garbage can if yours is full."

"It's not," Joe said. "I was just out there."

Arlene seemed puzzled. "Why did a B&B guest put trash in ours?"

"I've no idea," Judith said. "What was it?"

"I don't know," Arlene replied. "Carl saw someone dump a bag in our garbage can very early this morning. Why would anyone bother going around the hedge to do that?"

"Did he see who it was?" Judith asked.

"No. It was still fairly dark outside," Arlene said. "You know Carl likes getting up at the crack of dawn."

Judith let the subject drop. Maybe it wasn't one of her guests. There were homeless people who lived in the nearby parks on Heraldsgate Hill. Some of them were tidy by nature. The previous fall, an elderly woman had come to the front door asking for firewood and offering to pay for it by sweeping the sidewalk. Judith had given her some wood along with a food basket, but told her reimbursement wasn't necessary. The woman's grateful smile was sufficient.

"I should visit your darling mother," Arlene said, starting down the hall. "Does she know about the dead person? I don't want to distress her. She's such a sensitive old darling."

"Mother hasn't yet gotten the news," Judith admitted.

"Then I'll tell her," Arlene asserted. "I can do it gently. Oh—here she comes now. Gertrude! Guess what! A woman dropped dead as a dodo right outside your apartment this morning! Isn't that gruesome?"

Gertrude paid Arlene the courtesy of braking her wheelchair just beyond the threshold. "You think I'm blind?" she shot back. "I saw the stiff. Serves her right for eating my daughter's cooking. You should've been here to see what she did to her auntie Vance's beef noodle bake. I've had a bellyache ever since and I'm out of Pepto-Dismal."

"Mother," Judith said, "you know you made Renie come back to get seconds for you. I follow Auntie Vance's recipe to the letter."

"What letter?" Gertrude shot back. "X for X-rated? And where'd you get that ham this morning? It tasted like an old tire."

"I think I'll head home," Arlene murmured. "Bye, everyone."

"Hey, Arlene," Gertrude called, "stop in later and I'll let you have some of my Granny Goodness chocolates.

I only share them with people I actually like." She turned to Judith. "Well? Who croaked this time?"

"A guest," Judith replied. "Apparent heart failure."

Joe stood up. "Nothing to bother you," he said to Gertrude. "You don't have a heart. I'll check on Schmuck." He ambled out of the kitchen.

"What schmuck?" Gertrude asked.

"The guest whose wife died," Judith replied. "He passed out on the sofa after drinking a lot of bourbon to calm his nerves."

"Hunh. You sure he wasn't celebrating? I thought you'd do that after McMonigle blew up. I wouldn't have blamed you."

"Dan and I had some good times," Judith said quietly.

"Not often." Gertrude's wrinkled face was unusually sympathetic. "You worked your tail off while you were married to him. Oh, I'm not crazy about Dumbcluck, but I'll admit he's an improvement."

Judith smiled. "He's terrific and you know it. At least as far as I'm concerned. Do you really want some Pepto-Bismol?"

Gertrude rubbed her stomach. "No. I feel better now."

"I was about to come out to tell you when Arlene showed up," Judith said. "I suspect the wedding is off."

"Just as well," Gertrude declared. "If they're like most people these days, they won't stay married for long anyway. I read in the paper that almost half the couples in this country split up."

Renie and Sweetums arrived before Judith could speak. "Here comes the coz," she announced. "And Furball. Hi, Aunt Gert." She kissed the old lady's cheek. "It's five to eleven. I'm early. Where do I start?"

"You don't," Judith said grimly. "The bride's mother died this morning of an apparent heart attack."

"Right. Very funny. I'm not putting on an apron. You know I hate wearing—"

"I'm serious," Judith broke in. "Dead serious."

"Oh." Renie looked mildly upset. "That's a shame. You mean I got up half an hour early for nothing? Why didn't you let me know?"

"I've been kind of busy," Judith asserted, glowering at her cousin.

"Say," Gertrude said, "we could play three-handed pinochle. How about that, girls?"

The "girls" didn't look enthusiastic. Judith spoke first. "I still have a B&B to run, Mother. For one thing, I have to figure out how to store the . . ." She stopped as a scowling Joe came through the half doors.

"Woody just called my cell while I was trying to coax Schmuck into getting off the sofa. His scanner picked up your 911 call at his house. He's driving over here to check things out."

Judith was puzzled. "He doesn't need to interrupt his weekend to do that," she asserted. "Sondra won't be happy about it and I don't blame her. Didn't you tell him what happened?"

Joe grimaced. "Once the medics got the body to the morgue, one of them checked the inside of her mouth. He got suspicious about some residue. It turns out Millie may've been poisoned."

Chapter 4

J udith flopped down onto a kitchen chair. "I knew it was too good to be true!" she wailed. "Just for once, couldn't somebody die around here without getting murdered?"

"You'd be bored by mere natural causes," Renie remarked.

"You like pretending you're Sherlock Holmes," Gertrude declared.

"You keep out of it for once," Joe said sternly. "Let Woody handle it. He *is* the precinct captain."

Judith grimaced. "Did I say I wanted to get involved? Right now I'm just annoyed. And wait until Ingrid Heffelman hears about this at the state B&B office. She'll threaten to yank my license again."

Joe's expression was unreadable. "Whatever. I'm going to drag Schmuck for a walk around the cul-de-sac until Woody gets here. It shouldn't take him too long unless he gets stuck on the floating bridge."

Gertrude turned her wheelchair around. "If nobody wants to play cards, I'm going back into exile." She rolled off down the hall.

Joe had backtracked into the kitchen. "The patrol cops have arrived. I'll deal with them before I tackle Rodney. I'll make sure they cordon off Room One with crime-scene tape."

"You must keep some on hand," Renie called after him. "Would it be in one of the kitchen drawers?"

Joe ignored her and kept going. She regarded her cousin with a bemused expression. "Do you want me to stick around? I wouldn't mind seeing Woody. It's been a while. His kids must be in high school by now."

"The oldest is in college," Judith said. "If Woody's taking over, I'll sit this one out. I don't much like this current bunch of suspects . . . I mean, *guests*. They're really annoying. What I would like to know is why they came all the way up here to have the wedding. Apparently they don't have any friends or family in town."

"Did the bride and groom plan to honeymoon around here?" Renie asked, sitting down at the table.

Judith also sat down. "No, they're going to Japan."

"From here?" Renie looked puzzled. "Why didn't they get married in L.A. and fly from there?"

"How do I know?" Judith leaned back in the chair. "Maybe they got a cheaper flight from here. Maybe they're pathological liars. Maybe they came here to deliberately drive me crazy."

Renie laughed. "Dubious. Uh-oh. Here comes . . . somebody."

Judith turned to see a somber Cynthia Wicks entering from the dining room. "Mrs. Flynn?" she said, brushing stray strands of gray hair off her forehead.

"How can I help you?" Judith asked.

"As you may've assumed, the wedding is postponed," Cynthia said in a somber tone. "It doesn't seem right to celebrate a marriage under such tragic circumstances. How much of our money will be refunded?"

Judith stood up. "You intend to check out today?"

"Yes," she replied. "Stuart and I see no point in staying on."

"Mr. Schmuck paid for everyone's stay with his credit card," Judith explained. "We'll have to figure out a way to reimburse him so that he can give you a refund."

Cynthia frowned. "That sounds very complicated."

"It's not," Judith asserted. "It's a matter of sorting out who's staying and who's leaving. Have you discussed that with the other members of the wedding party?"

"No," Cynthia replied, again fiddling with her hair. "Stuart has a court appearance Monday afternoon in Los Angeles. We planned to take an early flight that morning. But leaving now will give him more time to prepare. This trip was rather inconvenient for us."

Renie, who had taken a sugar cookie out of the sheep-shaped jar on the table, looked up at Cynthia. "Not as inconvenient as it was for Millie Schmuck." She bit into the cookie with a vengeance.

"Sadly," Cynthia said, somehow growing even more melancholy, "Millie didn't take care of herself. She spent too much time fretting over her appearance. It's what goes on inside that counts."

"Right," Renie agreed—and stuffed half a cookie into her mouth.

"I do wonder," Cynthia went on, "what will become of her project. Oh, well." She turned away and left the kitchen via the half doors.

"What project?" Judith wondered out loud.

Luckily, Renie had swallowed the cookie. "A reclamation project for her looks?"

Judith heard voices. "I think Woody's here with Joe. They came in through the front door."

"Good." Renie got out of the chair. "Let's greet them before the official stuff starts."

Apparently Joe had managed to get Rodney on his feet. The cousins reached the hall, where Joe and Woody were watching the bereaved husband plod up the stairs. Judith winced, noting that Rodney had to clutch the handrail to steady himself. Joe rolled his green eyes at the sight, but Woody remained stoic, a familiar expression.

"Hi," Judith said, hugging Woody and kissing his mocha-brown cheek. "We've missed you and Sondra. You should've brought her along."

Woody waited for Renie's effusive greeting before he spoke. "Sondra doesn't like to get mixed up in my job if she can help it. I'm sorry about what happened this morning. The autopsy may prove the medics wrong, but we can't take chances, especially since . . . well, liabilities and all that."

Judith managed a faint smile. "Not to mention my reputation. You can skip being tactful. I've heard it all by now."

"Are all the guests on the premises?" Woody asked.

"I'm not sure," Judith admitted. "Shall I check?"

"I will," Renie volunteered. "It'll save you a trip upstairs." She immediately headed off, but paused on the first landing. "Where should I tell them the interrogation will be conducted?"

"The parlor?" Woody suggested, glancing at Joe.

"Sure," he said. "It's more private. The others can wait in the living room." He put an arm around Judith. "Hey, this is just like old times."

Judith winced. "Bad old times," she murmured. "Coffee?"

The two men had sat down on the matching sofas. "Not for me, thanks," Woody replied. "I've had my morning quota."

Joe also declined. Judith joined her husband. Woody asked if they'd mind being recorded. Both Flynns told him they didn't.

"Then," Woody began after setting up his taping device, "let's begin from the beginning. Who are these people?"

Joe deferred to Judith. "It's a wedding party from L.A.," she began, and then identified each of the guests. Renie returned halfway through the recital and sat down next to Woody. She didn't speak until her cousin got to the last name.

"Sophie took Belle with her to the spa," Renie said. "The doctor prescribed getting out of here for an hour or so as good medicine. They should be back soon, according to Clayton Ormsby."

Woody nodded faintly. "Do you know if all of your visitors were on the premises prior to Mrs. Schmuck's death?"

"I assume so," Judith replied. "Though some guests like to get up early and take a walk or just go out in the yard. But they were assembled for breakfast—except Rodney Schmuck. He didn't feel well."

"Hungover," Joe put in. "The whole bunch got back late from dinner. Millie came downstairs around six thirty to announce their bunch had some dietary restrictions."

Woody's dark eyes shifted from Joe to Judith. "Have you been up to their room this morning?"

"No," she responded. "I haven't had a chance. Will their room be a . . . crime scene?"

It was Woody's turn to grimace. "I'm afraid so, until we get an autopsy and a toxicology report. In fact, since the body was found in the backyard, that's a secondary crime scene. Did Rodney describe what happened to his wife?"

"Not really," Judith replied. "He was stunned and upset. Then he drank himself into a stupor."

Woody was silent for a moment, apparently considering his next question. "Could anyone else get into their room?"

Judith said they'd have to have a key. "But," she added, "Millie may not have locked the door when she came down here earlier. If you recall the layout, Room One is only accessed from the hall and is just off the front staircase. The guests have to share the bathroom between Rooms Three and Four."

"The place outside where the body was found has been marked off," Woody murmured, stroking his walrus mustache. "We'll have it processed as soon as we can, though it wasn't close to the walkway. Joe already brought down the juice glass, so Rodney can stay in Room One."

"That," Judith declared, "would be a help. I'd like to keep my distance from that guy."

"I don't blame you," Woody murmured. "Who's here now? Besides Rodney, that is."

"All of the men," Joe replied, then glanced at his wife. "Dr. Sophie and Belle went to the spa, right?"

Judith nodded. But Renie, who was beginning to feel left out, spoke up. "Why would the *surgeon* want a manicure? Aren't her hands too precious to be submitted to a rank amateur?"

"A valid point," Judith agreed. "Maybe she's having only a pedi."

Renie sniffed. "If she's so blasted brilliant, why can't she perform surgery with her feet?"

Although Woody looked amused, he changed the subject. "Let's start the questioning with the surgeon's husband. Clayton Ormsby?"

Joe stood up. "I'll go get him. I assume he's in his room." He paused by the coffee table. "Which room?"

"I told you, I don't know," Judith admitted.

"Just yell 'Suspect!'" Renie suggested. "Then see who comes out."

Joe shot her a disparaging glance before heading for the staircase.

"I assume," Judith said, "that's our cue to leave you alone, Woody."

He smiled. "It's my cue to go to the parlor." He also got to his feet.

The cousins trudged off to the kitchen. Renie sat down and again lifted the sheep-shaped cookie jar's lid. "Zilch?" she asked in a forlorn voice.

"I've been kind of busy," Judith replied. "Didn't you notice you ate the last one?"

"No. I just reach in and grab. I know what I want." Renie's disappointment gave way to a thoughtful expression. "When do you start eavesdropping?" she asked as the hands on the old schoolhouse clock ticked off eleven thirty. "Or finding me a snack?"

Judith, who was standing by the half door, ignored the request. "Joe's leading Clayton into the parlor. I suppose my husband will be allowed to sit in on the interview. That doesn't seem fair. He *is* retired from the force."

"Don't complain," Renie advised. "You know Joe will tell you what these bozos had to say for themselves."

"It's not the same," Judith asserted. "Men aren't as attuned to nuance and body language."

"True," Renie agreed rather absently, as if the statement wasn't worthy of further comment. "I don't suppose you have a prime suspect?"

Judith glared at her cousin. "This is where, if I happened to be a Brit, I'd say, 'It's early days.'"

Renie grinned. "Or early daze, as in—"

"I get it," Judith interrupted. "I should start making Mother's lunch. It's going on noon. And no, I'm not making you anything. What time did you eat breakfast?"

Renie made a face. "About an hour ago?"

"That's what I figured." Judith went over to the refrigerator. "It's a shame Mother keeps her eyes glued on her TV. She might've seen something in the backyard."

"Like what? Millie going ker-flop?"

"Well . . ." Judith paused before removing a bologna package from the refrigerator. "I don't imagine there *was* much to see, really."

"Go back over what you told me about Millie and the orange juice," Renie urged.

"I'm not sure it was orange juice," Judith admitted. "We keep at least three kinds in the fridge—orange, tomato, and cranapple. Of course the residue in the glass would show which of the three it was."

Renie looked thoughtful. "Allergies, food restrictions," she murmured. "I know all about the allergy part from my younger years. I assume Millie had a list of the verboten items?"

"She showed it to Joe." Judith scowled at her cousin. "What are you implying?"

"Well . . ." Renie paused. "I can only judge from my own experience with allergies. Even though I've outgrown some of the tougher ones like wheat, milk, vegetable oil, eggs, I still have the nut and peanut problem. Thus I'm *very* careful about what I eat when I don't know all the ingredients."

"Are you saying that Millie poisoned herself?"

"Maybe I am."

Judith sighed. "It'd be a weird way to commit suicide."

"Where's that list she showed Joe?"

"Millie must've taken it back to the room," Judith replied, moving away from the table to look out through the dining room and into the hall. "I haven't heard the cops come down yet. I'll try to waylay them before they leave."

Renie shook her head. "I'll do that now and save you a trip upstairs. Besides," she added with a grin, "I enjoy seeing a crime scene almost as much as you do."

"That does it!" Judith exclaimed. "I'm coming with you."

The two officers had just come out of Room One when the cousins reached the top of the stairs.

"Mrs. Flynn?" the younger and the shorter of the two said—and saw Judith nod. "The room's off-limits until it's been thoroughly processed. We have someone on the way to do that now."

"Okay," Judith conceded. "Wait—where did Mr. Schmuck go? I assume this was the room he occupied with the deceased."

"No idea," the other patrolman replied. "Maybe to one of the other rooms up here?"

"Maybe," Judith muttered. "Did you find anything of interest?" she asked in a brighter tone.

The older, taller cop frowned. "Such as?"

"A sheet of paper," Judith answered. "It was a list of dietary needs."

Both policemen shook their heads. "Sorry," the second cop replied. "Not even in the wastebasket. Did you need it?"

"My guests apparently do," she said. "Maybe it'll turn up somewhere later."

The cops both nodded, touched their regulation hats, and headed downstairs. Judith remained in place.

"You wouldn't," Renie whispered.

"It's *my* house," Judith asserted.

"No, it's not. It belongs to your mother. She inherited it from our grandparents."

"Well, it's *my* B&B," Judith declared. "I have a license to prove it."

"A license to snoop, you mean. Oh, go ahead," Renie said, sitting down on the divan next to the stair railing. "I'll stay out here and read the dog-eared magazines you leave for your guests."

"They're current!" Judith snapped. "That *Vanity Fair* just came out yesterday. I bought it at Falstaff's grocery store."

"Hunh," Renie grumbled. "I guess it was the picture of Charlie Chaplin on the cover that fooled me."

Judith ignored the comeback and went into Room One. She wished she'd worn gloves, but knew better than to touch the glass on the nightstand. At least, she thought, any residue would yield whichever juice Millie had poured for her husband.

But the glass was empty except for a tiny bit of water at the bottom. Someone—Rodney or Millie?—had emptied the glass and rinsed it out. Why? To get rid of any poison that might have been added?

She studied the rest of the room. Like all of the accommodations at Hillside Manor, the furnishings were rather sparse but comfortable. There was a double bed, a side chair, a dresser with a mirror above it, a wastebasket, and the nightstand. The bed was unmade, of course. Judith opened the closet. Millie's crimson robe immediately caught her eye. She checked the deep pockets, but came up empty. The only items on the floor were a pair of men's dress shoes and a pair of women's three-inch black patent leather pumps. The open suitcase on a stand at the end of the bed was tempting, but Judith heard voices in the hall. Maybe the crime-scene detectives had arrived. She felt panicky until Renie opened the door and peeked inside.

"Rodney wanted to get something out of the room," she said in a low voice. "I told him he'd have to wait. But I think I heard the 'tecs arrive. You'd better come out."

Judith was forced to comply. "Where did Rodney come from?" she asked, making sure the door was firmly closed.

"Room Two," Renie informed her. "I sent him back there. Who's staying in that room?"

"The would-be bridal couple," Judith answered. "But Belle and Dr. Sophie went off to the spa. I've no idea where Clark—the nerd—is, but he's probably not sure where he is either."

Clayton Ormsby was coming up the stairs. "My blog today will be about police brutality," he announced. "I've been badgered, belittled, and bedeviled by that precinct captain. Who does he think he is?"

"Woodrow Wilson Price," Judith said sharply. "He's a very intelligent officer."

Clayton now seemed faintly bewildered along with all the other words that began with a *B*. "Woodrow Wilson . . . I've already blogged about him. He couldn't make up his mind about the Great War. Maybe I'll take on Neville Chamberlain instead. At least that's not quite as dated for my readership." He wandered off toward Rooms Five and Six.

"His readership must be in their nineties," Renie murmured as the cousins headed down the stairs. "That figures."

They were heading for the kitchen when the crime-scene detectives arrived. Judith paused, but kept going.

"You aren't going to grill them before they go up-stairs?" Renie inquired.

"No. What's the point?" Judith glanced at the schoolhouse clock. "It's almost noon. I'd better finish up Mother's lunch or she'll pitch a fit."

"And I should head home," Renie said. "I've got a new graphic-design project from the county. Where'd I put my purse?"

"By the chair next to you at the kitchen table?" Judith suggested. "I think you . . ." She stopped, seeing Renie collect the big pewter-gray satchel that looked as if she could carry most of her household belongings inside. "I didn't see Millie's purse in Room One."

Renie gazed at her cousin. "Did she have one?"

"Yes, it was red patent leather. Didn't you notice it last night?"

"I was too busy trying to figure out how you could have Rodney declared insane on the spot," Renie replied. "Did you ever see his so-called proof about being your son?"

Judith looked chagrined. "No. That sort of flew by me. Damn. Maybe whatever alleged document he had was in the suitcase. I should've checked it out. Are you going out the back way? If so, I can hurry and finish Mother's lunch plate so you can deliver it to her."

Renie shrugged. "Did she see anything from the toolshed, such as Millie dropping dead?"

"Frankly," Judith said, adding potato chips and a sliced apple to the sandwich plate, "Mother rarely looks outside. She stays glued to the TV when she isn't doing her jumble puzzles or checking out the daily bridge hands or being talked to death on the phone by your mom."

"They have their own ways of getting under our skin," Renie remarked. "Mothers can do that, no matter how old their children are. But you've got to admit, they make us feel young."

"At least young-er," Judith pointed out. "It's been a long time since I hopped around on my pogo stick."

Renie took the plate from Judith. "Ever think that's why you had to have your hip replaced?"

Judith turned severe. "The surgeon told me it was congenital."

"It sure wasn't congenial," Renie said over her shoulder as she started down the hall. "But then I never had your sense of daring. You're the one who likes to take chances."

"Not this time," Judith shot back.

But by the time she'd said it, Renie had closed the back door.

Chapter 5

Judith managed to catch Joe in the front hall right after Dr. Sophie had returned from the salon and been ushered into the parlor. "How's it going?" she asked in a quiet voice.

Joe looked disgusted. "Bunch of bilge. Nobody knows anything. We've only got Pot-Head and Not-Quite-All-There Belle left to interrogate. Maybe after we're done with them you can rustle up some lunch for Woody and me."

"Gee, thanks," Judith drawled. "You can both have soup." She didn't wait for her husband's answer, but went through the front door.

And kept going, along the walk, around the giant hedge, and straight to Rankerses' garbage can. Lifting the lid, she spotted a plain brown paper bag on top. She opened it and saw shreds of damp paper. Was this a list of Millie's dietary needs? But the pulpy remains told her nothing. Judith wondered if the police lab could do anything to reveal what words had been on the paper. Following her whim—and her curiosity—she picked up the bag and returned to Hillside Manor.

It was going on one o'clock when Joe and Woody finally emerged from the parlor. They both looked weary.

"Hopeless," Joe said, slumping into a kitchen chair.

"Obtuse," Woody murmured, leaning against the counter by the fridge.

"Or cunning?" Judith offered.

Neither man commented. Judith persevered. "Are they free to leave?"

Woody shook his head. "Not until after the autopsy is concluded. That could take until midweek, maybe longer."

"They can't stay here past tomorrow night," Judith said. "I've got guests coming in Monday."

Joe frowned. "Can't you send the newcomers to other B&Bs?"

Judith gave him another dirty look. "And have to explain why to Ingrid Heffelman? Forget it!"

"Hey," Joe said, reaching out to take his wife's hand. "Woody's asked the patrol officers to stay close by. At least they'll be able to keep the media out of our hair.

So far, the press people don't know there's been an-oth—an unusual occurrence here."

Offering Woody a halfhearted smile, Judith thanked him. "It's just that . . ." She stopped to collect her thoughts. "I don't know how I find myself in these homicide predicaments."

Woody's dark eyes were sympathetic. "The only way I can explain it is that somehow there's an aura around you. It's like traffic accidents. Why do so many occur at the same intersections or parts of the freeways? It's a matter of how drivers respond or don't respond to certain road conditions. They're either inattentive or their vehicles aren't safe or they're reckless and thrive on danger because they're curious and risk takers by nature, so they . . ." He winced. "Maybe I should've quit while I was ahead."

Judith wished he'd quit before he'd started.

But when Woody was about to leave, she gave him the paper bag she'd found in the Rankerses' trash. "It may mean nothing," she'd told him. "But it's still an odd thing for a guest to do."

By midafternoon, calm had settled over Hillside Manor. In the wake of Phyliss's weekend absence, Judith never made up the beds or cleaned the guest rooms. That was up to the visitors, most of whom spent at least two nights and didn't check out until Monday morning. The B&B offered an economical three-night weekend package.

"Did everybody take off?" Joe asked when he came down from his den in the third-floor family quarters.

"I guess so," Judith said. "I saw the Kindreds leave. Maybe they've gone sightseeing since the wedding and reception have been called off."

Joe was looking bemused. "You really aren't sleuthing, are you? I'm surprised you bothered giving Woody that paper bag."

Judith couldn't quite look her husband in the eye. "With this bunch, if Millie was really murdered, I'd hope everybody did it, like all the suspects in the Agatha Christie train mystery."

Joe shrugged, took a diet soda out of the fridge, and exited the kitchen. Judith started choosing appetizer recipes for her loathsome guests' social hour. She was considering something simple—like cheese and crackers—when the front doorbell rang.

The broad-shouldered man a bit over average height wore a badge identifying him as Ethan Ethanson, city inspector. "Mrs. Flynn?" He saw Judith nod. "Sorry to bother you on a Saturday, but it seems you've had a couple of fires here lately. I thought I should check it out. It could be a wiring problem."

"It's not," Judith declared. "Both were caused by what was in the oven and it was only smoke. Or mostly smoke."

"Still, I'd better have a look. Lead me to the kitchen."

Judith had no choice since Ethan had put one foot inside the house.

"This is a B&B," she explained as they went down the hall and in through the dining room. "It can get hectic sometimes, especially in the kitchen."

Ethan didn't say anything, but went straight to the stove and took out a flashlight from the kit he'd carried over his shoulder. Judith tried to remain patient during the examination.

"Well?" she said after Ethan stood up and shut the oven.

"Everything seems to be in order," he replied. "Are your guests allowed to come into the kitchen?"

"They can, but rarely do." Judith was puzzled. "Why do you ask?"

"I work for the city," Ethan said without any expression on his round face. "I know an unmarked police car when I see one. What's happening around here?"

"A guest passed away this morning," Judith informed him, keeping her voice without inflection.

"Sad," Ethan remarked. "Elderly person?"

"Old enough to die suddenly," Judith said.

He nodded absently. "That's a shame. I'll be going now."

Judith followed him far enough to make sure he left the house. Maybe, she thought as he closed the front door behind him, she should have asked to see his license. But he'd worn a name tag that looked sufficiently official. Still, she couldn't help but wonder.

A few minutes later, Agnes Crump tapped on the half door to the kitchen. "Could I bother you for some ice? Charlie has a kink in his neck. He must've slept wrong last night. I'm afraid my husband doesn't travel well. He prefers staying at home, where he has his insurance agency in the basement."

"Come in Mrs. Crump," Judith said. "Do you want an ice bag?"

Agnes seemed nervous. "Well . . . if it's not too much trouble. I was going to use a towel, but an ice bag is best. I discovered that when I started volunteering as a Pink Lady at local hospitals in L.A. Oh—we're in Room Five. And please call me Agnes. Everybody else does," she added on a self-deprecating note.

Judith smiled. "Of course, Agnes. We haven't had a chance to visit. Is this your first trip to this part of the world?"

Agnes had entered the kitchen, but seemed uncertain about moving her plump figure farther than the counter next to the sink. "Yes. It's very green here."

"If we have water rationing, it won't be so green in August," Judith said, gesturing at a chair. "Do sit down. I enjoy getting acquainted with my guests. Usually, it's under more pleasant circumstances."

"Yes." Agnes wriggled her way into the chair. "Yes, I'm sure it is. But it had to be some sort of accident, don't you agree?"

"Of course." Judith sat down across from her guest. "I can't imagine exactly what, though." She refrained from suggesting Millie had mistaken Drano for tooth powder. "I understood that Mrs. Schmuck had some dietary restrictions. Or that another person in your group does."

"Well . . . some of us should," Agnes said, still in that self-deprecating voice. "Charlie should, too. But we're both so fond of eating."

Judith nodded. "I understand. I've always had to watch my weight. So does my husband since he hit middle age. It's a struggle. Did Millie have allergies or some other health problem?"

"I've no idea," Agnes said after a brief hesitation. "Charlie and I don't know the Schmucks all that well. You see, we're friends with Clark's family, especially his mother, Cynthia. I used to work for Stuart as a legal secretary."

"I see." Judith wasn't sure what she saw, except the anxiety in Agnes's cornflower-blue eyes. "Then you wouldn't know anything about Rodney's ridiculous claim to be my son."

"Oh, my, no!" Agnes looked horrified. "Charlie and I never heard of such a thing until he got here. Well . . . he did throw out some hints about a big surprise. But we thought it had to do with the wedding. Bear in mind we aren't intimate friends of the Schmucks."

Judith nodded sympathetically. "Are you acquainted with Clark's father as well?"

"Yes," Agnes replied with more certainty than some of her previous statements. "He's quite a fine man. He owns his own business. Ronald is involved with helping people find jobs."

"That sounds very worthwhile," Judith said. "I assume he lives in the L.A. area?"

"He travels quite a bit." Agnes's round face seemed to shut down. "I'd better take that ice up to Charlie. He's kind of miserable." She rose awkwardly from the chair.

"I'll get the ice bag," Judith said, getting up and going to the refrigerator. "I hope your husband feels better soon."

"So do I," Agnes murmured. "Men make such cranky patients." She accepted the ice bag and exited the kitchen.

Judith found two simple hors d'oeuvre recipes that she could practically make in her sleep. In fact, that's what she felt like she was doing as she put them together and slid two trays into the oven. The important thing, she reminded herself, was not to turn on the oven until it was going on six o'clock. She didn't need another visit from the firefighters—or the city inspector.

What she did need to do was figure out what to make for her family dinner. Her brain seemed empty when it came to ideas, despite having the larder well stocked. She decided to go out the back way and call on her mother. If nothing else, Gertrude could tell her what she didn't want for her so-called supper.

The sun had come out and it was a pleasant May afternoon. The sight of the crime-scene tape by the birdbath wasn't so pleasant. She'd asked Joe if the 'tecs had told him what they'd found in Room One. He'd insisted they hadn't told him anything. Judith thought he was lying in an attempt to discourage her from sleuthing.

Gertrude had the TV on overloud, blaring the dialogue from *Life with Father.* "*Can you turn that down?*" Judith shouted to be heard over William Powell.

"What?" Gertrude called back. "I can't hear you."

Judith lowered the volume. "There. It's a wonder the Dooleys in back of us don't report you for disturbing the peace."

Her mother took umbrage, waggling the remote at Judith. "With that big family, I need to turn up the TV to drown them out. I'm deaf, you know."

"When you want to be," Judith muttered, carefully perching on the arm of the small divan. "Being deaf, I don't suppose you heard or saw anything unusual in the backyard this morning."

Gertrude's wrinkled face was blank. "I'm not nosy like some people around here. And I sure don't go around looking for dead bodies. Say, what's that ugly yellow ribbon doing by the birdbath? Aren't the birds supposed to have a good soak? What's worse is I might get my wheelchair caught in that ribbon and have a tragic accident."

"It's not that close to the walk," Judith pointed out, "and I doubt it'll be there by tomorrow. The police should be done with their crime-scene investigation later today."

Gertrude shot her daughter a skeptical glance. "We'll see. The real crime scene is your kitchen. What gruesome thing are you cooking for supper tonight?"

"I haven't decided yet," Judith admitted. "You're an early riser. Are you sure you didn't look out to check on the weather? You often do."

Gerrude shook her head. "The weather is always the same," she replied doggedly. "It's either raining or it isn't."

"Mother . . ."

Gertrude knew when her daughter's patience was running out. "Okay, so I did see somebody out there. There was an idiot who looked like he was saying his prayers. Had his hands folded and kept looking up at the sky. Maybe he wanted to see if it was raining."

"That's the Reverend Kindred," Judith said.

"Kindred and his spirits, I suppose," Gertrude muttered. "Probably a religious wacko." She paused. "Earlier on, there was another, younger guy out there, but I forget when. He seemed to be taking notes. Of what, I couldn't say. Maybe he's a bird-watcher."

"Young, as in his twenties?"

Gertrude nodded. "I guess so. At my age, anybody under sixty looks young to me. I'm still waiting for you to grow up."

"But you didn't see Mrs. Schmuck's body?"

Gertrude scowled. "If I did, wouldn't I have mentioned it? The cops asked me the same dumb question."

"I didn't realize the police had interrogated you," Judith said, though in retrospect she should have known. No doubt Woody had told his subordinates that there was another possible witness on the premises. "I assume you gave the same information to them?"

Gertrude glared again. "No, I told them I'd seen Humpty-Dumpty fall off the wall and land on whoever it was who got killed around here this time. If those cops are as dumb as Lunkhead, they need all the help they can get. And I'm not gaga. Yet."

Judith couldn't suppress a smile at her mother's feistiness. "I know. You're a good citizen."

"I'm a Democrat, that's what I am," Gertrude asserted. "But I still do my duty, no matter who's running the government around here or in D.C. I always wished I could have voted for Harry Truman twice. Now, there was a man who knew his own mind and said what he thought."

"You and Truman would've gotten along just fine," Judith said, standing up. "It's too bad you didn't see who killed Millie Schmuck."

Gertrude gazed at her daughter with unblinking faded blue eyes. "Who says I didn't?"

Judith couldn't argue the point.

When she got back inside the house, Joe was in the kitchen with a red-faced Reverend Kindred. "I see no reason why I shouldn't conduct my Saturday-evening prayer service here. It's always open to all comers."

He pointed to a sheet of paper on the counter. "I'd only distribute my flyers to the immediate neighborhood. Now, will you allow me to use your copier or will I have to file freedom-of-religion and freedom-of-speech charges against you and Mrs. Flynn?"

"First of all, I don't think you'd get many takers right around here," Joe countered. "The Rankerses, the Dooleys, and my wife and I are all Catholics. The Steins are Jewish, the Ericsons are Lutheran, the Porters and the Bhatts are Methodists, and the new people in the rental don't seem to attend any church."

Kindred's jaw jutted. "You see? Fresh ground with souls to save! I'll personally call on them." Clumsily, he whirled around and left the kitchen.

Joe sighed. "Why did I think I could talk sense to a religious zealot?"

Judith laughed. "Because you're sensible?"

Joe, however, was looking beyond his wife. "Can it," he said under his breath. "Hi, Mrs. Kindred. Are you looking for your spouse? He just went out."

"Oh," Elsie replied without much interest. "No, I wanted to know if you people could help me find poor, dear Millie's project information."

Joe turned to Judith. "Not my line of duty. I have to check on the MG's progress at the repair shop." He made his exit via the dining room.

"Well?" Elsie asked, fists on hips. "Is there any chance you might've come across Millie's valuable data?"

"No," Judith answered. "I didn't realize she had a project. What's the purpose of it?"

The other woman folded her hands as if in prayer. "A program aimed at women who are seeking salvation. Very personal in its approach. The eye is the beholder of all unworldy and worldly things."

"It sounds . . . comprehensive," Judith said for lack of anything more cogent. "I'm sorry, but I have no idea what happened to Mrs. Schmuck's project information. Did you ask Mr. Schmuck?"

Elsie shook her head with its lank strands of graying auburn hair. "I don't like bothering him in his time of sorrow. Clayton Ormsby told me that Rodney is being badgered by the police."

"I think he may be exaggerating. The police have to follow procedure," Judith said in her most reasonable manner.

"The police!" Elsie exclaimed. "They're all corrupt. But I refuse to bribe them. I have no patience with them after they . . . Never mind. I'll only adhere to my conviction that all officers of the law are ungodly. They suspect the worst of even the most law-abiding, God-fearing people."

Judith feigned shock. "Surely you and Reverend Kindred have never been treated badly by the police."

"Well . . ." Elsie cleared her throat. "There was an incident about a year ago, but my dear husband was able to clear his name. It was all a silly mistake. There are some preachers who aren't quite all they should be, you know. Then there are some like George, who is more than a man of the cloth." She turned on her sensible heel and stalked self-righteously out of the kitchen.

Judith snatched up the phone and called Renie. "What are you doing this afternoon?" she inquired.

"I was working on this damned county design," her cousin replied glumly. "How do I convey changes in recycling rules? Dare I show the current county executive being stuffed upside down into a blue bin instead of a black can?"

"Probably not," Judith said. "I wondered if you could come over and help me do some research."

"Oh, no! I thought you weren't sleuthing."

"Well . . . I'm not, really, but I'd like to find out if these current guests are dangerous. They are, after all, under my roof."

"They paid to be there, right?" Renie retorted. "I suspect they'd just as soon head back wherever they came from." She paused. "It's a couple of hours before I have to conjure up dinner. Maybe I should pick up something easy at Falstaff's deli. Okay, I'll come by in a few minutes."

Renie's comment about where the Schmuck party had come from bothered her. She wondered why they had traveled from L.A. to hold a wedding in her B&B. They were headed for Japan, but Judith didn't think there were any direct flights to Tokyo from the local airport. She sat down at the computer and entered Rodney Schmuck's name. A few people came up with that surname, but no Rodney. That, of course, didn't mean he was using an alias. It only indicated he wasn't well known or into self-promotion via the Internet.

She typed in *Sophie Kilmore Ormsby.* As a surgeon, there should be a listing for her. No luck. She retyped the name, omitting *Ormsby.* The name appeared, but as a veterinarian over on the other side of the mountains. Maybe there was more than one Dr. Sophie Kilmore. Judith gave it one last shot, entering *George Kindred.* There were several, with some variations, but no reverends. Deciding her quest was hopeless as well as frustrating, she surrendered. She'd wait to see how Renie reacted to her futile efforts.

And realized she was indeed sleuthing. It seemed to be a habit she couldn't break. A bad habit, she told herself. And often a dangerous one. Yes, she'd been lucky over the years. But nobody's luck lasted forever.

Chapter 6

Judith conveyed the information—or lack thereof—to her cousin upon her arrival. Renie, in turn, reported that she'd seen the Reverend Kindred being chased off the porch at the rental house between the Ericson and Bhatt properties.

"Who lives there now?" Renie asked. "I don't think you told me who Herself's latest renters are."

"That's because I'm not sure," Judith replied. "They only moved in the first of May. Joe hasn't been in touch with his ex since then. Whoever they are, they seem like decent people, which is nice, considering some of the jerks Vivian has rented to in the past. Of course, she can't personally interview potential tenants when she's holed up with Jim Beam in Florida on the Gulf Coast."

"Understood," Renie agreed. "Oddly enough, the rev wasn't coming back here, but heading for the Bhatts on the corner. I don't think they're home. The SUV is gone."

"They're probably off with their kids," Judith said, ignoring her cousin's wistful look at the cookie jar. "It's a nice day. In fact, we should be out and doing."

"Doing what?" Renie asked with a faintly alarmed expression.

"Meeting the new neighbors," Judith replied, heading down the hall to fetch her jacket. "I think their last name is Clary or Cleary. Something like that. Try to be pleasant, okay?"

"Why do I always have to assume an uncomfortable demeanor?" Renie moaned. But she followed her cousin outside and across the cul-de-sac. "Gosh," she murmured to Judith, "I hardly recognize this big open space when it's not jammed with emergency vehicles. I feel disoriented."

Before they reached the curb, a familiar voice called out: "Yoo-hoo! Wait for me!" Arlene Rankers hurried to join the cousins. "I just happened to be standing on my toilet upstairs when I saw you heading to . . . the rental, correct?"

Judith nodded. "I thought I should introduce myself. And Renie."

"Of course," Arlene agreed. "I've come over to the Careys three times, but they're never home. They both must work. I've just happened to notice that they never take their mail inside until early evening. They shop at Gutbusters wholesale store and Nordquist's. Is Vivian really charging two thousand dollars a month to rent that rather small house?"

Judith didn't want to know how Arlene had found out the rental price. "That's really not exorbitant for Heraldsgate Hill," she pointed out. "Your Cathy should know that from her real estate dealings."

Arlene looked indignant. "What I'd really like to know is why Joe's ex didn't list the house with my daughter."

"Face it," Judith responded. "Vivian is a bit addled from drink. She's lucky she remembers she owns a house here on the hill."

"Hey, Arlene," Renie said as they started up the steps of the modest bungalow, "how come you spend so much time standing on your toilet? Doesn't it make you kind of dizzy?"

"The view," Arlene replied. "Do you realize how precious a view is? It adds immensely to the price of real estate."

"Right, right," Renie concurred. "We've got a view of the mountains and a good chunk of the city. But I've never yet stood on . . ." She shut up as a fair-haired young woman opened the front door.

Judith did the honors, introducing the trio. "We've been remiss," she went on. "We should've welcomed you to the neighborhood sooner."

"I tried," Arlene said, "but you and your husband must work. No one was home." Somehow she made their absence seem like a federal crime even as she put a foot down on the threshold.

Mrs. Carey offered her callers a strained smile. "My husband sometimes works nights. I'm Madeleine Carey. Call me Maddy. My husband is Jeb. Would you like to come in?"

"No," Judith replied firmly before Arlene could vault inside the house. "As you may know from the sign in our front yard," she went on, gesturing toward Hillside Manor, "I run a B&B. I was curious because one of our current guests was seen stopping off at your house a little earlier. I hope he didn't bother you."

Maddy's smile was more genuine. "No. Jeb was able to stop his salesman's pitch fairly fast."

"Good for him," Judith said. "That sort of proselytizing can be a nuisance."

Maddy looked puzzled. "Well, I'm not sure I'd call it that. I mean, it doesn't matter what he was trying to tell Jeb. As you probably know, we rent this house, so we couldn't sell it if we wanted to."

Judith couldn't suppress her surprise. "You mean he wasn't trying to evangelize?"

"No, no." Maddy shook her head. "He told Jeb he was a Realtor."

"Maybe," Arlene said, "he meant his kingdom wasn't of this world."

"I don't think so," Maddy responded. "He insisted we could get at least four hundred thousand for this house. He kept repeating, 'Location, location.' I don't think he meant heaven."

Arlene harrumphed. "My daughter, Cathy, could sell it for more than that. She's a very savvy Realtor."

Judith nudged Arlene. "That's not the point," she said. "I thought the reverend was in his preacher's mode. Sorry to have disturbed you, Maddy. We'll be going now. You must come over for coffee soon."

Maddy looked dubious, but smiled again before closing the door.

"That explains it," Arlene muttered as they reached the sidewalk. "Naomi Stein told me a man had come to their house earlier this morning asking if they were interested in selling. Did you know that, Judith?"

"No," she replied in a toneless voice. "I've been kind of caught up with other things, like having a dead body in the backyard."

"Oh, that's not so unusual," Arlene said with a dismissive gesture. "But door-to-door Realtors are. Usually they simply send you a letter saying how much they'd like to sell your house if you're thinking about a move. Of course we're not. Unless we do."

"Unh," said Renie, who had been remarkably quiet during the brief visit to the rental.

Arlene shot her a sharp glance. "Well? Are you put off because you live on the cheap side of Heraldsgate Hill?"

"No," Renie replied. "Our property taxes are lower. Ha ha."

Arlene didn't comment. Instead, she kept going toward the giant hedge. "I'm going to ask Cathy to check out this Kindred person's real estate credentials. He's probably not licensed to practice in this state. Heavens, he may not even be a preacher!" She disappeared around the huge mass of shiny laurel leaves.

"She's right," Renie murmured, "even when she's wrong. Damn—her manner of speaking is contagious. No wonder I like her so much."

"You're kind of contrary yourself, coz," Judith said, pausing by the driveway to the Flynn garage. "What do you think about calling luxury car rentals?"

Renie wrinkled her pug nose. "I don't really want to go anywhere. We might not get back in time so that I can fix Bill's dinner by six."

"I mean to find out where my guests were picked up," Judith explained. "I'd like to make sure they came from the airport. It puzzles me as to why they came here just to hold a wedding."

Renie kicked at a dead leaf. "That's different. I can deal with research. I'm calling it that because you're not really sleuthing, right?"

The cousins headed back into the house. "Damn it," Judith admitted, "I am. I can't help myself, especially when it happened on the premises. I can't believe the media hasn't shown up."

Renie laughed as they went into the kitchen. "They did. You might as well live in a gated community for the time being. Those unmarked police cars outside of the cul-de-sac diverted the media ghouls. Woody has clout. They stopped *me*. I had to prove I was family."

"How'd you do that?" Judith asked, slipping off her jacket.

"I called your mother. She grudgingly admitted we were all related."

"Amazing." Judith sat down at the computer. "Let me check limo rentals. You can man the phone."

Renie sat down at the kitchen table. "Do I get a snack?"

"Yes. I'll start the appetizers while you make the calls. Here's the number for A-List Autos."

Before Renie could punch in the number, Stuart Wicks entered the kitchen via the back hallway. "Excuse me," he said in a tone indicating he didn't give a hoot if Judith excused him for much of anything. "I've been informed that we can't leave until the autopsy is concluded, which may not be for several days. I have to be in court Monday afternoon."

Judith tried to look sympathetic. For all she knew, Stuart might really be a lawyer. "Can you ask for a postponement?"

"Not at this late date," he replied, his lean features grim.

"But," Judith pointed out, "you were booked through the weekend."

"We intended to take a very early Monday-morning flight out of here," Stuart said.

"To L.A.?"

"Of course."

"You'll have to talk to Captain Price," Judith informed him.

"I'll do that," Stuart said. "Please give me his number. I'll use my cell. I wouldn't want to be overheard on your personal line." He cast a disparaging glance at Renie, who was holding Judith's phone.

Judith scribbled the official—not the direct—line to the precinct captain on a Post-it note and handed it to Stuart. She knew he wouldn't be able to reach Woody since he was officially off duty. "Here. I hope the captain can be of help."

"He'd better," Stuart replied, closing his long fingers over the note as if he wanted to absorb it by osmosis. "My appearance in court involves a very serious case. Given my status in the legal community, I never deal with trivial matters." He stalked out of the kitchen.

"American Bar Association," Renie said. "Check him out in California and this state."

"I will," Judith assured her, sitting down again at the computer. "I should not only check for lawyers, but do the same with doctors and the AMA. I did find a Sophie Kilmore in the eastern part of the state, but it didn't say she was a surgeon."

"GPs can do fairly simple surgeries, especially the ones in small towns where they don't have specialists. I remember when . . ." The phone rang in Renie's hand. "I'll get it. Hello? . . . Yes, but . . . No kidding. You mean . . . How can we see through the Hedge That Ate the Early Settlers? . . . Sure, Arlene, I'll tell her." Renie disconnected. "Kindred showed up at the Rankerses' house while Arlene was with us. The rev was in Realtor mode. Carl told him to take a hike."

"He's working the entire neighborhood," Judith declared. "Now I'm beginning to understand the method to Rodney's kind of madness claiming he's my son. But what has any of that got to do with Millie being poisoned?"

Renie looked thoughtful. "She didn't go along with whatever scheme Rodney was hatching?"

Judith took even longer to say anything. The kitchen was very quiet. In fact, the entire house seemed unusually quiet, given that most of the guests apparently were upstairs. The only sound was the schoolhouse clock clicking its way to the three o'clock hour.

"Maybe Millie didn't," Judith finally said. "But what *is* the scheme? Pretending to be my son wouldn't get him far, even if it were true. He claimed he had proof, but I never saw it. For all I know, his mother *was* named Judith Grover. You told me a bunch of them came up on the Internet."

"Right, though with variations on Judith—Judy, Judi, Jude, and so on. Usually," Renie continued, "the people who are listed are well known—at least in a certain circle—or promoting their business or expertise."

"So one of them could be Rodney's Judith Grover," Judith mused. "Do you think we should check up on one or two of—"

"Don't even think about it," Renie interrupted. "I am not calling any of these women and saying, 'Hey, it's three o'clock and do you know where your illegitimate son is?'"

"I guess I won't suggest that after all," Judith murmured. She turned in her chair. "Did you hear the front door shut?"

"I thought it was the back door—with your mother forgetting to open it. Maybe she's stuck between the door and the screen."

Judith shook her head. "Joe's still at Ron's auto repair shop. He'd come in the back way. Let's check on the guests. It's too quiet upstairs."

She led the way down the long hall. "We'll grab some towels as our excuse for bothering this current bunch of weirdos."

"You need an excuse? Why not just walk in and tell them they're homicide suspects?"

"Most of them may be innocent," Judith responded. "At least I hope so. On the other hand, they may be guilty of something else. Oh, well." She gathered up a pile of towels from the built-in cupboards by the door that went up to the family quarters. Moving to Room Six, she knocked. "I'm not sure who's in here. They chose the rooms after they got back from dinner late last night."

There was no response. They moved on to Room Five—then Four, Three, and Two. Apparently, all the guests had left. The cousins stood by Room One with its crime-scene tape.

"We're going in," Judith announced. "I want another look at that suitcase. You can come with me or stay in the hall and sulk."

Renie heaved a resigned sigh. "I'll join you. Have you no respect for Woody?"

"I have enormous respect for him," Judith said as they entered the room. "I suppose that's why I'm trying to help him."

"You can't fool me," Renie asserted. "You're doing it for you because you like to sleuth. That's fine. Just don't get yourself—and me—into some tight spot where we get ourselves killed. I hate it when that happens."

"I'm not too fond of those situations either," Judith said, going through the suitcase. "Ah! Here's what looks like the sheet of paper Millie showed Joe." She stopped to read the typed words. "I'll be darned. It *is* recommendations for a gluten-free diet."

"You're disappointed," Renie remarked. "Me, too. I was kind of hoping for a threatening letter. Or at least blackmail."

Judith looked puzzled. "So what was destroyed and put in the Rankerses' garbage can?"

"Rodney's proof that you gave him birth without noticing it?"

"Maybe," Judith allowed. "If the so-called proof exists. Damn." She glanced again at the suitcase. "There might be a secret compartment."

Renie leaned against the bureau. "Go for it. But make it quick. I still haven't had a snack. I may pass out before dinnertime."

Judith barely heard her cousin. "Millie's purse— what became of it?"

"It turned into a briefcase?"

Judith scowled at Renie. "You're not helping. I know she had one; I saw it. It wasn't really big like yours or even mine, but it wasn't a little clutch type either. Give me a hand. I want to check under the mattress."

"Oh, good grief!" Renie cried. "Are you serious?"

"Yes. Come on, lift up the bottom end. I'll get the top."

But there was nothing to see—except the cousins staring at each other. Renie got down on her hands and knees to peer under the bed.

"I'm doing this before you ask me to because I knew what would be coming next. All clear except for some bedroom slippers." She stood up again. "Has it occurred to you that whatever you're looking for could've been burned and scattered to the wind?"

"Yes," Judith replied, "but I can only hope otherwise. It happens in mystery novels."

"This is real life. Let's go back downstairs where the food is."

"Let's not. If all the guests are out of the house, we can search the rest of the rooms. If anybody comes back, we still have the towels."

"Please." Renie held her head. "You can do this by yourself when they go out to dinner."

"Okay, okay." Judith picked up the towels.

Renie didn't say anything until they were back in the kitchen. "Do you still want me to call the limo services?"

"Yes." Judith opened the fridge while Renie dialed the first listing for upscale car services.

Five minutes passed while Judith wiped down the refrigerator's exterior and Renie kept making calls. "No luck yet with the car services?" Judith finally asked.

"I've still got two to go," Renie replied. She resumed dialing.

Judith listened with mild interest as she considered her family dinner entrée. Too late for pot roast. She'd thaw some salmon steaks that were in the fridge's freezer compartment. Her attention was caught by her cousin's expression of surprise.

"What do you mean?" Renie said into the phone. "Oh. I see. Has the limo been returned? . . . Who did you say rented it? . . . Spell that . . . Got it. Thanks." She hung up. "The limo itself was rented by someone named Floyd Kronk—that's with a *K*. Two *K*s, one at the beginning, one at the end. It was returned this morning. The limo, I mean. Not one of the *K*s."

Judith sat down across from Renie. "Floyd Kronk? Who is he?"

"Hey, I'm just the messenger. Whoever he is, he'd have to show a valid driver's license, right?"

"True." Judith was silent for a few moments. "Let me put that name into the computer." Without much hope of finding such a person, she moved to the far end of the counter. "Nothing," she said, "except for a Disney character."

Renie shrugged. "Too bad it wasn't Mickey Mouse. He'd be easy to pick out of a police lineup. Oh—Kronk has a local address. Let's try the old-fashioned way." She turned to the directory's white pages. "Here's F. F. Kronk. He lives over on the bluff."

"He does?" Judith was flabbergasted. "Now we're getting somewhere. Let me see that number. I'm going to call Mr. Kronk."

Renie handed over both the phone and the phone book. Judith punched in the number, but after eight rings she expected to hear Kronk's voice mail. Instead, a raspy male voice said hello.

For once, Judith didn't resort to fibbing in the interest of truth and justice. After being informed that Kronk had indeed driven the Schmucks to Hillside Manor, she asked where he'd picked them up.

"Bottom of the hill," Kronk replied in his gruff voice. "Right by that goofy-looking music museum. Tourists, right? Everybody goes to see all that stuff at the Center."

"Actually," Judith confessed, "I'm not sure they *are* tourists."

"Could be so," he conceded. "They didn't want to hear my usual spiel about the city. They were too busy yakking among themselves. That's fine with me, I get damned sick of giving all the blah-blah to visitors who end up moving here and ruining the place. Traffic! Specially when I have to drive that damned stretch thing. I might as well use a bus for my customers."

"Maybe," Judith said hopefully, "they were discussing their plans after they got here." She carefully avoided saying "schemes."

"Could be," Kronk agreed. "They were sure tickled with themselves. From the bit I heard, maybe they were bird-watchers, real excited about pigeons. Guess they don't have 'em where they live."

"Maybe not," Judith murmured. "Actually, they came here for a wedding. Did they mention that?"

"If they did, I didn't hear it," Kronk replied. "For all I know, they could've come to town for a funeral."

Judith didn't comment. The obvious remark would have evoked the tragedy in Hillside Manor's backyard. Neither she nor Renie needed any reminders of another death so close to home.

But she did catch the remark about pigeons. Apparently, she was supposed to have been one of them. At least they hadn't mentioned a dead duck.

Chapter 7

W hy," Judith said, "would anybody poison Millie? If, in fact, she and not Rodney was the intended victim?"

"Because they're both obnoxious?" Renie suggested.

"They're all kind of strange. If I didn't know better, I'd think it was some kind of act." She frowned. "In some ways, it is. Look at the reverend—he's got the real estate scam going on. Maybe he's not actually a preacher."

"He can't be both?" Renie tapped the table with a long fingernail. "If Kindred is really some kind of minister, it's a fringe sect. Those groups are usually small. The main man—or woman, for that matter—can't rely on the collection basket to make a living."

"Good point," Judith allowed. "Of course I originally believed they were from Southern California.

They have even more oddballs there than we have up here. Of course, they have a bigger population to draw from."

Renie nodded. "Bill's theory about our suicide rate—and San Francisco's—being so high is because all the crazy people from the East and the Midwest keep running farther and farther away from what they think is the source of their problems. They end up here or in the Bay Area and can't go anywhere beyond that. Both cities have all those attractive tall bridges, so they jump. It's terrible, because of course they've brought their problems with them. Counselors and shrinks like Bill can't really help that much because it comes from within. They can only provide a sympathetic ear."

"You're depressing me," Judith declared. "I didn't ask for a dissertation on mental illness."

"I have to live with it," Renie said. "I mean, Bill does talk about his job. He can't name names, of course. In fact, he usually can't remember them. Bill's not good with names. He's excellent with faces, though."

"Too bad he can't look at my guests and figure out which one of them is a killer." Judith sighed. "It'd help if I knew who was the intended victim."

Renie leaned back in the chair. "Go over the juice bit again for me, please. You weren't specific earlier."

"That's because I'm not sure," Judith replied. "The glass in Room One had been rinsed. The lab might come up with enough residue to figure out if it contained any poison. But nobody else at the dining room table—which is where Millie got it—was poisoned. That suggests that Rodney put the poison in the juice and then refused to drink it."

"While Millie was standing there watching him?"

Judith made a face. "I know, it doesn't make much sense."

"Nothing about this whole mess does," Renie asserted, getting out of the chair. "Hey, I figured out a way to convey recycling. I'll show one of your guests entering the B&B's front door and coming out the back way dead."

"That's awful," Judith asserted. "Murder isn't funny."

"Everything's funny," Renie shot back. "You know what Grandma Grover always said—'If I didn't laugh, I might cry.' Good advice."

Judith didn't argue.

Half an hour later, Judith heard the front door open. When she went out into the hall, she saw Dr. Sophie starting up the stairs. "Would you mind joining me for a moment in the living room?" she called to her guest.

The doctor's eyes were wary, but she complied. Judith gestured at one of the blue sofas, waited for Sophie to sit down, and then seated herself across from her guest.

"I'm sure," Judith began, "that you and your friends are all very upset over Mrs. Schmuck's untimely death. I know I am." She waited for a response, but Sophie's mouth remained in a tight line. "You must've been close to her."

"Fairly," the doctor finally allowed.

"Naturally, my husband and I are concerned about liability," Judith said, not without reluctance. "I don't know for certain if Millie took a glass of juice up to her husband, but I'm assuming she did, since she mentioned that was her intention. She didn't get it out of the refrigerator, so I suppose she poured some from one of the pitchers on the dining room table. Is that correct?"

Sophie seemed condescending in manner, but her answer was succinct: "Yes, I believe she used the glass that was at the vacant place setting—where Rodney would have sat—and poured the juice into it."

"Being a surgeon," Judith said, in an attempt at flattery, "you must have a very keen eye. Did you notice anything—however insignificant—about the glass itself?"

"Such as poison?" Sophie's expression was ironic. "Hardly. I admit I didn't scrutinize what Millie was doing at the time."

The doctor's detached attitude about the death of someone who was at least a traveling companion frustrated Judith. But the phone on the cherrywood table rang. "Excuse me," she said. "I must answer that. It might be a guest reservation."

It was, however, a fellow Our Lady, Star of the Sea parishioner, Norma Paine. Judith had barely gotten out "hello" before Norma broke in—and Sophie got up to make her exit.

"Arlene told me someone is offering to buy your properties in the cul-de-sac," Norma said in a booming, imperious voice that could rattle the china on the living room's plate rail. "I understand you and the Rankerses aren't interested in selling, but we are. I never thought Wilbur would retire from practicing law, but he has to cut down. His health, you know. In fact, we're thinking of retiring to Arizona. He needs more sun and less rain. Don't you, Wilbur?" The question was somewhat less ear-shattering, obviously being an aside to Mr. Paine.

"I didn't realize he was in poor health," Judith said. "I'm sorry."

"Oh, he'll be fine with a change in climate," Norma asserted. "Besides, I'm tired of keeping up such a big house for only the two of us. Anyway, I'd like to get in touch with those guests of yours who are buying up properties around here. Do you think they'll offer a good price? Real estate is ridiculously high on the hill right now, so we might take advantage of it."

Judith figured Norma would take advantage of just about anything and anybody, including cripples and small children. "Sure, I'll let them know. We'll miss you when you're gone," she fibbed.

"It'll be an adjustment for us as well," Norma admitted. "But retirement communities always have plenty of activities. As you know, I like to get involved."

"Yes—yes, you do, Norma," Judith agreed, glad that the other woman couldn't see her grimace. "In fact," she went on as Charlie Crump came into the entry hall via the front door, "I'll tell Mr. Crump right now."

"Crump?" Norma echoed. "That's an odd name. Oh, well. Thank you, Judith. I'll wait to hear from him."

Judith called to Charlie before he could start up the stairs. "What now?" he asked, plodding into the living room and looking put upon.

Judith explained the situation with the Paines. "I thought you might want to pass the news on to Reverend Kindred."

Charlie rubbed at his neck. Apparently he hadn't yet recovered from the kink. "We all dabble a bit in real estate now and then. It isn't easy for Georgie boy to get by passing the hat at church services. Have you got an address and phone number for these folks?" he asked.

"Yes," Judith replied, setting the phone down on the little table and taking the directory out of the drawer. She jotted down the required information on a pad.

Charlie scanned the slip of paper Judith had handed to him. He frowned. "Where is this from where we are now?"

"About six blocks west and closer to the top of the hill," she informed him.

He shook his head and handed the paper back to her. "No use to us. Too far away." He rearranged his comb-over before trudging out of the living room.

Just as Judith returned to the kitchen, Joe entered through the back door. He saw his wife's inquiring look and shook his head. "Don't ask about the cost of the repair job. It's worse than I thought and Ron's MG guru won't be in until Tuesday. It looks as if I'm without wheels for most of next week."

"That's okay," Judith said. "I don't have any big plans for the Subaru. Are you sure the MG is worth spending a lot of money to get it fixed? It's really old."

Joe's round face looked horrified. "Are you kidding? Do you know what that car is worth? It's a classic!

I bought it new in 1962. I've kept it up. I could probably sell it for at least fifty grand."

Judith resisted asking why he didn't do that. But his comment about the car being a classic made her think. She explained about the phone call from Norma Paine and Charlie Crump's reaction.

"It sounds to me," she went on, "as if the Schmuck gang wants only this specific bunch of properties. My question is why?"

Joe paused in the act of opening the fridge. "They think we have buried treasure around here? I'll admit, I've thought of burying your mother out there, but I suppose I should wait until she croaks. *If* she ever croaks." He removed a beer and flipped the tab.

"That's mean," Judith declared. "And your suggestion about buried treasure isn't worthy of you. Consider not just this small patch of the hill, but what's around it."

Joe took a sip of beer and leaned against the counter. "Lots of other houses. Apartment buildings. Condos. A fairly big park just up the hill from us. So?"

Judith nodded. "Exactly. No commercial properties once you get off of Heraldsgate Avenue. It's all residential, but condos are springing up in several parts of the hill, especially on top and over on the north side where Renie and Bill live. I think building a big condominium complex is the Schmucks' plan. But why they've put on this charade with who and what they are puzzles me. If anything, instead of claiming to be from L.A., they should admit they're more local. You know how most people here—especially natives like us—disdain California developers."

"Woody's checking their credentials," Joe said. "I gather they aren't listed in the local phone books. But a lot of people don't list anymore because of all the cell phones. I don't get that, unless it's because they keep changing cell companies and have to get different numbers."

"Some people never have a published number," Judith pointed out. "Bill and Renie have always been unlisted because they don't want calls at home from his goofy clients."

Joe drank more beer and then ambled over to the kitchen window. "Nobody in this cul-de-sac is willing to sell out," he finally said. "If anybody was, the Schmuck gang would lowball them. I wonder if they'd be out of here if Millie hadn't ended up dead."

"If they're local, why come here at all?" Judith asked.

Joe grinned at his wife. "To ingratiate himself as your son? You've got to admit that caught your attention."

"It was dumb," Judith asserted. "I still think he chose the wrong Judith Grover."

"Maybe." Joe sounded noncommittal.

Judith changed the subject. "Has the crime-scene processing finished outside?"

"Yes," Joe replied. "They were done over an hour ago." The green eyes twinkled. "They found a lot of fingerprints. It turned out they were your mother's. I wonder if I could talk Woody into busting her."

Judith refrained from gnashing her teeth. "Stop. I really get irked about how both of you constantly trash each other. Did the 'tecs find *anything* of interest?"

"I don't know yet," Joe replied. "Did you?"

"It's what I didn't find that's intriguing. Millie's purse. I don't suppose the cops turned it up?"

Joe's high forehead furrowed. "No mention of it. That *is* odd. Do you know what it looked like?"

"It was red patent leather," Judith replied, "which is hard to miss."

"Maybe," Joe mused, "one of the other guests swiped it. Millie might've had a lot of cash on her."

"That's dubious," Judith said. "Even if it were so, the purse still has to be someplace. Unless whoever took it stashed it during one of their neighborhood strolls. I wonder . . ." She stopped, staring at the phone. "Maybe I should call Tyler Dooley."

Joe looked bemused. "The Dooley grandson's a purse snatcher?"

"Hardly. But I'm going to call Corinne anyway to see if they were asked about selling their house. Granted, it's not in the cul-de-sac, but it's close enough to be included in what I should call this parcel of land. Tyler likes to play detective. Maybe his dog could sniff out the purse."

"Go for it." Joe polished off his beer. "I'm going to cut back some of the Rankerses' hedge on this side out back. It's shading some of those flowers you've got coming up across from your mother's witches' coven."

"Good idea," Judith murmured. But her mind wasn't on the garden. She picked up the phone and called Corinne Dooley. After a brief exchange of neighborly inquiries, the mother of the large Dooley brood asked if there'd been some trouble at Hillside Manor. Judith was candid; Corinne was matter-of-fact.

"My, that can be unsettling," she said. "Everything here has been fairly calm. Mary Lou fell off her unicycle and sprained her wrist this morning. Zach had his car dented rather badly up by Holliday's Drug Store this noon. Monica has hiccups that won't stop. Maybe I can get one of the other kids to scare her. It's too bad she didn't see the body in your yard. That might've done it."

Judith never ceased to marvel at Corinne's ability to cope so calmly with her huge family's misadventures. "What I was calling about," she explained, "is to find out if someone came by to ask if you wanted to sell your house."

Corinne laughed. "I don't think so. Tom and Johnny ripped out the front porch today. I doubt anyone would come around to the back. It's like a land mine with all the toys out there. If we had a body in our yard, nobody would be able to find it."

Judith didn't doubt it. "Is Tyler around, by any chance?"

"Let me think." Corinne paused. Judith could hear the shrieking of small children in the background. "He's probably riding his bike up at the SOTS playground," she said, using the acronym that stood for Our Lady, Star of the Sea. Do you want him to come by when he gets back?"

"Yes," Judith said. "I may have a . . . an assignment for him."

"Oh, that's wonderful! He does love to play detective. He wishes he could train Farley to be like a real police dog, but a mutt usually doesn't have those skills."

"True. But Tyler makes a good sleuth. He notices things."

"I'll admit he's observant, especially for a teenager. Both our sons were like that when you enlisted them to help with . . ." A crash could be heard in the background. "Oh, darn," Corinne said softly. "I think the bookcase in the hall fell over. I'd better make sure nobody's under it. Bye, Judith. Nice to talk to you."

The Dooley doyenne might have nerves of steel, but chatting with her could unsettle Judith. She gave a start when her name was called from the back hallway. Belle was languidly approaching the kitchen.

"I'm stressed," she announced. "Everybody keeps telling me that Mom's in a better place, but the morgue doesn't sound like that to me. Do you know where I can buy some weed? Clark and I are running out."

"They're talking about legalizing it here," Judith replied, "but it hasn't happened yet. Try hanging out by the high school or the junior high." For all Judith knew, the playground by the church and school might also be a good bet.

"Okay." Belle's gaze wandered to the high kitchen ceiling. "I don't suppose you could lend me a Big Ben? Or two."

"A what?" Judith asked, wondering if she was going deaf. Why not? Gertrude had claimed to be deaf for the past fifty years. Or so it seemed to her daughter.

Belle's eyes floated back down to gaze at her hostess. "You know—a couple of hundred dollars. For the pot. I thought Mom would have that much in her purse, but I can't find it. Do you know where it might be?"

"No," Judith replied. "As for a loan, I don't keep cash on hand."

"Bummer." Belle fixed her gaze on Judith's black purse that lay near the computer. "How about a check? Are there any banks open on Saturday around here?"

"I'm not writing you a check," Judith said firmly. "Key Largo Bank is only open Saturdays until four. It's ten after now. You're out of luck."

"I'm out of weed," Belle mumbled. "Maybe Clark can find an ATM. Is the bank around here somewhere?"

"It's up at the top of the hill and one block north. Are you smoking pot in your guest room?"

"Sure, where else? We like to kick back. But we keep the window open in Room Two. It's kind of small, but cozy. Except we didn't smoke while the cops were here." Belle shrugged. "Maybe I'll ask Dad. He's finally able to go back to his own room, but he's taking another nap in ours. I asked that older guy about Dad using his own pad and he said it was okay."

"What older guy?" Judith inquired.

"The one who was helping you make breakfast. I saw him in the hall when I went to the can."

"That's my husband," Judith said. "He's a retired police detective."

"Oh, darn!" Belle looked stricken. "Will he bust us for smoking weed while we stay here?"

"Probably not. He's got more important things to do right now," Judith added, though she wondered exactly what Joe was doing up on the third floor. Maybe he was checking backgrounds on the guests or talking to Woody on the phone. At least she hoped he was doing something to advance the murder investigation. Before she could say anything more to Belle, the nonbride wandered back down the hall.

Twenty minutes later, Tyler Dooley—and his dog, Farley—showed up on the front porch. Tyler's eager, round face lit up when he saw Judith. "Granny tells me you want me on the case. I heard you had another murder. That's amazing!"

"I wouldn't put it that way, exactly," Judith said, though Tyler's enthusiasm heartened her. After all, it was best not to dwell on the grimmer aspects of the tragedy. "Come in so I can tell you what happened."

Tyler hesitated. "Is it okay if Farley comes, too?"

"Sure," Judith said. "He's well behaved." She led the way back to the kitchen. It took her at least five minutes to recount the events, describe the people involved, and tell him what had transpired since the murder.

"Wow!" Tyler said softly when she finished. "This is all kind of confusing. But the scam idea to buy up the houses around here is the bottom line, right?"

"That appears to be so," Judith agreed. "I don't see what else could be their reason for this whole charade."

Tyler looked thoughtful. "This could be my last case," he said wistfully. "I'm starting college in the fall over at State U. That should be a real adventure, too." He glanced down at Farley and scratched the dog's head. "I'll miss this guy, though. So what's my first job? Surveillance?"

"You can do that anytime," Judith replied. "For now, I want you to look for Mrs. Schmuck's missing purse."

Tyler rubbed his chin. "Hmm. Any chance I could get a scent off of something that belonged to her? That'd help Farley."

"I'm not sure if Mr. Schmuck—Rodney—is back in his room. Let me check, okay?"

"Sure. I'll go out in the yard and study the crime scene." Tyler stood up. "Come on, Farley, let's go."

Upstairs, Judith noticed the yellow warning tape was gone from outside of Room One. There was no response when she knocked on the door. Cautiously, she stepped inside. Rodney apparently was still snoozing in Room Two, the smallest of the accommodations. Maybe Belle and Clark could put up with being so crowded only by smoking pot. Judith almost didn't blame them.

The crimson kimono was hanging in the closet. Judith slipped it off the hanger and went back downstairs just as Tyler and Farley came back inside. "This should do the trick," she said.

Farley sniffed tentatively at the shiny fabric. Tyler waited until he was sure the dog had taken in the scent. "Okay," he said. "We might as well start the search. It's clouding over so it might rain. Anyway, dinner's going to be late tonight. I think the stove broke. Again."

Judith didn't doubt it. If ever a stove was overworked, it'd belong to the Dooleys. If ever a mother and grandmother was overworked, it'd be Corinne. But she seemed to thrive on meeting her family's needs. Judith wished her own much smaller family was closer. But at least she had other diversions.

Once again, there was murder on her mind.

Chapter 8

Joe wasn't pleased to learn that Tyler was on the case. "The Dooley grandson's just a kid," he said, pouring drinks for Judith and himself. "It's bad enough that you keep putting yourself in harm's way, but I like it even less when you get a teenager mixed up in your crazy sleuthing."

Judith felt defensive. "You have to admit I've helped bring a few killers to justice."

"And damned near gotten yourself killed in the process," Joe reminded her. "Hey—don't you want us to be together into our dotage? What about that train trip back east we mentioned the other day?"

"I could forget about sleuthing, mind my own business, and get hit by a bus," Judith declared.

Joe smirked. "It'd probably be driven by the killer who was using it to get away from you."

"I don't want to argue anymore." Judith opened the oven. "It upsets me. I already grilled Mother's salmon first in case the guests actually show up for the cocktail hour. If she had to wait past six, she'd really be cranky. I'll take her meal out to her while you watch the rest of the food. And make sure the guests don't steal the silver. You are, after all, a private eye."

She hadn't bothered to put on a sweater before she left the house. Grimacing at the spot by the birdbath where Millie's body had been found, Judith felt the first drops of rain. She kept going, being a typical native and undaunted by the drizzle.

Gertrude was watching a baseball game. "No score," she announced. "Our starting pitcher is still scratching himself in places I won't mention. They're saying it might rain. So what? They always say that." She looked at the plate Judith had set down on the crowded card table. "Is this some unnatural species Dopey caught in Australia?"

"It's salmon from Alaska," Judith replied. "Could you shift some of your items so that there's room for the silverware?"

"I might be able to do that," the old lady replied. "I'm kind of crippled, you know." As if to prove it, she fumbled with the newspapers on the card table and sent them sailing onto the floor. "Now see what you made me do! I don't suppose you can bend over with your phony hip to pick them up."

Judith didn't answer. She was too stunned by the sight of what looked like a red patent leather strap peeking out from under the clutter. Hurriedly, she picked up a jumble puzzle book and the *TV Guide*. "That's Millie's purse!" she cried. "Where did you find it?"

"I didn't," Gertrude replied indignantly. "Sweetums was mauling it under the hydrangea by the garage this morning. Who's Millie?"

"The woman who was killed." Judith hesitated before touching the strap. But she realized that any fingerprints probably would be smudged by now. "I've got to give this to the police. They wondered why it wasn't found along with her other belongings."

Gertrude seemed disgusted. "There's not much in it. She only had about thirty dollars in her coin purse. I guess robbery wasn't the motive. She didn't even carry around a deck of cards like I always do. Are you sure she didn't die of boredom?"

"Some people aren't as keen on playing cards as you are, Mother," Judith said. "Enjoy your dinner."

"Ha! From the looks of this salmon, it wasn't caught, it was executed. How can you ruin a perfectly good piece of fish?"

Judith ignored the criticism. As she left the toolshed, she saw Sweetums sitting by the birdbath. She paused to stare at the cat. "If only," she said out loud, "you could talk, you'd be a good witness."

Sweetums responded by swinging his big orange plume of a tail and licking one of his paws.

What the hell . . ." Joe began when Judith came back inside. But he stopped and waited for her to enter the kitchen. Voices could be heard from the living room. "The guests did come down for the social hour," he said quietly. "Is that Millie's purse?"

"It must be," Judith replied, sitting down and opening the clasp. She removed a faux-leather packet to reveal credit cards and a local driver's license. "Her address is a street I don't recognize, but the zip code is in the north end. Is Rodney's license a phony?"

"Maybe," Joe allowed. "Or they could've recently moved here. What's the issue date on Millie's license?"

"March thirtieth of this year," Judith replied, "which is also her birthday. They *could* have moved here recently from California. A lot of people do that these days."

"Woody will check out the license Rodney showed you, of course," Joe murmured. "Are you joining the guests for the social hour?"

Judith shook her head. "No. I'm tired, I'm hungry, and I want to eat before the salmon gets dried out. Let's do it."

By some sort of minor miracle, the Flynns managed to get through dinner without discussing the murder case. But as soon as the table was cleared, Judith resumed her search of Millie's purse. She found a folded sheet of typewritten paper in a side pocket. Expecting something semisensational, she was disappointed.

"This is only a list of . . . I'm not sure what it is," Judith said, still keeping her voice down. The guests were still in the living room. "Take a look. Could it be medications?"

Joe studied the dozen unfamiliar words. "Temodar? It sounds like a title of some Mideastern potentate. Beats me." He handed the piece of paper back to Judith.

"I'll look up some of these on the computer later." She craned her neck to hear what was going on with the guests. "I think they're taking off for dinner. I hope they come back earlier than they did last night. Wondering about their return gave me minor nightmares. Of course what really happened this morning was much worse."

Joe didn't argue.

A little after seven, Judith called Renie to explain about finding Millie's purse and the list of exotic words. "I tried checking them out on the Internet," she went on, "but all I could find were warnings about side effects including everything but having your arms and legs fall off."

"The suits," Renie said. "Pharmaceutical-company lawyers are more concerned about being dragged into court than they are about helping patients."

"Being so breezy about it doesn't help me, coz," Judith admonished. "I could use a little empathy here."

"It's after hours," Renie said. "Bill and I are about to shut down our brains and watch mindless TV. Unless somebody else gets killed at your place tonight, do not disturb us."

"That's fine," Judith retorted. "I've got Tyler Dooley on the case." She sucked in her breath. "Oh, dear—I should tell him the purse has been found. Otherwise, his poor dog will end up trying to follow the scent to the toolshed and then into the house."

"Don't spoil the kid's fun—or Barley's. It gives them both something to do besides try to find sleeping space in the Dooley house."

"They have beds. Well, cots, anyway. Or sleeping bags. And it's Farley, not Barley."

"Whatever," Renie said airily. "Got to go watch some dumb movie I'll hate. Try not to let anybody kill you during the night. I'll see you in church."

Judith dialed the Dooleys' number. Someone other than Corinne answered. "Is Mrs. Dooley there?" she asked.

"Which one?" the youthful voice replied. "We got at least five of them."

"Never mind," Judith said. "Just tell Tyler that the purse has been found. I'll talk to him tomorrow. Or after Mass."

"Got it," the voice responded—and hung up.

The Schmuck entourage came back from dinner shortly after eight thirty. Feeling faintly guilty about her negative attitude toward the current guests, Judith got up from the living room sofa to greet the last trio of the group—Dr. Sophie and husband, Clayton, with a subdued Rodney in tow.

"Your cabdrivers take too many chances," Dr. Sophie declared. "Are they all Ethiopians? Don't they have real streets in Addis Ababa?"

"I'm sure they do," Judith said. "It's a huge city."

Clayton woefully shook his head. "I'll blog tomorrow about dangerous drivers. Especially the ones who take the wheel in a taxi. My nerves are shredded."

Judith didn't offer him any sympathy. Instead, she turned to Rodney, whose pallor worried her. "Are you feeling any better this evening?"

"Kind of," he replied. "Before dinner, I had a bit of the hair of the dog, as they say. But not too much. I'm still worn out. Dang, Mama, but all this stuff with Millie has upset your little boy. You and me are gonna have a little talk first thing tomorrow, okay?"

Judith's compassion took a hit. "That's fine, but I won't be able to do that until after I get home from church around eleven thirty. Of course, breakfast will be served as usual."

"Haven't got much appetite," Rodney muttered, clutching the banister as he followed his companions upstairs. "G'night, Mama."

Judith returned to the living room. Joe looked up from the spy novel he'd been reading. "I heard that," he remarked with a grin. "*I* should be disturbed. Rodney doesn't claim that I'm his father."

Judith sat down opposite her husband. "I thought maybe he'd given up on that 'Mama' part of their game. But the worrisome thing is how dreadful he looks. I wonder if he didn't drink some of the same juice Millie did."

Joe grew serious. "We don't know it was the juice, do we?"

"Well . . ." Judith's dark eyes were fixed on Joe's face. "Do you have a reason to believe otherwise?"

"We can't assume the juice contained the poison," Joe replied in his usual mellow, reasonable tone. "The autopsy results may indicate that's how the lethal stuff was ingested. But Woody won't have that information until at least Tuesday or Wednesday. Millie's death probably isn't the only suspicious one that will have happened over the weekend in a city this large. Keep in mind that a lot of relatives of people who apparently die of natural causes request an autopsy. That's becoming more common because of genetics and the need to know your immediate relatives' medical history. Of course, that's not a problem for you, because your mother will never die."

"Joe!" But Judith didn't want to get diverted from the original subject. "Is it possible that any of those drugs on that list I found in Millie's purse could have killed her?"

"Of course," Joe said. "But where are those meds? The cops didn't find any prescription drugs. Of course the killer may have disposed of whatever was used."

Judith's wide shoulders slumped. "I feel silly. I've been considering that Millie was poisoned by whatever must've been in the juice. I guess that was stupid of me."

Joe shrugged. "No, it was a logical conclusion. And God knows you're a logical person. But it's probably not what happened."

"Maybe," Judith said, "I should have stuck to my vow not to sleuth anymore. I think I've lost my knack."

Joe laughed. "You got sidetracked. You always have gone about solving cases by trying on one idea, finding out it's wrong, discarding it, and then moving on. It's sort of the way you buy your clothes."

Judith narrowed her eyes at her husband. "Are you discouraging or encouraging me?"

"Neither one," Joe asserted. "I know you, Jude-girl. You're going to do exactly what you want."

Judith didn't say anything for a long moment. "Maybe," she finally murmured, "I followed the wrong trail because that's what the killer wanted me—and the police—to do. What does Woody think?"

"Early days," Joe said. "You know Woody. He keeps his own counsel. He probably won't speak out until he gets the autopsy results."

"So what do we do about the guests? We can't keep them here under wraps."

Joe stretched and yawned as the grandfather clock struck nine. "You seem to think they actually live in the area. Let them check out Monday morning. It's too bad you didn't take a picture of Rodney's driver's license. I don't suppose you noticed if it had expired."

"I didn't." Judith was sinking into unaccustomed gloom, her eyes focused on the Persian carpet under the coffee table. She suddenly lifted her head and fixed Joe with a hard stare. "Go upstairs and ask Rodney for the damned license. Then you can see for yourself."

"No thanks," he replied. "Dealing with guests is your job, not mine. Except for making their breakfast, of course. Talk to him in the morning. He's probably already asleep. Rodney looked dead on his feet."

The description made Judith shiver.

As tired as she felt, Judith had trouble getting to sleep. Around midnight, she got out of bed and went into the den, where she called her cousin. Bill Jones went to bed around ten thirty, but his wife stayed up much later, often until going on 1 A.M. Renie swore that the later it got, the more creative she became.

"Is your house on fire—again?" she asked instead of saying hello.

"No," Judith said glumly. "Let me explain why I'm an idiot."

"I've known that since I was six," Renie shot back. "You couldn't play Monopoly with me because you couldn't read any of the cards. I had to wait a couple of years until you got to kindergarten."

"That was then, this is now," Judith said, mildly annoyed. "Although mentioning Monopoly is appropriate in regard to the Schmuck bunch. They seem to be all about real estate. Meanwhile, I realized tonight that I went off on a tangent."

"Not one of those 1961 Tangents. They ran backward, you know."

"Coz . . . don't joke. It's late, I'm tired and frustrated. Let me pass on what Joe said about the poison source."

"Okay," Renie responded. "I'll assume my professional mien and hear you out."

Judith unloaded. "Be honest," she added after finishing her spiel. "Am I getting too old to sleuth?"

"You're too old to run very fast from a killer," Renie said, "but you can still think just fine. So you got off on the wrong track. So did the cops if they thought the poison might've been in the juice. In retrospect, that was probably the wrong reaction. Millie probably wasn't the only one to drink whatever was on the table. Nobody else got sick, did they?"

"Rodney still isn't feeling very good," Judith pointed out, "but he drank a lot yesterday and probably the night before. Heck, he could even have flu. It goes around in good as well as bad weather."

"Don't I know it," Renie agreed. "I had it for three days last June."

"Speaking of being sick," Judith said, "I found a list of about twenty drugs I've never heard of in Millie's purse. Why would she be carrying something like that around with her?"

"For her alleged project? Maybe she planned to open a health spa."

The idea made some sense to Judith. "I'll ask Belle about that tomorrow. She must know. She might've been involved in the project." She winced, thinking of Millie's plans. Whatever was in the works, getting murdered hadn't been on the agenda.

Chapter 9

O n Sunday morning, Judith felt as if she were operating in a fog instead of the off-and-on rain that spattered the kitchen window. The guests seemed subdued. Reverend Kindred and his wife, Elsie, had been the first to come into the dining room. He'd asked if he could hold a prayer service in the parlor after breakfast. Judith told him she thought that would be . . . nice. She couldn't think of a better word.

Joe, however, was chipper. "I slept like a log," he told Judith. "You shouldn't get yourself all worked up over this latest disaster. You should be used to mayhem by now."

"I'm used to mayhem," Judith responded, "but how do you get used to murder? Even I can't do that."

"I did," Joe said. "I had to, working as a homicide detective. Woody and I both developed the skill of treating dead people as part of the human condition as well as part of the evidence. If we hadn't, we'd never have been able to solve our cases."

Judith didn't comment. She tried to smile when she brought the various breakfast items out to the dining room, but didn't engage the guests in conversation. She noted that Belle and Clark were the last to arrive, straggling in just as the reverend and his wife were almost finished. Judith overheard him tell the young couple that they might want to join the rest of the group for prayers. Belle rejected the invitation.

"What good will praying do for Mom?" she demanded. "If prayers didn't help her stay alive, they won't be of any use now."

"That's not the point," Elsie Kindred declared. "They're for the rest of us to know that our only help is with the Lord."

Belle laughed. "Hey, Nerd," she said to Clark, "I don't think the Lord can help *us*. We need help to find where we can get some more weed. Let's hit the stores on the top of the hill. There's got to be someplace that does pot business on the side."

Judith and Joe had overheard the conversation. "If," he murmured, "they have to go looking for pot, we can rule out drugs as part of the Schmuck scheme."

"I suppose," Judith said. "I'm going to ask Belle about Millie's project. I doubt it had anything to do with drugs, though I can't figure out why Millie carried around a list of meds I didn't even recognize. Maybe she planned to do something in the health field. For all we know, she may've had a medical background."

Joe chuckled. "Or she was a hypochondriac and knew a lot of doctors. The Schmucks brought one with them, after all." He glanced in the direction of the dining room. "I'll check Rodney's driver's license before we go to church. I can try one of your devious stunts and ask if he has a favorite photo of Millie in his wallet."

"As if," Judith sniffed, "you didn't have enough tricks of your own as a cop. I'll do it. Did you forget you don't like dealing with the guests?"

Joe shrugged. "You're right. They're all yours."

She had her chance when Rodney ambled into the kitchen fifteen minutes later. "Hey, Mama," he said, "any chance I can cadge a beer? It help settles my stomach."

"I've got some better remedies than that," she replied. "How about Mylanta?"

Rodney looked dubious. "Can you pour it in the beer?"

Judith refrained from rolling her eyes. "You don't need beer at nine thirty in the morning. Frankly, Rodney, you need to take care of yourself, especially now that poor Millie is gone. Would your prefer the Mylanta in liquid or tablet form?"

"Awww . . ." Rodney turned sheepish. "You're a good mother, Mama. Why weren't you around when I was growin' up?"

It wasn't easy for Judith to hold on to her patience, but she did it. "Sit down," she said, indicating a kitchen chair and realizing Joe had gone upstairs to change into his churchgoing clothes. "Let me get you a couple of the chewable tablets from the drawer. You must be overcome with grief, but drinking too much won't make it go away."

"It kinda does," Rodney murmured. "At least for a little while." He held out his hand for the tablets. "Okay, I'll do this cold turkey."

Judith sat down at the table and waited for him to swallow the meds. She decided to skip the ruse for looking at Rodney's wallet and cut to the chase. "Where did you get that California driver's license?"

"In California," Rodney replied with a flicker of indignation.

"Is it valid?"

"It was," he mumbled. "It expired at the end of March."

"Have you been driving with it?"

"Mama . . ." Rodney's expression was reproachful. "I'd never do that."

Judith smiled. "That's reassuring. So how do you get around?"

Rodney turned away. "Well . . . I have another driver's license. For this state."

"Is that because you actually live here?"

He grimaced. "We do now. I mean . . ." Rodney had turned back to look at Judith. "That is, *I* do now. Poor Millie doesn't."

"So you moved here recently," Judith said.

He nodded. "Earlier this month. I was born here, of course. Heck, you know *that,* Mama. But I moved to L.A. a long time ago. I had kind of a rough childhood without you."

Judith opened her mouth to insist that Rodney stop pretending she was his mother. But it occurred to her that maybe he really believed it. Rodney wasn't the first person she'd met who was delusional. After all, Renie and Bill insisted that Oscar, their stuffed ape, was real. Or so they claimed. Judith decided to shift the subject away from Rodney's youth.

"Do any of the other guests actually live in L.A.?"

"They all do," Rodney replied. "They're old friends of ours." His pallor took on a touch of pink. "It might sound dumb, but I thought it'd make more of a splash around here if Millie and I were still living in L.A., too. It does have what do you call it? Something like pancake, except in French."

"Panache?" Judith suggested.

"Yeah, right. That's the word." He hung his head. "Maybe that wasn't a good idea. I mean, it seems kinda silly now."

Judith glanced at the schoolhouse clock and stood up. "I'm leaving for church. I'm glad you told me the truth. That is, I was really confused about certain things. It made me uneasy."

Rodney had also gotten to his feet. "Hey, I couldn't go on lying to you, Mama. I always felt you'd give me a bad time if I did. I mean, I knew you were the kind of person who'd teach me about honesty being the best policy. If you'd been there to raise me, that is." He started back to the dining room, but stopped. "We got our own prayer stuff to do. I wonder if Georgie will pass the hat. Oh, well." He pushed open the swinging half doors and left the kitchen.

Judith hurriedly changed clothes up in the third-floor family quarters. She'd met Joe coming down. He told her he'd be waiting in the Subaru. He sounded a bit melancholy, no doubt because the MG was out of commission.

On the way up the hill to church, Judith told him about Rodney.

Joe wasn't particularly sympathetic. "The guy's probably an alcoholic. His brain may've gotten fried from booze a long time ago. All his pals may enable him, including the reverend. Rodney seems to have money from somewhere. Woody will check into that."

By chance—or bad luck—just after Joe pulled in to park on the parish school's playground, Norma and Wilbur Paine's imposing black Chrysler glided in next to the aging Subaru. The Paines' car always reminded Judith of a hearse. Norma's equally imposing body erupted from the passenger side.

"Judith!" she called. "What's going on? We haven't heard from your Realtor guests. Are they not diligent?"

"It's a long story," Judith replied, realizing that the Paines didn't know about the latest Hillside Manor disaster. "For one thing, Mr. Schmuck's not feeling very well."

"Well!" Norma joined Judith while the husbands took up the rear. "Maybe we wouldn't want sickly agents representing us. This Schmuck's problem isn't serious, I trust?"

"No," Judith replied. "But you have to do what's best for your situation. You know there are some fine real estate firms that are well acquainted with properties around here. As you may know, Cathy Rankers works for one of them."

Norma made a face. "I'd rather not deal with Cathy. You of all people know what Arlene's like. She's terribly opinionated."

If anyone could give Arlene a run for her opinions, it was Norma. A vision of pot and kettle danced in Judith's mind's eye. But she merely shrugged. "I thought you might want to deal with someone you already knew, especially a fellow parishioner."

"I think not," Norma said with a faint sniff of disapproval as they entered the vestibule. "It's not wise to do business with people you know. They take advantage. Indeed, consider what happened when I asked you to host the dinner for us that . . ." She stopped abruptly, seeing Carl and Arlene chatting with two of the adult Dooleys. "Come, Wilbur," Norma said, grabbing her husband's sleeve. "Let's find a place to sit that isn't near any of those dreadful Dooley children. They're such a nuisance."

Joe was smiling wryly. "Poor Wilbur. Why hasn't he strangled that woman? Or at least told her to put a sock in it. He's the poster boy for the henpecked husband."

Judith didn't comment. She spotted Renie and Bill sitting on the opposite side of the church. Coming from the hill's north slope, they always parked in the smaller lot by the rectory. Bill, as usual, was staring straight ahead, no doubt meditating, as was his custom. Renie, of course, was darting her eyes in every direction, probably trying to decide who was the least worst-dressed among her female fellow parishioners. She spotted the Flynns and offered them a small wave.

The organ played and the procession processed. As was often the case, Judith's mind occasionally wandered from the liturgy. But she did pray for the repose of Millie's soul and for Rodney to recover from whatever ailed him, even if it came out of a bottle. She also listened to Father Hoyle's sermon. The tall, chisel-featured, white-haired pastor always imparted something worth hearing.

At the sign of peace, Judith put on her friendliest smile to shake hands with the people nearby. When she turned around, she was startled to see Agnes Crump.

"I'm Catholic," Agnes murmured, giving Judith's hand a limp shake. "Charlie's not."

"Oh." It was the only thing Judith could say as the liturgy resumed. When Mass was over, she noticed that Mrs. Crump had already slipped away.

Joe hadn't seen the visitor. "I got caught up watching some of the Dooley kids across the aisle pummeling each other during the peace exchange. Agnes must've walked up to church. Maybe we can find her and offer a ride."

"There's something kind of pathetic about Agnes," Judith said after they were in the car. "As I recall, she and Charlie are actually friends with Clark Stone's father, though she did work as a legal secretary for Stuart Wicks. I wonder if Agnes and the Wickses are close. They're certainly different types of personalities."

"I don't see Agnes anywhere," Joe remarked after they pulled out of the parking lot. "Maybe she thought she could go straight down from the church to our house. I assume Agnes came up the hill via Heraldsgate Avenue since they must've arrived at the B&B that way. She'd have no way of knowing that the street by the church doesn't go all the way through because of the park."

"She can't get too lost," Judith said, also scanning their route. "Though some of the streets around here are oddly numbered."

Joe had turned onto the Avenue. "Agnes Crump's not a naive kid off the farm, she's a middle-aged woman from L.A. and a legal secretary. What does Charlie do for a living?"

Judith frowned. "Agnes said he did insurance work at home. His own agency, I gathered. I wonder if Cynthia and Stuart Wicks will leave for L.A. tomorrow. Or will Woody insist they stay close by?"

Joe shot Judith a quick glance. "You want me to bug my old buddy on the Sabbath? The Prices are Methodists. They probably won't get home from church until after noon. You know how Protestant services go on and on. Besides, Sondra teaches Sunday school and Woody spends time after church arranging food baskets for the poor and the infirm."

"Stop!" Judith cried. "Now I feel like I'm shirking my Christian duties. At least you work on some of the church and school repairs."

"Not if I can get out of it," Joe said, turning off the Avenue to head for Hillside Manor. "My back, you know."

"Your back? What's wrong with your back?"

"I have one. It could go out at my age. No heavy lifting."

Judith curled her lip at Joe. "You're a bit of a con man. You always were, in some ways."

"It's an inherent part of my good cop/bad cop persona," Joe declared. "While I was on the job I needed to con the occasional con to get a *confession*."

Judith shot him a withering look and didn't speak again until they arrived at Hillside Manor.

Gertrude had just exited the toolshed. "Well!" she called to Judith. "Are you two coming or going or do you know the difference?"

"We've been to church, Mother," Judith replied. "It's Sunday."

"It is?" Gertrude feigned surprise. "One day's the same as another when you're my age. Just one step closer to the grave."

"How close?" Joe asked in an eager voice.

Gertrude sneered at her son-in-law. "Not close enough to suit you, Lunkhead. I'm going into the house to get my meager lunch."

She revved up the wheelchair and sailed off to the back porch's ramp.

Joe poked Judith's upper arm. "I think I'll wash your car. Talking to your ghastly mother tends to warp my post-Mass Christian goodwill. If you need me, I'll be hiding in the garage."

Judith followed Gertrude inside. "It's only a little after eleven, Mother. Why are you hungry so soon?"

"Why not?" the old lady retorted. "I had to put up with one of your miserable guests just now. She sapped all my feeble strength."

"Who?" Judith asked as she took off her jacket.

"Some scrawny woman who claimed to be a doctor," Gertrude replied, stopping her wheelchair by the kitchen table. "I told her to examine my goiter and she wouldn't."

"You don't have a goiter."

"So? If she was a doctor, then she should have noticed that. Instead, she yapped about patient piracy." Gertrude frowned. "Or was it patient privacy or privilege or . . ." She shrugged her sloping shoulders. "For all I know, she was blabbing about a privy like the one up at the family cabin. I stopped listening. I just wanted to read the funny papers in peace. Why would she want to talk my ear off in the first place?"

"Good question," Judith murmured. "Do you remember anything she told you?"

Gertrude suddenly looked sly. "What's it worth to you? How about an early lunch? You shortchanged me on breakfast. I only got two pancakes with my egg and sausage."

Judith managed to hide her exasperation. "Okay. How about ham on rye with a slice of Swiss cheese, a dill pickle, and some celery sticks?"

"Skip the celery," Gertrude said. "The strings get caught in my dentures. Make that *two* dill pickles."

"Fine." Judith opened the fridge. "Now tell me what Sophie told you about her patients."

"Sophie? Is that what she's called?" The old lady looked as if she didn't think much of the name. "It was about your latest dead body in the backyard."

"I've never had a body in the backyard before," Judith declared. "A year or so ago there was one in Herself's garden, though."

Gertrude shrugged. "Close enough. The so-called *Doctor* Sophie wanted to know if I'd seen the dead woman alive in the backyard. I didn't see her at all, dead *or* alive. Unlike *some* people," she went on with an acid glance at her daughter, "I don't take up with hobbies that have to do with people who've been done in. I'll stick to my jumble puzzles."

"Is that all she mentioned?" Judith asked, sitting down at the table. "I gather Dr. Sophie said something about patients."

"My patience is being tried by all your goofy questions," Gertrude declared. "For a doctor, Sophie was kind of fuddled. In fact, she sort of admitted it." The old lady shrugged again. "It sounded to me as if she thought maybe she'd given somebody the wrong medicine. Or not enough. Or was it too much?" Gertrude now looked a bit fuddled, too.

"That's possible," Judith allowed. "I wonder . . ."

"You do that," Gertrude said. "You done making my lunch?"

"Yes," Judith replied. "Are you eating here or in the toolshed?"

Her mother grimaced. "And have Knucklehead show up while I'm eating? No thanks. That'd spoil my appetite. Anyway, he can't hide in the garage forever. Give me my plate. Then I'm out of here."

A moment later, Gertrude was gone. Judith remained seated, mulling over Sophie's remarks. Had Millie been under the doctor's care? Of course she might have been when the Schmucks still lived in California. And why had Rodney bothered with the ruse that he and Millie were still L.A. residents? It made no sense. Developers from all over the country were involved with projects in the city's nonstop construction.

Judith's musings were interrupted by a ringing phone.

"Where's Joe?" Renie demanded. "Bill wants to talk to him, but your husband's not picking up his cell."

"He doesn't take it to church," Judith replied. "He had to when he was still working for the city and it bothered him when it rang during Mass. It bothered everybody else, too."

"I didn't ask for an explanation," Renie said irritably. "The question was where's—"

"Joe's washing the car," Judith interrupted. "Can Bill wait until Joe comes inside?"

"You know Bill doesn't like to wait," Renie retorted. "Don't you remember how he didn't come out on the altar at our wedding until I reached the end of the aisle?"

"Actually I don't recall that," Judith said, trying to remain reasonable. "In fact, you're exaggerating. As your maid of honor, I was at the altar and Bill was there. But I did see him looking at his watch and shaking it a couple of times to make sure it worked. Why is Bill in such a tizzy to talk to Joe?"

Renie's heavy sigh carried over the line. "As you may have guessed, when we were at your house for dinner Friday, the husbands decided they should go on another exotic fishing trip. I got some stuff off the Internet for them last night, so Bill wants to confer with Joe."

"Oh, good grief!" Judith cried. " 'Exotic' translates as 'expensive.' How are we—and you guys—supposed to afford another big trip like that?"

"It wasn't all that expensive," Renie said, now sounding less fractious. "They wheeled and dealed to get a good price, remember?"

Judith wasn't giving in. "It still strained the budget."

"What budget? We've never had one. Bill and I are weak at math."

"Oh . . . Never mind. If Joe goes over to talk to Bill, do you want to come here? I need some help trying to figure out my current so-called guests. I've also learned some things you should know."

"Do I want to know them?"

"Yes. I firmly believe you should be as confused as I am."

"Well . . . Okay, I suppose that's only fair. Let's see what the husbands end up doing this afternoon."

Judith agreed and rang off. Ten minutes later, Joe came into the house. "You realize," he said, washing his hands in the kitchen sink, "that we have to buy a new car one of these days. The Subaru's twenty years old. Even a make as reliable as that one can't run forever."

"Eighteen," Judith countered. "And it runs fine. It's your fancy sports car that's costing us repair money now."

"That's different," Joe asserted. "It's a classic."

Judith shrugged. "Then maybe we can't afford you going with Bill on another big fishing trip to Peru or Thailand or Timbuktu."

"We've made no serious plans," Joe said, his round face innocent. "We might just go up to British Columbia or maybe Alaska. Those trips are comparatively cheap. By the way, I saw Agnes walk up the drive a few minutes ago, so she didn't get lost."

"You're trying to divert me." But Judith frowned. "I didn't hear her come in the front way. In fact, everything's quiet around here."

"Be thankful," Joe said, opening the fridge. "You fuss too much in general. Let Woody handle this case. He's an actual cop. Hey, where's the sandwich ham?"

"I gave Mother the last of it," Judith replied. "There's bologna and roast beef. You won't starve."

"But I had a yen for ham," Joe muttered. "Damn."

The phone rang again. Judith assumed it was Renie. "What now?" she asked after putting the receiver to her ear.

"That's *my* question," said a female voice that didn't belong to Renie. "In case you've forgotten I exist, this is Mavis Lean-Brodie from KINE-TV. You owe me."

"I do?" Judith gasped. "How can that be?"

"Because I saved you from a bunch of obnoxious media people yesterday," Mavis said in the voice that was well known as the longtime news anchor on the city's leading TV station. "As you're aware, I only go on air Monday through Friday. I want an exclusive this coming week on your latest murderous mayhem. I spent part of yesterday helping the cops shoo away some of my competitors from the cul-de-sac. I have friends in high places, kiddo. You and I go way back. I met Woody Price at the same time you did when the fortune-teller got herself murdered at your place."

"Yes." Judith saw Joe staring at her. "Of course, Mavis," she went on for her husband's enlightenment, "you're a local TV institution."

"Hunh. Some people think I should be *in* an institution by now," she declared. "Especially those eager, nubile young women who lurk around the station fondling their communications degrees. But enough of that. I want you to dish. How about meeting me for coffee up on top of the hill at Moonbeam's in half an hour?"

"I could do that," Judith replied. "Um . . . would you mind if my cousin joined us? She was coming over to see me this afternoon. You may remember Serena—or Renie, as she's known in the family."

"The one with the big mouth and the bigger teeth? Yes, I remember her. How could I forget?" Mavis said, sounding as if she'd like to do just that. "Oh, why not? You two seem to work as a team. Make it one o'clock. But don't let your cousin try to cadge lunch off of me because she figures I can put it on my expense account. See you soon." Mavis disconnected.

Renie, however, balked. "You know I almost never watch TV news unless you're on it," she said. "It's stupid, a bunch of people in heavy makeup—especially Mavis, now that she's older—reading the news off of a teleprompter and changing facial expressions frequently. They use so many filters for her close-ups that she's kind of a blur."

Judith didn't feel like begging. "So you won't join us at Moonbeam's? I hear they have some new pastries."

"What kind?" Renie sounded suspicious.

"I don't know," Judith admitted, "but someone at the drugstore said they were killer."

"Just your style," her cousin murmured. "Maybe I'd better come along after all."

Chapter 10

Judith's curiosity about what had become of Agnes Crump sent her to the front door. She looked outside to see her guest chatting with Arlene.

"Judith!" her neighbor called out. "Agnes has been telling me all about her years in the convent! Most intriguing—except for the nuns. I still have nightmares about them from my schooling at St. Radegunda's. Did I ever tell you about their cure for bed-wetting?"

"Uh . . . no," Judith replied, trying not to stare at a dazed-looking Agnes. "I mean, you did, a long time ago, but I—"

"Which," Arlene went on, "is how Agnes saved a man from the gallows." She took the other woman's hand and beamed at her. "How brave you were, my dear!"

Agnes apparently discovered that she still had vocal cords. "It wasn't as dire as the gallows. It was only a six-month prison term. A case of mistaken identity. I was a legal secretary for several years before I got arthritis in my hands and had to quit. But while I was still able to work, I recall when I typed up the information about the defendant—"

"Yes, of course," Arlene interrupted, patting Agnes's arm. "But it was so clever of you to notice Mr. Wicked's error. Not everyone would have caught that."

"Wicks, Mr. Wicks," Agnes said softly. "It wasn't so much his—"

"Whatever." Arlene tossed her short honey-colored curls. "But it would've been wicked for an innocent man to be sent to jail for something he didn't do."

"Yes," Agnes murmured. "So wrong." Her blue eyes looked misty.

Arlene gave the other woman one last pat. "You take care. I didn't realize you were at Mass. If I'd known, Carl and I would've driven you back here." She shot Judith a reproachful glance.

But Agnes came to her innkeeper's defense. "I left after the final blessing. I was afraid it might start raining again. I'm not used to wet weather."

"We have no other kind," Arlene declared. "You wouldn't want to live here. Please tell everyone you know back home about all the nasty rain we have and how miserable they'd be if they moved to the area. Have a nice day." She walked quickly around the hedge and disappeared.

"What a nice lady," Agnes murmured as she and Judith headed toward the front porch. "You're lucky to have good neighbors."

"We are," Judith assured her. "They've been next door since I was in my twenties. By the way, Rodney told me that he and Millie had moved back here not long ago. Why did they leave L.A.?"

"Oh . . ." Agnes's gaze roamed up to the entry-hall ceiling. "Millie had never lived here, but . . . I guess they both thought a change would be good for them." She didn't look at Judith, but lowered her eyes to study the Persian carpet.

"I understand Rodney was born here," Judith said, despite her reluctance to bring up the touchy subject of who had been his mother.

The blue gaze briefly met Judith's dark eyes. "He was. I know that's true. Excuse me, Mrs. Flynn," Agnes said, speaking more rapidly than usual. "I should lie down for a bit. After Mass, I rest and contemplate."

"Of course." Judith headed for the kitchen.

Joe was eating his lunch. "I'm going over to see Bill in a bit. You got any plans?"

"Yes," Judith said. "I'm meeting Mavis Lean-Brodie and Renie for coffee at Moonbeam's."

"Oh," Joe said, looking faintly chagrined. "I forgot to mention that Woody told me Mavis was outside the cul-de-sac yesterday shooing away the media competition. Why don't you drop me off at the Joneses' house? I can go on Bill's walk with him later and get some exercise."

"Good idea," Judith said. "Maybe I'll get something to eat at Moonbeam's. I still feel full from breakfast."

"You're not fussing about your weight again, are you?"

Judith put a hand to her abdomen. "I always gain a few pounds after Easter. I've lost some already, but I have two, three more to go."

"You're tall and fairly big-boned, so it never shows." Joe grinned. "Not even when you take your clothes off. You're too damned sensitive about your weight."

Judith carefully leaned down to kiss her husband's increasingly higher forehead. "You're really kind of sweet," she said.

"Don't tell anybody," Joe murmured. "It'd ruin my private-eye reputation. Oh!" The green eyes—magic eyes, Judith called them—lit up. "I forgot. While we were at church, I got a call on my cell for an assignment starting tomorrow. Missing person case. It should be easy. With your penchant for crime, the guy will probably show up here."

Judith finally sat down. "Who is he?"

"A city employee," Joe replied after swallowing the last of his sandwich. "I've got his name upstairs. He's only been gone a couple of days, but his wife is worried. She insists her husband's not the type to go off on his own. I've heard that line before. Have we got any pie left?"

"Only one slice of the boysenberry," Judith said. "Go ahead. I don't need it. I'm watching my weight, remember?"

"Do I hear something snide in your tone?" Joe inquired, one hand going to his slight paunch.

"I rarely nag," Judith said primly. "I would, however, suggest that if your stomach gets too big, it might bother your precious back."

"Touché," Joe murmured. And got up to fetch the pie from the refrigerator.

At exactly one o'clock, Judith was the first to arrive at Moonbeam's. The coffee shop was busy as usual, but she found a table that would seat three. Recognizing two couples from church, she smiled and nodded. Just as she was checking out the numerous varieties of coffee specialties, Mavis walked briskly through the door. At least a dozen heads swiveled to stare.

"I hate being a so-called celebrity," she muttered, glaring at a bald man at the next table who was virtually ogling her. "I'm a journalist, damn it. And unlike a lot of TV talking heads, I still chase news."

"I know that," Judith said, smiling again. "Otherwise, I wouldn't be here with you."

"Right." Mavis slipped out of her chic jacket. "Where's your bratty cousin?"

"Renie will be along eventually," Judith said. "Shall we wait for her or go get our orders now?"

"We order," Mavis asserted with a flip of her blond pageboy. "She can fend for herself. I know what I want—an espresso macchiato and some Greek yogurt."

The line was surprisingly short. Judith ordered a skinny latte and a ham-and-Swiss panini. As they took their items back to the table, Renie half stumbled inside. Apparently she was having trouble with the swinging door, which seemed to have declared war on her. Or, Judith mused, maybe she was cussing just for the heck of it. Acknowledging her cousin and Mavis, Renie barged past two stout older ladies and got ahead of them in line.

"She hasn't changed," Mavis remarked ruefully.

"She never does," Judith said. "But she's basically . . . decent. What do you want to know about my latest dead body?"

"How she got that way," Mavis answered. "Camilla Schmuck, correct? First, has her death been ruled a homicide or do the cops just figure it must be since it happened at your place?"

As much as Judith liked and respected Mavis, she was loath to tell her too much about the current B&B guests. "They came in a group to hold a wedding, all having known each other when they lived in the L.A. area. Yesterday morning Millie was found dead in the backyard. An autopsy was requested. For all I know, she died of natural causes."

Mavis smirked. "But you think otherwise."

"I'm not sure I do," Judith replied. "It *is* possible."

"Not with you," Renie stated, plopping down in the empty chair. "Hi, Mavis. What's that gruesome goop you're eating?"

"I call it lunch," Mavis snapped, staring at Renie's hefty chicken BLT sandwich. "It's not as grandiose as yours, of course."

"This isn't lunch," Renie replied. "I ate that at noon. This is snack."

"Egad," Mavis said under her breath. "You really are Petunia Pig. How come you're not fat?"

Renie, who had taken a big bite of sandwich, merely shrugged.

"Metabolism," Judith declared. "Some pigs got it, some pigs don't."

Mavis merely arched her pristinely plucked eyebrows. "As you were saying about your latest corpse . . . Did the wedding come off, by the way?"

Judith shook her head. "Millie was the bride's mother. They had to postpone it. Really, I don't see much news value since we don't know how or why she died."

"I like to be prepared," Mavis said. "Knowing you . . ."

"Stop." Judith had held up a hand. "Look, if it turns out not to be a natural death, I promise I'll let you know. But we may not find out until later this week. You know how long an autopsy can take. We've got too many people living—and dying—here these days."

"But," Mavis said, "most of them don't do it in your backyard."

The remainder of the get-together turned to other topics, mainly about other story lines that the KINE-TV crew was developing for future broadcasts. Shortly before two, Mavis announced that she had to change and head for a cocktail party at the mayor's residence. Renie decided she might as well go back to Hillside Manor, since the husbands were no doubt still planning fishing trips that could wreak havoc with their respective family incomes.

When they reached the B&B, Renie looked up at the clouds that had rolled in while they were at Moonbeam's. "If Bill and Joe are going to walk later on," she said, "they'd better both wear hooded jackets. Otherwise, they might get wet and shrink."

Judith glanced at her cousin as they went in through the back door. "Are you implying they don't know enough to keep from getting rained on? Joe's a native and Bill's lived here forever."

"I'm saying men don't always think," Renie replied. "Take Rodney Schmuck, for example. What's his point in insisting that you're his mother? It makes no sense."

Judith sat down at the kitchen table. "I've no idea," she said. "The only thing I can think of is that his mother really was named Judith Grover. Maybe she abandoned him at birth or gave him up for adoption. I don't even know *where* he was born, though he claims to have proof that I'm the one who gave birth to him."

"You'd probably remember it if you had," Renie said with a straight face. "Heck, I'd remember it. I'd have come to see you in the hospital. How come you haven't found Rodney's so-called proof during your searches of their guest room?"

"Good point," Judith conceded. "The only thing I can think of is that he's got it on him. Maybe in his wallet. You can get birth certificates shrunken down to that size and laminated for international travel purposes. I should've frisked him after he passed out yesterday."

Renie, who had sat down across from Judith, frowned. "Where are all the goofballs? It's really quiet around here."

"I don't know," Judith admitted. "With all the high-tech stuff, they could be watching movies on their phones. Maybe they rented a car. Or a van. Or a damned bus." She covered her eyes with her hands. "I just wish they'd never come here. They're a really annoying bunch of people. Except maybe Agnes Crump. She's merely kind of pitiful."

Renie was looking unwontedly serious. "I really think you should have Bill check out Rodney. He doesn't sound as if he's got it together."

"Of course he doesn't," Judith said. "His wife just died. Or do you mean the mama bit? And would Bill be willing to talk to him?"

"Probably not," Renie replied. "He doesn't like to work for free. In fact, Bill doesn't like to work. Since he officially retired from his psychology practice, he takes only very special cases, such as those who have not only mental and emotional problems, but enormous bankrolls."

Judith's face was wry. "He's all about the compassion, isn't he?"

"Skip the sarcasm. At least Bill is honest about his motives. Speaking of which, just in case Millie was whacked, have you figured out why anybody would want her dead?"

"No," Judith said. "I'm waiting for Joe to hear from Woody about background and such. Then there's the problem of these people sticking around inside. Unlike the usual guests, they seem to have absolutely no interest in seeing the local sights. But you'd think they might have personal errands to run while they're here. Somehow I don't see them as the type who'd use public transit." She leaned back in the chair. "That's what bothers me most. There's nothing typical about these people. Yes, they came for a wedding, but it got called off. They're stuck here—at least Rodney is—until the autopsy is finished. I can't put them up after tonight because I've got guests coming in Monday evening. They'll . . ." She shut up as Stuart Wicks came through the back hall and into the kitchen.

He didn't bother with a preamble to his news. "I finally heard back from a minion who works for your police captain. Price prefers that we remain in the city.

I am outraged," he concluded without inflection or expression.

Renie looked up at him. "How can we tell? Finger puppets might work. Or turning blue." She stood up. "I need Pepsi."

Judith felt obligated to speak. "Can you ask for a postponement?"

Stuart arched one dark eyebrow. "On a Sunday?"

"Oh." Judith's smile was feeble. "No, I suppose not. Could you delegate to someone in your office or do you practice alone?"

"I'm one of the senior partners in a large firm," Stuart replied with dignity. "We have over sixty attorneys just in our main office in Century City and three other offices in L.A. County."

"That's very impressive," Judith said, noticing that Renie had wandered back down the hall and was going outside. "I don't think Cynthia told me if your court appearance is for a criminal or a civil case."

"It's a civil matter." Stuart frowned. "That is, it's actually a hearing to prevent criminal charges being brought against my client." He sat down in Renie's vacant chair. "I'm rather shrewd at reading people's faces. You have a very sympathetic countenance, Mrs. Flynn. What do you make of the events that have transpired here since we arrived?"

"Tragic," Judith responded. "Puzzling, since Millie seemed in good health. You must know Dr. Kilmore. I assume she'd have some inkling if Millie had any serious health problems."

"I don't really know Sophie," Stuart said. "She's been friends with the Schmucks for some time. Bear in mind, I'm merely Clark's stepfather. I don't really know him all that well. Cynthia and I have only been married for three years."

"Did you know his father? That is, Cynthia's first husband?"

"No. They'd been divorced for . . ." Stuart's long, sallow face grew thoughtful. "I think about six or seven years. I believe he moved from L.A. after the decree was final. Cynthia lost track of him. A good loss, from her point of view. Unhappy marriages are only good for lawyers who handle the more contentious breakups. This is my first foray into matrimony. Cynthia and I have a most blissful union."

Judith tried to imagine the rigid Stuart Wicks succumbing to bliss. She couldn't. Nor did Cynthia seem like the type who would surrender to unbridled passion. *Of course,* Judith reminded herself, *you never really know about people. . .*

" . . . her own profession," Stuart was saying. "Don't you agree?"

"Well, yes, in general," Judith replied, not having heard the first part of whatever Stuart had been droning on about. In fact, she wondered how a judge or a jury could stay awake during his presentations. "How long has Cynthia held that job title?" she asked, hoping the question would enlighten her about whatever it was that Mrs. Wicks did for a living.

Stuart pondered briefly. "Six years? After divorcing Clark's father, she went back to school and earned her master's degree in family counseling at UCLA."

"That was smart of her," Judith said. "Her work must often be rewarding. Helping others, that is."

"Indeed," Stuart concurred, "though it is fraught with difficulties and sometimes even danger. The term 'family counseling' may sound benign, but I assure you that her job also has its hazards. Some of her clients are virtually deranged."

Judith saw Renie coming back into the kitchen. "Deranged?" Renie asked. "Hey, coz, how about your zany mother wrestling with Sweetums to stop him from destroying the stuffed donkey she got years ago as Democratic precinct committee woman? I stopped her just in time before she strangled the wretched beast. Sweetums must be a Republicat."

"Ah . . ." Judith began, "I don't think you've officially met Stuart Wicks."

"Probably not," Renie said in an indifferent tone as she tossed her empty Pepsi can in the garbage can under the sink. "I've never met Sidney Wicks either, though I watched him play basketball for UCLA and later in the NBA." She gazed disparagingly at Stuart. "You're barely six feet. You'd never make the team. If you could run, maybe you could get a job as a referee. That's what our Uncle Al did after his playing days were over."

Stuart took umbrage, his sallow face taking on a hint of color. "You are out of order! Have you no manners?"

Renie looked all around herself. "Gosh, I guess I left them in the toolshed. Maybe Aunt Gert will find them. She lost *her* manners seventy years ago. Does anybody here except me know how to spell 'pompous'?"

"Coz," Judith said in a beleaguered voice, "could you please not act like you came onstage in the middle of a really bad play? Stuart and I were trying to have a conversation."

Judith's guest got to his feet. "I believe that's my exit line. If," he went on, glaring at Renie, "we were in court, I'd cite you for contempt."

Renie merely stared unblinkingly at Stuart until he stopped glaring and left the kitchen.

"You," Judith said in her most severe voice, "can be a real twit sometimes. No matter what you may think about this current bunch of guests, can't you at least be civil?"

Renie let out a big sigh and looked pained. "I don't suffer fools gladly. Alas, you often do because you're so damned softhearted. Yes, I know these people are paying customers, but they're taking advantage of your good nature. I've spent my whole life watching out for you, but I can't always be around. When I am, I tend to be overly protective."

Judith's face softened. "I know. I appreciate it. But sometimes it's embarrassing."

"You're too darned sensitive," Renie said, though her tone was benevolent. "Anything new from Woody?"

"If there is," Judith replied, "Bill will find out before we do. Joe thought Woody might call him this afternoon. Of course it *is* a Sunday."

"Right," Renie agreed. "Even a police chief shouldn't have to work on the weekend unless the whole city is under siege. Other municipal employees don't work weekends."

Judith nodded. "That's true. In my job, weekends are usually the busiest . . ." She stopped, frowning. "That's odd. A city inspector came by yesterday to ask about the firefighters' call here. He wanted to find out what had happened and even checked the oven."

Renie grimaced slightly. "That *is* strange. Did he show you his license?"

"No, but he had a badge with his name on it." Judith paused, trying to remember what the ID looked like. "It looked very official, though I don't think it had his picture on it . . . Damn! I wonder if he was a phony. But why?"

"You're the sleuth," Renie said. "You work it out. Got any ideas?"

But for once, Judith didn't have a clue.

Chapter 11

S o," Renie said after she'd swiped some Brie out of the fridge and Judith had finished recounting the seemingly innocuous events of the day so far, "you're trying to solve what might not even be a murder. Why not just kick back and wait for the autopsy report?"

"Fact," Judith stated, one finger pressed on the table. "There were traces of possible poison in her mouth. What does that suggest to you?"

" 'Possible poison' is not a fact," Renie argued. "It's a surmise."

Judith was silent for a moment, but her dark eyes snapped. "What about my instincts? When have I ever been wrong about a homicide?"

Renie winced. "Wouldn't you like to be for just once?"

"Well . . . yes, I suppose I . . ." The phone rang. Judith got up to fetch the receiver off the counter.

Woody Price was the caller. He greeted Judith with his usual low-key warmth, then asked if Joe was available.

"He's at Bill's house," she informed him. "Can I take a message?" Her voice took on an eager note.

Woody chuckled. "I know you're as curious as that ornery cat of yours, but I have to deliver the goods to my old partner in crime. I don't want to bother him if he's visiting with Bill. Have him call me when he gets home, okay? I actually don't have all that much to tell him, since most of my out-of-town sources aren't available on a Sunday."

"You mean I get zip?" Judith said in a forlorn voice.

"Oh . . ." Woody hesitated. "I have an officer whose father is a Key Largo Bank executive. I found out that the Schmucks have quite a lot of money in that bank, both here and in L.A."

"I guess that's not a surprise," Judith said. "They showed up in a big limo. I had to admit that Rodney doesn't strike me as someone who could handle a job that made him wealthy."

"Actually, I don't know that he does," Woody responded. "The ten-figure account is in Mrs. Schmuck's name."

"Oh, good grief!" Judith exclaimed. "That's a lot of money! And only one bank reporting in so far?"

Woody chuckled again. "I only told you that so you wouldn't worry about them skipping out without paying—or if they already did, the check won't bounce and the credit cards are solid. I've got to go, Judith. Sondra needs some help in the garden. She's digging up a redwood. At least that's what it sounds like."

Judith thanked him and hung up. "That," she declared, "was most interesting!"

Renie pretended to yawn. "I guess so. How would I know, except from your gaga expression."

"Bottom line," Judith explained, "is that Millie is— was, I mean—worth ten figures."

"Really?" Renie said indifferently. "She wasn't in bad shape, but I didn't think her figure was that great. As for her bottom—"

Judith cut her off. "I'm talking about her bank account, dopey. She may have had at least a billion dollars in one account at Key Largo."

Renie shook her head in disbelief. "Nobody has a billion dollars in one account anywhere. Rich people have it stashed all over the place. Furthermore, it'd take more than a precinct captain to find out where the money was in such a short time."

"All I know is what Woody told me," Judith said with a touch of indignation.

"Even Woody can be bowled over, I suppose," Renie remarked. "Who was his source?"

Judith relayed Woody's explanation of how he'd found out about the Schmucks' wealth, but realized it sounded a little iffy. "Still, Woody's no fool," she added.

Renie nodded halfheartedly. "True. They had to have some big bucks to make offers for the properties around here. What did Rodney say he did for a living? If I heard, I've forgotten."

"He claims to be a motivational speaker."

Renie practically fell out of the chair. "That dim bulb couldn't motivate me to grab a lifeline if I were drowning! And I can't swim."

"I never figured out why you couldn't learn to swim," Judith said. "You took lessons before we sailed to Europe back in 1964."

"I wanted to be ready in case the ship sank," Renie declared. "It turned out I can't even float. The instructor told me I have no center of gravity. That's not a character flaw, you know."

Judith merely shook her head. "Never mind all that. Though I agree, Rodney doesn't strike me as . . . motivational." She tensed as she heard voices coming from the vicinity of the front hall. *The guests?* she mouthed at Renie.

Her cousin shrugged. A moment later the voices faded, but Elsie Kindred entered the kitchen via the dining room.

The reverend's wife was a tiny woman, barely five feet tall, pale and spare as a plucked chicken. Indeed, her graying auburn hair was combed into a wave that looked like an avian crest.

"Do you have any bandages?" she asked in a fretful voice. "My husband was injured while on his walk around the neighborhood."

"How did that happen?" Judith inquired, getting up from the chair.

Elsie flinched. "He encountered someone who was very rude. Out of good Christian charity, George asked why the man was so troubled. The poor soul shoved my dear husband and he fell on a garden gnome. The statue's pointed hat pierced his leg."

Judith went to a drawer at the far end of the counter. "I assume it's not a big puncture. That is, gnomes, being small, wear little hats."

"That's so," Elsie agreed, her hands fluttering a bit. "If you have some antiseptic salve, I'd appreciate it. Alas, I didn't bring my medical kit with me. An oversight, of course, but we made our departure in haste. I like to be prepared for any eventuality."

"Do you always bring along first aid when you travel?" Judith asked, handing over an assortment of bandages.

"Yes," Elsie replied. "I'm a nurse. You never know when you'll need emergency supplies." She smiled tremulously and went out through the swinging half doors.

"Holy crap!" Renie muttered. "Is she a real person—or just a human exigency?"

"She's a miracle maker," Judith said. "Somehow her presence made you keep your big mouth shut."

"I was too caught up in Elsie's 'be prepared' recital. Why did they leave in haste? Fleeing their creditors?"

"Good question." Judith sat down again. "Who has a garden gnome around here?"

If Renie was surprised by the question, she didn't show it. "Ah . . . offhand, I couldn't tell you. I've got only religious statuary and a curled-up cat sculpture in the yard. I think somebody on our side of the hill may have one, but that'd be a long trek for the reverend's walk. Are you thinking somebody coshed him for being overzealous?"

"It's possible," Judith allowed. "I understand the urge to do that."

"Was Kindred really proselytizing or making offers on houses?"

"He could do both, I suppose," Judith replied. "But I thought he only bothered people in the cul-de-sac. Maybe *we* should go for a walk. It's not raining. Yet."

"A walk?" Renie looked horrified. "You know I don't like to walk. I drive a car, and if I can't do that, I take a taxi, and if that's not possible, I stay home."

"You walked all over the beach when we were up at Whoopee Island in January," Judith reminded her cousin.

"That's different. It was mostly sand. That's why it's called a beach." Renie crossed her arms and turned sulky.

Judith stood up. "I'm going to take a walk. You can follow me in your car—you spoiled brat."

"Ohhh . . ." With great reluctance, Renie rose from the chair. "Fine. I'll go with you. But if I get blisters, it's your fault."

The cousins headed out through the front door. Gabe Porter was mowing his lawn; the cousins waved. The Ericsons were pulling into their driveway; the cousins waved again.

Renie still looked grumpy, but her tone was reasonably amicable when she asked if Judith had interrogated the neighbors.

"I haven't, really, except for Arlene," she said. "They got the spiel from Kindred about an offer for their house. But I don't think the reverend had gone farther than the cul-de-sac unless he expanded his web when he found out nobody close by wants to sell. Or maybe Kindred's seeking new members for his congregation."

"That may be *his* scam," Renie remarked as they reached the sidewalk of the east-west street. "Hey, why is that guy with the sunglasses sitting there in his car? Is he lost?"

Judith slowed her step, peering across the street. "He looks familiar. Now, where have I . . ." She stopped as the man started his white Chevrolet Camaro, pulled away from the curb, and drove off in a burst of speed. "What now? Did we scare him?"

"We don't look *that* bad," Renie said.

"Speak for yourself," Judith murmured. "As usual, your casual wear looks like a casualty. Why are you wearing a ratty sweatshirt that has Pluto on it?"

"Because I couldn't find one with Goofy?"

"*You're* goofy." Judith stopped in her tracks. "I think I know who that guy in the car is. I could be wrong, but even with the sunglasses, he looked like the city inspector who came yesterday."

"Was he driving a car like that?"

"I didn't see his car." Judith kept walking, but more slowly. "In fact, it should've been parked in front of the house. And if he was a real inspector, it would've had the city logo on it. I'd have noticed that."

"So," Renie said, "you got conned? But why?"

"I've no idea. All he did was look at the oven."

"Are you sure of that?"

The cousins had almost reached the corner. "I made sure he closed the door behind him. But I didn't follow him outside. Now I'm worried. I should have Woody check him out tomorrow. Hey, the Flahertys live here," she said, gesturing at the big white colonial house on the corner. "They're fellow SOTs. Let's ask them if Kindred stopped by."

"I don't think I know them," Renie said.

"Then you're about to get introduced. Be nice." Judith led the way up the steps to the front porch. She used the brass ring in a lion's mouth to knock on the blue front door.

A pretty, fortyish woman whose dark blond hair was in some disarray appeared after almost a minute had passed. "Mrs. Flynn?" she said. "Sorry to keep you waiting. I'm cleaning cupboards. Our oldest son, Peter, is coming back from his first semester at State University later this month. Neal is out in the backyard."

Judith recalled that Neal was Mr. Flaherty. Unfortunately, she'd forgotten his wife's first name. "This is my cousin Serena Jones," Judith said. "She and Bill are also parish members."

The two women shook hands. "Yes," Mrs. Flaherty said, "I've seen you at Mass. Your husband is a lector, isn't he? He has a wonderful voice. And it carries so well. Some of the other lectors tend to mumble. I don't think all of the elderly parishioners can hear a word they're saying."

Renie smiled graciously at the compliment. "He took voice lessons. His original intention was to become an actor, but he changed gears later on. Call me Renie. Your first name is . . . ?"

"Angie." She turned to Judith. "What can I do for you two? Is the parish holding some kind of event that I haven't heard about? Neal and I were gone for the weekend and just got back a little while ago. We went to evening Mass last night in Port Grumble."

"It's nothing to do with the parish," Judith replied, realizing that the Flahertys probably hadn't heard about her latest disaster. "You may know I own the B&B in the cul-de-sac. I hate to say this, but my current guests are a little odd. One of them is kind of a far-out preacher who's been bothering the neighbors around Hillside Manor. I was wondering if he'd been here, but of course you haven't been home."

Angie uttered a tight little laugh. "He *was* here. While we were gone, that is. The only reason I know is that he left a flyer under the mat. Frankly, his church sounds like a scam."

"I'm not surprised," Judith said. "I've never seen any information about his beliefs or practices. Do you still have the flyer?"

"Yes, in the recycling," Angie replied. "But we haven't yet taken the wastebasket out to the bin. Let me get it. Would you like to wait inside?"

Judith assured her they didn't mind staying on the porch. "You're behaving like a mature adult," she whispered to Renie. "I'm stunned. I hardly recognize you."

"You know I have excellent manners—when I need them," Renie declared. "How else do you think I manage to keep my clients so that I can earn a living with my graphic-design business? Egad, sometimes I have to deal with the mayor and the county executive and a whole slew of VIPs. Of course some of them have crappy manners, too. Did I tell you about the deputy mayor putting a whoopee cushion under the police chief's . . ." She stopped as Angie reappeared.

"It's kind of wrinkled," she said, handing the sheet of pale yellow paper with bright green printing. "I did skim what it says, but it sounded off-the-wall to me."

Judith smiled wryly. "The reverend is that way. Thanks, Angie. I'm sorry to bother you."

"No problem," the other woman insisted. "I see that car across the street is gone. The guy pulled up right after we got home, so it's been there for a couple of hours. I couldn't figure out what he was doing. Neal noticed that he seemed to be taking notes. Do you think he's a burglar?"

"If he is," Judith said, "he's driving a much nicer car than I do. In fact, it looked almost new."

"You may be right," Angie agreed. "He could be a real estate agent."

"Could be," Judith responded. But she didn't add that in the past three days real estate had taken on an unreal feeling for her.

Chapter 12

C an we go back to your house now?" Renie asked, sounding like a whiny six-year-old. "My feet hurt."

Judith looked down at her cousin's flimsy flats. "I'm wearing sturdy shoes. You are not. It's your own fault if you're in pain."

Renie's piteous brown eyes veered off beyond Judith. "I'm about to be saved. Here come the husbands. Bill, call me a taxi!"

"You're a taxi," her spouse shot back.

"Ha!" Renie cried. "Walking has dulled your wits. Your usual sharp intellect has vanished. Haven't I warned you that any kind of exercise is a bad idea?"

Bill made no comment as he and a bemused Joe walked over to the other side of the street and kept on going.

"What does he know?" Renie mumbled, kicking at a dry leaf. "I'm going back to get my car so I can drive home. Why are those goofy men we married still walking? Did Joe forget where he lives?"

"I think Joe's stopping across from the cul-de-sac," Judith said. "He probably wants to find out if Woody has called. Okay, we'll head for home, too. I want to find out what else Woody has to say besides what he revealed about Millie's wealth."

Sure enough, Joe and Bill parted company. Their wives picked up the pace while Renie's husband kept going.

"Hey," Joe called as he reached their side of the street by the cul-de-sac, "how come you two decided to go for a walk? Did the guests drive you out?"

"I was forced into it," Renie declared. "If we'd gone any farther, your wife would've had to carry me."

Joe laughed. "I'd like to see that." He turned to Judith. "Any word from Woody?"

The trio entered the cul-de-sac before Judith spoke. "Yes. I told him you'd call back. He says he found out something about the money . . . Oh, no! Rodney's climbing out the window in Room One!"

"Damn!" Joe cried. "He'll fall and break something and then sue us!" He trotted toward Hillside Manor.

"I'm leaving," Renie declared. "I'm taking my callused feet home." She stomped off to the Joneses'

Camry in the driveway without so much as a glance at Rodney, who was now straddling the windowsill.

"Mama!" he called in a frantic voice. "Help me! They want to send me away!"

Judith had followed Joe as far as the walkway, where he'd paused before hurrying on into the house. "Away where?" Judith asked Rodney.

"Somewhere I won't like," he replied, wiping what appeared to be perspiration from his brow. "A home for . . . people like me."

Judith wanted to say she'd never known anyone quite like Rodney, at least no one who had thought she was his mother. Instead, she invoked her usual compassion and smiled up at the distraught man. "That would be difficult for them to do," she said calmly. "They'd have to have proof that you were . . . unbalanced."

It was the wrong word to use. Rodney teetered on the windowsill. "I'm running away," he declared. "They'll never find me."

"Who are 'they'?" she asked, stalling for time and hoping Room One's door was unlocked.

Rodney's expression grew miserable. "My biggest enemies are Cynthia and Stuart Wicks," he said. "And," he added after a pause, "Belle, my sweet little girl! How could she betray her old man?"

"There must be some mistake," Judith said, wishing Rodney wouldn't keep shifting around on the sill and wondering what was taking Joe so long. "How does Dr. Kilmore feel about your . . . situation?"

"Sophie? Bah!" Rodney swung an arm in disgust, causing him to almost lose his grip. He righted himself and glared down at Judith. "She's on their side, I'll bet my boots. If I had any boots." He frowned at his stockinged feet. " 'Course, Sophie chimes in with Clark. He's going to college to learn to be a shrink. Thinks he can read my mind. Ha!"

"I wouldn't worry about what these people are . . ." Judith shut up as she finally saw Joe at the window. Apparently Rodney hadn't heard him come into the room.

Judith could hardly bear to watch, but Joe put Rodney in a headlock, and despite his prey's yelps of protests, the distressed guest was hauled inside. Feeling limp from the ordeal, Judith took her time to get into Hillside Manor. The house was eerily quiet. After collapsing on the sofa, she read the reverend's flyer that had been left at the Flaherty house.

"SAVE YOUR SOUL!" the headline read, with a subhead in smaller print that said "Do What Smart Folks Do—Stick with Stone."

After the first paragraph preached about Kindred's successful methods of bringing people to his Church of the Holy Free Spirit, the rev segued somewhat awkwardly into his pitch to buy the recipient's house. *I can make an offer that even the Good Lord Himself couldn't refuse,* he boasted. *If I could buy Heaven, God would jump at my offer! Call me or my associate Clark Stone at Stonehaven. The number is. . .*

Judith held her head. She didn't look up until Joe came into the living room, his ruddy complexion redder than usual.

"I'm out of shape," he declared, flopping onto the sofa next to Judith. "Rodney's no small thing. And the door was locked from the outside, so I had to go back downstairs to get the master key."

"Has he calmed down?" Judith asked.

"He's sort of weepy," Joe replied. "I told him to stay put. The rest of the gang seems to have gone somewhere. With any luck, they checked out. Are you going to call Woody?"

"Yes. Are you going to call him now?"

Joe sighed. "Yes. Hell, it's his case, so I feel obligated to do everything I can to help him." He turned to look at Judith. "I'd rather you kept your distance."

Judith smiled wanly. "You know I can't."

"Right." He nodded faintly. "That doesn't mean I have to like it, though." With another sigh, he got up and went to get the phone from the cherrywood table.

"Wouldn't it be easier if I listen in on the kitchen phone?" Judith suggested. "That way you won't have to repeat everything."

"Nice try, Jude-girl," her husband said. "Don't even think about it." He picked up the receiver and went into the front parlor.

Miffed, Judith sat on the sofa wondering what could be such a big secret about Woody's background information. The grandfather clock chimed four. Maybe, she thought, she should start making the guests' hors d'oeuvres and figure out what to have for dinner. Glaring at the closed door to the parlor, she got up and headed for the kitchen.

There was still a strange quiet inside the house. Granted, guests staying through the weekend usually spent Sunday afternoons enjoying the city sights or visiting people they knew. If there were incoming visitors, they didn't check in until five o'clock. Focusing on her current, troublesome batch of guests, Judith refused to spend a lot of time and effort on elaborate appetizers. She went down the hall to the pantry in search of canned smoked salmon. The only other items she needed were cheese and crackers. For all she cared, the Schmuck clan could graze in the backyard. Except, she realized with a guilty pang, that was where Millie had died. Attending Mass hadn't filled Judith with much Christian charity.

She was cautiously bending down to find the salmon when a voice startled her. She straightened up, turning to see Belle in the doorway. The young woman looked a bit dazed, but Judith figured she'd probably been smoking pot.

"Wow," Belle said softly. "We had the most amazing séance. You wouldn't believe the things my mom told us."

"Oh?" Judith felt strangely trapped in the small room. "That sounds fascinating," she said, joining her guest in the hall. "Come into the kitchen and tell me about it."

Belle traipsed after her, settling into a chair. "Your mother is marvelous," she declared in a voice filled with awe. "You should have told us she was a medium."

Luckily, Judith was opening the refrigerator and had her back turned so that Belle couldn't see her startled expression. "I . . . try not to advertise Mrs. Grover's powers. Some people misuse them. That is, they don't always correctly interpret what she has to say. How," she inquired, turning around, "did you find out about her . . . gift?"

"She told us," Belle replied. "Clark and I were smoking a joint in the backyard. Mrs. G opened the door and wanted to know why her apartment smelled funny. We told her we had no idea. Maybe it was because of that big orange-and-white cat. She said it was her familiar, so I asked if she was a witch. That's when she told us she was a medium. But a happy medium, she insisted. Clark and I thought that was deep. I mean, I figure most mediums must be way too serious."

Judith sat down, too. "I see. Did she—"

Belle spoke as if she hadn't heard her hostess. "I asked if we could have a séance and she seemed intrigued, so I told her it'd be amazing if everybody else could sit in on it because wasn't that the way a séance worked? I mean, a lot of people sitting around a table. She said she only had a card table, so it wouldn't work in her place. That's when we came inside and sat at the dining room table. I guess you and Mr. Flynn had gone somewhere, right?"

"Right," Judith murmured. "What did she tell you during the séance? I mean what did your mother tell you through . . . my mother?"

Belle gave Judith a loopy smile. "Mom was so happy! She hasn't been like that in months. I don't think she liked moving here from L.A. Too rainy and gray. She said it was really nice where she was, with lots of sun and warm weather. She has her own cloud. It's mauve."

"That sounds lovely," Judith murmured, always amazed at the many guises her own mother could come up with to sucker gullible people. "Did she mention anything about . . . ah . . . what happened before she got to her cloud?"

"Um . . ." Belle screwed up her face in the effort of recollection. "Not exactly. Except that her cloud never rains. It just floats. Like soap."

"That was it?" Judith asked.

"Pretty much." Belle frowned. "That was when the medium—I mean, Mrs. G—said she'd lost the connection."

"Yes," Judith murmured. "I'm sure she had. By the way, I didn't realize that Clark was involved with Reverend Kindred in real estate."

Belle nodded. "Oh, sure, we're all involved in that, really. But Clark's a brainiac, so he comes up with mega-ideas, especially for the rev. Preachers don't have much imagination, I guess." Her piquant face suddenly looked troubled. "Why did Mom have to die?"

Judith was taken aback. "Everyone dies eventually," she hedged. "It could've been an allergic reaction. It happens."

"No." Belle shook her head and stood up. "Mom didn't have allergies. She was still fairly young, she was looking forward to starting her spa project, she had megabucks, and Dad worshiped her. Mom had so much to live for. It makes no sense for her not to be around anymore even if she does like her cloud. It's . . ." She stared up at the high ceiling. "It's a mistake. It has to be."

Shaking her head, the befuddled Belle wandered out of the kitchen and down the hall to the back stairs.

Joe showed up a few minutes later while Judith was putting the appetizers on a tray. "Woody really didn't have a lot to tell me about the guests—or suspects, if you will—that we don't already know. They all seem to be who and what they say they are. Nobody has an arrest record." He put a hand on Judith's shoulder. "Sorry to disappoint you."

Judith pressed her cheek against her husband's before looking him in the eye. "Be candid. Do you think Millie was murdered?"

Joe held up both hands. "I honestly don't know. We have to wait for the autopsy. The EMTs are fairly sharp. If they detected poisonous residue in Millie's mouth, I have to believe that she ingested or at least tasted something harmful. But I also have to point out that poison is only fatal in sufficient doses, and even then it depends upon the victim—age, health, the whole nine yards."

Judith looked bleak. "That's not very reassuring, one way or the other."

Joe shrugged. "Sorry. It's the best I can do."

Judith hoped it wasn't the worst that could happen. And then realized it already had. There was nothing worse than murder.

Chapter 13

The rest of Sunday passed without incident. Judith set the cocktail items on the buffet, but didn't mingle with the guests. She was tired, sensing one of her migraines in the offing. From what little she could tell, the guests had seemed subdued. Maybe Millie's death had finally sunk in. Or perhaps the séance had given them food for thought. She couldn't detect Rodney's voice, so maybe he'd remained upstairs. If it was true that one or all of the others had locked him in Room One, he probably wasn't anxious to spend the social hour with them.

Shortly after six, the others left, presumably to go out for dinner. Judith assumed they'd called a cab—or cabs, given that there were too many for one car. She went upstairs to see if Rodney was hungry. He didn't answer her knock, so she quietly opened the door. He was sound asleep, snoring softly. An empty whiskey bottle lay on the floor by the bed. Judith decided that if he was hungry when he woke up, he could come downstairs and let her know.

When she went outside with Gertrude's "supper," she quizzed her mother about the séance.

"Saps," Gertrude declared. "I was bored. There wasn't much in the paper today, just a lot of bunk about people killing each other in the Middle East. Why can't those bozos get along after five thousand years? You'd think they'd all be worn out by now. Why don't they play cards to pass the time like I do? Or don't their religions believe in cards? No wonder they've got so many problems."

"It's all about religion and turf," Judith said. "It usually is mostly about turf when it comes to war."

"Turf?" Gertrude looked disgusted. "Isn't most of the Middle East a bunch of sand? Who fights over *sand*? That just shows how crazy they all really are."

Judith didn't want to argue with her mother, let alone go to war with her. She kissed the old lady's wrinkled cheek and bade her a good night.

Gertrude harrumphed. "There better not be another dead body out by my so-called apartment in the morning. It gets my day off to a bad start."

Judith didn't comment.

On a drizzly Monday morning, the guests still seemed unwontedly quiet when they gathered for breakfast. Cynthia Wicks informed Joe that she and Stuart had decided to stay on to help Rodney make arrangements for his wife's body. Stuart had asked one of his underlings to request a postponement of his case in Los Angeles County Court. The entire party planned to stay on at Hillside Manor.

Hearing the news, Judith groaned. "I'll have to ask Ingrid Heffelman to find other accommodations for the guests who had reservations for tonight," she whispered to Joe as he piled pancakes on a warming plate. "I hope she hasn't heard about our latest disaster. She could threaten to pull my innkeeper's license again."

"Don't worry about it," Joe said. "As far as I can tell, Millie's demise hasn't made it into the media. I assume that's thanks to your KINE-TV buddy, Mavis."

"I guess," Judith murmured glumly. "I hope the guests don't plan to hang out around here during the day. Phyliss will be cleaning and she'll insist on changing the beds and straightening up the rooms."

Joe shrugged. "No big deal. I'll tell them all to take a hike. If they balk, I'll say the cops have to search their rooms." He paused before taking the pancakes to the dining room. "Maybe Woody should have his crew do just that."

An hour later, Joe returned from upstairs, where he had changed into slacks and a sport coat. "I'm off to find the missing person. Call me if you have any problems."

"Where do you start looking for this guy?" Judith asked.

"City Hall," Joe replied. "That's where he was last seen." He kissed Judith and headed out the back door, but stopped. "Damn! I don't have the MG. I'll have to take the Subaru."

"Okay," Judith said. "If I need to go anywhere, I'll call Renie."

A few minutes after Joe left, Clayton Ormsby came into the kitchen, where Judith was cleaning up from the guests' breakfast. "We've rented cars and are going to the zoo," he announced. "Reverend Kindred feels as if the Spirit is not active in this neighborhood. The zoo will bring us back in touch with the primal world and salve our souls. My blog for the day will be on hyenas."

"I'm not sure if they have hyenas at our zoo," Judith said.

"That doesn't matter," Clayton declared with an airy wave of his hand. "It's the topic that makes the difference. My thought process is what's important. I'm extremely thought provoking. By the way, hyenas don't really laugh, you know. They have no sense of humor." He pivoted on his heel and made his exit.

Judith felt as if she'd lost *her* sense of humor. The Schmuck party was the grimmest, most arrogant group she'd hosted in years. With a sigh, she started loading the dishwasher. Five minutes later, Phyliss arrived in a dither.

"I saw your mother!" she exclaimed. "She told me somebody died in the backyard. Praise the Lord, at least it wasn't in the house."

"I don't think that was of importance to the deceased," Judith said. And wondered if in fact that was where Millie had breathed her last. "Mrs. Schmuck's family members and friends are still here and will be until the autopsy is finished."

Phyliss shuddered, her gaunt figure shaking as if a high wind had blown in through the back door. "Autopsies! Grisly ungodly things!"

Judith didn't want to get into a religious discussion. Maybe her cleaning woman would bond with the Reverend Kindred. She gave Phyliss instructions to start with the laundry, but not to change the beds, since the current guests were all staying on.

"Not all, I hope," Phyliss said, her gray eyes rolling like marbles. "The deceased must've been hauled off for decency's sake."

Judith assured her that the dead woman was in the morgue.

"The morgue," Phyliss muttered, stalking off down the hall. "Gruesome. Oh, well. They kept Grandpa Rackley in the attic for three weeks. Good thing it was winter." She disappeared up the back stairs.

Just after ten, Judith went outside with the garbage. The air felt fresh, with no hint of rain in the white clouds that moved lazily toward the west. To her surprise, Tyler Dooley was coming along the driveway with Farley at his heels.

"Why aren't you in school?" she asked.

"The power went out," Tyler replied. "They sent us home. I thought I should stop by to give my surveillance report."

Judith smiled. "Which is?"

"I hear you found the purse," he replied. "But this morning I looked out of my bedroom window . . . well, it's not *my* bedroom, since I share it with three other kids. Anyway, I saw a guy burning something in your barbecue. I thought that was weird."

Judith agreed. "What did he look like?"

"I never did see his face," Tyler said. "As for height, it's hard to judge, looking down from a distance. I figure he's middle-aged, kind of tall or at least average, and more skinny than fat. Whatever he was burning took him a couple of minutes. He kept looking around, maybe to make sure nobody was watching. I think it was paper, but one of my cousins . . ." He paused, frowning. "Or is he my uncle? He could be, I guess, even if he's five years younger than I am. Oh, well. Anyway, he—Kenny—busted my telescope. But O.P. can fix it when he comes home from college. He's getting an advanced degree in astronomy."

"I haven't seen O.P. or any of your . . . uncles in quite a while," Judith said. Two of the older Dooley boys had also been her neighborhood junior sleuths in their younger years. "What time was that?" she inquired.

"Eight-oh-three," Tyler replied. "I logged it. It's eight-oh-five when I always leave for school. I hang out with my choir buddies before class starts. Got to go, Mrs. F. I'm supposed to watch Aunt Cecelia's twins. She has to get a root canal. I wish somebody in the family would take up dentistry. Gran and Gramp are always griping about dental bills." He sauntered off, the faithful Farley pausing only to sniff the recycling bin.

After Tyler left, Judith went into the backyard and opened the barbecue. Sure enough, there was a considerable amount of what looked like paper ashes on top of the briquettes that had survived the winter. Unfortunately, there was nothing left to tell what had been burned.

When she went back inside, Clark Stone was in the kitchen, looking disconsolate. "Have you seen my wallet?" he asked.

"No," Judith replied. "I gather you lost it?"

Clark nodded faintly. "I guess. I didn't use it yesterday, but I know I had it Saturday, for sure. I used my Visa card to buy some . . . stuff when Belle and I were shopping up on the top of the hill."

"Did you have cash in it?" Judith inquired.

Clark shook his head. "Not much. Twenty bucks and change, I think. I card most stuff. But my credit cards are in the wallet."

"Have you called the stores where you made purchases?"

He shook his head again. "I'm not sure what they were called."

"Then," Judith said, trying not to sound severe, "you and Belle should go back to the business district and figure out where you might've lost your wallet."

"Can't," Clark replied, sounding doleful. "We're going to the zoo."

200 · MARY DAHEIM

"That won't take all day," Judith pointed out. "You'd better have your party drop off you and Belle up there on the way back from the zoo. By the way, how are all of you getting there?" In her mind's eye, she saw a circus train with the guests peering from the caged cars.

"My stepdad paid to have two rentals driven here," Clark explained. "They're parked out on the street. Stuart didn't think we should take up space from the neighbors here in the cul-de-sac. He's a lawyer, so he's always afraid of getting sued."

"Yes," Judith murmured. "I suppose he would be. Is Mr. Schmuck going with you?"

"I guess." Clark made a face. "He's kind of a drag."

"His wife just died," Judith said, forcing herself to remain cordial. "He's taken her death very hard."

"Yeah, right, it's a shame." Clark jammed his hands into the pockets of his designer jeans. "I guess I should cut him some slack."

"By the way," Judith said as Clark started to turn away, "did I hear or see something about you studying to become a minister?"

"Huh?" Clark looked mystified.

"I saw one of Reverend Kindred's flyers," Judith explained. "There was a mention of your name."

Clark laughed in a discordant manner. "Heck, no! I'm getting my Ph.D. in astrophysics. I only help out Kindred with his writing stuff for his sales and church pitches. He not only can't write, I don't think he can even spell. The rev dropped out of school in ninth grade. I better find Belle. We're supposed to leave for the zoo in a few."

Judith felt as if she were already there.

I won't survive another half hour if you don't come over here and save my sanity," she told Renie over the phone. "Even if the guests have left for a few hours, I'm getting by only on fumes."

"From what Belle and Clark are smoking?" Renie asked.

"Unfortunately, no. I might feel better if I smoked some funny stuff. Are you free to spend some time with me?"

"I just ate breakfast," Renie replied, "but I'm starting to wake up. Bill's got a patient coming by at noon, so he won't need the car." She paused. "I wonder if I'm supposed to be working on something?"

"It can wait," Judith declared. "I can't. But don't start out if you're still half asleep. I don't want to have to rescue you."

"Don't we always rescue each other?" Renie didn't wait for an answer, but hung up.

Judith was setting the phone on the counter when Charlie Crump peered over the half doors. "May I beg a favor?" he asked in a deep, yet uncertain voice that fit his rotund physique.

"Of course. Come into the kitchen," Judith said. "How can I help you, Mr. Crump?"

Charlie opened the half doors to reveal that he was bundled up for a winter day in Nome. Judith tried not to stare at the heavy black overcoat, the beige wool muffler or the thick hand-knit gloves.

"Would you happen to have any herbal tea?" he inquired. "I've run out of my own and didn't think to buy any when we were out yesterday."

Judith grimaced. "I'm sorry, I don't have any on hand." Seeing the obvious disappointment on Charlie's round face, she hastened to continue. "My cousin is stopping by shortly. I could ask her to pick up some at Falstaff's Market. Do you have a cold?"

The question may have seemed obvious, since Charlie had so obviously bundled himself. But he looked surprised. "Why, no. I find your climate here very damp. The air itself seems . . . moist."

"We do have quite a bit of drizzle," Judith said. "It rarely rains very hard, really. When are you leaving for the zoo?"

It was Charlie's turn for a pained expression. "In about fifteen minutes, I believe." He glanced at the schoolhouse clock. "Cynthia set eleven as our time of departure. Much of the zoo is outside, I assume?"

"I believe so," Judith replied, though she hadn't been to the zoo for twenty years. "Natural habitats for the animals, when it's possible."

Charlie shuddered. Or Judith thought he did, though it was hard to tell with all his heavy clothing. "Not the lions, I hope," he said. "I must join Agnes. She'll be worrying about me." He plodded out of the kitchen.

Judith picked up the phone and called Renie. "How soon are you leaving?" she asked her cousin.

"In about half an hour, I guess," Renie said. "Why? Are you that desperate for my company?"

Judith explained about Charlie Crump's request. Could her cousin come sooner?

"No, I can't," Renie snapped. "Why doesn't this bozo and the other wackos stop at the store and buy the damned tea? I'm not a shopping service."

"Doesn't Bill drink herbal tea before he goes to bed?"

"It's called Sleepytime tea," Renie declared. "Maybe it's herbal, maybe it's not. I don't drink it and all I know is that it has a bear in a nightshirt on the box. Stop talking to me so I can finish waking up or I won't be at your place until this afternoon." She banged down the phone.

It rang almost immediately. "Judith?" Woody said. "Is Joe there?"

"No," she replied. "In fact, he was headed for City Hall. He has a missing persons assignment for someone who works for the city. Did you give him the job?"

"No, that would come from the department that employed whoever's missing. I was calling to tell him we got the insurance data on Mrs. Schmuck."

"Do you want to give it to me so I can pass it on to Joe?" Judith asked in her most ingenuous voice.

Woody chuckled softly. "Well . . . oh, why not? She had three different policies, totaling twenty-one million dollars. One policy would've been worth three times that much if she'd been dismembered."

"Oh, ugh!" Judith cried. "I don't want to think about that!"

"Maybe you should," Woody said somberly. "That is, if foul play was involved."

"You mean because . . . Never mind, Woody. I find that idea upsetting." Judith paused. "I assume you don't have the autopsy report in yet?"

"No, but we could get it later this afternoon," he replied. "If we're lucky. What time do you expect Joe to come home?"

"I never know for sure," Judith said, "but unless he's on a stakeout probably around five thirty. You know what traffic's like these days."

He assured Judith that he certainly did and rang off.

Phyliss appeared in the kitchen, wielding a dust mop. "When can I start upstairs? Your heathen guests are milling around in the hall. Do I have to work around them?"

"Actually, one of them is a minister. In fact, he seems to be highly regarded among the others," Judith said, unable to resist the opportunity to see how her cleaning woman would react. "You might want to introduce yourself."

Phyliss's eyes narrowed. "What kind of minister?"

"The Christian kind," Judith replied.

The suspicion remained. "I'll see about that." Waggling the dust mop, she marched off down the hall. But before Phyliss could go farther than the back stairs, the Schmuck party came down the front stairs—and went out the door. Judith shrugged and thought about what to make for dinner. If the weather held, maybe they could barbecue. That would be Joe's job. With guests usually arriving and the cocktail hour ritual to oversee, she never had time to get the coals started properly.

Ten minutes later, Joe came in through the back door. Judith looked up from her recipe file. "What happened?" she asked in surprise.

"The missing person was found," Joe replied, shrugging out of his sport coat and coming into the kitchen to kiss his wife's cheek.

"Where did they find him?"

"On the job," Joe replied, pouring himself a cup of coffee. "He'd taken off early Friday and gone fishing for the weekend over in the eastern part of the state. His wife was out of town visiting her sister, so he decided to take off, too."

"Then who reported him missing?"

"The neighbor. They'd been asked by Mrs. Ethanson to take in the mail. When the wife went over there Saturday, she found Ethanson's official badge on the front porch. Mrs. Glubbet or whatever the neighbor's name is thought there was something sinister about it, so she panicked and called City Hall. Mrs. Ethanson isn't due back until tonight."

Judith stared at Joe. "Ethanson? Ethan Ethanson?

"Right." Joe looked puzzled. "How did you know that?"

"That was the name on the city inspector's badge who was here Saturday," Judith replied. "I wondered why he'd come on a weekend. This is all really strange because I think I saw him yesterday sitting in his car outside of the cul-de-sac as if he was keeping an eye on the immediate vicinity. How did he get hold of the real Ethanson's badge?"

"I don't know. I didn't ask. Weird," Joe muttered. "Why would anybody impersonate a city inspector?"

Judith shrugged. "I've no idea. Unless it somehow involves our peculiar guests."

Joe fingered his chin. "Maybe I should track down Ethanson and ask if he knows why his badge ended up on his front porch. Of course he's probably working in the field today."

"Maybe you can leave a call for him," Judith suggested. "Oh! Woody called about Millie's insurance policies." Her dark eyes widened at revealing the large amount. "Twenty million dollars."

Joe whistled softly. "The Schmucks must be loaded. How can that be? Inheritance?"

"That's possible," Judith allowed. "I can't imagine Rodney pulling in big bucks as a motivational speaker."

"Those guys do, though," Joe murmured. "It all sounds like bull to me, but what do I know? I'm a retired cop and a plebeian part-time PI."

Judith put her hand on his arm. "But I wouldn't love you so much if you weren't. Plebeian, I mean. After Dan died, I felt more like a pauper. He had no insurance and he'd never worked enough to have much Social Security or any kind of pension. You know that's why I had to turn my family home into a B&B to make a living. Librarians don't earn large salaries unless they're administrators. I'd have hated that part. I wanted to help readers, not supervise staff."

"That's because you're a real person, Jude-girl." He kissed her gently. "No autopsy report yet?"

"No. Woody thought maybe this afternoon."

"He'll be lucky if it's that soon. I'm going to change. Speaking of that, the Subaru needs an oil change. I'll take it to the Shell station over at MidBay after lunch. It's too bad we don't have a gas station on the hill anymore. I guess even the oil companies can't afford a site around here." Joe ambled out of the kitchen.

It occurred to Judith that apparently the Schmucks could afford to buy property on Heraldsgate Hill. She wondered where they got so much money. And, because her mind sometimes worked in devious ways, she realized that how they'd acquired their wealth could be through ill-gotten gains. Often, money was a motive for murder.

Chapter 14

Renie arrived shortly after eleven thirty. "Joe's home? Or did he take the bus to wherever he had to go on the 'tec job?"

Judith explained what had happened with the not-so-missing city inspector. Renie looked puzzled. "Do you think the real Ethan was set up by the guy who came to the house? Are you sure he was the same man sitting in the car across the street? And why was he doing that?"

Judith laughed. "You must be awake. You're asking a lot of questions."

"That's to keep my mind off the fact that you still haven't made cookies. I already checked." Renie went to the fridge and took out a can of Pepsi. "I'd cadge lunch off of you if I hadn't finished breakfast less than an hour ago. Pancakes and lamb kidneys. Yum!"

"Ick! Innards! How can you eat those things?"

"As fast as I can get them in my big mouth," Renie replied. "Well? Are you avoiding my queries?"

Judith poured a cup of coffee and joined her cousin at the table. "I think that was the phony inspector outside the cul-de-sac. I'm fairly good at recognizing faces—unlike you. Remember years ago when you didn't recognize your own mother at the Belle Époque Department Store?"

Renie winced. "Only too late did I realize it was Mom. I was taking back the hideous plaid jacket she and Dad had given me for Christmas. You got one, too. Your mother had gone to the same sale, but you didn't get caught returning yours. When Aunt Gert asked why you didn't wear it, you told one of your monster fibs. You said you'd been mugged and the thief had stolen it. Of course she believed you, even though she should've known no respectable crook would have been seen in a police lineup wearing that ugly jacket. What were our mothers thinking?"

"About the sale price," Judith replied. "They do love a sale."

"So do we have a plan?" Renie asked.

"A plan?" Judith paused. "I hadn't thought that far ahead. But maybe we should visit some of the stores to see if Clark Stone's wallet has been turned in. He thinks he lost it while he and Belle were shopping Saturday."

Renie seemed disinterested. "So? Why do you care? Let Clark Stone find his own blasted wallet. You're not his babysitter."

"I suppose you're right," Judith allowed, seeing Phyliss come into the hall from the back stairs.

"I'm saved again!" she exulted, entering the kitchen. "Hallelujah!"

"Oh, good grief!" Renie muttered, turning around to look at the cleaning woman. "How many times is this?"

Phyliss took umbrage. "You Catholics have some strange ideas about being saved," she declared. "All you do is show up and watch your priest say a lot of mumbo jumbo and make hand jive on the altar. I know, I went to one of your churches years ago. He finally talked in English for a few minutes, but his big message was needing more volunteers for bingo night. If that isn't gambling and a sin to boot, I don't know what is."

"No, you probably don't know," Renie responded. "That must've been fifty years ago. The Mass has been in English since the early 1960s. And we never played bingo in Latin."

Judith decided to intervene and looked at Phyliss. "I gather you met the Reverend Kindred?"

"I did for a fact," Phyliss replied, her gray sausage curls bobbing. "Fine Christian man. We had quite a coming-to-Jesus talk. I saw him before he went to the zoo. He made a comical joke about Noah and the Ark, but I can't remember how it went. Something to do with aardvarks. Maybe if I prayed on it, I could remember."

Renie feigned a yawn. "Spare me. Did the rev offer to buy the apartment house where you live?"

Phyliss scowled. "No. Why would he do that?"

The exchange between the two women was giving Judith one of her headaches. "Never mind, Phyliss. Have you made the guest room beds?"

"Just finished, praise the Lord," Phyliss replied. "Mrs. . . . Twix?" She shrugged. "Whatever her name is insisted I shouldn't bother, but I did up the rooms anyway after they went to the zoo."

"It's Mrs. Wicks," Judith murmured. "That's fine. By the way, I bought a new ironing-board cover, but I haven't put it on yet. It's next to the dryer in the basement."

"You should ask Reverend Kindred to bless it," Phyliss said. "He blessed my dust mop. He told me I reminded him of Martha in the Bible. You know, the one who did all the housework." Looking pleased with herself, Phyliss stalked off back down the hall.

Renie was looking bemused. Judith asked her why.

"Because I know what you plan to do," her cousin replied. "I'll help you search their rooms, of course. They can't stay all day at the zoo."

Judith glanced at the old schoolhouse clock. "I have to make Mother's lunch first. Why don't you go up to make sure Rodney left with the rest of them? If he stayed here, it doesn't matter, really. I've already gone over Room One."

"Sure," Renie said. "Why don't you whip up a batch of cookies while you're at it?"

Judith didn't bother to comment, but merely glared at her cousin.

I'd forgotten how small Room Two is," Renie remarked, glancing out the window. "When did you put a double bed in here? It barely fits. Is it made of sponge?"

"A couple of years ago," Judith replied, opening the top bureau drawer. "I can put only slim people in here."

Renie examined a bong. "Belle and Clark probably don't notice that the room's not much bigger than my master bedroom's closet. They may not know they're in a room."

"Nothing much in these drawers—just clothes," Judith noted before opening the small wardrobe. "Same here, except for a folder. Can you bend down to pick it up off the floor for me?"

"Sure." Renie obliged, but opened the folder before handing it to Judith. "Sheesh. Either Belle or Clark writes poetry—badly." She paused, scanning the hand-written words. "It must be Belle's. The first page is an ode to her mother. Oh, double gack! She must've been really bombed when she penned this crap. See for yourself."

Judith took a couple of sheets from her cousin. " 'Mom has a cloud for her shroud,' " she read to Renie. " 'I'd cry aloud if I didn't know she's proud of her cloud.' I don't think I can go on. It gets worse."

"How could it?"

Judith took a deep breath. " 'Mom's proud of her cloud, though it's not a shroud and the music's not loud, but sounds like tinkling bells and there are no smells. Sweet release and lots of peace.' Trust me. It doesn't get any better. What about the other stuff Belle wrote?"

Renie scanned a few more pages. "Just more mus-ings, unless you want to hear 'Ode to Grass' or 'What I See When I Get High.' There are writers who can put together some pithy stuff when they're smoking weed, but Belle isn't one of them."

"I don't see anything else of interest in here," Judith said. "Let's move on. And remind me to fumigate this room when the Schmuck party leaves or else the next guests could get high just being in here."

"It's a wonder Phyliss didn't comment about the smell," Renie said as they went into the hall.

"She has sinus problems among her many other complaints. Maybe she didn't notice."

"Who's in here?" Renie asked as Judith led the way into Room Three.

"Dr. Sophie and Clayton the Blogger." She paused. "Doesn't it strike you as odd that Belle didn't write something that conveyed her grief over her mother's death? She did say something to me about how . . . not sad, not tragic, but . . . *wrong* it was that her mother died so young."

"I don't know," Renie answered after they entered the room. "People grieve in different ways. Maybe Belle was high when she talked about Millie. Often, when someone who isn't elderly dies, their loved ones feel it is *wrong* that the person was taken away before he or she was able to live into old age. Remember how Grandpa Grover always read the obits first in the newspaper?"

Judith smiled at the recollection. "Yes. If the person—even if he didn't know the deceased—was younger even by a year, he'd gloat and I say, 'I managed to outlive that guy.' It was as if life was a game he was playing and he wanted to triumph over as many people as he could. But if it was someone who'd died much younger, he'd act puzzled, shake his head, and mutter that it wasn't fair."

"He could be gloomy, especially when Uncle Corky and Uncle Al went off to war," Renie remarked, searching through the closet. "There's a laptop on the shelf. I assume it's what Clayton uses for his blogs. Do you want to read any of his blather?"

"If I do, I'll check him out on my computer," Judith replied. "He may have had some comments about what happened to Millie unless he's doing a series on hyenas."

"For a supposedly well-to-do surgeon, Sophie seems to have shopped at Goodwill," Renie said. "Her taste in clothes is reprehensible."

"And your Wisconsin Badgers T-shirt is a fashion statement?" Judith retorted.

"Knock it off," Renie shot back. "You know Bill got his undergraduate degree at Wisconsin."

Judith opened the last of the dresser drawers. "So far, there isn't much . . . Ah! A metal box. Now, why would anyone bring a . . . It's locked."

"So? You have a knack for picking locks. Give it a shot."

"I can't." Judith looked sheepish. "Sophie's a doctor. It could be patient information. Peeking would be morally wrong."

"Are you serious? Since when did ethics get in the way when you're sleuthing?"

"Since now," Judith declared. "There *are* limits." Reluctantly, she put the box back in the drawer. "Face it, coz. Sophie may have patients who have questions. She may bring their histories when she travels."

"If you're right, her files may not be hard copies, but on disks or an external hard drive," Renie said. "That could complicate your snooping."

Judith put the box back in the dresser. "That's not the point. I won't violate my own brand of professional ethics. Let's move on."

"Your call. Do we access Room Four via the adjoining bathroom?"

"We might as well. That one belongs to Stuart and Cynthia Wicks. They decided to stay on after all." Judith opened the bathroom's second door. "Matching luggage," she noted, seeing two maroon hardside spinner cases at the foot of the bed. "They look very sturdy. And expensive."

"Fairly new, too," Renie remarked. "No big patches of ugly red tape like Bill put on all of ours so we can spot the luggage after it's been unloaded. These suitcases are locked, by the way."

"Of course," Judith murmured. There was no closet in Room Four, only a small rack for hanging up clothes.

She started searching the bureau. "Nothing. They've never unpacked. Let's hope the Crumps have something of interest in Room Five."

But except for Agnes's prayer book on the nightstand and several kinds of digestive aids, there was little of interest other than a phone number scrawled on a Post-it note.

"Where's the 213 area code?" Judith asked.

"Los Angeles," Renie replied. "Mainly downtown. The reason I know that is because the Saks store I go to when I'm in L.A. is in Beverly Hills and that's the 310 area code. Thus 213 would be mainly businesses and government offices. When I go to L.A., I try to never leave Beverly Hills."

Judith smirked. "Is that where you bought your Badger T-shirt?"

Renie sneered. "Ha ha. I bought it when we visited Bill's relatives in Madison six years ago."

"How long has the egg yolk been stuck to that sweatshirt?"

Renie glanced at her chest. "I'm not sure. Since Thursday, maybe?"

Judith shook her head in dismay. "When it comes to clothes, you're two different people. I don't suppose you know what the 874 prefix would be?"

"I sure don't. Do I look like Directory Assistance?"

"You look like you *need* assistance," Judith retorted.

Renie stuck out her tongue, but didn't respond. The cousins moved on to Room Six, where the Kindreds were lodged.

"The rev's flyers," Renie said, pointing to a small stack on the dresser. "Elsie's makeup case. She wears makeup? Then how come she looks so bad?"

"How do I know?" Judith searched the bureau drawers. "Here's some sort of kit. Oh, it's Elsie's. She's a nurse, you know."

"Didn't know, don't care," Renie responded. "What are you doing? Looking for poison?"

"Everything seems harmless to me," Judith replied, putting the kit back in the drawer.

"I found a Bible," Renie said. "It belongs to the rev. His name is inscribed in gold leaf on the cover." She flipped through the pages. "He's highlighted certain passages from both the Old and the New Testaments. Maybe they're for his sermons."

Judith found nothing else of interest. "We wasted our time," she mumbled. "An L.A. phone number and Belle's bad poetry do not advance us in our detection."

"Stop going all Sherlock Holmes on me," Renie said, still flipping through the Bible. "Some of these verses Kindred marked are kind of interesting. How about this one—'Charm is deceitful, and beauty is vain, but a woman who fears the Lord is to be praised.' At least that explains why Elsie's so homely despite her makeup."

"Not helpful," Judith said, her hand on the doorknob.

"Wait—there's more. 'In vain, you beautify your-self. Your lovers despise you; they seek your life.' Does that one grab you?"

Judith thought for a moment. "A reference to Mil-lie's project?"

"Maybe. Here's 'The getting of treasures by a lying tongue is a fleeting vapor and a snare of death.' I like the 'fleeting vapor' part. It's visual. I wonder how I could work it into one of my graphic designs?"

"Give it up." Judith opened the door. "Those quotes are no doubt intended for the rev's preaching."

Renie reluctantly closed the Bible. "They all seem to be about vanity and acquiring wealth," she said as they headed for the back stairs. "Do you really think there's no connection to what's going on with the real estate gig?"

"I can't see how," Judith replied. "Kindred seems as caught up in it as the rest of them." She paused at the foot of the stairs. "Unless the rev isn't the one who marked those passages. Maybe it was Elsie."

"You sense dissension in the Kindred marriage?"

"I've no idea," Judith admitted, "but I can see why a devout Christian woman wouldn't approve of mixing religion and moneymaking. That is, other than in support of her husband's calling. Nor would she be keen on Millie's alleged female improvement program. That might be why those verses were mainly about vanity and wealth."

"I take it you're convinced Millie was murdered," Renie said as they entered the kitchen, where Joe was finishing his late lunch.

"Well . . ." Judith began.

Joe turned around to look at his wife. "Go ahead, say it. The autopsy showed that Millie was poisoned. I think you're still batting a thousand when it comes to your homicide average, Jude-girl."

Judith wasn't exactly celebrating the news. "That's . . . tragic. Could Millie have committed suicide?"

"Possibly," Joe allowed. "An accident is always considered, too."

Judith sat down next to Joe. "Did Woody identify the poison?"

Joe used a napkin to wipe some mayo from his lower lip. "Aconitum. Highly toxic stuff. It works fast and wouldn't take much to be fatal. It's been around forever, going back to the Greeks."

Renie had also sat down. "The Greeks and the Romans liked taking poison. I assume Millie didn't.

Americans prefer guns to do themselves in. More efficient. But louder."

Joe shrugged. "True. Woody's initial pronouncement is 'accidental death,' though he isn't ruling out homicide or suicide. You know he's always cautious. He and I agreed we should herd the guests into the parlor and announce his findings to them. Their reactions could be interesting."

Renie feigned dismay. "And spoil their trip to the zoo? How crass! Hey, why not put a sign on the buffet for the cocktail hour stating that the appetizers may contain . . . what did you call it? Aconitum? If somebody avoids the cheese puffs or the salmon pâté, you'll have your killer."

"Not funny," Judith murmured. "I told you, murder isn't funny."

Renie made as if to slap Judith's arm. "And I told you it is. Laughter over tears has been the Grover mantra. Loosen up. If you tie yourself in a knot, you won't be able to figure out whodunit."

Judith glared at her cousin. "I'm thinking about Ingrid Heffelman's reaction. I don't want to lose my innkeeper's license."

Joe put his arm around Judith. "Relax. Woody's public statement only states that the tragedy occurred at a local hostelry. You're safe."

Judith wasn't appeased. "Ingrid will immediately suspect Hillside Manor as the hostelry."

"Get real," Joe said. "How many people have died or been killed at local hostelries of all kinds since you last had a corpse on the premises?"

"Joe's right," Renie chimed in. "Think about all the hookers who ply their trade at some of our less savory motels. The AAA on those places stands for Adulterous American Assassination Assignations. Oops! That's four *As*. You know I'm poor at math."

"Okay, okay," Judith said in a reluctant voice. "But it's still upsetting."

Joe removed his arm from his wife's shoulders. "I'm taking the Subaru to get the oil changed. You two keep out of trouble, okay?"

The phone rang just as he went out through the back door.

"So," Mavis Lean-Brodie said to Judith, "we've got an autopsy report. What else can you tell me?"

"Nothing," Judith replied. "The alleged suspects went to the zoo."

"Voluntarily?" Mavis asked. "Or are they part of an exhibit?"

"They're tourists. At least most of them are."

"Yes," Mavis said, sounding amused. "I'm aware that the victim and his wife recently bought a house in

Sunset Cliffs. If memory serves, you were involved in a murder investigation there several years ago."

Judith stiffened, causing Renie to stare at her. "Yes, Mavis, the gated community of Sunset Cliffs," she said for her cousin's enlightenment. "I hope they didn't buy that gruesome estate known as Creepers. That old mansion lived up to its name."

"No, they bought a twenty-two-room contemporary for a mere fifteen million. No water or mountain view, though. But it makes a person wonder why they didn't invite their California chums to stay there with them, doesn't it?"

"It does," Judith agreed. "But if you think I know why they came here instead, I don't."

"Maybe they didn't want the rest of your guests on their own expensive turf for a reason," Mavis suggested. "I have friends in high places—such as the owners of KINE-TV, who also live in Sunset Cliffs. I think maybe I'll pay them a call and take a look at the Schmuck property. Perhaps I'll get chummy with a neighbor or two."

"You *will* report back to me, won't you?"

"Of course. I *am* a TV reporter, thus I report. I may do that this afternoon, unless a big story breaks. Stay tuned." Mavis rang off.

Renie was looking irked. "Why didn't I listen in on the living room extension? Now you have to pass on whatever Mavis had to say."

Judith summed up what the anchorwoman had told her. "Oddly enough," she added, "after I found out that Millie and Rodney had moved here a short time ago, it never occurred to me to wonder why they stayed at Hillside Manor instead of at their own home. I guess I thought they were staying at a residence inn or some such place while they house-hunted."

"Maybe they hadn't furnished it yet," Renie said.

"That's possible. With over twenty rooms, that'd take some time." She frowned. "Or maybe we're overlooking the obvious. If buying up the cul-de-sac was their aim, then they had to stay here."

Renie nodded. "Still, the whole thing is kind of theatrical. Has Rodney stopped calling you Mama?"

"I haven't seen him today. He didn't come down for breakfast, but he went to the zoo with the rest of them." Judith was silent for a moment or two. "I'm curious about that L.A. phone number. I know the area code is 213, but do you remember the prefix?"

"Yes," Renie replied, digging into her huge purse and getting out her cell phone. "I may not do math, but I'm a wizard with phone numbers. Watch me."

She tapped in the required eleven digits. Her smug expression changed when the call was answered. "Yes," she said, "which section have I reached? I wasn't sure of the extension." Her brown eyes widened. "Oh, I meant to dial the dementia unit. Thanks, but I'll call later. I think I hear a burglar trying to break in."

"Well?" Judith said after Renie disconnected.

Her cousin's face was bleak. "It's the Los Angeles County Department of Mental Health. That was the extension for public guardians and committing people to asylums. Now I wish I hadn't asked."

Judith wished the same thing.

Chapter 15

J udith was startled. "Could the rev—or Mrs. Rev— be trying to get a guardianship of Rodney? Or worse yet, to have him committed?"

"Rodney does leap to mind," Renie replied. "But with this bunch, it could be any of them. Heck, it could be all of them."

"I wonder . . ." She stopped.

"What?"

"We assume Belle is the Schmucks' only child. What if that's not the case?"

Renie made a face. "Isn't one enough since it's Weedbella?"

"Our parents obviously thought one was enough, since we're both only children," Judith said. "Granted, it's odd that any siblings wouldn't be included in the wedding party, but maybe there's one in grad school or living abroad or who is estranged from the rest of the family."

"Maybe such a sibling isn't as strange as the rest of them," Renie suggested. "But does it matter?"

"It doesn't, I suppose," Judith conceded. "Damn, coz, I feel as if I don't have a grip on these people or this whole murder investigation. Maybe I *am* too old to sleuth."

"That's dumb," Renie declared. "The problem is the people involved. They're kind of unreal."

"True." Judith stood up. "I'm antsy. Let's go to the zoo."

Renie's jaw dropped. "Are you insane?"

"No. I'd like to know if that's where they really went. Even normal guests rarely go to the zoo. There's too much else to see around here."

"Fine. Take a cab." Renie crossed her arms and assumed her most mulish expression. "How can you tell if they're at the zoo? Do you know what kind of cars they rented? Could you distinguish them from the animals? Or do you think they're going to make an offer on the entire park area and turn it into one big residential development?"

Judith sank down slowly in her chair. "That's not all that goofy an idea. Not the zoo," she added hastily, "but that they're trying to find another parcel of land for condos. Property around the zoo isn't as expensive as it is here on the hill."

Renie uncrossed her arms and smiled. "Your customary logic has reasserted itself."

"I still feel as if I should be doing something," Judith said. "Except a phone number to L.A. County Mental Health and some Bible verses, we came up empty."

"You could check out some of Clayton's blogs," Renie suggested facetiously.

"Maybe I should," Judith said. "What would I do? Just put in his name and see what comes up?"

"Oh, good lord, I didn't mean . . ." But Renie knew better than to try to dissuade her cousin when she was in sleuthing mode. "Then do it. I'll take a nap. As for finding whatever bilge he writes, I have no idea how to look up a blogger."

Judith went over to the computer and typed in *Clayton Ormsby.* "Don't you want to see what showed up?" she asked.

"Not really," Renie replied. "Condense it for me. Like two, three words."

"He's got a website," Judith announced.

"Big deal. Who doesn't? You and I both have websites that I designed. They're necessary for doing business these days."

"Clayton calls himself 'A World-Class Act.' What does that mean?"

"That he's an idiot?"

"It's his bio," Judith said. "He was born in Lompoc, California, the Flower Seed Capital of the World. Where is that?"

"North of Los Angeles, toward the coast. I'm getting bored already."

"You have the attention span of a gnat," Judith declared. "Married Sophie Kilmore in 1988. Apparently no children."

"For that we can be grateful," Renie said. "Cut to the chase. Find one of his blogs and make it interesting or I'm taking my empty Pepsi can and going home."

"You are a pill." Judith clicked on *BLOGS*. "Wow. There are a ton of them. They're listed alphabetically by topic, not date."

"If you can't find a blog called 'Poison,' pick one in the middle, starting with *M*. I always do that when I'm confronted with stuff that's alphabetized. Usually what I'm looking for is toward the end of the alphabet, not the beginning. I don't know why."

Judith decided to humor Renie. "Okay, I've got 'Manliness,' 'Monkshood,' and 'Motor Sports.' You choose."

"I doubt Clayton knows much about manliness, and motor sports bore me. Go with monkshood."

"Okay," Judith said. "The monkshood blog is dated May fourth of this year. I'll print it out. It's a plant, you know."

"Right." Renie's boredom seemed to be glazing her eyes.

"It's only one page, single-spaced. Shall I read it to you?" Judith asked as the single sheet began to make its appearance in the printer tray.

"We can both read it at the same time. Jeez, you're making a project out of this. Now I'm getting hungry."

Judith had already glanced at the lead sentence. "Oh, no!" she cried. "Monkshood is poisonous. It's official name is aconitum."

Renie's interest was mildly piqued. "Is Clayton confessing all?"

"No," Judith responded, sitting down at the table. "He's using it as an example of toxic plants that grow in gardens and can cause serious problems for family pets. I guess Clayton's not worried about children, since he doesn't appear to have any."

"He's not the kid-friendly type," Renie said. "You don't have any monkshood in your yard, do you?"

Judith shook her head. "Not that I know of. See the picture? It's kind of a pretty blue flower, though."

"It's vaguely familiar," Renie said. "I suppose I've seen it around. A lot of ordinary garden plants are toxic. I wonder why he chose monkshood as an example?"

"Coincidence?" Judith mused. "Did it give someone an idea?"

Renie grinned. "You're assuming Clayton's pals read his blogs?"

"They might. Being his wife, Sophie probably does. Of course she's a doctor and might know about monkshood. You have to admit it's an odd coincidence that Clayton wrote about it only a short time ago."

"When did the Schmucks make their reservation to come here?"

Judith thought for a moment. "The last week of April. I remember because Easter came late this year and I spent the next week worrying because May wasn't filling up very fast except for the Memorial Day weekend. Then along came the Schmucks with their full-house request. It seemed like the answer to a prayer."

"A lesson in being careful what you pray for," Renie said.

Judith rolled her eyes.

After getting into a religious argument with Phyliss about where Noah could find penguins for his ark, Renie left shortly after two. Joe returned home a few minutes later. The repairs on the classic MG wouldn't be finished until Wednesday. Ron the Mechanic had to send away for parts.

"I've got a call in to that inspector," Joe told Judith as she was thawing spareribs for the barbecue. "I don't expect to hear back from him until close to five if he's on his rounds."

"Do you think he was bribed?"

"It's possible, I suppose." Joe grimaced at the spareribs. "It could rain. Maybe we should bake them."

"It doesn't look like rain to me," Judith said. "You just don't want to bother starting the barbecue."

"It takes so long for them to cook over the coals. The first time around is always iffy. I have to regain my knack." His round face turned puckish. "I can't remember if I filed it under *K* or *N*."

"Work it out," Judith said. But she smiled.

Mavis called around four. "Rich people give me a pain," she declared. "I think I'll do a series on why they're so standoffish with the media. Of course, it might dry up some of my sources."

"Don't tell me you of all people had trouble getting them to open up? You're more famous around here than most of them are."

"They don't want to be famous," Mavis responded. "They just want to be rich. But I'm relentless. I finally got a Mrs. Burnside-Smythe to talk after I made a fool of myself over her stinking little Pekingese, Horatio Alger. She told me she hadn't met the Schmucks, but her bridge partner, Mrs. Worthman, had spoken with Millie Schmuck a couple of times at the mailboxes. The quasi-modern house is mostly furnished except for the saloon—her word, not mine. It's in the basement."

"Did Mrs. Burnside-Smythe have anything interesting to say about Millie?"

"Not really," Mavis replied grudgingly. "But her tone indicated that the Schmucks were not One of Them, if you take her meaning."

"I do and she's probably right," Judith said. "In fact, I'm not sure the Schmucks and the rest of their crew are one of *us*. Anything else to report?"

"I hate to say it, but no. It really was a waste of my time," Mavis complained in a sour tone. "I should have been investigating corruption in city government."

"There is some?"

"There always is," Mavis replied wearily. "Got to dash and get ready for the evening news."

As soon as Judith put the phone down, she heard the front door open and a burst of angry voices. Hurrying into the hall, she found Cynthia Wicks berating Reverend Kindred.

"I don't give a rat's rear end about your stupid church, Georgie boy!" she shouted. "Keep religion out of this! We're on a mission, and don't you forget it!"

Stuart nudged his wife. "Mrs. Flynn," he said under his breath.

Cynthia turned to look at Judith. "A bit of dissension in the ranks," she muttered. "We're all still upset about Millie, of course. It makes us nervy. I'm sure you understand."

"Certainly," Judith said as Belle, Clark, and the Crumps started up the stairs. "How was the zoo?"

"Fine," Stuart replied. "There were a lot of animals." He took his wife's arm and followed the Crumps.

The others were right behind them. Except for one missing person. "Hey," Judith called after Dr. Sophie and Clayton, "where's Mr. Schmuck?"

Sophie glanced at Judith. "Asleep in the car. He's tired. He'll be fine." She kept going.

Judith returned to the kitchen to find Joe searching the cupboards. "Where's the lighter fluid for the barbecue?" he asked.

"In the pantry, top shelf," she informed him. "Do you know what kind of cars the guests rented?"

"No. I don't think they parked in the cul-de-sac. Why do you ask?"

"Because they left Rodney asleep in one of them," Judith said. "I want to check on him."

Joe sighed. "I'll go with you." He grabbed his wife's arm and started out of the kitchen. "Damn, but these people are a pain in the butt. Can't you evict them? They haven't paid for tonight, have they?"

"No, but I have Rodney's credit card on file and I'll charge their extended stay to that," Judith said as they went out the front door. "Is Woody insisting they stick around for a while?"

"He can't really do that without any evidence," Joe replied, gesturing across the street at a silver midsize Nissan sedan. "I think that's one of the rental cars."

The late afternoon had grown quite warm. As Judith and Joe waited to let a plumbing truck go by, she noticed that all the windows were rolled up in the Nissan. No one appeared to be inside, though.

"Maybe," she said to Joe as they recrossed the street, "Rodney's in that blue Honda parked just beyond the entrance to the cul-de-sac. I don't recognize it."

Joe led the way to the Honda. "Rodney's asleep in the backseat. There's an empty bottle of Scotch on the floor."

"How callous!" Judith cried softly as she peered into the car. "How could they leave him out here with the windows closed?"

"Damn those morons!" Joe pounded on the window. "What's wrong with them? Are they trying to kill off Schmuck now that his wife's dead?"

Rodney didn't stir, despite Joe's vigorous efforts. "He's breathing," Judith said. "He almost looks as if he's smiling."

"You'd be smiling, too, if you drank a quart of Old Grisly," Joe snapped. "I'll go get one of those jackasses to give me the car key. You stay put in case Rodney comes to."

Joe had barely reached the cul-de-sac when Arlene practically flew from the other side of the giant hedge and across the street. "Judith! Have you found another dead person? Who is it? Not the mailman, I hope. He's extremely late today."

"It's one of my guests," Judith said, stepping aside so Arlene could look through the window. "Have you met any of them except Reverend Kindred when he went door-to-door?"

"Not exactly," Arlene replied. "I did have to shoo that young couple off of our lawn Saturday. They looked as if they were going to take a nap. Was that the bride and groom who didn't get married?"

"Probably," Judith said, wincing as Arlene pounded on the Honda's window. She shouted Rodney's name, but to no avail.

"I give up," she said. "Those young people told me they were enjoying our grass. Or was it *their* grass?"

"Both, maybe." Judith made an impatient gesture with her hand. "What's taking Joe so long?"

"Maybe he's looking for Casper," Arlene said.

"Casper?"

"The new mailman," Arlene replied. "He tends to get lost, even in the cul-de-sac. I think he naps in our hedge. That's why he's often late."

Joe finally came into view. "Hi, Arlene. I had to find out which of the weirdos had the key to this Honda. It was Sophie. She was one of the drivers. I figure her for a real control freak."

"They're all freaks," Judith declared as she and Arlene stepped aside. "I wonder if you can wake up Rodney. He's probably in a drunken stupor."

"Great." Joe opened the rear door. He called Rodney's name several times, then shook him gently. There was no response except for a snuffling sort of snore. Joe shook him harder. "Damn! He's really out."

"I can get Carl to bring our hose over," Arlene offered. "We bought a much longer one this spring. I'm sure Mr. Schmuck would wake up if you sprayed him really hard."

"And I'm sure the rental agency would charge me for the damage to the car," Joe asserted. "Maybe Carl could help me haul Rodney into the house. Is he busy?"

"No, of course not!" Arlene exclaimed. "He's enjoying retirement so much. I love to see him relaxing and taking his ease." She tapped a finger against her cheek. "Now, let me think where I last saw him . . . Oh! Behind the washer and dryer. He's installing new outlets in another part of our downstairs. I hope he didn't get stuck against the wall. Look in the basement, Joe. I'll stay here with Judith in case Mr. Schmuck wakes up."

"We should get out of the street," Judith said to Arlene after Joe took off. "We're lucky nobody has hit us."

"It's not luck," Arlene asserted. "It's St. Christopher. Do you know some scholars say he never existed? What do scholars know? They only read books. Very dull books, I suspect. They have no imagination."

"I still have a St. Christopher's medal for travelers in my car," Judith said as they went back across the street.

"So do I." Arlene looked down at the gutter. "Somebody dropped something. Maybe Casper. He does tend to be careless." She bent down to retrieve what looked like some kind of pamphlet. "Hmm. It's for our state mental hospitals. Now, who do we know who's crazy? Let's start with some of our fellow SOTS parishioners. How about Francis Xavier Kloppenbluger? He wears a hairshirt, you know, and—"

"Let me see that," Judith interrupted. "It may belong to one of my guests. They may have dropped it coming back to the B&B."

"Which one of them is insane?" Arlene asked.

"All of them," Judith replied, seeing Joe and Carl appear from around the hedge. "Come on, Arlene, let's go open the front door. Our guys will have to cart Rodney up to Room One."

"Oh, dear," Arlene murmured, accompanying Judith through the cul-de-sac, "I hope it doesn't affect Carl's hernia."

"I didn't know he had one," Judith admitted.

"He doesn't, but he's always talking about getting one like his father did. I told him I don't think they're necessarily hereditary. Or are they?" She paused at the bottom of the porch steps. "My Uncle Woofy in Blue Earth, Minnesota, had one. He got it carrying his wife, Plethora, across the threshold when they got married. She was rather large. Unfortunately, he dropped her. It's a good thing she didn't fall on top of him or he'd have been crushed. Poor Uncle Woofy. He was always rather frail. Bowlegged, too, after that episode."

"I doubt that carrying his bride . . ." Judith saw Joe get into the Honda's backseat. Carl blocked her view, so she couldn't see how Joe was coping with Rodney.

"It's a good thing Mr. Schmuck isn't as big as your Aunt Plethora," she remarked. "I'd better open the door."

Both women went up to the porch. And waited. At least two or three minutes passed before they saw Carl turn around, bend down, and grab on to Rodney's legs. A few more seconds went by before Judith saw Joe emerge from the car carrying the rest of Rodney and kicking the Honda's door shut.

"At least they got him out of there," Judith said. "He still seems to be out cold."

"Maybe he's dead," Arlene said. "Have you ever had two married people die at the B&B before? I can't actually recall."

"Ah . . . no. It'd be a first." And for Judith, not a very pleasant thought. Nor was she pleased to see that Joe was quite red in the face and Carl was panting as they came up the porch steps.

"Gangway," Joe gasped as they carried the still-unconscious Rodney inside. "Sofa," he croaked to Carl after they entered the hall.

"Oh, drat!" Judith exclaimed. "I don't want Rodney in the living room. He might be sick after he comes to." She hurried inside with Arlene right behind her.

But Judith held her tongue when she saw Joe wiping perspiration off his forehead and Carl leaning against the mantelpiece. "Maybe," she said meekly, "a couple of the guests can take him upstairs."

Joe nodded curtly. "Fine. Come on, Carl, let's grab a beer and sit outside, where I don't have to look at any more of these crazy people." The two men headed for the kitchen.

Arlene stared at Judith. "Did Joe mean us?"

"Who knows?" Judith picked up an afghan from the back of the vacant sofa and tossed it over Rodney. "Would you like a glass of wine? I need a drink."

"No, thank you," Arlene replied. "I should go home and figure out what I'm going to make for dinner. Do take care, Judith. You look a trifle . . . frazzled."

"No kidding." But Judith hugged Arlene. "You and Carl are wonderful neighbors—and friends."

"Well, what are friends for?" Arlene asked. "Besides, you and your corpses do perk up the cul-de-sac. Most people tend to be rather dull."

Judith smiled at the statement. But she thought to herself that "dull" might be kind of nice for a change.

She'd never admit, of course, that dull didn't become her.

Chapter 16

Keeping to her word, Judith opted for simple appetizers: crackers, cheese, and smoked oysters. The guests could like it or send out for more exotic tidbits. Just as she was about to take the tray into the living room, Elsie Kindred tapped gently on the half door.

"May I trouble you?" she asked. "George got bit by a squirrel."

"That's too bad," Judith said. "Is he okay?"

Elsie timorously entered the kitchen. "No. He insists it's infected. It is quite red. Are the squirrels around her rabid?"

"I doubt it. Did it happen at the zoo?"

"The zoo?" Elsie's thick brown eyebrows shot upward, almost colliding with her scraggly auburn bangs. "No. It was quite a ways from here, by a lake.

There were lots of ducks there, too. They're very noisy, but otherwise, a very serene, peaceful . . . place. I can't find my antiseptic. I was sure I put it in my kit before we left home."

"Actually, there should be some antiseptic in the medicine chest of the bathroom between your room and the Crumps'."

"I checked there first." Elsie looked apologetic. "There wasn't any."

"I'll have to get some from the supply cupboard upstairs. Or you could get it instead," Judith amended. "Just pour some into a glass."

"Oh, yes, of course. There are glasses in our room. Thank you. I'll do that now. I hope George has finished his prayers. He's trying to pray away the pain. Bless his heart." She scurried off through the half doors.

Joe came through the back door. "I called Ethan Ethanson on my cell after Carl left. He was conned."

Judith's curiosity was piqued. "Conned? How do you mean?"

"As in duped." Joe opened the fridge. "I need another beer. Do you want me to make you a drink?"

"Yes, please. I was going to do that, but Elsie Kindred interrupted me. As a minister's wife, I wasn't sure she'd approve of her innkeeper hitting the sauce. How was Ethan conned?"

Joe removed the cap from a Molson's Ale. "He was contacted last Friday by a guy who said a Jim Johnson had told him Ethan's boss was his relative and he'd gotten his okay to play a practical joke on a builder friend. All he needed was to borrow a city inspector's badge over the weekend. Ethan didn't see any harm, so he obliged. He was too excited about his fishing trip to give it another thought."

"It sounds plausible," Judith said. "The reason, that is. But Jim Johnson? How many of those are in the phone book?"

Joe's expression was wry as he handed Judith her Scotch. "Enough to make the one who suckered Ethan hard to trace."

Judith sipped some of her drink before asking what the impostor looked like.

"A little over average height; brownish hair; pleasant face; no distinguishing marks. What are you thinking?"

"About the so-called Ethan Ethanson who came here," Judith replied. "He fits that description. Not someone who would stand out in a crowd, but he could also be the guy I saw sitting in the car as if on surveillance."

Joe grinned. "So he came to spy on you—or your zany guests?"

"The latter, I assume. For all I know, he may've been spying on them from the time they got here. Maybe he's a PI. Hey, you might've run into him at some point."

"Only if he's another retired cop," Joe said. "We PIs try to keep out of each other's way. I'll go check to see if the coals are hot."

Judith set out the appetizers in the living room. She had returned to the kitchen when the phone rang. To her surprise, the caller was Jack Hardy, the longtime funeral director from across the ship canal who had handled most of the Grover family's burials over the past half century.

"Jack!" Judith said in surprise. "I thought you'd retired."

"I did," he replied in his usual cheerful voice. "But once in a while my sons need Dad to give them a hand. We had three funerals over the weekend and already two more for this coming week. So many of these folks have moved here from other places—but you know that. If you read the obits, ninety-five percent of them were born somewhere else."

"I'm well aware of that," Judith said wryly. "In the past five years, I've heard from at least two dozen guests who visited here, liked it so much that they pulled up stakes and moved to our now bulging city."

Jack chuckled. "It's good for business, though. At least my business. But that's not why I'm calling. One of my sons had a funeral out north today at Land of Eternal Repose. Afterward, when Jeff was in the cemetery office, the guy behind the desk asked if any of the funeral party had lost a wallet. Jeff had no idea, but he took a look, didn't recognize the name, but noticed whoever it was had one of your B&B cards in it. Does Clark Stone ring any bells with you?"

"It does," Judith replied. "He's a guest who thought he'd lost his wallet while shopping up on top of the hill. He's here now, so I'll tell him to pick it up. Will you be around for a while?"

Jack chuckled again. "I'm not around now. Our office is closed. I'm at home. Say, my other son, Jake, has a meeting tomorrow up on the hill near Holliday's Drug Store. He can drop it off there. You know the Hollidays, right?"

"Sure. I'll let Clark know. He may be checking out tomorrow." Or so Judith hoped. She thanked Jack and rang off.

Shortly after six, the guests straggled down in twos and threes. According to Joe, the spareribs weren't done and his gruesome mother-in-law was pitching a fit in the backyard. Judith poured a half inch of Scotch into what was left of her melted ice, took a big swig, and headed for the living room. All of the Schmuck party had gathered except Rodney. Joe and Carl had finally managed to get him upstairs after they'd finished their first Molson's.

Clark and Belle were seated at the baby grand piano, picking out some discordant chords. The rest of the party was engaged in desultory conversation and not necessarily with each other. The Reverend Kindred appeared to be delivering a sermon to the grandfather clock.

Judith smiled a greeting as she ran the gauntlet of guests to reach the far end of the long living room. She had to tap Clark's shoulder to get his attention.

"You wallet's been found," she said, hoping to sound amiable. "It was at the cemetery north of the city, but it's been dropped off at Holliday's Drug Store on top of the hill."

"Oh." Clark looked puzzled. "What cemetery?"

"The one just north of the city," Judith replied.

"I thought that was a golf course." Clark looked at Belle. "Did we go to a cemetery since we got here?"

"I don't think so," Belle replied. "But then I nodded off some of the time we were driving around checking out . . . the scenery."

"Never mind that," Judith said. "You can get your wallet back tomorrow."

Clark wasn't perturbed. "That's okay. I don't need it now anyway. Sophie's picking up the tab tonight when we go out to dinner. Hey, Belle, what were those last chords you played? Was it the theme music from *Harold and Kumar Go to White Castle?*"

Judith didn't want to know. She made her way back to the kitchen without any of the guests bothering to speak to her. That suited her just fine. But she felt gloomy, not being able to remember a time when she felt so distanced from her visitors. Except maybe Rodney. Even if she wasn't his mother, she realized she was taking a maternal interest in the poor drunken sot. She took another swig of Scotch.

Judith and Joe were still outside at seven o'clock, not having eaten dinner until six thirty. Gertrude had slammed the door on her toolshed apartment after stating that if the Flynns were trying to starve her to death, she was going to report them to CPS.

"Doesn't the old bat know that CPS is for children?" Joe asked.

"Maybe she thinks she can report her daughter and son-in-law to them for abusing her. You know Mother likes to tease us."

"Tease us?" Joe's green eyes sparked. "How about torture us?"

"She finally consented to eat dinner," Judith pointed out.

"But not with us," Joe reminded his wife. "She took it inside her so-called ramshackle dwelling."

"You know that was her choice after we got married. Mother refused to live under the same roof with you."

"The feeling is mutual," Joe muttered.

The phone rang before Judith could defend either her mother—or Joe. Judith picked up the receiver and heard Renie's voice.

"Hey, coz," she began, "I forgot to ask if Rodney ever produced the birth certificate or whatever proof he has that you're his mother. I assume you never found it while you were pillaging Room One."

"No," Judith replied. "For all I know, he had whatever the document is inscribed on the head of a pin. I don't think what I found burned in the barbecue was it, though. That looked like the remains of ordinary typing paper."

"Nothing ordinary about Rodney," Renie remarked. "Did he and the rest of the gang ever come back from wherever they went?"

"Unfortunately, they did." Judith proceeded to relate the afternoon's adventures at the B&B while Joe dozed in the lawn chair.

"Gosh," Renie said in mock surprise, "was that as much fun for you as it was for them?"

"Don't ask," Judith replied. "They seem subdued tonight. They've been that way all day. Maybe they really are mourning Millie."

"It *is* possible that they were fond of her. Or do you think they're merely hangers-on?"

"I don't know what to think," Judith admitted. "But now that you brought it up, I'll ask Rodney about his proof that I'm his mother. If he ever sobers up enough to know what I'm talking about."

"Do you think he's really drunk?"

Judith started to say yes, but paused. "That's an interesting question. Are you suggesting he could be doing drugs?"

"Well . . . no. But someone could've drugged him."

"That's true," Judith said in a thoughtful tone. "An empty liquor bottle doesn't mean he drank it. I wonder . . ." Her voice trailed off.

"Keep speculating. I have to watch *Lonesome Dove* with Bill for the fourteenth time. It's a good thing I enjoy it as much as he does." Renie hung up.

The guests left for dinner shortly after six. Judith hoped they'd stay away for hours. But she wondered if Rodney had gone with them. A little after eight, she went upstairs and rapped on Room One's door. There was no response. She tried the knob. It turned easily in her grasp. The room was still light enough so that Judith could see the bed was empty. Apparently Rodney had recovered sufficiently to join the others for dinner. Relieved that he wasn't still in an alcoholic stupor, she went back downstairs to join Joe in the living room.

"Well?" her husband said, looking up from an espionage novel he'd been reading. "Any sign of chaos upstairs?"

"No," Judith replied, sitting down on the sofa next to Joe. "I will say this for the current guests—they're fairly tidy."

Joe gave a slight shrug. "Good for them. You want to watch TV?"

"Not really. I'd rather just sit here next to you and be quiet."

Joe put his arm around her. "Go for it. You've been under a strain. Any way we can take a break for a few days and maybe go up to Canada or down to the ocean?"

"I'd have to get Arlene and Carl to sub for us, but about now it sounds like a wonderful idea." She snuggled closer. "In fact, just sitting here with you is kind of wonderful."

"Kick back. The last few days have been rough."

Judith nodded. In fact, she felt as if she could nod off. And did. When she woke up, it was almost ten. Joe apparently hadn't moved, but he'd finished his book. "I hate it when the good spy turns out to be a bad spy who is a double agent and the villain is a robot. Dumb book. Why don't we go to bed?"

"That's a good idea," Judith said—and smiled.

The Flynns were both asleep by eleven o'clock. They never heard the guests come back. Tuesday morning brought a light drizzle, the kind that wouldn't last long, but might return later in the day.

Judith felt refreshed as she and Joe prepared breakfast. When eight o'clock rolled around, no one had yet appeared at the dining room table. As the schoolhouse clock ticked to eight thirty, she remarked that the guests must have made a late night of it. By the time it was going on nine, Phyliss Rackley had arrived. After a litany of her latest bodily aches and pains— and praise to the Lord that she could still stand up on her own two feet despite fallen arches—she started upstairs.

"The guests haven't yet come down," Judith called after her. "Why don't you do the laundry first?"

"You know I have my routine," Phyliss declared. "I'll tidy up the guest bathrooms. If they want to use them, they can ask. The Good Lord gave them voices, didn't he?" She clumped off down the hall.

Judith's good mood was going bad. "The food will be inedible by the time they finally get down here," she griped. "Are they all hungover?"

"Maybe not the rev," Joe said. "Why do you care? You don't seem overly fond of them."

Before Judith could reply, Phyliss came back into the hall. "Now, don't go calling me snoopy," she said with a wag of her bony finger. "But the door to Room Six was ajar. I figured nobody was in there, so I had me a peek. I was right. Empty as the tomb on Easter Sunday. I went through the bathroom to take a peek into Room Five. Empty, too. In fact, all the rooms are empty. Maybe Satan took them in their sleep. Except the minister, of course."

Judith didn't think that was the case. In fact, she didn't want to think about what had happened to her missing guests.

But she knew she had to do something. The guests weren't mere guests—but suspects.

Chapter 17

A t least," Joe said, trying to console his irate wife, "they didn't stiff you for the bill, right?"

"That's not the point!" Judith yipped. "They're a bunch of crooks, they're up to something, they're running away!"

"What," Phyliss demanded, "do you expect of godless people? They probably did in the poor minister."

Judith shot her cleaning woman a baleful glance. "Hardly. He's as big a criminal as the rest of them. He's a phony."

Phyliss's face sagged. "That's a terrible thing to say about a man of the cloth! I talked to him. He's a sincere Christian preacher who knows his Bible." She flounced off in a fit of high dudgeon.

"Face it," Joe said, still sounding reasonable. "You should be glad they left. You're only upset because you can't grill them to find out who poisoned Millie. If anyone actually did, of course."

Judith stared at her husband. "You think she poisoned herself?"

"No, not really, but it could've been an accident."

"I don't encounter accidents, I encounter murder," Judith declared. "You're a cop. You should know the difference."

"I may be a *retired* cop," Joe said, still calm despite the warning look in his green eyes, "but I've always needed evidence before I consider foul play. Woody's hedging his bets, too. Be reasonable."

"I need to talk to Renie," Judith muttered.

"You can't. She's still unconscious."

Judith acknowledged Joe's statement with a faint nod. It wasn't her style to get so upset. There was something about the Schmuck bunch that was—as Renie had put it—unreal. That gave her food for thought. But after mulling while cleaning up from the uneaten guest breakfast, she dismissed the long weekend from her mind. She was never one to dwell on life's more unpleasant aspects.

"You idiot!" Renie yelled over the phone two hours later. "Don't tell me you don't give a hoot about

Rodney and his not-so-merry band of loony hangers-on! Have you lost your mind?"

"Of course not," Judith replied indignantly. "What's the point? They're gone. I'm done."

Renie was uncustomarily silent for a moment or two. "Okay. You want to have lunch someplace? I skimped on breakfast. I overslept and didn't get up until ten thirty."

"I'm waiting to hear back from Ingrid Heffelman," Judith said. "I had her move the four reservations for tonight to other B&Bs. She's supposed to tell me if she has anybody who might want to stay here."

"So I'm supposed to pass out from malnutrition because of Ms. Heffalump?" Renie grumbled. "She can call on your cell. I'll meet you at Heraldsgate Café in fifteen minutes. Wait. I just realized I'm not dressed. Make that twenty-five. Maybe I'm not really awake yet. I'd better look in the mirror to see if my eyes are open. But if they're still closed, how can I tell?"

"Try pinching yourself. And avoid driving in your sleep." Judith rang off.

A little after eleven thirty, Judith noticed that it was drizzling again. Sweetums came through the cat door and meandered down the hall, looking miffed. Apparently Gertrude had not granted him admission to the toolshed. Checking to make sure his dish in the pantry had food and the bowl had water, she headed outside.

The Subaru wasn't in the garage. Irked, she went back inside, where Phyliss had just come up from the basement. "Do you know if Joe left?" Judith asked.

"About half an hour ago," Phyliss replied. "He couldn't find you, so he told me to tell you he had to investigate some evildoers. Oh, he said you'd better fix lunch for your mother because she's on the warpath."

"About what?"

Phyliss shrugged. "How would I know? Isn't your mother always on the warpath? If you ask me, she's a troubled soul. I've tried to save her, but she resists hearing the Word. She just waves those beads of hers at me and says to get lost. Doesn't she know I've been found?"

Judith didn't attempt to defend her mother. That was a lost cause not unlike Phyliss's appraisal of her mother's soul. Instead, she called Renie. "I have no car," she told her cousin. "Joe took it. He has to work. Do you want to pick me up or shall we eat here?"

"Ohhhh . . ." Renie's sigh was audible. "Jeez, I'm practically passing out from hunger. Okay, I'll be there as soon as I can. Meet me out front."

"Don't rush," Judith said. "I have to make lunch for Mother."

"In that case, make it for me, too. Forget about the café. I can't wait that long." Renie slammed down the phone.

Judith took off her jacket. She was making an egg salad sandwich for Gertrude when the phone rang.

"Some rich people," Mavis Lean-Brodie began, "are starstruck. Or at least they like to get chummy with so-called media celebrities. Mrs. Burnside-Smythe, she of Sunset Cliffs, called minutes ago to tell me that Mrs. Worthman told her she'd seen two carloads of people drive through Heaven's Gate. How's that for breaking news?"

"You mean they went over a cliff?" Judith asked in a shocked voice.

"No, no," Mavis responded sharply. "That's what the Schmucks call their house."

"Oh! Well, that solves the puzzle here. They checked out without giving me notice. They're a little short in the consideration department."

"You mean you got stiffed?"

"No, I have Rodney's credit-card number," Judith said. "Thanks for letting me know, Mavis. Have you put your story together yet?"

"Are you kidding?" Mavis shot back. "I'm not sure there *is* a story. Your old pal Woody Price isn't calling Millie Schmuck's death a homicide yet. Or do you know something I don't?"

"I don't," Judith replied. "You're the one with the latest news on the Schmucks. Maybe they got the mansion's saloon furnished. Those people should call it the saloony."

"I'll take your word for it," Mavis said. "I won't interview them until it's murder." She hung up.

Renie showed up right after Judith returned from taking lunch out to Gertrude. "Is my sweatshirt on backward?" she asked Judith. "I got dressed in a hurry."

"It's blank," Judith replied. "Both sides."

"Oh. Then it doesn't matter. I thought it said 'Something Stupid.'"

Judith frowned at her cousin, "Like what?"

"I've got three purple sweatshirts," Renie responded. "This one's blank, another one has the University's logo on it, and the one the kids gave me for Mother's Day says 'Something Stupid.' When they asked me what I wanted, I told all three of them I needed new sweatshirts, but not ones that said something stupid." She shrugged. "Of course that's what my perverse children had put on the new purple sweatshirt. If Bill and I had any money, we'd disinherit them."

Judith opened the fridge. "When it comes to being perverse, I don't think your apples fell too far from the tree. I haven't made our lunch yet. Ham, egg salad, tuna, or baloney?"

"Ham, with cheese—Havarti, if you have it." Renie sat down at the table. "So the guests took off?"

Judith related what Mavis had told her. "I assume," she concluded, "Woody is investigating, but he probably thinks the guests are still here. Maybe I should call him."

"Don't bug him," Renie cautioned. "He'll let you know if he sends a detective to question the loonies. Frankly, I'd try to forget about the Schmucks. I'll bet the Californians are heading back to L.A."

Judith gave her cousin a sheepish look as she handed her a plate with a sandwich and potato chips. "That may be so, but it's why I can't help dwelling on them. I worry about what will happen to Rodney."

"Sheesh." Renie rolled her eyes. "Hey, you're really not his mother."

"I know," Judith said, making an egg salad sandwich for herself, "but he's so vulnerable. What if they really do plan to commit him? Maybe one of that bunch is applying for a guardianship or else they're talking him into voluntary commitment."

"That's not your problem," Renie declared before taking a giant bite out of her sandwich.

Judith sat down across from her cousin. "You're the one who suggested Rodney might not be drinking as much as it appears. What if he's being drugged?"

Renie started to argue, but frowned instead. "I guess you can't put much past his so-called pals. They have access to drugs—a doctor, a nurse, not to mention Clark and Belle with their dealer connections. Weed may not be the only funny stuff those two do for recreation."

"I hate to think Belle might be in on a conspiracy against her own father," Judith said. "She's so spacey that I can't get a handle on her."

"How upset was Belle over her mother's death?" Renie asked.

Judith considered the question. "At first, she couldn't believe what I was trying to tell her. Then, when she realized that Millie was in fact dead, she burst into tears. Later, she talked about her mother being too young to die, which, of course, she was. Much of the time Belle wasn't quite planted firmly on the ground. You saw her poem with the allusion to the cloud that my mother dreamed up in her phony séance."

Renie laughed. "I'd like to have sat in on that."

Judith remained serious. "I wish I had. It might've revealed a lot of things about the guests. Do you know anyone who lives in Sunset Cliffs?"

"Not offhand," Renie replied, wiping butter off of her short chin. "I've done some design work for CEOs who might . . ." She stopped and narrowed her eyes at

Judith. "Are you looking for an entrée into the gated community? What about the family at Creepers where we got stuck with another corpse?"

"I don't know if any of them are still around," Judith replied. "After all the awful things that happened there, they might've moved away. Surely you must have a connection to somebody who lives there."

Renie looked mulish. "I don't think so."

"You're lying."

Renie chewed on several potato chips. "Tevah Boy, mehba."

Judith managed to translate what her cousin said through a mouthful of food. "Trevor Boyd—from Key Largo Bank?"

Renie nodded—and swallowed. "Right. But we aren't exactly close. I designed the bank's calendar two years ago in exchange for wiping out my nine-hundred-dollar overdraft. How was I supposed to know what I had in my account? I'd been Christmas shopping."

"You can't balance your checkbook when it's Arbor Day," Judith said.

Renie wrinkled her pug nose. "When *is* Arbor Day? I forget."

"Never mind. Let me think—what excuse could you give for calling on the Boyds?"

Renie gazed up at the ceiling. "My mind's a blank."

"Come on, coz," Judith coaxed. "You don't have to actually go see him, we just need an excuse to get inside the Sunset Cliffs gate."

"Boyd wouldn't be home during the day anyway," Renie said, holding her head. "Okay, Mrs. Boyd . . . Have I ever met her? I forget. Oh, right, I had to go to the bank's Christmas cocktail party, where the new calendars were handed out instead of bonuses. Boyd's kind of cheap. Mrs. Boyd has corns. I remember she had to take off her shoes right after her fifth kamikaze. We can be her new podiatrist or some damned thing. I mean, I can be the podiatrist. You're my assistant."

"Do podiatrists usually have assistants?" Judith asked.

"They do now," Renie replied. "You're it. Maybe I should use a phony name. Do you remember Dr. Foot? He was Grandma and Grandpa Grover's dentist. I always wondered why he wasn't a podiatrist."

Judith felt a headache coming on again. Sometimes her cousin had that effect on her. "Are you done eating?"

"Unless you've got dessert," Renie replied.

"You don't usually eat dessert," Judith said.

"I do if you have pie. Remember how my dad always asked my mom, 'What kind of apple pie have you got?' It was his favorite." Renie stood up. "Never mind. We should go now in case Bill needs the Camry after his walk."

After checking in with Gertrude, the cousins headed north to Sunset Cliffs. The drizzle had stopped and the sun was flirting with the clouds as the two women avoided the always busy freeway and kept to side streets. Their destination lay just beyond the city limits, overlooking the Sound.

"You," Renie said, glancing at Judith, "should be telling the lie to the guard. I don't do as well at that sort of thing."

"I suppose I could lean over to talk to him if you want to pretend you're mute."

Renie turned off by the golf course, slowing down as they approached the woodsy entrance shielding Sunset Cliffs from prying eyes. The guard stepped out of his booth. He looked as if he was barely old enough to vote, let alone confront troublesome visitors.

"Hi," Renie said in a bright voice. "We're here to see Rodney Schmuck at Heaven's Gate. My cousin and I want to make sure they're getting settled in, since they only arrived this morning. Rodney drinks, you know, and he doesn't always know what's going on."

To Judith's amazement, the guard opened the gate and waved them inside. "I don't believe it," she gasped. "How did that happen?"

"Sometimes telling the truth actually works," Renie replied. "Now, how do we figure out where Heaven's Gate is located? This is a huge property and most of the houses are tucked away from the road."

"I remember that. The mailboxes are up ahead," Judith said. "Maybe we can figure it out from the addresses. Or do they have addresses? As I recall, they're too discreet for anything so intrusive."

"You're right," Renie agreed. "We'll have to drive around until we see two cars that look like their rentals. Do you know what they had besides the Honda?"

"A silver Nissan—I think," Judith said.

"Close enough," Renie murmured. "Unless they put the cars in the garage."

"Don't ask for trouble," Judith said as they pulled up by the mailboxes.

Renie got out to have a look. "Just names. Darn. There's a blank box. I'll bet that belongs to the Schmucks. Hey—these suckers aren't locked. Let me see if Rodney and company have any mail."

Judith started to protest, but reconsidered. "Well?" she inquired as her cousin sorted through what looked like mostly circulars and junk mail. "Anything of interest?"

"A couple of bank statements from California," Renie answered. "A county utility bill. Something from an L.A. doctor's office. Maybe that's a bill, too." She shoved the mail back in the box and got back behind the wheel. "No clue where the house is, though."

"We'll find it," Judith said as she spotted a big colonial with a tasteful sign on the lawn that read FARQUHAR'S FARM. "Some farm. What do they raise? Hundred-dollar bills?"

"Rich people don't use real money," Renie declared. "It's too vulgar."

After ten minutes, it seemed to Judith that they were going in circles as they wound around the narrow road, uphill and down, an occasional elegant mansion in the distance, a glimpse of the Sound and the snow-covered mountains beyond.

"Remember," Judith said, "we're looking for a fairly modern house."

"Most of these homes are more traditional," Renie pointed out as a pair of chipmunks scampered across the road in front of them.

"I feel as if we're lost," Judith complained after another five minutes had passed. "Have you any idea where we are?"

"Still in the USA," Renie replied. "Or not. That house on the hill looks like a French château. Maybe we should've brought our passports."

But a moment later Judith saw what appeared to be the blue Honda. "There's another car in front of it in the drive. Yes, it's the Nissan. But I can't see much of the house from here."

Renie reversed enough to turn off of the road. "Shall I drive up to where those cars are parked or do we arrive by stealth?"

"We're not burglars," Judith asserted. "Go ahead and pull in."

As they approached the parked cars, the large, rambling house became more visible. "It looks like a ranch house on steroids," Renie remarked. "Whoever built it should've had their architect committed."

"Maybe that's why somebody was calling the L.A. County Department of Mental Health," Judith said.

Wide concrete steps led up to the front porch, which was surprisingly small given the size of the house. A large picture window was at the right of the front door, but the drapes were closed. Renie used the sleek brass ring that served as a knocker.

"Listen," she said in a low voice. "It set off chimes."

Judith leaned closer. "Not very melodious, just a few notes," she murmured.

"It's the Fate motif from *Carmen*," Renie whispered. "The previous owners must've been opera buffs."

Elsie Kindred opened the door. "Mrs. Flynn!" she exclaimed. "What a surprise. We were expecting the fumigator." Her eyes darted to Renie. "Is she it? I mean . . ." Elsie grimaced.

"I'm the podiatrist," Renie declared. "But never mind that now. How's Rodney?"

"He's resting," Elsie replied, looking ill at ease. "The poor man is utterly worn out from the trauma of losing his wife. George was praying with him, but Rodney nodded off. I'd ask you in, but everything is in such a muddle. Dear Millie—rest her soul—hadn't yet finished furnishing all of the rooms."

Judith moved a step closer and put a hand on Elsie's arm. "I was so sorry you all left without giving me a chance to say good-bye. Did Clark get his wallet back? I've been worried about him. I hope his money and credit cards were all there."

Elsie frowned. "I have no idea. Clark and Belle were in the other car. We all got here within a few minutes of each other, though."

"Would you mind if we came in so I could talk to Clark?" Judith asked in her warmest tone.

"Ah . . ." Elsie darted a glance over to her right. "Clark has joined some of the others in the sitting room for prayer with my husband. Perhaps I could have Clark call you when you get home."

"Oh." Judith's expression conveyed deep disappointment. "But I so much wanted to say good-bye to

Rodney. I feel just terrible about having Millie die at my inn. I've never had such a terrible thing happen to me. It weighs on my conscience. I'm sure the reverend would understand."

Elsie's round face expressed mixed emotions. "My, I don't know what to say. I can't interrupt the prayer service, you see. It may be a while because they only began to pray a few minutes ago."

"That's all right," Judith said, putting one foot on the threshold. "We're in no hurry. Since you all left without any notice, I may not have any guests coming this evening and . . ." She stopped and bit her lip.

Renie put a hand on Judith's arm. "It's a financial hardship for my cousin. She depends on having the B&B occupied every night of the year to make ends meet. She supports her aged mother, you know. I believe you met Mrs. Grover at the séance."

"Oh, yes, of course!" Elsie exclaimed. "Mrs. Grover is very gifted. She told us that my husband would someday become the second Martin Luther. Or," she said suddenly, frowning, "was it Martin Luther King? But wouldn't George have to change color?"

"All things are possible with God," Renie declared solemnly.

Elsie still seemed puzzled. Judith took advantage of the minister's wife's uncertainty to squeeze past her and go inside. "If we could wait until everyone finishes praying . . . it would make me feel so much better to have a word with Rodney in particular, though I don't like to disturb his rest. All of you went through a harrowing experience under my roof."

Elsie nodded vaguely. "Please make yourselves comfortable in the drawing room," she said somewhat timorously. "Would you like a cup of hot tea?"

"That would be wonderful," Judith said with a smile. "Traffic was busy this afternoon. My nerves are frayed."

Elsie nodded and disappeared via the hall.

"Sheesh," Renie muttered, flopping onto an orchid-damask settee. "Who furnished this room? Everything looks like it came out of the back end of the warehouse. It's beyond eclectic, it's a symptom of decor madness."

Judith's eyes roamed over her surroundings. Modern, Victorian Provincial, and a few odd-lot pieces that might have come out of the Great Depression littered the room. "I thought I had some diverse items. Of course I inherited most of Grandma and Grandpa Grover's furniture."

"It suits your house," Renie asserted. "This stuff doesn't fit even a poorly designed ranch house. I wonder if they brought it from L.A.—or Goodwill."

Judith stood up. "Stay put. I'm going to eavesdrop."

"Don't," Renie urged, also getting to her feet. "You'll have to bend way down to listen at the keyhole. If there is a keyhole. I'll do it." She hurried off across the hall.

Judith tried to relax, but the mohair armchair felt lumpy. After a minute or so had passed, Renie returned, grinning.

"They're not praying," she announced. "They're playing—bingo. I heard two winners shout at the same time. Is that Agnes's idea? She's the only Catholic and heaven knows we love our bingo."

Judith laughed. "Could be. It's a wonder they didn't try a séance."

"I wonder if the reverend is playing," Renie said, sitting down. "It might be against his religion."

Judith started to speak, but heard voices. "The games must be over," she whispered, trying to glimpse her ex-guests.

A moment later, Stuart Wicks sauntered into the drawing room. He paused in midstep when he saw the cousins. "My word," he said in a disapproving tone, "what are you two doing here?"

"We just happened to be in the neighborhood," Renie replied. "We have old friends in Sunset Cliffs."

"They don't live in Heaven's Gate," Stuart snapped.

Judith thought it best to intervene. "We felt remiss at not saying good-bye to you and the others, especially Rodney. He worries me."

Stuart shrugged. "Rodney is not to be worried about. He drinks, therefore he's fine."

"Nobody who drinks to excess is fine," Judith asserted. "Have any of you and his other friends tried an intervention?"

"Neither my wife nor I believe in meddling in other people's affairs," Stuart declared with a lift of his sharp chin.

"But," Judith said, "Cynthia is a family counselor. Surely she's concerned about Rodney's reliance on alcohol. Your wife must feel duty-bound to help him. Unless," she added, "it's only Millie's death that has temporarily unhinged her husband."

Stuart sneered. "You're meddling. I must ask you to leave."

Renie stood up. "Gladly. There's a noxious air in this dump and I don't think it has anything to do with booze. Come on, coz, let's get out of here and call the cops."

"I beg your pardon!" Stuart shouted. "On what grounds? I'm an attorney, remember?"

"We can't forget," Renie shot back. "So what? I'm a podiatrist."

The cousins made their exit, leaving an uncharacteristically bewildered Stuart Wicks behind them.

Chapter 18

T hat," Judith declared as they got into the Camry, "was not our finest hour."

"Can't win 'em all," Renie muttered. "Stuart may be the biggest jackass in the bunch."

"He's not a likable guy," Judith conceded. "You know, I think you're right about Rodney. Yes, he may drink too much, but someone—maybe several someones—may be keeping him drugged. But to what purpose?"

"Money?" Renie responded as they reached the main road. "That's the usual reason."

Judith nodded. "They may try to convince him he should sign everything over to Belle. Then, given his daughter's space-case history, they'll fleece her. Of course, if she marries Clark, she'll become Cynthia and Stuart's daughter-in-law. That's a frightening scenario."

"I'll bet that was the original plan," Renie said, driving much faster than Sunset Cliffs' twenty-five-mile-per-hour speed limit. "But Millie dies and the wedding's postponed. Maybe Mr. and Mrs. Wicks are afraid Belle will back out at the last minute."

"You don't think she's in love with Clark?"

"I don't know," Renie admitted. "They *seem* like a real couple. But they're young and they might decide to live together. I get the impression they've been doing that all along or they wouldn't have shared the same bed at the B&B. If Belle would stop puffing the funny stuff, she might wise up and tell her would-be in-laws to take a hike."

"Young people these days have—slow down! There's someone . . ." Judith held her breath as Renie swerved to miss a woman who had been walking on the road rather than on the verge.

"Moron!" Renie cried. "Why are rich people too tight to have sidewalks? Or don't they ever walk any-where except on golf courses?"

"Slow down," Judith said, this time more calmly.

"I already have," Renie snapped. "I didn't hit any-body, did I?"

"No, but I think that was Belle." Judith turned to look behind them. "Yes, now I can see her head-on. Pull over. Let's find out what she's up to."

"She was almost up on Cammy's grille," Renie declared, annoyed.

"It wouldn't be the first time you put somebody up there," Judith shot back. "Remember the forest ranger by Snosalamie Falls?"

"I thought he was a mailman," Renie said, pulling over to stop. "Or was that up by the family cabins?"

"Never mind." Judith opened the car door. "Your adventures behind the wheel are a cross between watching NASCAR and *COPS* on TV. Here comes Belle."

"Here goes Renie," her cousin murmured. "I wish."

Judith ignored the comment and got out of the car. "Hi, Belle. Do you need a lift?"

The young woman halted in midstep and peered at Judith. "Mrs. Flynn? How come you're here?"

"I wanted to check in on your father," Judith replied. "But he was resting when we stopped at Heaven's Gate. How is he coping?"

Belle shrugged. "Okay, I guess. Worn out. Who wouldn't be?"

Judith noted that Belle's eyes seemed normal, though she looked faintly haggard. "Of course. Will your mother's funeral services be held here or in L.A.?"

"I don't know," Belle replied in a heavy voice. "Reverend Kindred insists we have a memorial for Mom at his church down there, but . . . well, she wasn't all that religious and I hate funerals. I mean, who likes them, really? They're always so sad."

"They're supposed to bring closure," Judith said.

Belle's eyes sparked. "Isn't being dead enough closure for anybody?"

"It's not for the person who died, but for the loved ones they leave behind." Judith felt faintly hypocritical. Her mind flashed back to Dan McMonigle's service. He'd died at forty-nine, all four hundred and five pounds of him, virtually bedridden for the last few months. Judith had felt only relief—not just for Dan to be out of his misery, but for her husband of nineteen years to be out of her life. She forced a slight smile. "You know your mother is . . . on her cloud."

Belle made a face. "I guess. I wrote a poem about it." Her expression changed to quizzical. "Where are you going?"

"Home," Renie replied, staring straight ahead.

"Can I have a lift to that shopping area south of the golf course?" Belle asked. "It's kind of a long walk from here."

"Sure," Judith said before Renie could say no. "Hop in the backseat. Where do you want to be dropped off?"

Belle didn't respond until she was inside the car. "Actually, the place I want to go is about a half block off the main drag on the left. You don't have to turn off. I can walk that far."

Judith didn't make a further offer, lest her cousin pitch a fit. "Do you mind walking back?" she asked as Renie hit the gas and once again broke the speed limit to get out of Sunset Cliffs.

"No," Belle answered. "It's what? Less than a mile. I guess I should have taken one of the rental cars, but I felt like walking."

Renie pulled over by the cross street. "Watch out for traffic. Some people drive too fast around here." She ignored Judith's glare.

"Thanks," Belle said, opening the rear door. "I'll be fine."

"Will she?" Renie asked as Belle headed for the crosswalk.

Judith sighed. "I can't worry about everybody."

"Yet you do," Renie said with a smile as they drove on. "I wonder where she's going. There aren't any businesses on that street."

"No commercial enterprises," Judith agreed. "But you recall the two-story building that looks like a business, but has no sign?"

"Vaguely," Renie responded. "Why?"

"It's a rehab center," Judith responded. "I wonder if she's checking it out for her father."

Right after Renie drove off from Hillside Manor, Tyler Dooley pedaled his way up to the B&B. Farley was running behind him. "Hey, Mrs. Flynn," he shouted before she could reach the front steps, "what happened with your guests? Their rentals were gone this morning when I left for school. Did they check out? My cousin Petey got up before I did and he told me he'd seen some of them outside. Two of the men were carrying another guy over to the Nissan."

"What time was that?" Judith asked.

"I'm not sure," Tyler replied. "Petey just turned five and he can't tell time yet. But it was light enough that he could see outside when he got up to go to the bathroom. I checked the computer and the sun rises this time of year around four thirty."

"It would've been earlier than when Joe and I wake up at six," Judith said. "We never heard them leave. The Schmuck party must've sneaked out while most people in the neighborhood were still sleeping."

"Except Petey," Tyler pointed out.

Judith smiled. "Yes. Good for Petey. When he gets a little older, maybe you can recruit him as a junior sleuth."

"He's a curious little guy," Tyler said. "Do you mean the Schmucks skipped on your bill?"

Judith shook her head. "I've already charged them on Mr. Schmuck's credit card for the nights they stayed here. I'm good on that."

Tyler looked disappointed. "So they won't be back?"

"I don't think so," Judith replied. "They all went to the house in Sunset Cliffs that Mr. and Mrs. Schmuck bought earlier this year. I'm afraid this sleuthing episode is over. I'm sorry, Tyler."

"That's okay," he said, after a pause. "Maybe next time."

"I'd just as soon there wouldn't be a next time," Judith confessed.

Tyler shrugged. "But there usually is, right?"

Judith grimaced. "If there ever is, let's hope the body isn't found on my property."

"Right." Tyler grinned. "Did you say Sunset Cliffs?"

"Yes. Why do you ask?"

"My dad's boss at the construction company lives there," he replied. "Mr. Quincy. Well, he's not the boss on the jobs, but he owns QQQ Construction. In fact he calls his house Quincy's Quaint Quarters. I guess it's kind of like one of those big mansions in England. My parents have gone to a couple of big parties there."

"Interesting," Judith murmured.

Tyler's face brightened. "You think Mr. Quincy knows something about the Schmucks?"

"He probably hasn't even met them," Judith said. "The homes out there are spaced quite far apart."

But she mentally filed away Quincy's name. Just in case she was still on the case.

The first thing Judith did when she got inside Hillside Manor was check her phone calls. Ingrid Heffelman of the B&B association had left a brusque message: "I have two reservations for you tonight. Irwins, retired couple from Topeka; two widows from Boston, Schuster and Brewster. No, I am not kidding. What happened to your full house? Did your crazy housekeeper scare them away?"

Judith was grateful that Ingrid obviously didn't know one of the recent guests had died while staying at the B&B. After pouring herself a glass of ice water, she sat down at the counter to see if she had received any reservations via e-mail. There were none, but there was a message from Key Largo Bank. Judith read through it with a sinking sensation.

We regret to inform you that the credit card in the name of Mrs. Rodney Schmuck was canceled as of midnight Sunday, May 21. The charge of payment to Hillside Manor cannot be honored.

Judith grabbed the phone and dialed Renie's number. The phone rang four times before her cousin answered in a gasping voice.

"What's wrong?" Judith asked.

"I had to stop off at Falstaff's to pick up some sockeye salmon for dinner tonight," Renie replied, still out of breath. "I just came in the door. Bill must have gone on his walk. Why are you calling me? I just saw you ten minutes ago."

"Fifteen," Judith said. "But skip that. The Schmucks stiffed me on the B&B charges. I got an e-mail from the bank. The credit card was in Millie's name, not Rodney's, and they must have canceled it right after she died. I never saw the actual card. I only had the number and the other information I always need."

"That's weird," Renie responded. "Why would anyone rush on a weekend to cancel a deceased's credit card? Especially if the spouse had it in his possession. Or did he?"

"I told you, I never saw the damned thing. I took it over the phone when Rodney called to confirm the reservation. That was a couple of weeks before—wait. It wasn't over the phone. It was via e-mail."

"But don't you usually ask for an imprint of the card when the guests show up?"

"Yes," Judith replied, "but between Rodney insisting I was his mother and all the craziness that followed, I never got around to doing that. Then the next morning Millie was dead. I guess I got distracted."

"You always were kind of ADD," Renie remarked drily. "Too bad I wasn't there that morning to bail you out. But as you well know, I don't do mornings."

"Right," Judith agreed glumly. "If you'd stumbled over Millie's body in the backyard before eleven o'clock, you'd probably have kept going and crashed into the birdbath."

"So? Aunt Gert would've come out to rescue me," Renie shot back. "She has a good heart under that crusty facade."

"If you can cut through the crust to get to it," Judith grumbled. "What really bothers me is that the Schmucks seem to be loaded with money and yet they cheated me. Wouldn't that make you mad?"

"I never work for people, only big corporations," Renie replied, sounding serious. "If any of them tried to gyp me I'd call Bill's brother, Bub, and sic his firm's underlings on them. I am not without resources when it come to business."

"Maybe *I* should call Bub," Judith huffed. "I do know him fairly well after all these years."

"Go ahead," Renie said. "Don't forget he was the first one to get the zoning laws changed on the hill so his high-flying builder client could put up those big condos above your property."

"I had forgotten that," Judith muttered. "Oh, well, it was bound to happen with the city growing so fast. Speaking of high-fliers, how well do you know Trevor Boyd from the bank?"

"I told you, I've met him a couple of times," Renie said. "He may not remember me. I was just another peon doing a job for him."

"You're not the forgettable type," Judith declared. "There are times when I'd like to forget you, but I can't. Besides, I assume you were on your best behavior when you were with him."

"I was—except for the deep-fried prawns incident. I dropped one in his bespoke pants cuff. Luckily, he didn't notice it at the time. He was too engrossed with my cleavage."

"That's kind of what I meant," Judith said.

"But he probably wouldn't recognize my face," Renie pointed out.

"Then ditch the crummy sweatshirt and wear something with a V-neck," Judith urged.

"Hey!" Renie yipped. "You've got some loony idea about getting inside the Schmuck house! Why don't we just pitch a damned tent in the woods around there and pretend we're Indian scouts? That wouldn't be any goofier than me playing the role of a bodacious boob. Or should I say, 'showing off my—' "

"Okay, okay," Judith interrupted. "Maybe it wasn't one of my smarter plans. I keep forgetting we're kind of old."

"So's Trevor Boyd," Renie retorted, "but that doesn't mean I'd do it. You'd be better off having Bub get your money back and forgetting about the Schmucks."

Judith sighed. "You know I can't do that."

"Yes, I do." Renie's sigh was audible over the phone line. "We need a more inventive plan. Hey, who do we know who could play gardener?"

Judith considered the idea. "How about Tyler Dooley?"

"You want to put your neighbor kid in harm's way?"

"Well . . . no, I suppose that's wrong." Judith paused. "Arlene and Carl? You know how fussy they are about their yard. They could actually do some work while they're spying."

"Would they go for it?" Renie sounded dubious.

"They might," Judith said. "You know Arlene has rampant curiosity. Besides, they're both game for a little adventure. I think I'll go over there now before the two sets of new guests arrive."

Renie wished Judith good luck and hung up.

Arlene was in her kitchen, cleaning out cupboards. "Where," she demanded, clutching a trio of nesting bowls against her bosom, "do all these old dishes come from? Most of them are ugly. Why do I need them taking up space?"

"We all collect too much stuff over the years," Judith said. "Give them to St. Vincent de Paul's."

Arlene was horrified. "I can't!" she exclaimed. "I'm sentimental about these precious items. They hold so many memories."

Judith thought she recognized one of the bowls as a missile Arlene had hurled at her better half during one of their heated arguments. "Would you and Carl like a mysterious job?"

Arlene's blue eyes brightened. "Do we get to wear disguises?"

"Sort of," Judith replied. "You'd be gardeners at Sunset Cliffs."

"We don't need disguises for that," Arlene declared. "We always wear our regular clothes when we're working in the garden. Why Sunset Cliffs? That's a very exclusive area. They must have their own gardeners."

Judith explained about the Schmucks and their entourage leaving the B&B. "I've no idea whether the rest of that crew intends to stay, but since they reneged on their B&B payment to me, I'd like to find out what they're up to."

Arlene smiled. "You'd also like to find out if Mrs. Schmuck was murdered. And if so, who did it. I know you too well, Judith. How do Carl and I get into Sunset Cliffs? It's a gated community."

"I'll think of something," Judith said. "In fact," she went on as inspiration struck, "I have Rodney's cellphone number. You can call and tell whoever answers that before her untimely demise, Mrs. Schmuck asked you to do some gardening for them."

"That's a lie," Arlene stated. "I never tell lies."

Judith knew that her neighbor's integrity was beyond reproach. "I can call for you," she said.

"I couldn't let you lie for me," Arlene declared. "That's wrong."

"We're seeking a higher truth here," Judith said solemnly. "And justice. Think of it not as a lie, but as merely taking a fabrication to a new level." It was, after all, the attitude she adopted for her own so-called fibs.

Arlene, who had put aside the bowls, fingered her chin. "Yes, I can understand that. When you put it like that . . . Do you have the number with you?"

Judith nodded, removing the Post-it note from her slacks pocket. "Here. It's an L.A. area code, so I'll reimburse you for the call."

"Nonsense!" Arlene cried. "It's in the line of duty. But I'll have to talk to Carl first. He's painting the furnace. Teal. Very nice."

"You keep up your house so beautifully," Judith said, rather wistfully. "It's like a showplace."

"Oh, Judith! It's such an old house, built at the same time yours was over a hundred years ago. Raising five children in it has caused a great deal of wear and tear. And I don't mean just on Carl and me, but to the house. Still, it's home." She smiled.

Judith smiled back—this time not so wistfully.

Joe arrived home just after Phyliss had left for the day. "I got stuck at City Hall," he said, looking faintly out of sorts. "It turned out to be a record search for one of the doofuses I'd kept under surveillance a couple of months ago. But I finished around four, so I stopped in at the precinct station to see Woody. He got the final autopsy report this afternoon."

"And?" Judith asked, wide-eyed.

"The poison—aconitum—isn't hard to come by," Joe replied. "Are you sure we don't have some of the plants growing in our yard?"

"I know just about every flower, shrub, and plant we've got," Judith said. "Many plants are poisonous. But I don't think we have aconitum or monkshood.

On the other hand, I might not recognize either plant unless I saw them in bloom. What else did Woody have to say?"

Joe was opening the cupboard. "Let me make us some drinks first. Have you got any guests coming in tonight?"

"Yes," Judith replied, and told him about the two reservations.

"They don't sound like perps," he said, setting a couple of glasses on the counter. "Any news from the Schmucks?"

Judith avoided her husband's gaze. She'd wait to tell him about the visit to Sunset Cliffs. "The Schmucks won't be back. There's no way Woody can keep the Californians from returning to L.A., is there?"

Joe shook his head. "He's already talked to them and he has no evidence. Woody turned the investigation over to a couple of 'tecs."

"Anyone I know?" Judith asked, taking the glass of Scotch Joe had poured for her.

"No, a couple of newbies," he replied sitting down at the kitchen table. "I don't know them either. I suppose they'll come by to talk to us."

"I'd think they would've done that already," Judith said, joining Joe at the table.

"They were only given the assignment today. They have to do their homework first. Besides, there's not much we can tell them that isn't in Woody's case notes."

The doorbell rang. "That must be the first of the guests," Judith said, getting up.

Annabelle Brewster and Suzanne Schuster were white-haired, dowdy of dress, and thin as matchsticks. Judith wondered if they were sisters, but didn't ask. She had them sign the registry.

"Are you interested in seeing any of the city sights?" she inquired of the newcomers.

"Only the bars," one of them replied somberly.

"We have quite a few of those," Judith said, not sure which woman was Brewster and which was Schuster. "Would you like a map of the city?"

"No, thank you," the same widow responded. "We prefer to be surprised. That's part of the adventure while visiting other cities. We dislike having preconceived notions."

"That's very . . . wise of you," Judith said, for lack of a better comment. "I'll show you to your lodgings." She led the way up the stairs and stopped at the door to Room Five. "Feel free to open the window. Our nights are mild this time of year. As you may recall from the information I sent you, there's a social hour at six. I serve wine and appetizers."

"We don't drink alcoholic beverages," the other woman asserted, perhaps proving that her vocal cords worked. "However, fruit juice would be refreshing."

"I'll put some out in the dining room just off the hall." Judith gave them her friendliest smile and went back downstairs.

"The widows don't drink," she reported to Joe, who had migrated to the living room in her absence. "But they want to visit the local bars. Is that weird or what?"

"It's an 'or what,'" Joe said. "Maybe they like to watch. Or they're trolling for men. Speaking of drinks, I put yours on the coffee table."

"Thanks." Judith sat down on the opposite sofa. "Did Woody have anything else to say about the case?"

"He got the rest of the lab results back," Joe replied. "As we figured, the glass that contained the juice also had the poison in it." His green eyes glinted. "Both Millie and Rodney's DNA was on it."

Judith stared at Joe. "Did they both drink the juice?"

"The DNA was on the rim," he replied. "Of course it'd depend on when the aconitum was put in the glass."

"Oh, dear!" Judith exclaimed. "Then it would have to be Rodney or Millie, right?"

"So it would seem," Joe said. "But maybe one of them only took a sip and the other drank the rest. And some people have higher tolerances than others. Were all the rest of the guests at the table? I don't remember. I was too busy cooking."

"Let me think." Judith's high forehead furrowed in the effort of recalling the morning's events. "Yes, I think the five other couples were all in the dining room. Of course, any one of them could've briefly left the dining room and gone upstairs. We really can't see who's at the table from the kitchen."

Joe allowed that was true. Fortified by the Scotch, Judith revealed the visit to Sunset Cliffs.

"You took that long trek to find out they were playing bingo?" He merely shook his head and asked what was for dinner.

Earl and Minnie Irwin of Topeka didn't arrive until almost six. They'd rented a car at the airport, gotten stuck in rush-hour traffic, tried to take a shortcut they found on a map, and discovered the street was under construction. Before they could figure out exactly where they were, they'd ended up across the ship canal staring at the giant stone sculpture of a gnome holding a real VW under the bridge.

"Nothing like that in Topeka," Earl murmured before Judith led them to Room Three. "Kind of strange."

Judith hadn't argued.

Both sets of guests had gone out to dinner. As the Flynns were relaxing in the living room, the phone rang. Judith got up to grab the receiver off the cherrywood table.

"Mrs. Flynn?" a hushed female voice asked.

"Yes, who's calling?"

"Belle. Belle Schmuck. I'm scared."

"What's scaring you, Belle?" Judith raised her voice to alert Joe.

"I'm not sure," Belle replied, still keeping her own voice down. "We never got Clark's wallet back. The drugstore wasn't open when we drove by this morning. It was too early."

"Can't you take one of the cars tomorrow and collect the wallet?"

"I don't know," Belle said. "I don't think they'll let us."

"Who won't let you?"

"Um . . . mainly Sophie. She's sort of in charge here. She was mad because I went out this afternoon. Do you think I'm in danger?"

Judith considered the question carefully. "Since the police aren't sure if foul play was involved in your mother's death, they may think all of you are in danger. Has anyone in your party talked to Captain Price or his detectives since you left the B&B?"

"Ah . . . I don't think so," Belle replied. "I haven't seen any police cars around here."

"The detectives may not drive cruisers," Judith said, thinking that the Sunset Cliffs residents might ban anything as crass as a cop car inside their enclave. She looked at Joe, but he merely shrugged. "Look, Belle," Judith continued, "don't worry about something that will probably never happen. Oh—I almost forgot. Mrs. Grover found your mom's purse by her apartment. I should've brought it with me today. Maybe I could deliver it to you tomorrow."

"No!" Belle's tone was sharp. "I mean, it's too much trouble. I doubt she had much money in it. Seeing her purse would only make me sad. I have to go now. Clark's mom wants to talk to me. Hi, Cynth—" The line went dead.

Judith hoped Belle wouldn't end up the same way.

Chapter 19

B acon sizzled in the skillet, ham slices heated under
the broiler, and the waffle-iron light registered
green. Joe paused with his hand on the mixer controls.
"The Rankerses are going to do *what*? Are you insane?
Are they insane?"

"They like adventures," Judith replied, holding tight
to the carton of eggs she'd taken out of the refrigerator. "The Schmuck bunch won't recognize them. What
could possibly go wrong?"

Joe clapped a hand to his forehead. "Can I count the
ways? Belle calls and says she's scared spitless, meanwhile, you con our favorite neighbors into playing spies,
and knowing Carl, he won't be armed. Hell, he doesn't
even own a gun."

Judith set the eggs on the counter before moving across the kitchen to put her hands on Joe's shoulders. "Arlene and Carl are savvy. They won't put themselves in harm's way. Besides, are you convinced that Millie was murdered by Rodney or one of their so-called friends?"

"As a former cop," Joe replied, "I'm damned suspicious. Millie didn't strike me as a suicidal type. She was pretty full of herself as far as I could tell. Didn't she have big plans for some kind of spa?"

Judith let her hands fall away. "Yes, she did. But that could be a motive for murder. I mean, what if one of the others in their party wanted in on the project and she turned that person down? What if the Schmucks moved up here to get away from those hangers-on? There was something wrong about all this from the start."

Joe's expression was wry. "You realize you're arguing against yourself about whether or not the Rankerses could be at risk?"

"Well . . . I see what you mean," Judith admitted, "but I still think there's no harm if they pose as gardeners. Why would anyone think they were suspicious?"

"Because that's the nature of the beast," Joe replied, checking the bacon. "Your ex-guests struck me as not only difficult people, but paranoid. Maybe Belle isn't wrong to think someone's out to get her."

Judith started to respond, but hearing voices in the dining room, she went out to greet her visitors.

"How was your evening out?" she asked Brewster and Schuster.

"Fascinating," replied the widow who seemed the more loquacious. "So many bars, so little time. We had no idea."

"Did you go downtown?" Judith inquired, not knowing what else to say.

"We stayed in this neighborhood," Widow Number One said. "We found a half dozen within a few blocks right on top of this hill. We don't drive, you see."

"That's . . . just as well," Judith murmured, still bewildered by the women's interest in bars, but not wanting to seem nosy. "Will you see some of our other sights today?"

"Perhaps," the same widow replied. "We don't go to taverns, which are sometimes seedy, only to establishments that serve hard liquor. We discovered that the restaurants here open their bars early, so we might get started on our rounds after breakfast. Oh! I see you have a pitcher of that lovely cranapple juice we had last night. Quite bracing. Suzanne and I had never tasted it before."

Judith hid her relief at finally learning which widow was which. The Irwins entered the dining room, looking faintly disgruntled.

"Good morning," Judith said, even if Earl and Minnie didn't look as if they agreed. "Did you have a restful night?"

"Restful, yes," Minnie replied, her eyes zipping to the buffet, where Joe was setting out waffles and ham. "But we didn't realize we were on such a steep hill. It's very disorienting. Are you sure it's safe?"

"The hill's been here for quite a while," Judith said. "In fact, this is the house in which I was brought up."

Earl scowled. "Well, 'up's' the word for it. We're way up here. What about those earthquakes you people have?"

"They don't happen very often," Judith assured them. "The last one was five years ago."

Joe smiled pleasantly at the Kansans. "If you're here when everything starts to shake, the best place is under this dining room table. It's solid oak, so watch out for your heads." He returned to the kitchen.

Minnie put a hand to her large bosom. "My! That doesn't sound very comforting!"

"Believe me," Judith asserted, "that table has withstood many an earthquake. It's seventy-five years old."

"So am I," Minnie retorted. "I never thought I'd see the day that I'd have to crawl under a table to keep from getting killed in an earthquake."

Judith smiled kindly. "The chances of having one while you're here are unlikely. Really." She kept smiling as she joined Joe in the kitchen.

After finishing his cooking chores, Joe informed Judith that he was going to see Carl and Arlene to tell them not to go to Sunset Cliffs. Judith started to argue, but saw from his stern expression that she couldn't change his mind. Three minutes later he was back in the house.

"They've already left," he said grimly. "I forgot what early risers they are. Damn. How come they've never had a cell phone?"

"I suppose because they don't want one," Judith replied. "Stop worrying about them. You're making me crazy."

Joe refrained from commenting.

"Only two rooms full?" Phyliss looked elated. "Hallelujah! The Lord has been good to me again. Less hard labor today. My trick knee is acting up again. It goes out for no reason, as if Satan grabbed my leg and was trying to drag me down into the Netherworld."

"That's a shame," Judith said vaguely. "Since you only have two rooms to make up, why don't you go through the drawers and closets to make sure they're free of cobwebs and dust? I've noticed a few spiders coming into the house now that it's May."

Phyliss grimaced. "Spiders! They're Beelzebub's tool! They terrify me."

"Then grab a can of bug killer out of the cupboard upstairs and spray the closets first," Judith said. "You'll be giving Beelzebub's familiars an afterlife in Hades."

"I *will* do that, the Good Lord willing," Phyliss declared. And off she plodded, singing "Onward, Christian Soldiers" in her shrill, off-key voice.

The Irwins had offered the widows a ride. Schuster and Brewster had accepted, feeling they'd be remiss if they didn't visit the downtown area. That was fine with Earl and Minnie. They'd go from there to the adjacent Civic Center to see the sights.

Judith checked her Wednesday reservations. She had three, so if the unscheduled widows and Kansans wanted to stay another night, that was fine with her.

A few minutes after eleven thirty, Phyliss came downstairs into the kitchen, sneezing and coughing her head off. "Dust!" she exclaimed. "Satan's relentless. He's trying to weaken my resistance in his battle for my immortal soul. Oh—when I was making up the bed in Room Two," she continued, digging in her apron pocket, "I found these Post-it notes. Lots of scribbles I can't make out."

"Thanks," Judith said, taking the notes from Phyliss, who was blowing her nose with what sounded like the Seventh Angel's trumpet in Exodus.

As soon as the cleaning woman left, Judith picked up the phone and called Renie to tell her about the Rankerses' ruse as gardeners.

"So," her cousin said, "Arlene and Carl are on the case. I was wondering why you hadn't already called to ask me to join you in another fruitless visit to Sunset Cliffs."

Judith kept her voice down, lest Phyliss suddenly reappear. "My pious cleaning woman found some notes in Belle and Clark's room. I haven't looked at the contents. Want to check them out with me?"

"Why don't you take a picture of them with your cell?" Renie responded. "I've got work to do."

"You never start until afternoon."

"Ohhhh . . . why not? I have to buy more Copper River sockeye at Falstaff's before it goes out of season. I almost swooned when we had it last week. Bill thought he'd have to get the smelling salts. Or wait until I came to so I could bring him his dessert. You want me to pick up some sockeye for you?"

Judith hesitated. "It's quite expensive, isn't it? I saw the ad, but they didn't list a price. That scares me."

"And facing off with killers doesn't. I'll get enough for you, Joe, and Aunt Gert. My treat, though I don't know why I'm so damned goodhearted. It's early yet. Maybe I should look in the mirror and make sure I'm me." Renie hung up.

Though tempted to read the notes, Judith exerted supreme self-control. Luckily, Renie staggered in the back door ten minutes later. "I'm worn out," she announced, flopping onto a chair in the kitchen, where the Flynns were eating lunch. "I practically had to arm-wrestle some snooty old bat to get the last of the sockeye. She was asking the fish man all sorts of inane questions about how the fish are caught, how they're shipped, how they spawn, how they got along with their in-laws. I finally stepped on her foot and asked for the last pieces they had. Ha ha. I won. But I twisted my knee when I stepped on her."

"Serves you right," Judith declared. "But I'm glad you persevered."

"So am I," Renie said. "If she didn't know anything about fish, she's not from around here. I bought halibut cheeks, too, along with gulf prawns and a couple of rainbow trout. By the time I was done, she looked like she was having an aneurysm."

Joe made a face. "I should arrest you for assault. How come nobody's ever tried to kill you?"

"It's my charm," Renie asserted. "I'm irresistible. And, as you may recall, there were times when outraged murderers tried to kill me—and your sleuthing wife."

Joe passed a hand over his forehead. "Don't remind me."

Judith decided to change the subject. "Would you like a sandwich?"

"No, thanks," Renie replied. "I had my usual late— and big—breakfast. I don't suppose you've baked any cookies yet?"

Judith shook her head. "I really haven't had time. If you're going to stay for a while, maybe I'll do it while you're here."

"I can help," Renie said. "I'll be your taster. I love raw cookie dough. Where are the notes?"

"I think," Joe said, getting up, "that's my cue to leave. I've got to see a man about an MG." He exited the kitchen and the house.

"How much do I owe you for the fish?" Judith asked Renie.

"Zip. I told you I was treating. It's in my purse. I'll put it in your fridge. I assume you don't want to freeze it? Since it's fresh and I paid for it, I advise you to have it tonight."

"I thought by a treat you meant . . . Never mind. Are you sure?"

Renie feigned indignation as she removed the sockeye in its brown wrapping paper and opened the fridge. "Am I ever not sure about what I say? Even when it's really weird?"

Judith smiled. "No, you're not. I mean, yes, you are." She frowned. "Now I'm not sure what *I'm* saying. Let's have a look at those notes."

Placing the Post-its on the table, she saw Renie's brown eyes grow curious. "I bet Clark made those. My artist's eye tells me that's not feminine writing."

"You can probably figure these out for yourself once you get used to the chicken scratches," Judith said.

Renie was looking in her big purse. "Damn! I forgot to bring my glasses. You'll have to read them to me."

Judith scowled at her cousin. "You rarely remember your glasses."

"I don't need them except for really small print— and chicken scratches," Renie replied in a reasonable voice.

"Okay, fine. The first one says 'beer.' Got that?"

Renie looked vague. "I don't have any beer."

Judith ignored the comment. "Next is 'bank' or 'bunk.' This one says . . ." She frowned. "I *think* it's 'dud.' That sounds right for this bunch. Here's 'get renal' . . . no, 'get rental.' The cars they rented, maybe. 'Learn prayers.'" She looked at Renie. "Do you suppose that's to help Kindred with his ministry?"

"Probably," Renie said, appearing bored.

"'Read Bibble.'" Judith paused. "He must mean *Bible*, right?"

Renie nodded vaguely.

"There are three or four I can't make out at all," Judith said. "The last one is 'talk 2 crumb pol claws.' What does that mean?"

"Huh?" Renie was staring off into space.

"You heard me. See for yourself." She shoved the Post-it across the table. "Well?"

Renie peered at the notation. "I honestly can't tell. Unless he means Crump, not crumb. Would 'pol' refer to the police? They don't have claws, though. Just handcuffs."

Judith took back the note and studied it again. "Yes, it must be Charlie Crump. But what's 'pol claws'?"

"I have no idea," Renie admitted. "Police is a good guess. Or politics of pollution or . . . any word that starts with those letters. Give it up, coz."

"What's not among these notes is any reference to the wedding," Judith said, still staring at the Post-its as if she were willing them to reveal more information.

"Wouldn't you think a groom-to-be might have some reminders of what he had to do before the ceremony?"

Renie's expression was wry. "The groom being the spaced-out Clark, yes—as in remember to show up. But the bride's also a flake. What are you implying?"

"I'm not sure," Judith said. "There's something about all of this being very . . . theatrical. Maybe my imagination has gotten the better of me, starting with having the wedding here in the first place."

Renie looked thoughtful. "We know now that Belle's parents had already moved up here to a gated community that has its own chapel. It'd be reasonable to think the Schmucks would hold the wedding there."

Judith smiled. "You're using my kind of logic, but these people are illogical in . . ." She stopped and stared at Renie. "Who has the marriage license and where did they get it? They arrived here Friday night. Belle told me they didn't get in until after five. Most government offices close at five and stay that way over the weekend. Belle and Clark came from L.A. along with the others. They couldn't use a California wedding license in this state, could they?"

"No," Renie replied. "Mom, being a legal secretary by trade, once told me you have to have a valid license from this state or it's not legal."

Judith sighed. "Another reason why so much of what's gone on doesn't seem real. By the way, I forgot to tell you that Belle called last night to say she was scared. She couldn't explain why, but she didn't sound as if she were exaggerating."

"Not an unreasonable feeling," Renie pointed out. "Her mother may have been murdered."

The phone rang. Judith reached behind her to pick up the receiver from the counter. After she said hello, there was dead air. "Yes? Who's calling?" she inquired.

"Adam and Eve," a familiar, if hushed, voice finally answered. "We're in the Garden of Eden."

"Arlene?" Judith said.

"I can't say. I borrowed Abel's cell and it may be tapped."

Abel, Judith figured, must be one of the Rankerses' two sons. "Have you something to report?"

"Yes. The clergyman and his wife just left in one of the rental cars. I recognized him because as you may recall he'd come to our house."

"I'd forgotten that. But where they're going probably isn't sinister," Judith said. "Anything else of interest going on?"

"They put a large trunk in the backseat of the car," Arlene responded, still keeping her voice down. "It wouldn't fit in the trunk. That is, the trunk they were carrying, not the car's—"

"I get it," Judith interrupted. "Did it seem heavy?"

"The minister and another man I didn't recognize carried the trunk," Arlene said. "A rather tall, distinguished-looking man. In fact, someone else has just come out of the house."

"The man with Kindred sounds like Stuart Wicks," Judith said. "Describe whoever you're seeing now." She waited for a response. But after almost a minute passed, she spoke up. "Arlene, can you see what the man looks like? Arlene? . . . Arlene? . . . *Arlene* . . . ?"

There was no answer.

Chapter 20

W hy," Renie demanded, "do I have to drive to Sunset Cliffs? Why can't we go in your Subaru? Why do I have to do all the driving?"

"Stop whining," Judith snapped. "I assume Joe took my car up to Ron's to check on the MG. But he may've walked. Go see for yourself if the Subaru is in the driveway or the garage."

After glaring at Judith, Renie tromped off down the hall. "Subaru's in place," she announced. "We'll take your car. I don't know if Bill needs ours this afternoon, but I won't leave him in the lurch if he does. You can follow me to our house. We might as well go now. I don't see you baking any cookies."

"I got distracted," Judith said.

"Right." Renie grinned. "Dead bodies trump piggy cousins."

Ten minutes later, Judith and Renie were on their way north in the Subaru. The sky was cloudy, the temperature mild. It had drizzled earlier in the day, which was good, Judith thought. The new geraniums on the front-porch steps needed watering.

"Should I call Arlene to tell her we're coming?" Renie asked as they turned off from the main route to the street less traveled.

"Darn," Judith muttered. "I forgot to note the cell phone's number. It belongs to one of their boys."

"We'll have to pretend we don't know the Rankerses," Renie said.

"Of course. I hope they haven't had a serious problem. The grounds seem fairly expansive. They may not be right by the house."

"Are you kidding? How can Arlene and Carl spy if they're not up close and personal?"

"Good point," Judith said, slowing for the turn into Sunset Cliffs. "Let's hope the same young guy is at the sentry post today."

But a grizzled older man stepped out to greet them. "Destination?" he inquired, peering at both cousins.

"Heaven's Gate," Judith replied. "We're here to see Mr. Schmuck and his daughter, Belle."

The guard nodded once. "I'll call to let them know. Please wait." He went inside his sentry shack.

Judith frowned. "Maybe I should've fibbed."

"What would you have said?" Renie asked.

"That I was here to consult with the Schmucks' gardeners?"

"Not bad," Renie murmured.

The guard came back to the Subaru. "Go ahead," he said—and opened the gate.

"Wow." Renie kept her voice down. "That's impressive. I was eagerly awaiting a convoluted lie from you."

"You mean a mere fib. Now let's see if I can remember how to get to the house without driving in circles. Am I going the right way so far?"

"I think so," Renie replied. "We can't really get lost."

A few drops of rain sprinkled the windshield. "This part looks familiar," Judith said after they turned a lazy curve. "Yes, it's just up ahead on the right."

As Judith approached Heaven's Gate, she saw the Rankerses' SUV parked off on a paved area next to the drive. "I don't see the rental cars," she said as they drove up the slight incline to the front entrance. "Maybe they're in the garage."

"I don't see Arlene and Carl," Renie said, looking in every direction. "There's not enough rain to keep them from working outside."

"Maybe they took a break," Judith suggested, coming to a stop. "Maybe it's silly to worry about them. Cell batteries run down."

The cousins got out of the car. Renie paused, looking off toward a rose garden. "It looks like their gardening gear is over there, but I don't see any sign of Arlene and Carl."

Judith grimaced as they walked up to the front door. "Let's hope they're okay." She grasped the brass ring that set off the chimes. For over a minute, there was no response. She gave the brass ring another try. "I don't like this," she murmured. "There's something creepy about this whole setup. That chiming reminds me of a death knell."

"Don't say things like that," Renie snapped. "I don't like your premonitions. They're often right. And the chime is Bizet's fate motif, which seems . . . bizarre."

Almost another minute passed before the door swung open. Judith and Renie both gaped as Arlene gaped back. "What are you doing here?" she asked, her blue eyes wide.

"What are you doing opening the door?" Judith asked.

Arlene shrugged. "They all left a while ago. They had to call a cab to get everybody in. I guess there wasn't room for all of them in the car the minister and his wife drove away. The trunk, you know. Only four of them could fit in the Honda. Those Crumps are very stout."

Relief swept over Judith. "Is Carl in here, too?"

"Of course," Arlene replied, leading the way down the hall. "He found some beer in the refrigerator. We decided to have a look around. This is quite a nice house, in its way, but I wouldn't want to live here. It doesn't feel like a home."

"That's not surprising," Judith said—and immediately was repentant. "I shouldn't say that. Rodney and Millie seemed . . ." She couldn't come up with the right word and looked at Renie for help.

"How about noncombative?" her cousin suggested.

"That works," Judith mumbled before greeting Carl, who was drinking from a can of beer and holding a salami-on-rye sandwich.

"We spies need nourishment to stay alert," he declared. "How come you showed up here?"

Judith glanced at Arlene. "You disconnected while we were still talking. I was worried about you two."

"Oh!" Arlene cried. "I dropped the cell while I was trying to get a better view of what was going on. What do you suppose was in that trunk? A body?"

"Hardly," Judith replied. "Did you do a head count of the people who left the house?"

"I did," Arlene asserted. "It was all eleven of them. That's why they needed the cab. That trunk took up the backseat of one of the cars. It was quite large. Yes, a body would fit. Unless it was someone very tall. You know—like one of those eight-foot basketball players. That's *too* tall, don't you think? Unless you don't like to spend money on ladders."

Carl was looking bemused, as he often did when listening to his wife. "I don't think any basketball player is eight feet tall," he said.

Arlene turned to stare at him. "How would you know? Have you ever measured a basketball player?"

"No. Unless you count our kids." He frowned. "Where *is* our ladder? I was looking for it the other day when I wanted to check the gutters."

Arlene turned thoughtful. "Mrs. O'Hurley borrowed it."

Carl looked surprised. "Mrs. O'Hurley? Isn't she over ninety?"

"So?" Arlene huffed. "She wanted to look in the neighbors' window."

"What neighbors?" Carl asked. "She lives behind a bunch of cedar trees across the street. Who could she possibly see?"

Arlene's face turned faintly pink. "Umm . . ." She darted Judith an embarrassed glance. "It was a man trying to climb out the window at the B&B early Tuesday morning. She'd seen him try to do that once before, but she didn't want to go up on her roof again. It was still a bit dark."

"Rodney!" Judith said under her breath. "I wonder how they cajoled him into leaving. Belle, maybe. The gang might've needed Rodney to get inside this house. I assume any of the guards would recognize him as the owner. Did you notice if Rodney was in one of the vehicles?"

Arlene grimaced. "Honestly, I can't be sure. Those cars may've had tinted windows. Except for the taxi. But I've never seen Rodney up close. Still, I could count heads. Does the total of eleven include all of them?"

Judith nodded. "What cab company was it?"

"Not Yellow Cab, not Farwest, not . . ." Arlene paused. "I didn't recognize the colors or catch the name. Maybe one of those gypsy cabs?" She turned to Carl. "Do you know?"

"I didn't see the taxi leave," he replied. "I was trying to figure out if some of those roses had black spot."

Arlene threw up her hands. "You see? Carl takes yard work seriously, even when he's not getting paid. Except in our garden, of course."

"Yes, right," Judith murmured.

Renie, who seemed to have lost interest in the exchange, was looking in the fridge. "Hey, they've got pancetta. Maybe I'll have a snack."

"Coz," Judith said, "don't. We'd better get out of here before the others show up." She turned back to Arlene. "In fact, I wish I hadn't let you and Carl come here. Why don't you leave, too?"

"But we're not done!" Arlene exclaimed. "We haven't finished weeding the area by the reflecting pool."

"You aren't getting paid," Judith asserted. "They didn't hire you, I did. I mean . . . you know what I mean."

"A job's a job," Arlene stated. "Isn't that right, Carl?"

"You're always right," he replied, having finished his sandwich and coming to stand behind his wife. "Except when you're wrong. But you never are, my darling Arlene."

The cousins saw Carl roll his eyes and make a face. Judith checked her watch. "It's almost three. You must've gotten here quite early. It seems to me that you've put in a full day. Especially for free."

"We have another hour to go," Arlene said. "We didn't take a lunch break until now. We want to earn our money."

"What money?" Renie asked.

"From the people in the house," Arlene replied. "We're billing them. Why not? We earned it. They can give us cash or a check."

Judith knew when to give up when arguing with Arlene. "Good luck with that," she said. "But be careful!"

The cousins left Heaven's Gate and returned to the Subaru. The drizzle had stopped, though the clouds still hung over Sunset Cliffs. Neither Judith nor Renie spoke until they were outside the security gates and on the southbound street.

"You're either still worried about the Rankerses or you're mulling," Renie finally said. "Which is it?"

"Both," Judith replied as they paused at the first stoplight. "I'm also wondering what's in that trunk."

"I don't suppose it's Millie," Renie remarked.

Judith shuddered and her foot almost slipped off the brake. "Don't say things like that! It's too gruesome."

Renie shot her cousin a sly glance. "Don't tell me it didn't cross your devious mind."

"Well . . . I suppose it's a natural thought, given the circumstances," Judith allowed, "but I honestly don't think so. How about gold bullion?"

"That's unworthy of you. And boring."

"Okay. Maybe it's Millie's wardrobe. They may be donating it to a charity."

Renie leaned her head back against the seat. "Aaaargh! That's so goody-goody that I can't believe you said it."

"You've got a better idea?" Judith shot back.

"I don't have ideas," Renie asserted. "I have concepts and designs."

"Then conceive and design a viable explanation," Judith said. "Maybe they're shipping something from the house. Or getting rid of things they don't need anymore, especially now that Millie's dead."

Renie sighed. "I'm beginning to like that gold bullion a lot better."

"Look, coz," Judith said in a reasonable tone, "there's probably nothing sinister about that trunk. It isn't as if . . ." Her voice trailed away as they approached the bridge over the ship canal.

"What?" Renie demanded.

"They never left Sunset Cliffs," Judith said.

"Who didn't? What do you mean?"

"The Schmuck bunch," Judith replied. "If they had, the security guard would've known. He'd have told us nobody was home."

Renie looked incredulous. "Are you nuts? You think he counts heads of everyone who comes and goes through the gates?"

"Yes, I do," Judith declared. "That's part of his job. He's their security person, he wants to make sure everyone is safe and accounted for. Besides, what else has he got to do all day?"

"You might be right," Renie conceded, "but where did they go? And why did they need a taxi?"

"As you may recall from when we were here several years ago, Sunset Cliffs is a large area, all the way to the Sound on the west and the golf course to the north. If memory serves, there are well over a hundred homes and most of them aren't within sight of one another. Not to mention that the Schmucks haven't lived there all that long to familiarize themselves with their surroundings."

"Okay," Renie said. "I get that. But we still don't know why they were all heading out into the wealthy wilds of their gated community."

"I admit that," Judith responded as they began the climb up Heraldsgate Hill. "It irks me."

"You'll figure it out eventually," Renie asserted. "I'm serious, you know."

"I hope so," Judith said, pulling up in front of the Joneses' Dutch colonial. She smiled. "I appreciate your confidence in me."

Renie shrugged before opening the passenger door. "Why? You've done it before and you'll do it again."

Judith's expression turned grim. "I also hope I do it in time. I keep having an eerie feeling that someone else is in danger."

"You mean Belle?"

"I don't know who I mean. That's the problem. But the killer—assuming there *is* a killer—does know."

When Judith pulled into her driveway, she noticed that the MG wasn't in sight. Maybe the repair job hadn't been finished. She entered the house through the back door to find Phyliss in the kitchen, scrubbing the backsplashes by the sink.

"Did Joe come back with the MG?" she asked.

"He came and he went," Phyliss replied. "He wanted to—as he put it—air out the car. Whatever that means. If he put the top down, wouldn't it get plenty of air just sitting in the driveway?"

"He meant the engine," Judith said. "He'd better get back before rush hour starts or he won't be able to go more than ten miles an hour on the freeway. Anything else I should know?"

"Yes," Phyliss responded. "One of your guests showed up. He's in the living room."

"Mr. Irwin?" Judith asked in surprise.

Phyliss shook her head, the gray sausage curls bobbing. "No. One of those peculiar people who was here over the weekend."

"Oh, no!" Judith rushed off through the kitchen. When she reached the living room, she saw a bedraggled

Rodney Schmuck collapsed on one of the matching sofas.

"Hi, Mama," he said in a ragged voice. "I came home."

For once, Judith chose not to reprimand him for calling her Mama. She noticed there was a rip in his pants and his sport shirt was dirty. "How did you get here?"

"The bus," he replied. "Two buses. Or was it three? I forget. Can I have a drink, Mama? I'm beat."

Judith hesitated. "How about a mug of hot coffee?"

Rodney shook his head. "Coffee gives me a gut ache."

Judith relented. "Just a short one, okay?"

Rodney frowned, but nodded. "Mama knows best. I guess."

Phyliss was finishing up in the kitchen. She saw Judith reach for the bourbon bottle. "No!" she cried. "You're not going to drink Satan's brew, are you?"

"I am not," Judith declared. "But Mr. Schmuck is. Moderation in all things, Phyliss. Jesus drank wine."

"It was grape juice," Phyliss asserted. "They didn't have wine or any filthy alcoholic beverages. That's why they called it the Holy Land."

If Judith knew when to give up arguing with Arlene, she also surrendered trying to reason with her cleaning woman. Pouring a scant inch of bourbon into a small glass, adding ice and water, she returned to the living room.

Rodney looked as if he were about to nod off. "Oh, Mama, just what the doctor ordered. You're really swell."

"Don't gulp it," Judith ordered, sitting down on the other sofa. "Now tell me exactly how and why you ended up here at the B&B."

"I jumped out of the car," he said after taking a reasonably small sip of his drink. "Then I climbed over the fence and went off to get a bus that would take me here. I got tired of them bossing me around."

"They didn't try to chase you down?" Judith asked.

He took another sip of bourbon and shook his head. "They probably thought I was going back to the house."

"Who's being so bossy?"

"Sophie and Cynthia, mostly," Rodney answered. "But Stu's got a yap on him, too. Millie had some really weird pals."

"You don't mind leaving Belle alone with that crew?"

For just an instant, Rodney seemed alarmed. "Well, she's got the nerd to look after her. Though he's kind of a sad excuse for Superman."

"Why were they bossing you? I mean," Judith clarified, "what kind of demands were they making on you?"

"Every kind." Rodney paused to drain the glass and then shot an appealing look at Judith. "I don't suppose . . . ?" He let the query die away.

"Not right now," Judith said kindly. "As you were about to tell me? The demands, that is."

Rodney sighed, resting the empty glass on his stomach. "What to do for Millie's funeral, where to hold it, how to honor her memory, ways to make me go nuts."

Judith pounced on only one of the complaints about his companions: "What kind of memorial are they talking about?"

Rodney scratched his neck. "It was . . . some kind of fund. A . . . an endowment, Cynthia called it. To help people. She likes doing that. She's a sort of social worker."

"Yes, I heard she's a counselor," Judith said. "Who would actually get the money to establish whatever this project was for?"

"I'm not sure," Rodney replied. "They got to arguing about that part and I sort of nodded off. That's the dangedest thing. Ever since Millie died, I feel tired all the time. You might not believe this, Mama, but your boy is usually pretty lively. I guess it's stress. That's what Sophie told me. She gave me some pills for it."

"What kind of pills?"

"White ones."

"Do you know what they're called?"

"No. What difference does it make?"

"Do you have any with you?"

Rodney shook his head. "Sophie gives them to me, four times a day. I don't know if they cure stress. I'm not sure what stress means, Mama. But I miss my Millie."

"I know," Judith said. "You mustn't let Sophie give you those pills. You're a grown man and you can't let people push you around. How can you give motivational speeches when you're not motivating yourself?"

"Good point," Rodney murmured. "I haven't done any speaking gigs since we moved here. I should get out and hustle, huh?"

"That's right," Judith agreed. "You can't let those hangers-on tell you what to do with your money either."

Rodney grimaced. "It's not my money. It's Millie's money. She was rich. I didn't have much when I married her."

"But you're her husband," Judith pointed out. "Both Washington and California are community-property states. You get everything she had. Did she have a will?"

The grimace turned to gloom. "Yeah, she did." He gulped and lowered his eyes. "Everything goes to Belle. I'm sunk." Finally looking at Judith with piteous eyes, he seemed on the verge of tears. "Will you take care of me, Mama?"

For one fleeting moment, Judith almost wished she could, but sanity overcame her. "No, Rodney, you have to do that for yourself."

He shook his head. "Can't do that. I'd rather be dead."

Judith wondered if someone was planning to grant Rodney's wish.

Chapter 21

Rodney wanted to stay at Hillside Manor. Judith told him he could spend the next two nights, but the Memorial Day weekend was coming up and the B&B was booked. Rodney asked if the Flynns had a private guest room. They did, of course, though Judith wasn't going to admit it.

"I heard you tried to escape from here again Tuesday morning," Judith said, hoping not to sound as if she were reprimanding him.

Rodney seemed chagrined. "Yeah, I did. I didn't want to go back to Heaven's Gate without Millie. It doesn't seem right."

"I understand. You can stay in Room One," she went on. "I haven't put anyone else in there since you left."

"Thanks. It feels like home." He smiled faintly. "Your hubby's about my size. Do you think he could lend me some duds?"

"I'll ask him when he gets home," Judith said. "I do have a problem. Your credit card was canceled over the weekend. You and the others owe me for the three nights you stayed here."

Rodney's jaw dropped. "Oh, dang! How'd that happen?"

"I thought maybe you knew."

Rodney shook his head several times. "No idea. It was in Millie's name and . . . Would that be an automatic thing because she's . . . dead?"

"Not unless the credit-card company was notified," Judith replied. "I assume you didn't call them."

He shook his head again. "How am I going to pay for anything? I've only got about twenty dollars on me."

"Have you checked with your bank?"

"No." Rodney brightened slightly. "We opened an account at a Key Largo branch not far from Sunset Cliffs. I think I saw one of their other branches on top of the hill. Can you give me a lift up there?"

"I could, but . . ." Judith paused, hearing the back door close. "I think Joe's home. I have to make hors d'oeuvres for the guests. Maybe he can do it. You can ride in his classic MG."

"I'd like that," Rodney asserted. "I didn't know you had one of those snazzy old foreign cars."

"My husband bought it new just before I met him," Judith said as she leaned forward to listen for Joe to show up in the living room. "Maybe he went upstairs," she murmured. "I'll go see where he is."

Joe was in the kitchen staring at the refrigerator's contents. "Hi," he said. "Do I want a beer or a serious drink?"

"Don't ask me," Judith replied. "Can you take Rodney up to the bank? He escaped from Sunset Cliffs this afternoon via bus."

Joe closed the fridge. "Those rich people have their own bus? What's he doing back here? I thought we'd seen the last of those jackasses."

"It's a long story," Judith said. "Would you mind taking him up to Key Largo? He hasn't got much money, and as you may recall, his credit card was canceled."

"Hell." Joe scratched his head. "Okay. But I'd rather take him back to Sunset Cliffs."

"He's got some problems with the rest of those people. I'll explain later. Or maybe he'll tell you while you're on the way to the bank."

"No doubt he will," Joe said resignedly. "I suspect his so-called friends are taking him to the cleaners."

"You got that right," Judith replied.

Judith started making the appetizers—stuffed spinach and crab in mushroom caps, Brie on crisp English crackers, deviled eggs with Pacific shrimp. She'd just finished setting everything out on small platters when there was a knock at the front door. Glancing at the schoolhouse clock, she noted that it was almost four thirty. Maybe her new guests had arrived ahead of the usual check-in time.

When Judith opened the door, Belle Schmuck staggered across the threshold. "Help me!" she gasped. "I may've been followed!"

Judith grabbed Belle's arm to steady her. "What happened?"

Belle waved a hand and shook her head as she took some deep breaths. "Let me sit," she finally said.

Judith held on to the young woman's arm as she steered her into the living room and eased her onto one of the matching sofas.

"Thanks," Belle said with a ghostly smile. "I sneaked out of the house and asked the security guard to call a cab for me. May I have a glass of water?"

"Of course. I'll be right back." Judith hurried to the kitchen, poured out a glass of water, and added three ice cubes from the freezer. "Here," she said to Belle, handing her the glass. "What happened?"

Belle took a deep breath and a sip of water. "I was in the hall when I heard George and Elsie Kindred arguing in the den. He mentioned my name, saying I was just like my mother—really stubborn. Elsie didn't agree. Then she said, 'What do you plan to do with the daughter?'" Belle stopped, pressing her lips together. "Then he shouted, 'Never mind! She's in the way.' That's when I decided I had to get out of there."

Judith tried to hide her shock. "Was that right before all of you drove away with the trunk?"

Belle frowned. "What trunk?"

"Ah . . . someone told me that the Reverend and Mrs. Kindred drove off from Heaven's Gate with a large trunk in the backseat."

Belle shrugged. "Maybe they did. So what? Elsie Kindred and Agnes Crump have been doing some work around the house. I guess they like to keep busy. They're a really dull pair of women."

Judith changed the subject. "What did you all do when everybody drove around Sunset Cliffs?"

"Got acquainted with the neighborhood," Belle replied. "I'd never been there before. After Mom and Dad moved up here, I stayed in L.A. with Clark. I had a job at a coffeehouse in Beverly Hills where I got to meet some celebrities." She made a face. "Most of them aren't good tippers. Clark was working on his thesis.

In fact, he usually hung out at the coffeehouse all day while he came up with ideas."

"It must've been interesting," Judith remarked, hoping she sounded sincere. "Did you know your father also ran away?"

Belle's eyes widened. "No! What do you mean?"

"I take it you weren't in the same car with him on the drive?" She saw Belle frown and shake her head. "Your father jumped out, somehow managed to get to a bus stop, and came here. He's gone to the bank with Joe. They should be back soon." She glanced at the grandfather clock, which had just chimed the quarter hour. "In fact, they should be here by now. They've been gone quite a while."

"Poor Dad!" Belle exclaimed. "He's had a terrible time since Mom died. Those other people treat him like a child. Is he going to stay here?"

"I told him he could, at least for a night or two," Judith said. "But I have a full house over the long weekend. How long do you think the rest of your party will stay on at Heaven's Gate?"

Belle's head drooped. "I haven't got a clue. They seem to be settling in. I don't like any of them, especially Clark's mother. Cynthia's a witch. Sometimes I think marrying Clark is a bad idea. But it wasn't *my* idea in the first place. If two people love each other, what does a ceremony have to do with it? Besides, I don't really . . ." She seemed close to tears.

"Whose idea was it to have the wedding?" Judith asked.

Belle made an effort to compose herself and wrinkled her nose. "Cynthia and Stuart's. They want my money. I don't think Clark cares about my money. I'm not sure he knows I have any. Of my own, that is."

The comment puzzled Judith. "You have your own private fortune?"

"Mom set up a trust fund for me before I started college," Belle replied. "It wasn't megabucks to start with, but I dropped out of Pepperdine in my second year. I'd met Clark at a party—he went to undergraduate school at Pepperdine—and he was already living off campus. I moved in with him a few months later. Mom was wild."

"Because you were living with Clark?"

"No. Mom liked Clark—in her way. But she thought he was weak and could be manipulated by his mother. Mom didn't trust Cynthia—or Stuart. She told me they were greedy." Belle drank more water. "Cynth told Mom that as long as Clark and I were living together and sharing expenses, he should be added to the fund as co-owner. Mom told Cynth to buzz off. Meanwhile, the fund kept growing. I rarely took anything out after the first year. Mom was shrewd about money and financial stuff."

"I assume," Judith said, "Clark's mother and his stepfather put pressure on the two of you to get married? Or was it also a moral issue?"

Belle nodded. "They thought we were living in sin. And Stuart is kind of religious. That's how he got hooked up with the rev. He's a bad influence, but then I've never been into church stuff."

Judith heard the back door open. "Excuse me," she said, getting up. "I think Joe and your father are back."

She met a weary-looking Joe in the kitchen. "Where's Rodney?" she asked.

"Hauling his new clothes upstairs," Joe replied in disgust. "The Schmuck bank account had been closed. I had to take him shopping on the Avenue and buy something that didn't look as if a bum had been wearing it. I need a drink."

"You'll need a double," Judith informed him. "Belle's here, too. She ran away from Heaven's Gate."

"Crap!" Joe said under his breath. "Are we going to end up with the whole gang coming back here?"

"I doubt it," Judith said, putting a hand on his arm. "The two Schmucks seem to be the outsiders."

Joe's usual mellow disposition appeared to have deserted him. "You're not running a hotel. Schmuck and his kid live in a mansion, for God's sake! He can't be completely broke. His wife was stinking rich."

"All the money goes to Belle," Judith said, keeping her voice down. "I don't know if she's aware of that yet. Still, she can afford to pay us for their stay over the weekend and for now. Belle and Rodney are scared. They think the others want them out of the way—permanently."

Joe expelled a big breath. "Damn. You and your heart of gold. Maybe Woody should assign someone to watch that house in Sunset Cliffs. If those rich snobs let him. They might sue the city for violating their privacy. That place is a fiefdom." He paused. "What happened with the Rankerses and their gardening job?"

"Oh!" Judith exclaimed. "I forgot to check in with them. Could you go over to see them now? I'll have your drink waiting for you."

Looking beleaguered, Joe agreed. "Be right back. Start pouring the Scotch." He dashed down the hall and out the back door.

The phone rang before Judith could pick up the bottle.

"Hey," Renie said, "why don't you and Joe come over to dinner after you make nice with your guests? We've got enough sockeye for four. I overbought. You can save yours for tomorrow. Bill actually told me he could wait until six thirty to eat as long as he had a snack first. His ulcer, you know."

"Bill hasn't had an ulcer in thirty years," Judith declared. "We can't. Things have gotten complicated here. Rodney and Belle showed up. Separately, that is."

"Oh, dear." Renie paused. "You need backup. Why don't Bill and I come over and bring our sockeye? I'll cook the food, you coddle the guests. Okay?"

"That's a lot of bother for . . ." Judith saw Gertrude roll into the house. "Here comes Mother. Okay, fine. I'll see you soon." She hung up as the old lady stopped her wheelchair just short of the stove.

"When do we eat?" Gertrude demanded in her raspy old voice.

"Your dinner will be ready at six," Judith replied, hearing the doorbell ring. "That must be the new guests. I'll be right back."

As Judith went to the front door she heard Rodney calling to her: "Mama! Where are you?"

She realized he must have come downstairs while she was in the kitchen. Judith ignored him and opened the front door to greet Ronald and Jeanne Chang, a middle-aged couple from San Francisco who were in town to visit their grandchildren. Trying to drown out more shouts from Rodney and an argument between Joe and Gertrude in the kitchen, Judith somehow managed to get the Changs registered before directing them to Room Three. For once, she didn't feel as if she could manage the stairs to take them up in person. Her conscience was soothed when they seemed to be a pleasant, unflappable pair.

Judith paused in the doorway to the living room. "I'll be back in a few minutes, Rodney. Please be patient."

He pointed to his empty glass. "Another shot, please, Mama?"

"I'll see if I have any left," Judith said between clenched teeth before heading to the kitchen. "Well?" she queried Joe. "What did the Rankerses have to report?"

"They aren't home yet," he replied, pouring drinks. "They probably got stuck in traffic." He turned to Gertrude. "You want to get tanked, you goofy old bat?"

"Up yours, Knucklehead," Gertrude shot back. "I want my supper."

"It's only five twenty," Judith pointed out. "Renie's making dinner here tonight."

"Why?" Gertrude asked. "Did my daffy niece set fire to her kitchen? It wouldn't be the first time."

"She only did it once," Judith said, "and that was on Easter when the duck she was roasting blew up in the oven."

"Oh, right, I remember that," Gertrude mumbled. "We all had to eat burgers from the joint at the bottom of the hill."

The doorbell rang again. Judith found two young girls who looked as if they should still be in high school. She was only partly wrong—they were from a small town near the Oregon border and were in the city to check out the University. She handed over a map of the campus and sent them upstairs to Room Four. Finally, she went into the living room, where Rodney was wearing a new plaid short-sleeved shirt and equally new tan pants. He was sitting across from his daughter and looking petulant.

"It's not right," he declared. "Belle and I shouldn't be the ones to have to run away from *my* house."

"Actually, Dad," Belle said, "it's *my* house. But you're right. This is all wrong."

Judith cleared her throat to get her guests' attention. "Perhaps you two would like to go out to dinner," she suggested, hoping to sound sympathetic. "You've both been through so much."

"Gosh, Mama," Rodney said in dismay, "I was hoping for a home-cooked meal. You know—like you would've made for me if you'd had the chance to bring me up."

"I'm sorry, I can't do that tonight," Judith responded. "I have family coming and my cousin is making the dinner. There are several nice restaurants on top of the hill."

Rodney didn't look happy about that idea. "I'm not family?" he asked in an injured voice.

Before Judith could respond, Belle reached out to touch her father's knee. "Hey, Dad, why not eat out? I can pay. I've got money, remember?"

"Right." Rodney still looked unhappy. "I should be the one paying. Oh, well—a man's gotta eat when a man's gotta eat. Pick one that serves booze. Mama doesn't seem to want to bring me a refill."

Judith discreetly withdrew. Ten minutes later, the Joneses arrived.

"Make way," Renie called out from the hall. "Here comes the sockeye! Oops!" She tripped over her own feet and would've fallen if Bill hadn't caught her by the arm.

"It's a good thing she can cook," he muttered. "She sure as hell can't walk."

Renie snarled at him before setting the package of salmon on the counter. "I need vegetables and potatoes. I'll make hash browns. They go well with fish. By the way, Aunt Gert is out in the backyard trying to run over Sweetums with her wheelchair."

"She often does that," Judith said. "He's too quick for her."

Bill was gazing around the kitchen. "Where are the drinks?"

Joe reached for the cupboard. "Sorry. I needed mine sooner. My lovely wife inflicted one of her goofy guests on me this afternoon."

Bill shot a wary glance at both cousins. "Our wives get some oddball ideas. They just like to do that. Why did we marry into this crazy family?"

"Because *we're* crazy?" Joe retorted, handing Bill a shot of Scotch over ice. "Let's go outside. It's clearing up. We can let Judith's mother verbally abuse us instead of trying to cream the cat."

Judith watched the husbands decamp from the kitchen before turning to her cousin. "Let me catch you up on what's happened since I saw you. I don't think Joe cares and I know Bill doesn't."

"Go for it," Renie said, rinsing asparagus spears under the tap. "You need to vent."

And Judith did, focusing mainly on the Schmucks. By the time she finished, Renie had chopped up the raw potatoes in the food processor. "So," she said to Judith, "Rodney may be broke, but Belle has all the money. What's their problem? Their so-called friends can't stick around the area forever. Father and daughter can wait it out."

"They can't wait it out here," Judith asserted. "I feel sorry for them, but I can't play nursemaid. I've got a B&B to run."

"They can stay at a hotel," Renie said. "Where are they now?"

Judith moved to the half doors. "I can't hear them. Maybe they left to eat dinner elsewhere. They have no car, so they might've called a cab."

Renie placed the salmon in the oven under the broiler. "Then relax. You've really let them ruffle your fur. Unless," she added with a puckish expression, "you want to adopt Rodney."

"Oh, good grief! Never! I've given up trying to tell him he is *not* my son, but he pays no attention. He's fixated and that's that. But the Mama bit is driving me nuts!"

Renie's face grew solemn. "Could that be part of a plan?"

Judith leaned against the kitchen counter. "I never thought of that."

"Maybe," Renie said, still serious, "you should."

While Renie prepared the food, Judith visited with her guests in the living room. The widows informed her they'd be leaving in the morning right after breakfast.

"We've done all we can about the bars," Schuster declared. "There's only so much we can absorb in a single city."

"Absorb?" Judith echoed. "How do you mean, if you don't drink?"

"Oh!" Brewster exclaimed. "I don't think we told you about our mission. Like you, we're in the travel business. We write guidebooks. The one we're working on now is on drinking establishments in the country's twenty largest cities. We have our own method of grading them, which, of course, has nothing to do with the quality of their potables."

"I see," Judith said, trying not to smile. "Have you ever written a guidebook to B&Bs?"

Schuster nodded. "That was our first ever, over ten years ago. We're doing a revised and expanded edition now." She glanced at her companion. "We haven't yet graded Hillside Manor. In fact, we always wait two or three days after we leave to evaluate any establishment we visit. I will say this—it's been remarkably quiet and very pleasant so far."

Judith did smile, but she felt it was a trifle forced. "That's a very reassuring assessment. I hope it stays that way."

"It probably will," Brewster responded. "After all, what could possibly go wrong at a B&B?"

Judith wasn't about to tell her.

Gertrude declined eating with the rest of the family. She had to watch her favorite TV programs, though Judith wasn't sure what—besides the news—came on in the six to seven o'clock slot. For all she knew, her mother could be watching mud wrestling.

There was still no sign of Rodney and Belle Schmuck, so Judith assumed they were dining elsewhere. The Flynns and the Joneses had just finished dinner when the phone rang. Judith rose from the table to answer it while Bill muttered something about phone calls never being taken at their house between six and seven o'clock.

"Judith," Arlene said, "how are you?"

"Fine," Judith replied, mouthing Arlene's name for Renie's benefit. "I've been wondering how you got along at Sunset Cliffs."

"Not all that well," Arlene answered. "We were discovered. I'm afraid we're being held prisoner at Heaven's Gate. At least they didn't confiscate my cell—"

For the second time in the day, the line between Judith and Arlene went dead.

Chapter 22

They can't be in any real danger," Joe declared. "You know how Arlene tends to dramatize things."

"I don't think she's doing that now," Judith retorted. "What's wrong with you? These people aren't exactly benign. For all we know, one of them poisoned Millie. And by the way, I don't see Woody's 'tecs pulling any rabbits out of hats with their investigation. In fact, I wonder if they're doing their job."

"Hey," Joe shot back, "Woody always does his job and so do his people. What's he supposed to be doing? Putting your favorite suspects on the rack?"

Judith didn't back down. "You said yourself that there might be a problem with investigating a crime in Sunset Cliffs. Why wouldn't I be concerned, especially when it involves the Rankerses?"

"I still say Arlene may be exaggerating," Joe asserted.

Bill nodded. "She just likes to do that."

Renie let out a squawk. "Quit saying that! You're driving me nuts!"

"Short trip," Bill muttered, gazing at the high ceiling.

Joe stood up. "Let's go watch a baseball game in the living room, Bill. I'm sure my wife feels one of her migraines coming on."

The men left the kitchen. "Great," Judith grumbled. "Now we have to clean up the mess."

"I didn't make a mess," Renie said. "I clean as I cook. I can't work in chaos. It disturbs my artistic temperament."

"Well . . . we still have to clear off the table and put stuff in the dishwasher." Judith paused. "No, we don't. We should go check on Arlene and Carl. What if they *are* being held against their will?"

"Call her."

"I can't. I don't have her son's cell number. I only have the one for their regular phone."

"The number didn't show up on your phone when she called?"

Judith shook her head. "My landlines's so old that its features are really limited."

"Drat." Renie frowned. "I suppose we should make sure they're okay. If our ornery husbands are watching baseball, they won't know we're gone."

"True." Judith ran a hand through her salt-and-pepper hair. "Okay. Let's do it. Shall I take my car?"

"Yes," Renie replied, standing up. "If Bill wants to go home, he may've forgotten I was with him. *He just likes to do that*," she said in a loud voice. Nothing. "Damn," she whispered. "They're so caught up in the game that Bill doesn't even know I'm taunting him. To further quote my husband, 'Let's move on out. Boppin'!' "

The cousins left via the back door. A quick look at the Rankerses' driveway verified that their car was still gone. Judith paused before leaving the cul-de-sac as a big black SUV went by on the through street. Five minutes later, they were going down the north side of the hill and taking a right to the six-way stop.

"Don't look now," Judith said, "but I think we're being followed. Did you see a white Camaro parked anywhere near the B&B?"

"No," Renie answered. "I was watching you watch traffic. Wait—wasn't the phony inspector driving a Camaro?"

"He was. I think he's two cars behind us. I first noticed the Camaro up on the Avenue at the arterial by the bank, but I didn't think much about it. Of course I may be wrong."

Renie twisted around to look. "All I can see in back of us is a red car. Why don't you avoid the big bridge and take the smaller one across the ship canal? That way maybe we can lose him."

"Good thinking," Judith agreed as she went through the intersection and around under the big bridge. "Hey, once we get to the bottom of the hill, I'll keep going on this side of the canal all the way to Fisherman's Bridge."

"Brilliant," Renie said. "After that first stoplight, gun it."

"You want me to get arrested?"

Renie grinned. "Hey, that's not a bad idea. You could really lose the phony inspector, then."

"And end up with a fat speeding ticket? No thanks."

"Come on, coz," Renie urged as they waited for the light to change by the forested college campus at the foot of Heraldsgate Hill. "I don't see the Camaro yet," she said, looking behind them. "Maybe it's not him. There must be several white—uh-oh. Here he comes."

The light turned green. "Oh, what the heck," Judith muttered. "They don't patrol this street except when classes are in full session." She pressed the gas pedal. "Is he still behind us?"

"I can't tell," Renie replied. "A couple of other cars are in the way now. It's starting to get dark."

The wide street that ran along the canal wasn't very busy. Judith suddenly grew reckless, pushing the pedal even harder. She felt a sense of liberation from all of the past few days' frustrations. "Whee! That headache I felt coming on is gone."

"Good. You've been tying yourself into knots ever since the Schmucks showed up. You need to kick back."

"You can't blame me for being upset over . . ." Judith heard a siren close by. "Damn! Is that the cops?"

Renie turned around again. "It's not a parade float. You better pull over before we get to the bridge turnoff."

"Damn it!" Judith exclaimed, spotting a place to park by a lumber store. "Just as I was starting to feel good again. Can you see if the cop's pulling up, too?"

"I'm afraid so," Renie said. "Should I fake near-death symptoms so you can tell him you're taking me to the ER?"

Judith shook her head. "I was speeding. My husband's a former cop, as you may recall."

"He was never a traffic cop. In fact, did Joe ever walk a beat or . . ." Renie shut up as the officer appeared next to the car and Judith rolled down her window.

"Excuse me, ma'am," the tall, fresh-faced policeman said, "do you know the speed limit on this street?"

"Yes," Judith replied, "and I know I was going too fast. I'm in a hurry because my neighbors are being held hostage in Sunset Cliffs."

The cop blinked and removed his hat. "Really. That's quite an explanation for speeding."

"It can't be helped," Judith asserted. "But as long as you're here, why don't you follow us out there? We could use your assistance." She noted his name stitched into his uniform's shirt: *D. Frolich.* "My cousin and I would really appreciate it."

Frolich looked taken aback. "Ah . . . May I please see your driver's license?"

"Of course." Judith rummaged in her purse. "I'm Judith Flynn. My cousin is Serena Jones. Here." She handed her wallet to the cop.

"Okay," he said, returning the wallet. "But I still have to cite you for going fifteen miles over the posted limit."

"That's fine," Judith responded. "Just write it up quickly so we can be on our way. You will follow us, won't you?"

"I can't do that," Frolich said. "I'm on patrol."

Judith stared at him. "If I call 911 and ask for help, will you respond?"

Frolich looked askance. "But I'm already here."

"Exactly," Judith agreed. "So please follow us. Or lead the way. You choose. Otherwise, I'll have to call another policeman when we get there."

The officer still seemed conflicted. "Let me make a call of my own." He stepped away from the Subaru.

"Why," Renie asked, keeping her voice down, "didn't you tell him you're Mrs. Joe Flynn and have him call Woody? Or do you just like torturing the poor guy?"

"I don't want to use clout," Judith declared. "It'd make me sound . . . pretentious. Besides, he probably wouldn't believe me."

Frolich returned. "I'm sorry, ma'am. My desk sergeant says I have to write you up."

Judith didn't argue. "Fine."

"It's seventeen dollars over the basic fine," Frolich replied. "The total—"

"Just do it," Judith broke in. "I told you, I'm in a hurry."

The officer scowled. "But you don't want to get pulled over again for going too fast, Mrs. Flynn."

"Of course not," Judith retorted, "but I want to get where I'm going before somebody gets killed."

"Right." Frolich looked unmoved as he began to fill out the ticket. "Is that your current address on the license?"

"Yes."

"Is the photo correct?"

"Yes."

"Well . . . your hair's a different color than it is on the license."

"Aaaaargh!" Renie screamed. "She colors her hair! Write the stupid ticket, you . . . you *Frolich,* you! We've got lives to save!"

The cop's face flushed. "Okay, okay, I'm doing it."

Two minutes later, the cousins were on their way again. "Is he following us?" Judith asked Renie.

"Not yet," she replied. "I don't think he remembered he was driving a cruiser. Maybe he's waiting for a taxi."

"Speaking of being followed, that Camaro must've passed us when I pulled over," Judith said. "Did you see it?"

"No," Renie replied. "I was watching the cop car. Gosh, coz, this is the second time you've been picked up for speeding in the last year."

"At least I didn't have to pay a fine when we were up on Whoopee Island in January. That county deputy had common sense."

"He found out you were FASTO," Renie said.

Judith grimaced at the reference to the nickname admiring fans had given her when they'd learned of her detecting skills. It stood for Female Amateur Sleuth Tracking Offenders, which was bad enough. But ocasionally when the acronym was misspelled as FATSO, she'd get angry. Judith had always been self-conscious about her weight.

"Right," Judith said. "But he stopped regarding us as suspects."

"I still think you should have pulled rank and had Frolich call Woody. How much is the ticket?"

"Eighty-seven bucks," Judith replied as they headed over Fisherman's Bridge. "My main concern is Arlene and Carl. Now it's getting dark. Maybe that's good. It might be smart to park the car away from Heaven's Gate and sneak up on the place."

"But the guard will have to call the house," Renie said.

"No, he won't. You're going to tell him we're calling on the Key Largo bank president."

Renie looked dismayed. "I am? No—you tell them. You're a much better liar than I am."

Judith considered. "Okay, I can do that."

"I can't wait to hear what you'll say," Renie said, grinning.

"I can't either. I'll wing it when we get there."

Eight minutes later, they were pulling up to the gatehouse. A young, dark-haired man stepped up to the car. Judith assumed her most businesslike expression.

"I'm Ms. Dooley," she said. "We're here to meet with Mr. and Mrs. Quincy about some details of the project our company is working on."

The young man nodded politely, then reached inside the gatehouse for the phone. Less than a minute passed before he gave them the high sign and opened the gates.

"Who on earth are Mr. and Mrs. Quincy?" Renie demanded. "And when did you adopt Tyler Dooley? Isn't Rodney enough of an extra son?"

Judith explained about the construction project that Tyler's father had been involved in. "I thought about using the Key Largo bank president instead, but I figure Tyler will get a kick out of my little ruse."

"Little ruse? How about a big fat lie?" Renie leaned back in the seat. "Sheesh. You're teaching the poor kid nefarious ways to navigate the world. Doesn't that bother you?"

"Of course not," Judith retorted. "Everyone is some-times forced to tweak the . . ." She frowned, slowing the Subaru down to a crawl. "Aren't we by Heaven's Gate? I don't see any lights."

"It's a big house," Renie said. "Keep going. Maybe they're all in some other part we can't view from this angle."

To Judith's relief, several amber lights glowed on two floors of the Schmuck mansion's west side. Pulling into the drive, she tried to spot the Rankerses' SUV, but couldn't see much beyond her immediate surroundings. Clouds blotted out the moon; a lazy breeze ruffled the shrubbery near the porch; between the tall trees, patches of the darkening sky could be seen to the west.

"No welcome light on," Judith murmured, unbuckling her seat belt. "Let's do it."

Renie sighed. "Sure, why not? Nothing bad can happen to us. We're invincible. Aren't we?" She didn't expect an answer and vaulted out of the car to head for the house.

As they reached the steps, a frog croaked nearby. Judith wondered if it had come from the reflecting pool. Except for the soft rustle of leaves, it was very quiet. Unnaturally so, she thought, accustomed to the bustle of a city neighborhood. Maybe the rich could buy quiet. The thought disturbed her in some way as they went up to the porch and Judith did the honors with the chime.

And waited. "Somebody had to hear that," she said softly, her hand still touching the brass ring. "Should I try again?"

"Wait. It's a big house. They may be a long way from the front."

Another minute passed. Judith was about to have another try with the chime when the door opened.

"Arlene!" she gasped. "What are you doing?"

"Opening the door—again," Arlene replied. "Hello, Judith; hello, Serena. Would you like to come in? Wait—I'd better find a light switch."

"But," Judith said as wall sconces suddenly illuminated the hallway, "I thought you and Carl were hostages."

Arlene shrugged, leading them into the sitting room. "We are," she replied. "But none of these people know how to cook. They asked if I could, so I had to make dinner. Now they want us to stay over and make breakfast. I have no idea how they've managed the last few days. Maybe they eat out or have food brought in." She shrugged again. "I'm sorry. I should've called you, but my cell battery went out. Oh—would you like some lemon meringue pie? I made three and there's some left over. Unless someone was a pig. That wouldn't surprise me."

Judith was still flummoxed. "We were worried. That's why we're here. I was in such a rush that I got an eighty-seven-dollar speeding ticket."

"Add it to the Schmucks' bill," Arlene advised.

"That's another thing," Judith said. "They stiffed me for the B&B charges."

Arlene looked shocked. "No! That's criminal. Can't Joe have them arrested?"

"That's a bit extreme," Judith murmured. "But I should talk to them about it as long as I'm here."

Arlene nodded. "Of course. In fact, they want to talk to you."

"They do?" Judith asked in surprise. "Who? Or all of the above?"

"I'm not sure," Arlene replied. "It was the woman with the unruly gray hair who said 'they' wanted to speak with you. She claims to be a doctor. I wonder what kind. For birds, perhaps. They could roost in her straggly hair while recovering. I suppose one of them will talk to you. One of the people, I mean. I haven't seen any birds in the house."

Renie, who was slouched in a leather club chair, finally spoke. "I'd like to talk to *somebody*. I wouldn't even mind somebody talking to *me*. My puppet strings are kind of frayed."

Judith glared at her cousin. "Stop being a brat. Try to remember you're a grown-up. Good grief, you've been on Social Security for over a year."

"So what?" Renie shot back. "I still work, so I'm still paying into the system. Wait two years until you get to be my age."

A man's voice interrupted before Judith could respond. "Mrs. Flynn?"

Judith turned to see Charlie Crump in the doorway. "Yes. Please join us. I was making sure everything was going well with you and your friends. Somehow I still feel responsible for the tragedy you all experienced while staying at my B&B."

Charlie eased his bulk into a green-and-gold-striped armchair. "Terrible thing, of course," he murmured. "Poor dear Millie. Poor old Rodney. Damned shame." He shook his balding head.

"How is Rodney?" Judith inquired, wondering if Charlie or any of the others realized that the Schmuck father and daughter had fled the premises.

"Oh . . ." Charlie gazed at the ceiling. "He's coming along. Takes time, of course. Heals all wounds, as they say. Which reminds me," he said, reaching into the pocket of his argyle sweater, "I've got an insurance form here I'd like you to sign. I'm in the business, you know."

"Yes," Judith said. "Agnes mentioned that. Why do you want me to sign this form?"

Arlene waved her hand in a dismissive gesture. "Mr. Crump's probably selling you a policy you don't need. Really, Judith, he's a *salesman*." Her tone suggested the word was an obscenity.

Judith smiled faintly. "I'm sure he can explain what this is all about." The smile stayed in place, but became coaxing. "Can't you, Mr. Crump?"

"Of course! Of course!" he asserted, looking offended. "I'm not pulling a fast one here. It's for the purpose of Rodney filing a claim on Millie's life insurance.

I want to avoid any blame on Mrs. Flynn's part for the poor woman's tragic demise."

Arlene's face was set, but she didn't comment. Renie looked bemused. But Judith shook her head as she accepted the form from Charlie.

"I'll have to take it with me so Bub—I mean, my attorney, can see it," she said pleasantly. "I'm sure you understand."

Charlie chuckled. "Now, Mrs. Flynn, just sign it now. It's a simple disclaimer."

"But I'm not a simple person," Judith responded, still in a pleasant tone. "I'm a businesswoman. I always run any legal document past my lawyer."

Charlie's jowly face hardened. "Maybe I should make you an offer you can't refuse. For your property, that is. How does a million bucks sound to you?"

Judith drew back on the sofa. "Are you kidding? Do you have any idea what property costs on Heraldsgate Hill's south slope?" She glanced at Arlene. "What's your house worth?"

Arlene gazed off into space. "According to my daughter, Cathy, who's in the real estate business . . ." She paused to gave Charlie a hard stare. "We could ask two million for our property. Our lot is larger than the Flynns'. No offense, Judith," she murmured, "but you know it's true."

"Okay, okay," Charlie said to Judith, "then sign the gol-darned form and be done with it."

Judith got to her feet. "No. We're leaving now. I'll get back to you in a day or so. You'll still be here, I assume?"

The color rose in Charlie's face as he clumsily stood up. "Yeah, we've got some unfinished business. You better not be trying to wiggle out of what happened at your place, Mrs. Flynn, you hear that?"

"I heard," Judith declared with a lift of her strong chin. "Arlene, are you and Carl leaving, too?"

"Oh, no," she replied. "I told you, they want us to stay overnight to make breakfast. Then we can finish the front part of the garden. Don't worry, we'll be fine." She shot Charlie a warning look.

Judith hesitated, but Renie was already heading for the hall. "Okay. Call if you need anything."

Arlene nodded—and glared again at Charlie Crump.

"Well?" Renie said after the cousins were back in the Subaru. "Are the Rankerses being held against their will?"

Judith sighed. "Their so-called employers may think so, but I think Arlene and Carl are having the time of their lives. Well, maybe not quite, but they *are* in the thick of things. That's not all bad."

"Do you think Rodney and Belle have come back here?" Renie asked as they headed along the dark, narrow road.

"I doubt it. I still think they went somewhere for dinner. We should find out when we get back to Hillside Manor."

"Are you really going to ask Bill's brother to look over that insurance form?"

"Probably not," Judith replied, slowing for the gate that had swung open at their approach. "It can't be very complex. What I want to know is why Charlie asked me to sign it in the first place. I didn't poison Millie."

"So who did?"

"That," Judith said, "is what I'm still trying to find out."

Chapter 23

"Where have you been?" Joe demanded when Judith came in the back door. "Bill went home twenty minutes ago."

"I dropped Renie at her house. She figured Bill might've taken off. He keeps to a rather rigid schedule, you know."

Joe still looked irked. "Just answer the question," he growled, following his wife through the kitchen.

Judith kept on going. She didn't reply until they'd sat down on the living room's matching sofas. "I was worried about Arlene and Carl. They seem fine, but they're staying overnight at Heaven's Gate."

Joe looked skeptical. "Of their own volition?"

Judith winced. "Not exactly. It's kind of hard to explain."

"Damn!" Joe leaned his head back on the sofa and looked up at the ceiling. "Now you've got our favorite neighbors putting themselves at risk. What next? You send Tyler Dooley out to Sunset Cliffs on his bicycle to make sure Arlene and Carl are still alive?"

"I hadn't thought of that," Judith admitted—and immediately rued her words. "I mean, I wouldn't do that. It's a long bike ride."

Joe sat up straight and peered at his wife. "Okay, what happened when you got to the gated community's House of Horrors?"

Judith recounted their adventures, though she left out the part about her speeding ticket. That could wait until Joe's mood improved.

"Damn," he said when she'd finished. "I wonder if Woody could get a cop inside Sunset Cliffs to keep an eye on the house."

"That's sort of what Arlene and Carl are doing," Judith pointed out. "Undercover, as it were."

Joe made a face. "That's not the same."

"But . . . never mind. Hey, what happened to Rodney and Belle? Did they ever come back from dinner?"

"No. Do you want them to?"

"Joe . . ." Judith paused to collect her thoughts. The entire Schmuck group had been a big pain, but she felt sorry for Rodney. And being kindhearted by nature, she even spared some pity for Belle. "They're sort of pathetic. They may also be in danger."

Joe rubbed at the back of his head. "Who isn't in the Schmuck lash-up, including the Rankerses? Save your sympathy for them and not a bunch of screwballs you'd never met until last Friday."

Judith didn't speak for a few moments. "I know a way you could put a cop in Sunset Cliffs," she finally said. "Arlene and Carl could give permission for a plainclothes officer to get through the gate."

"And how would you go about arranging that?" Joe asked, his skepticism returning.

"I could call them," Judith replied. "I don't have the cell's number because it belongs to one of their boys, but their daughter, Cathy, could give it to me." She rose from the sofa to check her telephone listings. But before she reached the hall, the phone rang. "Drat," she muttered, hurrying to the cherrywood table, "I'll get that."

"Judith?" Mavis Lean-Brodie all but barked into the phone. "I've been banned from Sunset Cliffs. What's going on out there?"

"Nothing newsworthy," Judith hedged. "How could you, of all people, get banned? Everybody knows you."

"That's the problem," Mavis replied grimly. "I was recognized and someone with clout—of which there is plenty in that gated community—put my name on the Do Not Pass Go list. Can you meet me for lunch tomorrow? Go ahead, bring your lippy cousin along. But this time let's meet at Chez Fred on the Avenue."

"Okay," Judith said. "Shall I make a reservation?"

"No. I can do that. I still have clout with restaurants. I'll see you at noon." She rang off.

Judith glanced at Joe, who had picked up the latest issue of *Sports Illustrated* from the coffee table. While he seemed engrossed, she suspected otherwise, but she took a chance and called Renie.

"I can't go," Renie said on a reluctant note. "I'm meeting with some dweeb from a software company with a name I can't remember. Heck, I can't remember the contact's name either. I'll just ask for Mr. Dweeb when I get there. The maître d' will know who I mean. Unless they've got more than one computer type coming for lunch."

"Darn. I'd hoped you could come along. Oh, well—I guess I can deal with Mavis by myself."

"Coz," Renie said, sounding serious, "you could deal with King Kong. Your knack for connecting with other people is an art form."

Judith was touched. "That's . . . really kind of you to say."

"It was. But I don't do 'kind' very often, so I'm out of practice. And I just ran out of 'kind.' I'm hanging up now to prove it."

Renie was as good as her word. The phone rang again before Judith could replace the receiver.

"Mrs. Flynn?"

"Yes?" Judith replied, noticing that Joe had dozed off.

"This is Belle Schmuck," the young woman said in a low voice. "Dad and I've checked into a hotel downtown. We want to be incognito for a while. I'm hanging up now, but we thought you should know we're okay. So far."

Judith heard the disconnect before she could say anything.

"Why," **Renie** asked, "are you calling me at eleven o'clock?"

"All the guests have come back to the B&B and Joe just went to bed," Judith replied. "You stay up late. My husband's being a pill."

"Husbands do that," Renie conceded.

"I know, and I even understand why this time," Judith said, and went on to tell her cousin about Belle's phone call.

"So you don't know which hotel. Do you think they registered under assumed names?"

"I gather they did," Judith responded. "They're on the run from the rest of their so-called chums. Not that I blame them."

"No."

"I knew you'd agree with—"

"I mean," Renie broke in, "I'm not going downtown with you tonight to check out hotels and look for frightened Schmucks."

"I did not intend to do that!" Judith cried. "Honest!"

"You're such a good liar," Renie remarked. "But this time I think I believe you. Maybe you can get Mavis to speculate on all of this when you lunch with her tomorrow."

"I don't know how good she is at speculating," Judith said. "She's a news type, she deals in facts and— oh, good grief! I forgot to look at that insurance form! Can you hold on while I get it out of my purse?"

"Sure," Renie replied. "It's after eleven, my husband's sound asleep, my lop-eared bunny's in his cage in the basement. What else have I got to do?"

Judith took the phone into the kitchen where she'd left her purse. "Let me see . . ." she said, sitting down at the kitchen table and flipping through the pages. "The policy is in Millie's name . . . The first part goes on and on with standard life insurance information . . . Oh, yes, it's definitely for twenty million dollars. I wonder what the monthly premiums are for that much."

"How would I know?" Renie said, sounding bored. "Hurry up. I suddenly need a snack."

"Hey, it takes time to—ah! There's a rider or whatever they call it. Ohmigod! The policy doesn't cover—and I quote—'death by misadventure.' So *that's* why they want me to sign off on this thing!"

"Of course." Renie yawned. "What do I crave? A BLT or a vat of vanilla ice cream with caramel-butterscotch topping?"

"Coz! Stop being a twit. If I'd signed this, I could've perjured myself."

"But you didn't sign it," Renie said in a reasonable tone. "Tear up the damned thing and go to bed."

"No. I'm saving it. It's evidence."

"Of what?"

"I don't know yet," Judith admitted. "That is, I suppose they want the insurance. But I wonder who the beneficiary is . . ." She leafed through the few pages and gasped. "It's Agnes Crump!"

"Agnes?" Renie sounded mildly surprised. "Why Agnes?"

"Charlie Crump is the one who probably sold this policy to Millie," Judith said. "Who knows what he told

Millie? Or maybe she never knew. The policy is dated September tenth of last year. I wonder if Rodney—or Belle—even knew about it."

"Ice cream," Renie said. "That appeals to me more than a BLT."

Judith started to speak, but thought better of it. Instead, she hung up on her cousin. There were times when Serena Marie Grover Jones could try even Judith's almost limitless patience. But she did take Renie's advice and went up to bed.

Unfortunately, she couldn't get to sleep. Her brain refused to shut down. All she could think of was Charlie Crump's insistence that she sign the insurance waiver to exonerate herself of any liability. The rider specified foul play. Judith knew she hadn't caused Millie's death. But did the request imply that someone else had? Of course she'd assumed it was possible that Millie had been murdered. Judith had grown accustomed to being associated with homicide victims. Maybe she was wrong this time. Given that most deaths were caused by natural causes, maybe that was how Millie had died.

Yet Judith's history with dead people strongly suggested otherwise.

Clouds hung over Heraldsgate Hill Thursday morning when Judith came downstairs. "Say," she said to

Joe, who was cracking eggs into a big bowl, "I thought the autopsy report was due by now."

"I told you it might be later in the week," he responded. "The more people who move to this city, the more deaths we get. Haven't you noticed how many obits are in the newspaper these days? That means more autopsies."

"Not every death requires an autopsy," Judith pointed out.

"Right." Joe turned on the mixer, obviously not interested in discussing postmortem procedures.

Judith took two pounds of bacon out of the refrigerator. Before she could open the first package, Sweetums scrunched his big, furry body through the cat door and strolled down the hall. "Mother must be up early," she murmured. "I'll try to make her breakfast now. Oww!" She glared at the cat, who had just raked her leg with his claws. "You ornery pest! Didn't Mother feed you this morning?" She started down the hall to check his dish. "Claws!" she exclaimed. "That's what Clark meant."

Joe turned off the mixer. "What?"

"Some notes Clark had in their room," Judith explained, moving away from Sweetums, who was poised for a second attack. "It looked like 'claws,' but I'll bet it was *clause*. Clark may not be a very good speller."

Joe turned the mixer back on. Judith shook her head and went to the pantry to get more cat food. Her husband didn't seem interested in what might be possible clues.

It wasn't until she'd taken Gertrude's breakfast out to the toolshed and the current guests were seated in the dining room that Judith asked Joe why he seemed so grumpy.

"It's simple," Joe said, putting his hands on her shoulders. "I love my wife. I tense up when I think she's putting herself in harm's way." The green eyes flashed. "Is that so hard to understand?"

"No," Judith mumbled. "But when it happens under our roof, it's hard for me to avoid wondering how and why."

"But we don't really know what happened," Joe asserted. "How about this? Until Millie's death is ruled a homicide, you butt out. Okay?"

Judith frowned. "Um . . . I suppose I could do that. I'm having lunch with Mavis Lean-Brodie today. She's been following what . . . happened here as a possible TV news story."

Joe's hands fell away from Judith's shoulders. "Oh, hell! That means you and the B&B will be broadcast all over the region. Do you really want that kind of publicity? What will Ingrid Heffelman think?"

"Maybe Ingrid's too busy running the state B&B association to watch TV."

"Ingrid'll hear about it one way or another," Joe said, lowering his voice to keep from being overheard by the guests in the dining room. "She'll be on your case again and you know it."

Judith's temper finally came to the fore. "You want me to interfere with freedom of information?"

"I want you to use common sense. When you see Mavis today, tell her you don't want publicity. It's bad for business. Maybe she can understand that."

"I doubt it." Judith paused. "I can give it a shot, though."

"You do that," Joe said, picking up the bowl of eggs.

Judith decided to shut up and check on the guests. The current group seemed more congenial than her husband on this cloudy May morning. And at least none of them had been murdered.

Yet.

Judith had never been to Chez Fred before. It was a relatively new restaurant on the hill, but had received good reviews. Mavis was already seated when she arrived a couple of minutes after noon.

"They have a very fine rosé from Provence here," Mavis said in greeting. "I ordered a bottle. I hope you like it."

"I don't drink wine very often," Judith admitted. "I serve it to my guests during the social hour, though. I tend to buy whatever's on sale."

Mavis raised her eyebrows, but refrained from sneering. "Really, Judith, I thought you were a woman of some culture."

"You and your family stayed at my B&B years ago," Judith said. "I don't remember you complaining about what I served."

"I was probably too busy complaining about my family," Mavis replied. "As it turned out, I was justified in one instance."

Judith thought back to what had been her first encounter with a dead body. Like the currently deceased Millie, the victim had died on the premises. "Let's skip the old history," she said. "What do you know that I don't about the Schmucks?"

"Probably not as much as you do," Mavis admitted. "My spies tell me you were at Sunset Cliffs last night."

"Your spies?"

Mavis nodded. "Gate guards can be bribed for information, if not for access onto the sacred grounds. By the way, I ordered tartines for both of us. Duck confit,

Brie, fig preserves. If you don't like it, you're out of luck. They only offer three different tartines at lunch, but the chef—Maurice—is in one of his moods and only did duck."

"I'm sure it'll be fine," Judith said meekly.

Picking up the bottle of rosé, Mavis announced that she'd already sampled the wine and it was adequate. "I'll pour. Move your glass a bit closer. What's the latest?"

"Not much, really," Judith replied. "Rodney and Belle have moved to a downtown hotel. The rest of them seem to be in a holding pattern."

"That's it?" Mavis looked incredulous. "What's wrong with you?"

Judith shrugged. "I suppose they're waiting for Millie's body to be released. I gather she'll be buried here, not in L.A."

Mavis grew thoughtful as she sipped her wine. "I guess that makes sense. I wonder if some of the Sunset Cliffs residents are buried somewhere on the grounds. They have their own chapel, as you know. Very High Church, very WASP. Of course." She sipped more rosé.

"A very handsome chapel," Judith remarked.

"What's with the autopsy report?" Mavis asked. "It's taking a long time, isn't it?"

"Not according to Joe," Judith said.

"Can't he get his old pal Woody to hurry up the process?"

"My husband isn't inclined to put pressure on his former partner," Judith replied. "Really, I don't know much more than you do. How about your own investigation?"

The tartines arrived. "I had one of my peons do deep background on the people involved. Unfortunately, nothing much turned up. Those hangers-on are all who and what they say they are. Very discouraging. I'm beginning to wonder why I'm following this story in the first place."

Judith nodded vaguely. The duck confit was delicious, but she wouldn't admit she'd never eaten one before. "I don't suppose any of your spies mentioned seeing the Schmucks with a large chest."

"A couple of the Schmucks have a large chest—or stomach," Mavis said. "Why do you ask?"

"I mean a big box type of chest," Judith clarified. "They were seen carrying it out of the house and putting it in a car before they all drove off somewhere in the woods."

Mavis narrowed her eyes. "Hmm. That's rather intriguing. But those guards wouldn't have seen that happen. I wonder . . ." She looked beyond Judith out toward the Avenue.

"Yes?" Judith coaxed.

"If someone could search the grounds . . ." Mavis began. "Say, I heard they hired some gardeners. I wonder if they could be bribed? The guards would know the name of the firm that sent them."

Judith grimaced. "It was Carl and Arlene Rankers—my neighbors. You may remember them."

Mavis laughed. "I do. I liked them. They have a lot of moxie. Well? Can they get back inside?"

"That's the problem," Judith confessed. "They can't get outside. It seems they're being held against their will. Or not," she added, suddenly feeling very Arlene-like. "I mean, I was worried about them, but they seem rather . . . complacent about the whole situation. I suspect it's quite an adventure for them, really. Arlene, especially, has boundless curiosity."

"Interesting," Mavis mused. "And yet Joe won't ask Woody to help?"

"No. In fact . . ." Judith sighed. "He's grounded me."

"Really." Mavis's tone was dry. "Lance was often penalized for intentional grounding when he played pro football. My husband was always afraid of getting tackled. That's also why his nickname was Out-of-Bounds Brodie. And speaking of beyond borders, there's one other possibly intriguing thing I found out about your current suspects. Rodney and Millie flew to Switzerland in February for a week."

"Skiing?" Judith asked.

"Dubious. They stayed in Zürich the entire time. The trip struck me as odd, but I don't know why. There wasn't anything special going on in the city that would have a big appeal for American tourists."

"Maybe they have friends there," Judith suggested.

"It's possible." Mavis checked her watch. "I should be getting back to the station. Is there anything else I should know?"

Judith shook her head. "Nothing I can think of. I'd like to avoid any publicity linked to my B&B. As you mentioned, Millie's death was probably an accident. We've heard nothing to indicate otherwise. That makes your news story a dead end. So to speak." And wished she hadn't said it in the first place.

Back at Hillside Manor, Judith checked her Friday list of incoming guests for the Memorial Day weekend: a family from Rapid City, South Dakota, with two teenage daughters; two older couples from Appleton, Wisconsin, traveling together; a pair of Lewiston, Idaho, brothers who were checking out West Coast graduate schools; and a baseball scout and his wife from Dallas.

They all sounded benign to Judith. But she reminded herself that so had the Schmucks.

Joe had left to do some shopping, mainly at the hardware store. Around three o'clock, Judith called Renie. "What do you know about Zürich?" she asked her cousin.

"As much as you do," Renie replied. "Z for Zürich, Z for zilch. When we were in Switzerland, you may recall our only stop was Lucerne. Nice lake, creepy covered bridge, good food, and a friendly piano player in whichever bar we were hanging out in that night. Why do you ask?"

Judith explained what Mavis had told her about the Schmucks' February trip. "She thought it was odd."

"The Schmucks are odd," Renie said. "Why do you care if they went to Zürich?"

"I looked up the city on the Internet," Judith replied. "It's famous for its medical clinics."

"You feel sick?"

"Hardly. But it *is* suggestive, don't you think?"

Renie didn't respond right away. "Well, I suppose it could be. You found that list of drugs, right? Maybe one of them was ill."

"That's what crossed my mind," Judith said. "Millie, I figure. Unless . . . let's face it, Rodney is a mental and emotional mess. I wonder if he was like that before his wife died. His obsession about me being his mother might indicate that."

"Didn't you think it was a ruse to butter you up so they could get their paws on your property and the rest of the cul-de-sac?"

"Yes, and I still think that's part of it. I never saw the birth certificate, though Rodney claimed to have it. I wonder if he was lying." Judith sighed. "I'm frustrated. Joe told me to butt out. Maybe I should."

"You know you can't," Renie said quietly. "Even if no crime has been committed, you still feel responsible in some way for Rodney. Don't argue. You've got a kind heart and you know he's being railroaded by his so-called friends. I don't care what Mavis found out about their backgrounds, I still think they're a bunch of con artists."

The doorbell sounded. "Somebody's here," Judith said. "I'll call you back, okay?" She hung up.

When she opened the front door, a gray-haired woman of about sixty stood at almost military attention. Judith expected her to salute. She wasn't carrying a purse, but what appeared to be a large briefcase. "Mrs. Flynn?" the stranger queried in a deep, rich voice.

"Yes? Can I help you?"

"Perhaps." The woman looked to her left, right, and behind her. "Yes, I'll come in, if you don't mind."

Judith ushered her into the living room, indicating the newcomer should sit on one of the blue sofas. "I'm Judith Flynn, the owner of this B&B. Are you interested in reserving a room?" she asked, sitting down on the other sofa.

"I know who you are," the woman replied, shaking out the pleats in her long, plain skirt. She cleared her throat. "My name is Judith Grover."

Chapter 24

J udith thought she hadn't heard correctly. "I beg your pardon?"

The other woman's thin mouth hinted at a smile. "I'm Judith Grover," she repeated. "Yes, I understand that was your maiden name as well. I've never married, but I've borne a son. I immediately put him up for adoption. His new parents called him Rodney Schmuck. I've been trying to find him for some time."

Judith leaned back against the sofa cushions. "I see. Yes, of course. He was staying here at the B&B, but he's gone now. I mean, he's still in town, but not here." She paused, watching the other Judith's face react with only a slight twitch. "Did you hire a detective to find him?"

"I did." She gazed up at the high ceiling before looking again at Judith. "I swore I'd never do that. You see,

I wasn't married when I gave birth to Rodney. I was only seventeen and his father was much older. He was out of the picture as soon as I discovered I was *enceinte*. And please call me Jude. I was never a Judy type of person and I feel Judith is rather stilted."

Despite thinking the formal version fit her visitor more accurately, Judith smiled. "Of course, Jude. But you changed your mind about finding Rodney?"

"I turned sixty-two in March," Jude responded. "I retired from my government job at the end of April and I decided it was time to review my life. In retrospect, it seemed right that I should try to find the only real legacy that I have. By that, I mean my son."

"That's understandable," Judith said.

Jude offered a slight nod of agreement. "The detective traced him to an exclusive neighborhood north of the city, but when I called there, I was told he'd left. Are you certain you don't know where he is now?"

"Rodney and his daughter—your granddaughter—moved into a downtown hotel," Judith replied.

"Granddaughter?" Jude showed a hint of curiosity. "What is her name?"

"Belle," Judith said. "Actually, it's Arabella."

"That's . . . that's rather nice." Rodney's mother actually looked pleased. "I suppose I could start calling the hotels."

"You could," Judith responded, then reluctantly added, "but they may be registered under assumed names."

Jude frowned. "Why would they do such a thing?"

"Ah . . ." Judith hesitated. "There was friction between them and their traveling companions over a business venture. It seems the main reason they came here was to buy up property and build condos."

"How odd. I was told Rodney is a motivational speaker. My informant turned up nothing about any involvement in real estate."

"All I know is what I learned while they were here." Judith paused again, wondering how candid she could be with the woman who called herself Rodney's birth mother. "Did you keep his birth certificate?"

"Of course," Jude replied. "I brought it with me. Would you like to see it?"

"If you don't mind," Judith said.

Jude opened the case and removed a slightly wrinkled sheet of blue paper. "I moved away from here not long after I gave birth to Rodney. I've been living in Denver for many years," she said, handing over the certificate. "I worked for the U.S. Mint there."

Judith smiled as she scanned the information. "Your son was born in the same hospital as mine. My Mike is several years younger, though. He works for the forest service and is currently in Maine."

"A commendable type of job," Jude remarked, taking the certificate from Judith. "You're certain you have no idea where Rodney is?"

"I'm afraid I don't," Judith said as they both got up from the sofas. "Where are you staying?"

"At one of those residence inns not far from here," Jude replied as they went into the hall. She bit her lip. "Please don't think me fanciful. Over the years, I did something rather foolish." She stopped, looking uncertain.

"Don't we all do foolish things from time to time?" Judith asked softly.

"I suppose." Jude stared at the Persian carpet before looking again at Judith. "While working at the mint for almost forty years, I saved the new coins that were made there. Be assured, I paid for them and acquired a great many. I have no idea what the amount totaled." She paused once more. "The coins were for my son, should I find him. When I found out he was living in a wealthy community, I realized he probably had money of his own. All the same, I anonymously shipped the coins to him in a large wooden chest. Do you think that was folly on my part?"

Judith tried not to show her surprise. "Of course I don't. You intended that he should have them. It was very thoughtful of you."

Another faint smile touched Jude's thin lips. "You're quite a sympathetic person. I must go now. Thank you." She opened the door and marched down the steps.

Judith half expected to hear a drumroll.

Five minutes later, Renie came through the back door, announcing that lunch with the dweeb had been so tiresome that she'd had to cheer herself up by buying a new handbag at the local accessories store. After ten more minutes and another futile attempt by her cousin to raid the cookie jar, Judith had unloaded her account of Jude's visit to the B&B.

"Well," Renie said after one last resentful glare at the sheep-shaped cookie jar, "you solved the part about the chest. That's a big house with tons of storage room, so why would they bury the chest in the woods?"

"Who knows?" Judith responded. "It might have been some goofy idea of Rodney's. He wouldn't know where it came from, and unfortunately, I never asked him about it. When I deal with that poor guy, I feel as if I'm going from one debacle to the next."

Renie laughed. "Being grounded by Joe isn't hampering your style. Just stay put and see who shows up next."

"You did," Judith said.

"Don't sound so disappointed," Renie retorted. "As long as you have to stick around here, why don't you make some cookies?"

Judith glanced at the clock. "It's after four. I still haven't figured out what kind of appetizers to fix for the guests."

"Are any of this group suspicious?" Renie asked.

"No, just ordinary folks, and more to come for the holiday weekend." Judith got up from the kitchen chair. "I could make salmon pâté. Where's the new purse you bought?"

"I left it in the car," Renie said. "It's puce, with silver studs. I haven't got a thing to go with it. Oh, well. Where's Joe? I didn't see the MG in the drive."

"He went to the hardware store," Judith replied. "You know how men can take forever at a hardware store. It's like kids in a toy shop."

"Boys and their toys," Renie murmured. "How come Joe isn't working much this week?"

"Good question. Of course he had to wait to get the car fixed and then deal with that, but we could use the money."

"Who couldn't? Bill hasn't seen any clients the last few days. I asked him why and he told me they were all nuts. I refrained from mentioning that's what brings in the big bucks. I still think he should have a sit-down with Rodney."

"I'd like to listen in on that one," Judith said as she went down the hall to fetch a can of smoked salmon from the pantry. When she returned to the kitchen, Renie asked if she'd heard from Arlene.

"No," Judith replied, opening the can. "That bothers me. I wonder if their kids have any idea that they're still at Heaven's Gate."

"They've actually only been gone for a full day," Renie pointed out.

"True, but the Rankerses' offspring stop by fairly often for one reason or . . ." The doorbell rang again. "I hope that's not guests arriving early," she said, heading out of the kitchen.

"Let me come with you," Renie volunteered. "If they're early birds, I'll shoo them away."

"No, you won't," Judith asserted. "It does happen once in a while."

To both the cousins' surprise, a grim-faced Reverend Kindred stood on the porch. "We need to talk," he said.

Judith stepped aside. Kindred moved purposefully into the living room, but didn't sit down. He cleared his throat and spoke in his most formal manner. "In the name of our Lord, where is Rodney?"

"Not here," Judith replied. "Go ahead, search the house."

Kindred shook his head. "I believe you. But I think you know where he is. The Lord despises subterfuge. Tell me where I can find him."

"I don't know," Judith said. "That's the truth. Why did he run away from his own home in the first place?"

"Because he's unwell up here," the rev replied, tapping his temple. "Demon rum. It ruins the brain cells along with the disposition."

"Really?" Renie said. "Is that what happened to you? I'm so sorry! No wonder you got religion."

Kindred's long face darkened. "Of course not! Lips that touch liquor will never touch mine!"

"Good," Renie retorted. "Then I'm safe from any lecherous advances you might make." On that note, she flounced out of the living room.

Judith ground her teeth before she spoke. "My cousin sometimes speaks without thinking. I apologize."

"She's very rude," Kindred declared. "But I forgive her, as the Lord commands me. Maybe, like poor Rodney, she suffers from her own demons. We're trying to find him so he can get help."

"What kind of help?"

The rev suddenly seemed fascinated with the view from the bay window. "You know—a place where he could improve his mental health."

"Do you think that's his only problem?" Judith asked, wishing Kindred would look her in the eye—or at least sit down.

"We all have problems," he murmured, now studying the grandfather clock.

Though tact was always preferable, Judith opted for candor. "Has Rodney always been a heavy drinker?"

"Anyone who imbibes liquor has a problem," the rev replied as the clock struck the quarter hour. He flinched before finally looking at Judith. "Doesn't that hellacious noise drive you insane?"

"No. I like it." Judith's patience was fraying. "I thought you might consider sending Rodney to a place that treats alcoholics."

"His problems go deeper than that," Kindred said. "The soul, you know. It's for his own good, and should be done as soon as possible."

"Would he consent?"

The rev shrugged. "Maybe, maybe not. But the Lord—and the law—make provisions if he doesn't agree."

"Then I gather someone in your group has a power of attorney."

Kindred flinched again. "I believe Stuart Wicks, being a lawyer, may have that. Why do you ask?"

"Just curious," Judith said. "Excuse me, I have to get ready for my guests. I'll see you to the door."

If the rebuff bothered the rev, it didn't show. "Bless you, my dear Mrs. Flipp. I'll keep you in my prayers and see myself out."

Judith stayed in the living room until she heard the door shut.

"What a jackass," Renie declared when Judith returned to the kitchen. "How did you keep from telling him to stick it?"

"It wasn't easy. I assume you were listening from the hall."

"Of course."

Judith opened her recipe book. "Hey—what happened to the smoked salmon? The can's empty!"

"The cat," Renie said with a shrug.

Sweetums, however, was entering the hall through his little door. "*You* ate it!" Judith cried. "How could you? Did you take it with you to pig out while you were eavesdropping?"

"No, I scooted back to the kitchen and grabbed it. I'm quick."

It was useless to get mad at Renie. Judith started for the pantry, but the phone rang again. "You answer it," she said, and kept going.

When she returned, Renie handed her the receiver. "It's Cathy Rankers. She wants to know where her parents are. She says there's two days' worth of stuff in their mailbox."

"Damn," Judith said under her breath, but took the receiver from Renie. "Hi, Cathy. Your folks are still working at Heaven's Gate. It's a big job, big yard, big—"

"Judith," Cathy broke in, "I don't get it. Dad and Mom aren't professional gardeners. Why did they go out there in the first place?"

"It's kind of a long story," Judith began. "You know how curious your mother is. The guests who stayed here over the weekend are now living out there, but they canceled my payment for the B&B. Your parents, being so goodhearted, decided to—"

"Stop." Cathy's tone carried authority. She was, after all, a successful Realtor. "This isn't some kind of dangerous setup, is it? Don't take me in the wrong way, but I know your history, Judith. You have a way of finding serious trouble even if you don't go looking for it."

Judith didn't waste time defending herself. "Have you tried calling your parents?"

"Yes, of course," Cathy replied. "But the cell battery must've run down. She left the charger here. I'm picking up Dick and we're going out to Sunset Hills to see what's going on."

"How will you and your brother get through the gate?" Judith asked, noting that Renie had left the kitchen. No doubt she was going to listen in on the phone in the living room.

"One of my former clients lives there and Dick's done repair work for them in the last year or so. Don't worry, we know how to handle this."

Judith didn't doubt that claim. "Okay, but keep me posted."

"Me, too," Renie said.

"Who's there?" Cathy demanded. "Is that Serena?"

"Who else?" Judith retorted. "She's on the living room phone. Please be careful, Cathy. These people may be . . . sketchy."

"Ha!" Cathy exclaimed. "I've been in real estate for almost thirty years. You think I don't know sketchy? Talk to you later." She hung up.

"I think," Renie said, returning to the kitchen, "the cocktail hour has arrived early. I'll make us each a short one."

"Why don't you and Bill have dinner with us again tonight?" Judith suggested.

"I'd have to go pick up Bill," Renie replied. "He's probably still taking his postwalk nap." She smiled. "You're antsy. You don't want to be left alone."

"I won't be alone," Judith said. "Joe didn't run away from home."

Renie was still smiling. "You know what I mean. You need your older if not always wiser cousin to prop you up while you're grounded."

Judith smiled back. "You're right. 'Closer than sisters.' Isn't that what we've always said?"

Renie nodded. "And the good part was that when we got mad at each other, we could ask our mothers to send the other one home."

Before Judith could respond, Joe came through the back door. "I squelched your latest harebrained idea," he announced, hanging his jacket up in the hall.

"What idea?" Judith asked.

"Tyler Dooley," Joe replied, entering the kitchen, where Renie was getting the liquor out of the cupboard. "Oh, hi. I should've guessed you'd show up to cheer your cousin."

"What about Tyler?" Judith asked. "I haven't seen him today."

"Are you sure about that?" Joe asked, his green eyes narrowed.

"Yes!" Judith snapped. "The only time I left the house was to have lunch with Mavis. I've been here ever since. Ask Renie. She knows what I've been doing."

"It's true," Renie said to Joe. "Stop acting like Torquemada. Your wife hasn't had a very good day. In fact, why don't you get back in the MG and pick up Bill? We're having dinner here tonight."

"Again?" Joe said.

"Hey!" Renie shouted. "Are Bill and I imposing on you? I provided the sockeye salmon last night, you jerk."

Joe sighed. "Okay, okay. I can't take on both of you."

"What about Tyler?" Judith asked.

"He called to me from over the fence just now," Joe replied in his more normal tone. "One of the older kids—I can't keep all of that brood straight—was heading out north after dinner to see one of his buddies. Tyler said he was going with him and getting dropped off at Sunset Hills so he could snoop around. I told him that was a bad idea." He kept his gaze on Judith. "Was that *your* idea?"

"No," Judith said. "I agree with you about Tyler going out there. Did you convince him not to pull a stunt like that? How would he get in?"

Joe shrugged. "Climbing the fence, maybe. It could be done by an agile kid. Hell, for all I know he could pole-vault over it."

Renie had picked up her purse. "I'm off. I've had a good time, but this wasn't one of them." She started for the back door.

"Coz!" Judith cried, following her cousin into the hall. "Are you going to pick up Bill?"

"No," Renie replied, her hand on the doorknob. "I know when I'm not wanted. I intend to make beef Stroganoff for my husband and pamper him to pieces. Sometimes it's hard to tell, but Bill actually likes me." She slammed the door behind her.

Judith returned to the kitchen and glared at Joe, who was pouring Scotch into two glasses. "Now see what you've done. You hurt Renie's feelings."

"No, I didn't," Joe asserted. "She's just mad because I got . . . cross with you." He put his arms around Judith. "Are you going to walk out on me, too?"

Judith leaned against him. "Of course not. But Renie's right. I really didn't have a very good day. Where were you all afternoon? I don't see any bags from the hardware store."

"That's because I left them in the garage," Joe said. He kissed her forehead and let go. "After that, I went to see Woody."

"Oh?" Judith's dark eyes brightened. "Did he have any news?"

"He did," Joe replied, after taking a sip of Scotch. "The autopsy report on Millie came in around four."

"And?"

Joe set his glass on the counter. "The cause of death was confirmed as an accidental poisoning. But that wasn't all that was in the findings. Millie was suffering from . . ." He paused, then slowly continued: " . . . cra-ni-o-pha-ryn-ge-o-ma."

"What on earth is that?"

"In Millie's case," Joe answered with a pained expression, "it means she had an inoperable cancerous brain tumor. Millie had only a few months—maybe weeks—to live."

Chapter 25

Judith's suspicions were confirmed. There had been so many things that pointed in the direction of a serious, possibly fatal illness: the sheet of paper with cancer-related items; the trip to Zürich; the comment Belle had made about why her mother had to die—as if it were inevitable. And it was.

After dinner, Judith felt upset. It was pointless to unload on Joe, so she called Renie from the kitchen. "I sensed something like this," she said after giving her cousin the latest news. "I haven't been able to come up with a viable motive for killing Millie. Not jealousy, not hatred, not even the money angle works because the one who benefits from her death is Belle and she's already extremely rich. Besides, Belle doesn't seem all that fond of money, so I can't see her killing her mother to get even more. I suppose I should just forget about the whole thing, right?"

"You can't do that and you know it," Renie shot back. "It's either suicide or murder. If it's the latter, then a crime has been committed. Do you think Millie knew she was dying?"

"I don't know," Judith admitted. "Maybe she was never told. Does it matter now?"

"Hey," Renie argued, "you know it does. To you, if to no one else. Seeking truth and justice is your forte. Don't quit now."

"This situation is different," Judith said. "Every time I've gotten involved in a murder investigation, the killer has had one of the usual motives. You know what I mean—greed, jealousy, passion, revenge—whatever. But this was a mercy killing."

"I get that," Renie agreed. "But who did it?"

Judith was surprised by the question. "I assume either Rodney or Millie. Maybe the others didn't know she was sick."

"Coz! That's not worthy of you. Judging from what you just told me, Belle knew. If she knew, probably Clark knew, and so on down the line. You're feeling sorry for the Schmucks right now. But you still don't know the identity of the poisoner."

"You're guilt-tripping me," Judith said glumly. "Woody apparently doesn't think it was a homicide. It's been ruled an accidental death."

"I know, but that's because he has no evidence to indicate otherwise." Renie's sigh was audible. "You're right. I should shut up."

"That's okay." Judith paused. "If someone else put the poison in Millie's juice, what's the motive?"

"Gain?" Renie suggested. "They're doing their best to make sure Rodney can't access his money. Now Belle seems to be the wealthy one."

"And she's as scared as Rodney," Judith mused. "We have to assume that Millie inherited money. I wonder what her maiden name was. It might be on the death certificate."

"If you hear from Rodney or Belle again, you could ask one of them."

"But they might not contact me. I wonder . . ." She broke off.

"What?" Renie asked.

"Did Jude hire a P.I. to follow me?"

"Maybe she thought you could lead him to Rodney?"

"Dubious," Judith responded. "The problem is that the P.I. had already found out that Rodney lived in Sunset Hills. Jude sent those coins to him a month or so ago. I'm wondering if her private eye is not the guy calling himself Ethan Ethanson, city inspector."

"Two P.I.s?" Renie sounded skeptical.

"It's not impossible," Judith said. "But the phony inspector may not be a P.I. His reason for checking out the Schmucks could be personal. They might have a history of scamming people out of their property. He might be seeking revenge."

"Anything's possible that involves the Schmuck bunch," Renie allowed. "Hey—I've got to go. Bill's ready for *Munich*."

"He wants to go to Germany?" Judith asked in surprise.

"No, the movie," Renie replied. "It's about a counterattack on the terrorists at the Olympics in . . ." Bill's voice could be heard in the background. " . . . *Ja, mein Führer*, I'm coming!" Renie hung up.

Judith left the kitchen and went into the living room, where Joe was on the sofa reading an espionage novel. She sat down across from him and picked up the latest issue of *Vogue*. After a couple of minutes, she realized she hadn't really taken in any of the first hundred pages she'd leafed through.

I can't focus on a single thing, she thought to herself. *All I can think of is those Schmucks and their so-called friends. If I try to stop, I worry about Arlene and Carl.*

Did Cathy and Dick go out to Sunset Hills? Even if they got in, what happened after that?

"What's wrong?" Joe asked, finally looking up from his book.

"Everything," Judith replied. "I mean, everything about what's gone on around here this last week. I'm going to call Cathy." Ignoring her husband's baleful look, she got up and went back to the kitchen.

There was no answer. Judith knew Cathy had only the cell and her landline at the real estate office. But they closed at five. In all the years of living next door to the Rankerses, Judith had only Cathy's office phone number. She flipped through the directory, but found no listing for Dick. In fact, the only Rankerses in the book were her parents and the real estate business.

The doorbell rang. Judith wondered if one of her guests had forgotten to take the house key. But of course the door was unlocked. She and Joe never closed up the house until they went to bed. Glancing into the living room on her way down the hall, she noticed that Joe had nodded off. Apparently espionage wasn't always riveting reading.

Judith opened the door a bit warily to see Clark Stone standing on the welcome mat. "I stole a car," he said.

"You did?" Nothing that a member of the Schmuck group did could surprise Judith. "Come in," she said, leading him into the parlor. "Have a seat. Whose car did you steal?"

"One of the rentals," Clark replied, sinking awkwardly into one of the two high-backed armchairs. "Have you seen Belle?"

"She's with her father," Judith informed him. "They left here and went downtown to stay at a hotel. I don't know which one."

"Darn." Clark scowled. "My father thinks she skipped out on me. Maybe she doesn't want to get married. He says that's probably why she left. Oh, well."

"You mean . . . Stuart Wicks? Your stepfather?"

"No," Clark said. "I mean my real father. He's staying downtown, too. At that big old hotel. I forget the name."

Judith didn't blame him. The name had been changed over the years and recently had become a Four Seasons hotel. "I didn't realize your father was in town."

"He's been here a few days, I guess," Clark said vaguely. "He travels a lot in his job. I guess he talks to recruiters who're looking into backgrounds for people they might want to hire."

"Right," Judith said, sounding almost as vague as Clark. "Does he also live in L.A.?"

"Santa Monica. Dad's got a yacht. He likes to sail out of there. He's got moorage."

"That's . . . nice for him. Look, Clark, I really don't know where Belle and her father are staying. Did you know she'd come here?"

"Not really," he replied. "But Belle told me she wanted to find her dad. I don't think she knew much about the city, so I figured she might've come here to ask if you'd seen him. Mr. Schmuck mentioned that you'd been really kind to him after Mrs. Schmuck died." He lowered his eyes. "I don't suppose you have a spare room vacant?"

"I don't," Judith said, again feeling guilty about the guest bedroom in the third floor family quarters. "If your father's at the big, old hotel downtown, why don't you stay with him?"

Clark's face brightened. "I never thought of that. Maybe I will. I don't want to be accused of stealing the rental, so I'll turn it in. They must have a downtown office. I probably can walk from there to the hotel."

"That sounds like a plan," Judith said, smiling encouragement. "I assume you got your wallet back?"

"My . . . oh, right. I had a messenger bring it out to me from that drugstore. It cost a lot, but it was worth it. Hey, I better go now. Thanks for your help, Mrs. Flynn. Oh—how do I get downtown from here?"

Judith told him to go back to the Avenue and *down the hill.* She was careful to emphasize the direction, for fear of Clark going the wrong way. "Turn *left* when you leave the cul-de-sac," she said at the door. "After two blocks, you'll be at Heraldsgate Avenue. Then turn *right* and you'll end up downtown."

"Sounds like a no-brainer," Clark responded.

"It is," Judith said. As long as he used his brain, of course.

Joe headed up to bed early. Judith locked the front door, but though she was very tired, she wasn't ready to settle down. The grandfather clock told her it was ten forty. Her mother would still be up, watching whatever was on TV.

Going out the back door, she realized that the evening air felt almost balmy. Maybe there would be good weather for the Memorial Day weekend. A crescent moon hung over the hill, though Judith couldn't see many stars. There were a couple of lights on at the Dooleys', but of course the Rankerses' house was dark. The only nearby light was from the B&B's back hall. She'd forgotten to hit the switch for the back porch. Sweetums joined her near the birdbath, leading the way to Gertrude's toolshed apartment.

"What now?" the old lady demanded when Judith came inside. "Don't tell me you finally split up with Lunkhead. It's about time. Now I can die happy."

Judith ignored the remark. "You're watching *ER*?" she practcally shouted. "Would you mind turning the sound down?"

"What? I'm deaf, you know. Speak up!"

Judith grabbed the remote and hit the mute button. "I didn't think you liked hospital shows," she said.

Gertrude looked puzzled. "Is that what it is? I thought it was a comedy. No wonder so many of the people are wearing masks. How come you're here and not there?" she asked, gesturing at the house.

"I haven't had much time this week to visit with you," Judith replied. "Are you and Aunt Deb playing bridge tomorrow?"

"You bet. We're going up against Gilhooly and Fiasco. They're a couple of hard cases, but we'll kick their fat fannies."

"Those names aren't real, are they?"

"I never remember their last names," Gertrude admitted. "But I know from seeing them at SOTS that the Irish blabbermouth counts her cards out loud and the Italian can't see so good. I like our chances."

"Good for you and Aunt Deb," Judith said, patting her mother's stooped shoulder. "Say, what else do you remember from that séance you had with the people who were here last weekend?"

Getrude looked blank. "What séance?"

"Mother . . . you remember it just fine. Give. Please?"

Gertrude frowned. "They all seemed to want to know about money, especially the porky little coot with the comb-over."

"Charlie Crump," Judith murmured. "Do you mean as in getting more of it?"

"I guess so," Gertrude replied. "It was like they expected a big windfall. Maybe they bought lottery tickets. After I came out of my trance, one of those nincompoops asked me why you wouldn't sell the house. I told him it was because you don't own it, I do."

"Was that Rodney, the husband of the woman who died in the backyard?" Judith asked.

"No. It was the idiot who blogs," Gertrude replied. "He asked if I wanted to read some of the stuff he wrote. I told him my jumble puzzles would make more sense."

"Clayton Ormsby," Judith murmured. "They want the whole cul-de-sac for condos."

Gertrude shrugged. "Speculators. California's full of 'em."

Judith didn't argue. Nor did she remind her mother that there were plenty of speculators in their own state. Of course Gertrude already knew that. She could see what had happened in their own neighborhood and it wasn't all good. But was any of it worth killing for? Judith wasn't sure.

It seemed even darker outside to Judith after she left her mother. She walked carefully, always aware that even stepping on a pebble could throw her off balance. Just as she passed the statue of St. Francis, she gave a start. Someone was standing at the edge of the driveway by the house. The figure moved closer. Judith could see a man—a fairly tall man—and something about him looked familiar.

"Hello?" she said softly, though her voice sounded strained.

"Mrs. Flynn?" the man responded.

"Yes." Judith stopped a few feet from the porch. "Can I help you?"

The man came closer. She recognized the phony inspector. Even in the darkness she was certain he was the same person who had been watching from the white car parked outside the cul-de-sac. Forcing herself to sound natural, she decided to go along with whatever game he was playing. "Mr. Ethanson?"

He frowned, adjusting the collar of his blazer. "That's not my real name. I'm Ronald Stone. I think you know my son, Clark. He was a guest here recently. I'm afraid I pulled a bit of a stunt on you over the weekend."

Judith felt her shoulders slump with relief. "I wondered who you really were. I found out who you were *not*. Would you like to come inside?"

He nodded. "I tried the doorbell, but no one came to answer it."

"My husband must not have heard it," Judith said, leading the way inside. Ronald Stone might seem harmless, but she knew from experience that first impressions weren't always accurate. In fact, sometimes they were downright dangerous. It was better to let her latest visitor think Joe was still up and about. Since her guests should be returning from their evening adventures, she decided it'd be more private to sit in the kitchen.

"Your son told me you were in town," Judith began after they were seated at the table.

Ronald looked surprised. "You've seen him recently?"

"He was here earlier," Judith replied.

"Why?" Ronald asked, his expression tense.

"He thinks Belle wants to break off their engagement."

Ronald looked relieved. "I hope so. I don't want Clark mixed up with that bunch. I told him that before he ever agreed to come on this trip with my ex and her jackass of a husband."

Judith started to speak, but stopped as she considered Ronald's words. "I'm confused," she admitted. "I was told that the purpose of the trip and staying here was to hold the wedding Saturday at my B&B."

Ronald burst out laughing. "That's crazy! Clark hardly knows Belle. That is, one of those casual 'let's move in together to save on rent' situations. When my son told me they'd broken up, I didn't get it. I didn't even know they were dating. I figured it was all some kind of lark. But I played along. When I came here pretending to be a city inspector—and I *am* sorry about the deception—I was hoping to see Clark and make sure he was okay. But he wasn't around that day. I kept watching for him, but every time I saw him, he was with Belle or the rest of those people."

"You couldn't call him?" Judith asked.

"I tried," Ronald replied. "But I never got through. I suppose he lost his cell. Clark's always losing things. That's one of the many reasons Cynthia and I split up. She had very peculiar ideas about child raising, such as never disciplining him or teaching him to take responsibility. To my ex, that was old-school nonsense. She wanted our son to raise himself so he could achieve personal freedom. It's a wonder he didn't go off the rails and end up in prison."

Judith was dismayed. "This was before Cynthia became a counselor?"

Ronald nodded. "God only knows what kind of advice she gives. Cynthia has always had weird ideas. That idiot doctor friend of hers—Sophie—egged her on. They went to a private girls' high school together."

"Yes, fast friends forever," Judith remarked. "That's a tough bond to break. Would Clark have gone through with the wedding?"

"Probably," Ronald said with disgust. "He's easily led. But I doubt that Kindall or Kindick or whatever he calls himself is a real minister. He's another weirdo."

"I wondered," Judith said. "I couldn't figure out how they got a marriage license since they'd just arrived in town."

"They probably didn't have one," Ronald responded. "What I can't figure out is what's really going on with this lunatic bunch, especially after Belle's mother died. I didn't know about that when I came here that day. I was stunned."

"You must've missed the EMTs and the cops," Judith said. "Did you have any idea before you came here that a wedding was planned?"

Ronald shook his head. "I only found out about that after I got here. When Clark told me last week he was traveling with Belle and the rest of them, I was sailing in the Santa Lucia Islands north of here. I decided I'd better head down to the city to keep an eye on things. He'd never mentioned that a wedding was in the offing. Maybe the poor kid hadn't been told about it until they got here. I never knew the Schmucks. My only connection with that bunch is through Cynthia and Sophie."

"I don't know what to say," Judith admitted. "I *have* considered that so much of what happened with them has been some kind of charade. You followed me to Sunset Hills, didn't you?"

"I did," Ronald said. "I saw their rental cars were gone. I didn't want to try another impersonation stunt with you, so I finally followed you out there. I had no idea such a place like that existed around here. Of course I'm not familiar with this area. As you might guess," he continued with a chagrined expression, "I couldn't get inside. The only people I know there are Clark's so-called friends and I figured Cynthia would make sure I'd be sent on my way."

"So what are you going to do next?"

"At least Clark's out of there now," Ronald replied. "If only he had a cell . . ."

"He left here for your hotel," Judith said. "He may be there now, waiting for you. Assuming he . . . he found the right hotel, of course."

"Of course." Ronald's smile was wry. "I'd better go. Thanks for hearing me out. You must think I'm crazy," he added as he stood up.

Judith also got to her feet. "No, I don't. Believe me," she said as they went through the dining room to the hall, "this past week I've experienced a lot of crazy with Clark's traveling companions. They all seem rather strange."

At the front door, Ronald put his hand on the knob and sighed. "To be fair, I don't know most of them. But money may motivate whatever they're up to. You'd be surprised what greed can do to people. It's pernicious."

Judith merely smiled and wished him good luck. She didn't say there wasn't anything about greed or the other deadly sins that would surprise her. She'd had too much experience with most of them. Especially with the ones that led to murder.

Chapter 26

Judith slept better than she expected. The early morning passed without incident. While Joe visited with the guests in the dining room, Judith called Rankers Real Estate shortly before nine. To her relief, she was immediately transferred to Cathy.

"Dick and I were refused entry," she declared in an irate voice. "The guard obviously had been warned about letting in visitors. Bribed, I'll bet. I'm calling the police. Or would it be the county sheriff? Sunset Hills isn't inside the city limits."

"Good luck with that," Judith said. "Gated communities have their own security. I suspect they're a jurisdiction in themselves. I take it you haven't heard from your parents?"

"No," Cathy replied, now sounding glum. "Even if Dick's cell died on Mom, why can't she pick up one of the landlines where they're being held prisoner?"

"Some people don't have a landline these days," Judith said. "You don't."

"True," Cathy admitted grudgingly. "But I still may call the police. Unless . . ." She left the sentence unfinished.

"Unless what?" Judith finally asked.

"Unless you go out there today," Cathy said. "You've gotten in before. Maybe you can do it again."

Judith made a face and was glad Cathy couldn't see her. "I'm not sure I can do that. I've got a full house all through the long weekend."

"But your guests won't show up until late this afternoon, right?"

"Right," Judith agreed reluctantly. "I'll try, okay?"

Judith never told Joe what she called her little fibs. But she knew he'd pitch a fit if she revealed her intentions. Thus she called Renie to ask if she'd like to go to lunch, maybe somewhere other than in the neighborhood. Renie thought that was a good idea.

"How about one of those new places in the mall by the University?" she suggested to Judith. "I've got some Father's Day shopping I could do at one of the men's stores there."

"Sounds good," Judith agreed. "I'll stop by around eleven thirty."

"Make it twelve fifteen," Renie said. "I'm not dressed yet. It's barely eleven. I've only been up for half an hour. If we get there later, we'll miss the noon rush. Besides, I won't be hungry that soon. I had trout for breakfast. Yum!"

"Lucky you," Judith said.

Joe entered the kitchen just as she put the phone down. "Not another Schmuck call, I hope," he said.

"No. Renie and I are going to lunch and then to do some shopping," she said. "I'll see to Mother before I leave."

"Okay." Joe started scraping a frying pan. "I've got a surveillance job starting tonight. It's out of town, in the state capital. It may last through the weekend. Will you be all right without me?"

"Yes, of course," Judith said. "You rarely leave town on those jobs. Has it something to do with our government down there?"

"I guess," Joe replied. "Sometimes I don't get all the details. My job is to report on what the subject does while I'm watching. They don't tell me more than I need to know."

Judith understood. It had been over a month since Joe had been given a round-the-clock surveillance assignment. She never really minded his being gone for a few days. But this was the first time he'd had to leave town.

"When do you start?" she asked.

Joe looked sheepish. "Now. As you know, it's a long drive and in weekend holiday traffic at that. I'd better get packed."

Her gloomy feeling returned. She was silently lecturing herself when the back door opened and she heard a familiar voice: "Your cat has a seagull in the hedge."

"Arlene!" Judith rushed to her neighbor and hugged her. "How did you escape?"

She felt Arlene shrug. "We just left. Our job was done. I really don't think those people know what they're doing. If they're some sort of criminals, they have a peculiar way of showing it. Shouldn't at least one of them carry a gun? In a holster, I mean. Why, they don't even lock all their doors at night! Really, I doubt they even know we're gone."

"What are they doing?" Judith asked.

"They play a lot of board games," Arlene replied, leaning against the kitchen counter. "Scrabble, Risk, Monopoly. I've never understood why they don't raise real estate values for Monopoly. Imagine buying a property for sixty dollars!"

"That's it? I mean, they weren't doing anything . . . unusual?"

Arlene turned thoughtful. "I think someone said one of their cars was missing. A rental, I mean. They probably parked it somewhere and forgot. I suppose they'll have to get at least one taxi when they go to the airport."

"The airport?" Judith said in surprise. "You mean some of them are leaving town?"

"All of them, from what I happened to overhear through the keyhole while I was down on my hands and knees dusting the door to the parlor. It sounded as if they planned to take a flight this evening."

"Oh, no!" Judith cried. "I mean . . . I'm not sure what I mean. Maybe I figured they were in for the long haul here."

Arlene seemed puzzled. "What do you think they plan to haul?"

"I mean I thought they were going to stay . . ." Judith shook herself. "Never mind. The main thing is that you and Carl are safe."

"I think we always were," Arlene said. "But that doesn't mean we weren't concerned at first about their intentions. It was rather rude of them to insist we stay until Carl finished the yard and I cooked and cleaned the house. Of course, it was a change of pace to be undercover servants. Mrs. Kindred gave us a very nice check."

"That's great," Judith said. "I've been feeling guilty for putting you and Carl in harm's way."

"Nonsense," Arlene asserted. "It was a break in our routine. That's always good. Unless it's bad. Aren't you going to do something about your cat? He was making quite a mess with that crow."

"I thought it was a seagull," Judith said.

Arlene frowned. "Maybe it was. As I just told you, it was quite a mess."

"I'll tell Joe about it," Judith said vaguely. "Oh—do your kids know you're home?"

"Yes." Arlene looked disgusted. "I wondered why the mailbox was empty, so I figured one of them must've stopped by. I called Cathy right away. Honestly, why must children fuss so? It wasn't as if we'd fallen into a den of thieves."

Judith didn't contradict her. But she felt Arlene was wrong.

Ten minutes later, Joe came downstairs. He set his valise by the back door and came into the kitchen. "I really hate leaving you alone for so long," he said, putting his arms around Judith. "Promise you won't do anything reckless while I'm gone?"

Leaning her head on his shoulder, she avoided looking in her husband's eyes. "I won't. You be careful, too."

"Sure." He kissed her lingeringly before letting go. "You make me want to get back home in a hurry."

"Do that," she said, smiling. "I'm already missing you."

An hour later, she picked up Renie. "We're not going to the shopping mall," Judith told her cousin.

"We're not? How come?"

"Apparently the nut jobs are leaving town," Judith declared, and related the rest of her evening and morning conversations.

"Wow," Renie said softly. "You get a lot done, even when you're at home. Hey—does this detour mean we aren't having lunch?"

"We'll have a late lunch," Judith responded.

"What if we're dead?"

Judith glanced at Renie. "That's about the only thing that could make you stop eating."

"I plan on eating in heaven. If I get there, of course. I'd rather not go to hell, because of all the fires. The meat there must be really well done. So overcooked, no natural juices. I wonder if they have waiters in hell. I've known some who should be there."

"Stop it," Judith said. "I'm not in a very upbeat mood."

"Okay." Renie yawned. "Do you have an attack plan for the residents of Heaven's Gate?"

"No. I plan to play it by ear."

"Hmm. Playing things by ear always sounds odd to me. Have you ever tried to strum a guitar with one of your ears? Or put your head on the piano keys and just thump away?"

"*Please* don't try to cheer me up," Judith snapped.

"You couldn't strum a guitar with both of your ears. At the same time, I mean."

"Stop. Now. Just be quiet."

Somewhat to Judith's surprise, Renie shut up until they were turning off to Sunset Hills. The guard at the kiosk was the one who'd been on duty the first time they'd arrived. Judith rolled down the window. "Mr. and Mrs. Wicks at Heaven's Gate," she announced. "We're here for a business meeting."

To Judith's relief, he nodded and opened the gates.

"No call to the house?" Renie said as they moved on.

"Maybe he remembered us from before," Judith replied.

"But you lied about why we were here."

"I did not lie," Judith asserted. "I told a slight fib. The guard probably remembered only that we'd been here recently. He's not about to ask for ID or pat us down."

Renie squirmed in her seat. "I'm not sure I like doing this."

"Then you should've stayed home."

"I thought we were going shopping. And out to lunch. You deceived me. See? More lies."

Judith slowed down as they approached Heaven's Gate. "Only one car parked in the drive, which means they should be on the premises."

"Which also means we're outnumbered," Renie muttered. "Why aren't we armed? I could've brought one of Bill's guns."

"You'd end up shooting yourself. Or me. Please get out of the car."

Renie complied, but let Judith go first. They waited a full minute before the door was opened.

"Mrs. Flynn!" Agnes Crump exclaimed, clutching her throat. "I thought you were the police!"

"What? Why?" Judith asked, startled.

"Because . . ." Agnes lowered her eyes. "I confessed."

Judith wondered if the poor woman had lost her mind. "Confessed to what?"

Agnes stepped aside. "Come in. Please." She didn't close the door behind the cousins until she'd scanned the roadway. "No police cars in sight. Oh, dear. Maybe we should go into the study."

Judith and Renie followed Agnes. The study was halfway down the hall on the left. It was a fairly small room, with bookcases lining both walls. Except for a few reference volumes and some popular paperback novels, the shelves were bare. Apparently Rodney and Millie Schmuck weren't avid readers.

The only furnishings consisted of a bare table, a desk with a serviceable office chair, and two upholstered armchairs. Agnes moved behind the desk, indicating that her visitors should sit in the armchairs. When Judith and Renie were seated, Agnes sank into the office chair, clutching its arms as if she were afraid of sliding onto the floor.

"It's terrible," she said through lips that barely moved. Taking a deep breath, she turned her cornflower-blue eyes first on Judith, then on Renie, and back again to Judith. "I killed Millie."

Judith forced herself to sound casual. "Why did you do that?"

Briefly, Agnes closd her eyes and her lips moved slightly, as if in prayer. "Millie didn't know she was dying of brain cancer. Rodney took her to a clinic in

Switzerland, but told her it was for him—he said he was having dizzy spells and the doctors he'd gone to here and in L.A. were no help. He told Millie she might as well get checked out while they were at the Swiss clinic. The doctors told him there was nothing they could do. Of course Millie had no idea she was so sick. It wasn't until lately that her headaches really bothered her. She'd hardly slept the last few nights, I guess. I just wanted to help ease her pain."

Judith nodded. "So how did you help her?"

Agnes flexed her fingers. "With wolfsbane. I take it for my arthritis. It's an old-fashioned remedy. But honestly, it helps."

"Wolfsbane," Judith murmured. "Aconitum, right?"

"What?" Agnes looked blank.

"The scientific name for wolfsbane or monkshood is aconitum," Judith said, still in a conversational tone. "Why did you give it to Millie?"

"She'd complained of a headache from the time she and Mr. Schmuck met us with that big limousine," Agnes explained, flexing and unflexing her fingers. "I've used wolfsbane because it helps me. I know it's an old-fashioned idea, but it really does. After we arrived at your B&B, I asked Millie if her headache was better. She told me she still had it. I told her about wolfsbane, but she dismissed it as folklore."

Judith didn't argue the point. "So what did you do then?"

"I went out in your garden while the others were drinking wine in the living room," Agnes replied. "I used to work in my garden for hours until my hands became so crippled. I saw that you had wolfsbane growing there, so I picked some."

"I do?" Judith felt a twinge of guilt for having the lethal plant in her garden. But that was hard to avoid when so many common plants, shrubs, flowers, and trees were poisonous. "Go on," she urged Agnes.

"The next morning when Millie went upstairs to see to her husband, I followed after her to ask if she still had her headache. I didn't want to embarrass her in front of the others. I had the wolfsbane in my pocket and told her to mix some in water if she hadn't gotten rid of the headache. She just laughed, so I left, thinking the headache must've gone away overnight. But I guess it hadn't. Millie wasn't one to complain." Agnes lowered her eyes and started to cry.

Judith patted Agnes's arm. "You meant to help, not harm her. In the long run, it was a mercy killing. Don't feel guilty. Please, Agnes."

"But . . . ," Agnes snuffled, "she's still dead!"

"You spared her a lot of misery," Judith asserted. "Think of what you did as a blessing. Where was Rodney when this happened?"

Agnes sniffed some more and wiped her eyes with a rumpled handkerchief. "In the bathroom, I guess. He wasn't in the room."

"I thought the juice was for Rodney," Judith said. "I don't know why Millie drank it. If the amount was lethal, then either Rodney refused . . ." She stopped. "Any way you look at it, it was an accident."

"I should go to confession," Agnes declared, still dabbing at her eyes. "In fact, I thought maybe there'd be a priest hearing confessions at your church last Sunday."

"No," Judith replied. "With the priest shortage, we only have our pastor, Father Hoyle, at the rectory. But there's a parish a mile north of here. Tomorrow's Saturday, so they'll probably have confessions."

Agnes looked bleak. "We're leaving tonight. What if the plane crashes and I die with this sin on my soul?"

Renie, who had grown restless in the armchair, waved a hand. "It's not a sin to make a mistake. Get over it. If you're worried about flying, get loaded like I do."

"Coz!" Judith cried. "Don't offer bad advice. It's embarrassing when you stagger onto an airplane and cackle like a chicken." She turned back to Agnes. "Why are you all leaving now?" she asked.

"I don't know. Charlie told me it was time to go home. He said we were finished here." She blew her nose before tucking the handkerchief back in her pocket. "I suppose I should pack."

"Do that, Agnes," Judith advised, standing up. "Keep busy. My cousin's right, if a bit blunt. You performed a merciful act, so you have to stop feeling guilty. Please."

Agnes didn't say anything. Realizing there was nothing more she could add, Judith started out of the room with Renie right behind her.

"Poor woman," Judith murmured when they were out in the hall.

"Cut it," Renie snapped. "She's one of those gloomy Catholics who enjoys wallowing in guilt. You're right to tell her to go to confession. The priest will be bored and half asleep. He'll give her some prayers to say as penance and send her on her way. Maybe then she'll feel better. Or not."

"Now *you* sound like Arlene," Judith chided.

"Arlene's contagious," Renie said. "In a good way, of course."

"Right." She grinned at Renie. "Or not."

Renie laughed. "Now who do we confront?"

"Whoever we see first. I wonder where the rest of them are?"

She'd barely gotten the words out when Elsie Kindred appeared from a room off to their right. "What are you doing here?" she asked in an anxious voice.

Judith chose candor. "Your group reneged on the payment to the B&B. I'd like to get a cashier's check. I'm not leaving without being paid. Where's Stuart Wicks?"

Elsie's dark eyes darted in every direction. "He . . . he left a few minutes ago. With some of the others. They had some business to do."

"What kind of business?" Judith asked.

"Outside." Elsie frowned and bit her lip.

"You mean in the garden?"

"Well . . . in a way. But they went somewhere else first."

"How come?"

The color rose in Elsie's face. "To get some equipment."

"Equipment?" Judith glanced at Renie.

Her cousin took the cue. "What kind of equipment?"

"I don't know for sure," she replied. "Clayton mentioned renting a truck—a pickup truck, I think." Elsie grimaced. "As the Good Lord is my witness, I'm not sure what they're doing."

Judith nodded faintly. "Who else is here now?"

"My husband, George; Sophie, along with Agnes," Elsie replied.

"Yes, we talked to Agnes," Judith said. "You're a nurse, Elsie. I'm curious about Rodney's drinking. It bothers me. Has he been addicted to alcohol for a long time or were his current bouts with the bottle triggered by Millie's death?"

Elsie frowned. "I haven't really known the Schmucks for all that long," she said, nervously rubbing her upper arms. "Of course George and I rarely imbibe except for a glass of wine on social occasions. Now that I think about it, I don't believe I've ever seen Rodney take more than one drink of any kind."

"So," Judith suggested, "his recent drinking is an aberration."

"I guess so," Elsie allowed. "When I mentioned it to Sophie—since she's a doctor—she told me it was good for him, given his grief. A temporary release from reality, is the way she put it. In fact, Sophie seemed to encourage him, now that I look back on the last few days."

"Sophie's another self-serving twit," Renie declared. "You all used both Millie and Rodney in your real estate schemes."

Elsie's face crumpled. "That's harsh," she asserted in a tremulous voice. "Despite what you may think, George does try to be a good Christian. He discovered that Rodney still had the Swiss clinic's findings in his luggage. None of us wanted Millie to realize she was so ill. My husband destroyed the official diagnosis and removed what was left from the premises."

Judith thought back to the residue Carl and Arlene had found in their garbage. "I wondered what had been . . ." she began, but stopped as she heard a commotion outside.

The front door flew open. A dozen men, half of them armed and in uniform, charged into the house. "Police!" they shouted. "Please stand against the wall."

Renie moved closer to Judith. "Does that mean us?" she whispered.

"I guess," Judith said—and followed instructions.

The uniformed cops began opening doors. Judith realized they were state patrol officers. Two men in plainclothes asked Elsie to identify herself and if she was a resident of the house. In a nervous voice, she told them she was a visitor. The men moved on to the cousins.

"And you?" the taller of the two men said to Judith.

"Judith Flynn," she said. "I'm also visiting."

"Me, too," Renie chimed in, at her most ingenuous. "I'm Serena Jones and I reserve the right to talk as much as I want. But not right now." She gave the officer her cheesiest grin.

"Idiot," Judith growled at Renie out of the corner of her mouth as the duo kept going down the hall.

Elsie turned to the cousins. "Where *is* Agnes?" she asked in a worried voice.

Judith gestured at the study. "In there. Maybe you should get her to come out."

Elsie looked at the half-dozen cops who were by the front door. "Dare I move?"

Judith shrugged. "I don't see why not. We've identified ourselves. Do you know why they're here?"

"I don't want to know," the preacher's wife said grimly. "I'd better see to Agnes. She's been rather upset lately." Elsie headed for the study,

Renie stared at Judith. "Well? What's next on your battle plan?"

Judith smiled. "I think our work here is done."

"What grounds are they busted on?"

"*The* grounds," Judith replied. "As in digging up that chest of coins, for one thing. I hope they catch them in the act. I'm guessing that's why they rented a truck. But there may be other, more serious charges. Extortion, maybe fraud."

"You mean trying to inveigle people out of their property for unfair prices?"

"That's my other guess," Judith said. "I suppose we could ask."

Renie looked skeptical, but she followed her cousin to the front door. Judith approached one of the state patrolmen.

"What's the problem here?" she inquired.

"Sorry," the dark-skinned young man replied. "We're not allowed to give out information."

Judith nodded, noting that the officer's nameplate identified him as L. B. Hermanson. "I understand. But would you call Captain Woodrow Price in the city's first precinct? I can give you his direct number."

Hermanson seemed taken aback. "Captain Price? You know him?"

"Yes," Judith said. "He used to be my husband's partner when they worked as homicide detectives."

"Excuse me," the officer murmured. "I have to check with someone." He walked over to another state patrolman who, judging from his brass, slashes, and the two bars on his uniform, was his superior. The senior officer stared at Judith, then spoke into his cell. After a brief exchange, he motioned for the cousins to come down from the porch.

"You're free to leave," he said. "We've been in touch with Captain Price as well as the chief of police."

Judith smiled. "Thank you." She started down the steps.

The captain turned as she walked past him. "Are you really FATSO?" he inquired under his breath.

"No," she answered—and kept on going. Sometimes, Judith thought, the usually reticent Woody Price talked too much.

After a stop for lunch to shut up a suddenly hungry Renie, Judith got home a little after three. She immediately checked phone messages. The first was for a reservation in late June. The second was from Belle.

"Dad and I checked out of the hotel," she said. "I tried to call Clark, but I got a recording. Then I phoned Heaven's Gate. Nobody answered. Oh, well. I'm taking Dad back there anyway. It *is* his home and we have to plan Mom's services. They'll be private, though. I don't want to see any of those other people ever again, not even Clark. Hey, you were really nice to both of us. Dad misses you and told me to give Mama his love."

Judith had barely hung up the phone when Joe came through the back door. "What on earth . . . ?" she cried. "Did the MG break down?"

"No," he replied, putting his arms around her and grinning. "You're in one piece. I'm only semisurprised."

Judith assumed an innocent expression. "I told you I wouldn't do anything that might upset you. Renie and I had lunch at . . ." She saw the glint in Joe's green eyes. "Magic eyes," she'd always called them. "What?"

"I went to see Woody," Joe said. "How were things at Heaven's Gate?"

Judith stepped away from her husband and glared at him. "You didn't go to the state capital."

"I didn't have to," he replied airily. "Woody called them, along with some other law enforcement types. The California cops and the feds have been onto your former guests for some time. They make a nasty habit of trying to scam people out of their property all over the West."

Judith slumped onto a kitchen chair. "But their backgrounds were checked."

Joe sat down on the other side of the table. "That's right. They're who they say they are. But that doesn't mean they aren't a bunch of crooks. Ever hear of white-collar crime?"

"Of course I have," Judith retorted. "I thought you'd disassociated yourself from what was going on, especially after you told me to butt out. How long have you been working this case behind my back?"

"Oh . . ." Joe ran a hand over his high forehead. "Only since Monday, really. That is, after I talked to

Woody. He'd heard something about the gang's operations. This was the first time they tried to pull anything around here, though."

Judith was still annoyed. "How come you didn't start interviewing them while they were still here? I mean, in a casual way."

Joe shrugged. "I hadn't been really chummy with that bunch from the start. Switching gears and chatting with them might've made them suspicious. Besides, they were gone by Tuesday morning."

"Were Millie and Rodney part of the scam?" Judith asked, beginning to simmer down.

Joe shook his head. "They always pick a pair of local pigeons as a front. Maybe they had to wait until somebody they knew who had money moved here from L.A. The Schmucks suited their purposes to a T."

"*T* for Traitors," Judith murmured. "Belle didn't know, did she?"

"No," Joe said, "but she was still in L.A. finishing up her last college semester down there. Belle was their link to the Schmucks."

Arlene burst through the back door. "I'm furious! I took the Wickses' check to the bank. I asked the teller to make sure it was good. But it wasn't."

Judith forced herself not to laugh. "They suckered you, too?"

"Yes," Arlene said. "Imagine! All that hard work we put in out there! They even wanted me to polish the heirloom sterling silverware."

"Did you?"

"No," Arlene replied indignantly. Her blue eyes suddenly sparked. "I decided to bring it with us instead."

Judith couldn't hide her surprise. "To clean it?"

Arlene shook her head. "To keep it." She glanced at Joe. "Of course you might call that stealing." She paused. "Or not."

Just before the guests started arriving, the phone rang. "Mama!" Rodney shouted. "Guess what? Everybody's gone from our house! What happened? Never mind, you probably don't know. But I wanted to tell you that it's really great to be living so close to you, Mama, and I hope we can see a lot of—hold on, Belle's calling to me . . ."

Judith took a deep breath and shook her head. Would she never get rid of Rodney and his misconception about her identity? She could hear faint voices in the background, and after a couple of minutes, she was tempted to hang up. Or have her phone number changed. But that would be bad for business. She was still mulling over her options when Rodney came back on the line.

"The dangedest thing just happened," he said in a wondering voice. "Somebody who calls herself Judith Grover just showed up and says she can prove she's my mother. How can that be? Wait, she's got a birth certificate . . . Well, I'll be a . . . Hold it . . ."

He turned away from the phone. "Coins? . . . No kidding! For me, Mama? Oh, wow! Hey," he said into Judith's ear, "gotta go! But I'll always remember you, even if I'm not your little boy!"

"That's so kind of you, Rodney. It was nice to meet . . ."

But Rodney had hung up. Judith smiled ironically as she set the receiver on the counter. Yes, it was sweet of him to say he'd remember her.

But Judith would prefer to forget.

About the Author

MARY RICHARDSON DAHEIM is a Seattle native with a degree in communications from the University of Washington. Realizing at an early age that getting published in books with real covers might elude her for years, she worked on daily newspapers and in public relations to help avoid her creditors. She lives in her hometown in a century-old house not unlike Hillside Manor, except for the body count. Daheim is also the author of the Alpine mystery series and the mother of three daughters.

www.marydaheimauthor.com

HARPER LUXE

THE NEW LUXURY IN READING

We hope you enjoyed reading
our new, comfortable print size and found it
an experience you would like to repeat.

Well – you're in luck!

HarperLuxe offers the finest in fiction and
nonfiction books in this same larger print size and
paperback format. Light and easy to read, HarperLuxe
paperbacks are for book lovers who want to see
what they are reading without the strain.

For a full listing of titles and
new releases to come, please visit our website:

www.HarperLuxe.com